To Solve for X: A Christian Fantasy

To Solve for X: A Christian Fantasy

Roberta Symon

To Solve for X: A Christian Fantasy

© Roberta Symon 2018

This book is a work of fiction. Named locations are used fictitiously, and characters and incidents are the product of the author's imagination. Any resemblance to actual events or places or persons, living or dead, is entirely coincidental.

Published by
Lighthouse Christian Publishing
SAN 257-4330
5531 Dufferin Drive
Savage, Minnesota, 55378
United States of America

www.lighthousechristianpublishing.com

Romans 5:1—Therefore, since we have been justified through faith, we have peace with God through our Lord Jesus Christ.

Chapter 1 – Betrayal

The lethal palm-laser pointed at her heart looked like state of the art, which didn't help Yancey at all. *What a stupid thought to have in the split second when I'm dying!* But she thought it. And she died. She knew it with certainty.

My heart burst. The pain was stunning. That much is clear.

The split second elongated and horrified her more than her death had.

I remember…how can a dead person remember?
Panic clawed at her.

The torture in her mind spun out and lived on.

Again she saw Jason Thomas, eyes glazed with his most recent "hit" of rynlyn, the latest designer drug on the street. He giggled aimlessly into the air as he depressed the thumb-sized trigger on his *Las*, as the kids called them. It was a popular weapon, evolved from a harmless, twentieth century tool used for pointing at graphs and charts to catch people's attention. Not harmless, and still an attention-grabber, this one pointed, too—*right at me!*

Yancey had heard tales of heads severed during the French Revolution yet blinking their eyes and trying to speak;

maybe my brain is refusing the death message from my heart. Whatever this was, the impossible instant replay continued.

With the slow-motion clarity sometimes exaggerated in the mind by extreme crisis, she again watched Jason's beardless mouth form into an "O" at the pretty green stream of light that boiled the moisture in her tissues and exploded her heart. *The laser jolt burned like lightning and touched off pain that felt like three-tons of fireworks exploding inside my chest.*

Mindless, he stood there, in her memory as he had in real-time, gurgling as spittle ran down his smooth chin. Again, she saw his eyes with their pinprick pupils looking much like the round, delighted orbs of a two-year-old who had just discovered his latest marvel.

I heard him giggling as I fell to the floor. It ticked me off.

This much is fact. My head bounced. Then, what?

The second fiery ordeal of pain torched all my cells systematically, a scanning probe slicing and dicing my body in sections from the top of my head to the soles of my feet.

What scan? Whose scan? Was it a scan? And WHERE IS HERE?

Yancey wrestled her thoughts away from that mental abyss—*dying twice?*

Her mind, or whatever this was—she had for decades boldly taught her students and anyone else who would listen that she had no more soul than a squirrel scrounging for nuts— had stubbornly registered new sensations of burning agony *after* she had died.

WHAT IS ALL THIS?

To relieve stress from that imponderable, she mentally quipped, *Great!* Now *I find out zombies are real. I must be the latest model: deadpan sense of humor intact.*

Yancey's mind groped for another angle.

This can't be the Christian archetype of hell—I'm still in my same body—now, where did those outdated notions come from? Yancey shuddered, felt herself cramp from fresh pain, and shook off the thought and the fear that came with it.

Jason Thomas blasted me into what should be oblivion; only, I haven't landed.

So, WHERE IS HERE?

Unreasonably, her brain re-asserted her death but continued firing thoughts. Physical sensations of being flooded and then of beginning to float in liquid inundated her. *This is a load of bull!*

Panicked further, an event she hadn't thought possible, Yancey forced her mind to fumble for another wisecrack. A headline came to mind: *English teacher dies on dry land by drowning from a* Las *blast. Yeah, that might keep them guessing.*

As white opacity rose above her head, Yancey's mouth and lungs filled with liquid while she tried to suck in the air needed to scream. Trying to master this new terror of drowning, she forced a fresh headline into her mind: *English teacher dies three times; Ripley's and Guinness vie for body in a fight to the finish…again…again… and again.*

Maybe this third round is some weird, congestive heart failure from the sac around my heart— the third time I've died; maybe I don't have the hang of it yet! Maybe it's just a nightmare. But she knew pain like hers would have awakened any sleeper.

The milky emulsion superimposed itself around her shrieking nerve cells and began to dull and finally cut off her pain, but not her consciousness. *That's better.*

Of course, I'm still the liveliest corpse I ever heard of—uh, except for Lazarus and Jesus. Disturbed by her second allusion to the Bible she had dismissed from her life except as great literary fiction, Yancey thought, *I guess death might bend one's imagination that way.*

Where is HERE?

Physical comfort increased with the soothing liquid; she abandoned her dead-alive conundrum and began again to distract herself with tomorrow's headlines.

The disinterested paper-video tomorrow, she thought, *will routinely report one more teacher fatality. It will say, "Thursday, 15 March, 2376: (Ah, man! The ides of March!) Just outside her classroom, 7-301of Public School # 17 of the Dayton-Cincinnati Metroplex, Ms. Yolanda Philips, sixty-year veteran, was terminated by…blah, blah, and blah."*

Yancey figured she wouldn't be listed as **DR.** Yolanda Philips—*Well, Dad,* she sniped, *you warned me a degree was a waste of time and money.*

Any publicly educated city dweller who bothered to read or listen further to the vid article, she knew, would easily visualize the crime scene or one just like it: the long, beige, metallic, tubular Corridor 7B, "Language Arts" wing—like all the other tubular corridors in all the other "Metroplex Combined Schools: Serving Citizens with Technology."

Probably, she thought, *the bored reporter will stop there.*

At least my obit picture will show a healthy thirty-seven-year-old, not my real, eighty-seven-year-old self; thank you, Daddy, for paying for all those virtual-age injections. To be so ignored and to appear as an old coot at the same time would really expose me as a loser.

One more death like all the other school deaths. My violent demise won't even make Page One. A shame!

How fitting. Well, Dad always said, "You'll die at your crazy job," or "They'll have to carry you out." Score one more for you.

I hoped to accomplish so much more. I had so much more to see, to do, to teach, if the truth be known.

Oh, this is too soon. Not fair!

Thinking of "fair," Yancey experienced a jolt of grim satisfaction when she thought of her Dad and of Jason Thomas. By midnight both Jason and the kid who sold the rynlyn to him would be a little history lesson of their own: don't mess with crime boss Duke Silva's daughter.

The kids' families, too, might become history if Daddy Duke thought them deserving. She felt grimly appalled at her gut reaction: pleasure— *my father's daughter, after all.*

After sixty years as "the great educator hoping to make a difference," I discover I want only revenge! Couldn't I have gone brain-dead before I caught myself savoring the grisly vision of Jason Thomas' head in a sack delivered to Dad by midnight tonight?

In the very end, I betray myself: just another savage cut down by some other drooling savage. She tried to scream; it emerged as a clay-like gurgle in the thick, cold, milky goo, and she nearly retched.

This isn't fair, either! I might've died happy without knowing this. Her despairing thoughts continued.

They would, she groused.

Exasperated, she snorted, and felt thick bubbles blurp from her nose. *Humiliating, that's what this is.*

Angered by her self-betrayal in this grim moment of truth, for she had been sinned against, never the sinner as she saw it, she framed an inelegant word in her mind. *Oh, that ticks me off worse. An English teacher, purveyor of beautiful thoughts, and that's all I've got?* The triviality of that thought ramped her temper higher—*the summation of my life: a confusing plot lacking resolution.*

Oh, this death is just one horror and comic routine after another! Come on! Where's the sweet nothingness I've believed all my life? Grimly, she experienced all feeling receding from her limbs and then the trunk of her body and silently rooted, *Come on, oblivion! My life has been nothing; let's conclude it in the nothingness it deserves!*

But no, no decent, split-second ending for me! This is some macabre comedy farce directed by someone I can't see and have never known.

Immediately, she chided herself: *I'm reverting to superstition again: first, hell; then, God? What's next, a devil? Oh, I know—little green men!*

WHERE IS HERE? Hysteria beckoned her.

O.K., Yancey, enough of that!

Objectively and uneasily, Yancey's mind again registered that this much thinking represented an unreasonable success of one's brain in terms of denying its own demise. *Those Frenchmen would be jealous!* No person's mind should be able to exist this long after the red heart which fed it had been blown to smithereens by some dolt of a druggie.

WHERE IS HERE?

When everything went black, finally, Yancey thought she sighed with relief. Dead but not dead was too large an equation to solve while in the act of dying. To solve for that X required living, but she appeared to have run out of time.

Chapter 2 – The Tank

After an indefinite amount of time, awareness barged its way through the blackness she had hoped would be the end.

I have no physical sensations.

WHERE IS HERE? Her scream emerged as a gurgle which made her want to retch. *Correction, I have some physical sensations, although gagging and puking wouldn't have been my first and second choices.*

Outside stimuli came suddenly. HERE suddenly involved sets of small hands, not hers. They reached impersonally into her chest cavity, and she could feel them. Fascination held her still.

Yancey's mind told her, "open-heart surgery." Her exploded heart and its blasted nerve endings vibrated, and she recognized she must certainly still have a torso; the ministrations of the hands tickled. Light pricks, perceived by her with great satisfaction as brighter whites almost like welding arcs, began to stimulate her limbs, and she knew her legs and arms moved in reflex.

Her mind tried insisting it was the paramedics—*they got here in time—* but she knew she lied. *Little green men do NOT exist! My mind's all I have left under my control. I need to keep it!*

Yancey's impressions of the small hands terminated.

At a console outside Tank Sixteen, Chief Medtech P'shan finished his clinical tests. "Repairs to the subject's heart are successful," he commended his crew. "Well done."

Scrambling against panic inside the Tank, with reasoning her only weapon, Yancey told herself, *just because two opposite things look impossible to be true at the same time, it doesn't mean that one truth cancels the other. Both might be real.*

Gravity holds objects to the ground, but aerodynamics lets airships overcome it. The heavy crafts refuse to fall from the air to obey the laws that rule the ground. She reasoned stubbornly. *Aircrafts follow a higher law.*

Maybe it's like this for me: dead—she resisted the threatening panic—*but not dead. I have little, or wacky sensations at most, but I am still thinking…so, not exactly dead.*

She experienced absolute silence.

What a hoot! I never believed in absolutes.

PANIC won. If there are med-tubes, I'll jerk them out. I can't feel my body responding, but my brain still works. She willed herself to convulse—to buck and kick and gyrate—to destroy. She felt her neurons giving way.

A thought arrested her, *Is it Hell? Is it Heaven?*

Whichever, it's going to be a dead bore. Her mind slurred, *I wanna speak to the Management!* Sarcastically she tried a mental snigger to counter the dread that she might have entered eternity.

Ambivalence arrested her suicidal gyrations and affored P'Shan a critical second. Yancey sorrowed as she felt her mind fall apart—*too late to pull myself together.*

One of the two asserted itself: death, or the blackness she figured passed for sleep in this undulating, alien environment. *What to hope for?*

P'shan, Chief Medtech on *Catchcraft P-17*, looked up from monitoring the brain waves from Catch Number Sixteen. He'd responded in a blur to the alarm. *The anesthetic worked. Her brain is viable; her heart still beats*; thus, the Catch is a success. *She will live.*

Reproducing cells faithful to the patterns dictated by the diagnostic scan he had run on earth a fractal of a second after her official death, the Tank would rejuvenate her physical body during the trip. P'shan leaned back in his small chair, closed his eyes, and sighed with relief. Only one more to go on this trip—the Craft Number indicated the total Tanks onboard—and he and his crew could return Planet-side.

P'ruhn entered with a welcome mug of tea.

The *P*'s before each crew member's name indicated their permanent ship assignment. The single, small, gold tab on her collar's edge marked P'ruhn as Captain of the ship. It was a matter of course in their culture that the greater in rank served the lesser. P'ruhn had decreased to her highest level of service.

Each crew member felt deep pride and satisfaction to be in the Service on a Catchcraft. The excitement of making a successful Catch could never be exaggerated. These were souls of the Watcher's making. He watched over them to do them good. To serve him in this pursuit was to be part of the highest order.

A low, melodious tone halted the two crew-mates' review of Number Sixteen's progress. At odds with the pleasant, harmonious sound was the controlled chaos it catalyzed. The crew, Captain P'ruhn and Chief Medtech P'shan included, scrambled to make Catch Number Seventeen a success for the Watcher who had thus signaled.

At 11:34 P.M., the elliptic, ebony curve of the sleek *P-17* began to reverse itself as it tore from black space back towards Earth to make its last Catch on this trip.

Two in one day! P'shan exulted. *The Watcher is good.*

Chapter 3 –Planet-fall

P'treth, navigator of *Catchcraft P-17,* calculated the angle of entry and degree of speed at which to reverse the ship's ellipse in order to bring her safely to her home berth. This was no easy task. The ellipse had to invert precisely to produce the ship's own unique acoustics.

Energy and objects that did not resonate with the planet's own harmony of sound would find themselves repelled. This was why earth probes in this far quadrant had dubbed their bit of the creation the dull designation of quadrant *X 27217.* No planets were visible there. P'treth smiled and thought, *Planet X is here, all right.*

Unlike the elite, compact race of slender humanoids called Spacers, who comprised ninety-eight percent of crew members for Catch ships, navigators tended to come from any number of races on Planet X. Typical Spacers' hands tended to be too short-fingered to run the simultaneous operations required to pilot the complex ellipses called Catchcrafts.

Navigator P'treth was a Gimzo, one of a coastal race born to master positional and technological intricacies, whether terrestrial or spacial. Perhaps four inches taller than the average, five-foot tall Spacer, whom he otherwise resembled except for a reddish-brown cast to his skin, P'treth now let his long-fingered hands fly over the lighted squares in the console portions overhead and to his right. With the ellipse in correct configuration, the exact sequence tapped on the correct squares would produce a harmonious resonance between these and the remaining console to his left.

When the two sound waves converged in matching compression and expansion rhythms, P'treth would press the central square on the panel at desk height before him. The joined sounds would then focus, and, like negative electrons seeking a positive feeder to create Earth's lightning, would acquire their unique, matching sound from the ship's berth beacon. Like a sort of automatic pilot, *P-17's* individual berth-sound would first guide and then land its craft home.

Planet-fall for a *Catchcraft,* done well, was one of the most satisfying experiences in the fleet. As the ship acquired the signal, the joined sound waves would cross the threshold of audibility for the entire crew. There could be no sweeter sound, and no other was like it, the unique sound of home.

If one were not the Captain, preparing the ship for cross-down, or the Chief Medtech, zealously finishing his final tasks with the seventeen Tanks—the final two on this voyage successfully filled in a single day—one could find a viewport. Black space spangled with stars would give place to bright air and then blue-gold sky.

Spacers never tired of the view. Home is beautiful. Past the two suns, turquoise water with whitecaps rolling up would caress or crash below on the massive, irregular cliffs of stone like black basalt. Dockings planet-wide for Catch ships all lay hidden in natural, fortress-like areas. No other ships or areas on Planet *X* could resonate with the sound beacons unique to their splendid crafts. The Watcher secured His special messengers.

The landing would feel like stepping on some gigantic gel sole. The black body of the ship would settle into a perfect oval crafted for its berth.

The glorious music of home would crescendo. P'treth knew all the crewmembers' hearts would resonate with the glad sound and feel thanksgiving for another safe Planet-fall, just as his did at this moment. He thought of what the morning stars must have sounded like at the speaking of creation; perhaps, he mused, the Catchcraft's berth- song captured a string of it.

P'treth had a few more tasks. *P-17's* black ellipse, now barely discernible against its jet-black berth, descended smoothly down through the interior of the Service's docking hub. As singing hydraulics in the natural cliff-tower transported the ship below the reach of the elements, the Navigator began running his checks. The last all-clear before power could be cut would come from Medtech P'shan, and then Captain P'ruhn would give the crew the signal.

Chief Medtech P'shan, like most of his crewmates, unconsciously hummed along with the ship's berth song. Once the sound reached the ship, it traveled more swiftly through *P-17's* alloy than it had through the atmosphere. Humming allowed one to become a small part of the beauty and, as multiplied experiences had shown, actually increased productivity.

Spacer P'shan's small, stubby fingers fairly glided over the gauges, dials, and colored squares that comprised the controls for each of the Tanks. For this moment—the unique gift for the Chief Medtech on each Catchcraft— P'shan was the maestro conducting under the direct authority of the All-Ruler.

Re-surfacing of each individual was a masterful, eagerly awaited business. P'shan would flush each Tank in order of maturity. As zealously as any new Mother with her precious infant, the machines counted fingers and toes, and hearts and other organs, then ran tests, which Tank occupants like Yancey, in her Tank Sixteen, should feel as stimulating electric shocks necessary to "jump-start" neutralized and newly fabricated neurons.

Humming to himself before draining the environment and releasing their its offspring, the Chief Medtech waited till each Tank's system resonated perfectly with the unique Life-melody the Watcher pulsed through for that Tank's occupant.

P'shan had apprenticed a dozen years before he had mastered the matching of the Rejuvenates' songs.

P'shan never tired of this process. *If one ever doubted the Watcher is infinite, he ought to ask a Medtech,* he thought. *Each Rejuvenate's song down through the ages is unique. I remember from Tech School a multitude of logs where previous Techs also marveled at this fact.*

Sensitively adjusting the appropriate frequencies, tones, and volumes, Tank by Tank, P'shan knew each of the Rejuvenates should experience this as pleasurable, even thrilling vibration after the degree of sensory deprivation needful to shelter them from pain during the revival and reconstruction process.

In ideal conditions, seventeen Catch-conductors would be poised to board the Catchcraft when it reached the bottom of its protective crater. A Tank with no Conductor present to receive its occupant had to be carefully sustained until one arrived. This was part of the harmony.

P'shan's hands with their blunt, capable, sausage-fingers stilled over the indicators for Tanks Four and Twelve. Sad, but true to most Catch voyages, he'd had to inform two of the Conductors that their services would not be needed.

Why do they do it? he asked himself for the thousandth time. Two Tank occupants this trip—and it had nearly been three—had willfully refused to continue co-operation with the rejuvenation process. Willfulness was the only force that could thwart a Catch-tank: each individual was, even after an initially successful catch, mysteriously free to choose rebellion. Catch-subjects could practice stubbornness so deep and pride so selfish, they had rather terminate their own existence than submit to life.

P'shan faced this Catch-trip's two catastrophes, the Medtech's worst nightmare: failed Tanks. The biological clean-up of sloughed-off tissue, atrophying organs, and soured rejuvenate fluid in a failed Tank required disgusting, extra duty for designated medical assistants.

Adding to the difficulty was the oppression of silence. Only the emotionally hardy and physically stable could endure the performance of the required tasks in that desolate void.

The med-assistants and P'shan mourned the losses. Although not morally responsible, the vibrant Spacers inevitably felt the Watcher's grief over the lost life-songs.

Why would humans choose self-destruction rather than accept the Watcher's love?

To cut off his experience of horror over such failures would mean to cut off his corresponding capacity for the beauty and the glory of the Watcher's will. P'shan sighed and re-focused on his humming. Surrendering his grief, he cleared himself to receive the remaining Rejuvenates' life-melodies.

When he finished with Tank Seventeen, P'shan contacted the fifteen Conductors waiting for the living 'Juvies,' as the rest of the Spacers irreverently called his miraculous Rejuvenates. Soon, each one of the Catchcraft's precious cargo would join the companion Conductor whom the Watcher had lovingly appointed.

Yancey awoke and felt relief. With pleasure she experienced a distinct, mild shock disrupting the blankness. Her body, which she had correctly surmised, felt the liquid/gas in which she floated answer by expanding and contracting.

Intuitively, she felt sure the shock and the waves comprised a Word. For the first few seconds, however, she heard no sound. *Pretty tough without ears,* she impatiently wisecracked. Her little joke fell flat; tensely, ridiculously, she snapped at herself, *of course I have ears!*

The expansion and contraction repeated and became regular. The waves brought pleasure to Yancey, like riding in a kayak in a light swell. Suspended and floating on her back, she soon internalized the motions and began experiencing a sensation like a humming deep inside her.

What a delight to begin to hum along with the strange, stimulating sound waves and actually feel bubbles escape from her real lips! *Humming*, she thought, *a tune with no words; but this has words. I just can't make them out yet.* As one who had built her life around words, she felt bereft.

The white opacity that was liquid-gas floated her down as it receded from around her. Her bare buttocks lost their last cushion of whiteness and came to rest on cold metal.

I can feel cold!

Turning her head to one side, she retched the last of the liquid as her lungs filled with air.

Wanting a look at herself, Yancey blinked to clear her sight-starved eyes. *They're not clearing easily.* Yancey saw her hands first.

Could those be my hands? A tangled roadmap of fine wrinkles crisscrossed by upstanding blue veins and prominent tendons covered the tops and pointed the way to long, thick, curving fingernails. Suspiciously, and almost with a sense of horror, she strained to look now at this body of hers which she had just begun greeting with such thankfulness.

Her road-mapped, paper-thin skin sagged all over. Her tummy splayed across her hip bones like a rounded pillow in a wrinkled pouch. When she tightened her arms and legs, despite some aches, her muscles responded, but her skin did not follow; instead, it curdled into sun-damaged folds. She gasped.

Craning her neck made it and her back pop and crack in hurt protest.

The aged skin and the pain angered her. She levered herself upright. Gritting her teeth against the ensuing physical distress minimized that difficulty but made room for the next unwelcome revelation.

Wait a minute. My upper teeth are missing. Aaagh!

I have my real teeth, but my beautiful, top-of-the-line synthetic bridgework is history. Boy, is Daddy gonna be mad! That work cost him a bundle even back when I was only nine.

As tongues do (*I have a tongue!*), hers poked and probed the four empty holes where her top front teeth should have been but weren't.

Shifting explorations, Yancey reached for her hair, which dribbled white goo over her.

She finished peeling the disgusting, long strings off her shoulders and back, held it away from her body, and strained to look at it. Long, wet and gray, the hair was not bleached, butched and gelled as she had worn it when dying as a spry, albeit artificially maintained thirty-seven-year old. The hair made her shiver in more than one way.

Yancey continued to hold the limp, cold mass away from her torso and inspected it with growing alarm. Savagely, she wrung it out. Her scalp hurt from the effort.

So much gray! Unless it's just the goo? But it would take a lifetime to grow such a mop!

To calm herself, Yancey determinedly switched her attention from her hirsute dilemma back to her chilly posterior to note *I'm naked.* Her mouth twitched. She shrugged and figured *whoever put me in this tank has already gotten an eye full if they wanted it. In my present condition, who'd want it?*

Well-modulated words from a surround system now reached her ears and halted her alarming self-inventory. Her nervous tongue scraped her empty sockets involuntarily as she concentrated. The sounds, though not as pleasant as what she unconsciously dubbed the "creation song," were immediately intelligible.

The disembodied voice instructed, "Ms. Phillips, please exit the Tank through the portal now opening at the front. A hot, cleansing shower will meet you just before you reach the hatch. You'll dry off and find clothing provided."

Buster, she thought, *I'd do way more than exit wherever HERE is to get a hot shower and get this stringy mess of hair off my back.*

Feeling weighted down, her bones and sinews responded grudgingly as she walked. Sharp pain clawed her knees, and her muscles protested. She moved laboriously. The sensations were new and sharply unpleasant.

So, she thought as she wrestled her recalcitrant body toward the opening portal, *what happens if I can't make it out to the shower?*

She had to force her legs, suddenly grown like tree trunks insistent on rooting at each step, to move. *Six decades of receiving stem-cell injections from the finest, fresh placentas and umbilical cords Dad's money can buy have spoiled me. I THINK THESE JOKERS HAVE RESTORED ME TO MY CHRONOLOGICAL AGE OF 87!*

I know eternal youth isn't available even to the very rich back in the good ol' U.S., but our science maintained my eighty-seven-year-old body functionally at thirty-seven. What's the problem with these guys? They've already shown they're way past our technology. My heart is beating again. No Earth treatment could do that.

Pain-racked, she now grudgingly acknowledged another disturbing reality: *I died, but this certainly isn't oblivion.* She steadied herself with a quip, *This ain't Kansas, either, Toto.*

Yancey paused and patiently stretched muscles that protested to the tune of popping bones and joints. *Being dead for even a short while might reasonably make a girl's muscles feel a bit cranky when first awakened. I've heard jokes all my life about* rigor mortis.

Plucking up her nerve, she quirked her mouth at her gallows humor. She finished flexing and stretching her stiff muscles as she had always done for her work-out sessions on Earth. The process took longer, *and all I'm trying to do is walk.*

The simple stretches produced painful cramps. Anger at these unseen experimenters' refusal to help their lab project, as she now styled herself, helped Yancey hobble and scrabble her way toward the promised shower. *Maybe the shower will limber me up.*

Hmmph, to think I was complaining about lack of sensation.

The hot shower rained down hard on her from above while more water jets rose to meet her from the floor; others pummeled her from the side walls. The water stung as it shot from all sides of the small, cylindrical, transparent chamber where she shakily stood by clinging to two metal bars rising from the middle of the shower.

It was a welcome, impersonal massage. White gook melted and sluiced off as the waters pounded her.

Yancey noted the membranous walls that had risen around her in response to her body weight on a rubbery surface different from the rest of the floor. The touch of her bare feet—*veined, bumpy, and my toes are crooked*—on the circular pad embedded in the floor about three feet from the Tank's exit had initiated the growth of the chamber and now maintained the delightful water barrage.

One foot off the pad decreased the flow. She stepped back quickly and stood delightedly on the pad.

Shampoo and scented soap smelling like lavender joined the wonderful massage without hands. She felt her pores open and unclog. The steam soothed and expanded her lungs and gentled her breathing. When the wet phase ended with no help from her, powerful, warm jets of heated air dried her.

The membranous walls rescinded, and she stepped curiously off the pad. *No more stalling,* she thought as a smooth panel opened in the floor to the left of the doorway.

From the cavity rose a small ledge which could be either a seat or a shelf. Thankfully, she eased her way down onto it.

Looking at everything through a fuzzy film which she now attributed to lingering steam, Yancey hopefully pulled her hair, now free of its white residue, once again over her shoulder for a closer look.

She huffed out a silent scream. Her hair, always coarse, still had washed-out streaks of its native auburn, but the predominant colors were ugly shades of gray and white.

Newly cleaned, the stuff frizzed and snaked wildly to her waist. She slumped down on the ledge-seat. This hair would never be free from white residue again: its whiteness belonged to her. She jerked it back behind her violently.

She, Yancey Philips, sat exposed, naked in her real age: not thirty-, but eighty-seven.

The pain in her joints returned in force as Yancey dully rose and donned the powder blue robe which waited in a niche behind the little seat. She started to creak her way to the door, but the same mellifluous voice said, "Ms. Philips, the sandals will help."

Dispiritedly, she turned her blurry eyes to the simple shoes which had remained unseen below the robe. When she tried to focus on how they might fasten, an audible sob finally escaped her. Her gnarled, blue-veined hands groped blindly for the fastener.

The kind, masculine voice said gently, "Just place your feet in the shoes and touch the straps together. They'll stick." They did.

The sandals did help. Large bunions on her feet experienced a generous cushioning action and lessened the pain in her knees a bit as she labored her way to the next portal.

They are watching me. Fear helped slow her steps even further. *What else will these weird scientists do to me?*

One forlorn tear escaped her cloudy left eye. She brushed it angrily away with her crooked fingers, careful to avoid raking her eye with her long, yellowish fingernails. *How long was I in that tank?*

Everything about herself disgusted her. *I was there long enough to re-grow my body in all its natural eighty-seven-years, but not long enough to augment it?*

Yancey squared her bent shoulders as well as she could. *I already died once. What do these... people... want from me?*

To restore me like this—why not just leave me dead? She shook off the black thoughts and stretched her misshapen, sandaled foot through the hatch. Behind her, the door slid hissing into its side pocket in the wall.

Chapter 4 – Conductors

A muscular Being not quite six feet tall and in his thirties or forties, by her earth reckoning, reached out his well manicured hand and took her own hand and stick-like arm, which wrinkled in diagonal lines under the contact. He supported her over the raised bottom of the hatch, and gently released her when he saw she was steady.

Yancey thought, *Being, not man. He seems too perfect to be human.*

He had short, sandy hair cropped close to his beautifully shaped head. Even his ears were perfect. His complexion seemed California-golden. He placed his face very near to hers where she could see him despite the cloudiness of her vision. His eyes drew her own to them.

Almond-shaped, hazel in color, fringed with thick, brown lashes, his eyes exuded peace and compassion. She had started angrily to jerk herself away from his alien nearness. One close look at his eyes had stopped her.

Those glorious eyes with their tawny gold, rich brown and mossy green colors really saw her. She knew it and felt more naked than she had in the Tank.

After she began to teach, she had allowed no one, ever, to look into her eyes as through a window to her soul. Eavesdropping, learning of others, she looked into their eyes but faked whatever she wanted them to see in her own. She counted this ability a great asset. *I don't get this guy.*

She swept her lashes down. *Closed to inspection, Thank you.* He did not move. Surprised, she raised her eyes to study him again.

Then he spoke, and the deep, calm tone let her know closed eyelids or cloudiness, either, was nothing to him. Yancey felt exposed and unnerved by his proximity. The unfamiliar haze over her eyes disadvantaged her and made the encounter more terrifying.

His voice, definitely the melodious one from the Tank, drew her to him. He inclined his head and closed his own eyelids briefly as if she were someone special, not to close her out as she had tried to do to him, but to take her in and hold her safe. He said, "Welcome to Planet *X*."

Her lined, wrinkled lips twitched at that. Yancey didn't know if cloudy eyes could twinkle; if they could, hers did. *Is that the best you can do? Planet X?* Years of teaching kept the thought silent in her mind and quickly returned her face to a bland expression so as not to give offense in this bizarre situation where she did not know the rules.

She was not quick enough. He said, and his tone was approving, "I am glad to have amused you. It is a good sign and breaks the stress of arrival."

You think that relieved "the stress of arrival?" Yancey wanted to roll her eyes at the understatement but she had learned how keenly he watched her. She bit her bottom lip to ambush her new amusement. He smiled in return as if he knew. *This guy is good!*

"My name is Elbraith, and I am your Conductor. Please come with me. We'll talk as we walk, and I'll try to answer your questions. Before we proceed, however, let me assist your vision, your nails, and your dental problem."

Yancey stood rock still, not daring to believe. He leaned toward her with a tool no larger than a Chap Stick. She felt a quick puff of air in her right eye; after she involuntarily blinked, another in her left. Each time, she saw a flash of light and felt that liquid-gas sensation again.

Each stung. Tears running—just like that—her vision cleared.

To her hands and feet he pressed an innocuous semi-circle. Her nails stayed thick and yellow, but with a low, humming sound, the gizmo trimmed and shaped them.

Next, he extended to her an opaque dental bridge. She applied it as one might a mouth-guard. Fitting perfectly, it adhered to her gums and filled the unsightly spaces. Her tongue informed her it felt like teeth.

He smiled. With no fuzziness, Yancey experienced it full-wattage, as it were. For a moment she forgot where she was, wherever that was, and a dim memory fragment stirred. It passed so quickly, she promptly forgot it.

Thus tangled up, she nearly missed it when he said, "Now you look more natural."

She inclined her head to him as he had to her. It was another familiar trick from various combat skirmishes which the Board had humorously called "Teacher Merit Evaluations," or, sometimes simply, "Office Chats." Here, as there, she was the nervous party. If she modeled peace, followed her own rules, and mirrored his own calm actions, she would listen better and, perhaps, learn more than he intended. *I can do this.*

She stood still instead of following him when he moved. She covered each eye in turn and looked curiously around her. Her far vision was surprisingly better than her near. *I hope these folks have discovered bifocals along with their snazzy cataract sticks.*

Numerous other exit portals from Tanks like hers appeared to face into the room. Her escort noticed she had not followed and politely waited half-way across the area from her. Encouraged, she observed strange markings above each portal.

The first figure in each was alike for all doors. She formed the impression, "Tank/Container/Reservoir." The second characters differed. Correctly, she surmised they were numbers.

Two portals remained locked. This piqued her curiosity, but instead of voicing the question, she put her hand to ease her lower back and gave her closest attention to this strange companion of hers.

He stood watching but not staring at her. His blue tunic matched hers exactly in color, though not in length—hers was floor-length and split from the hem to the knee on both sides. Noting his knowing smile as she delayed and inspected him, Yancey finally followed her strangely attractive and courteously waiting escort.

As they approached the exit from the area, Yancey heard voices. Emerging into the next space, silver, curved, and much larger in area than the one they just left, she saw fourteen other Beings in mid-thigh-length robes like Conductor Elbraith's, and fourteen other humans in floor-length robes like hers.

Taken together, the robes' colors offered a kaleidoscopic array. In each case the Conductors' robe colors matched that of the person whom they shepherded. *I guess that's what Elbraith is doing to me, shepherding me.*

Fifteen pairs. Seventeen portals in the last room. So, the Beings, whoever they are, are not perfect.

Chapter 5 – Theatre

As assorted as the charges they bird-dogged, the Conductors seemed to vary in age and size. Some older Juvies, the short form for "Rejuvenates," paired with younger Conductors, as with her and Elbraith.

Other Juvies' partners ranged from impossibly young, almost childlike, to older, more mature partners like the Red Conductress. Sexually, partners might be paired with the same or the opposite sex. In age disparity, there seemed to be no pattern either.

Yancey felt glad Elbraith was, at least, middle-aged as near as she could tell. *What a drag it would be to be saddled with a kid or an older person who needs more help than I do. I bet the teenaged human robed in grassy green over there feels like a babysitter to his diminutive Conductor.*

Across the room the fifteen odd pairs, themselves included, provided splashes of color so pleasant to the eye that the colors seemed almost to seep into her being in the way a one-in-a-million sunrise or sunset might sometimes do on earth. Grassy green, mossy green, pastel peach, deep orange, flaming red, deep burgundy, sunshine yellow, straw-pale yellow, both deep and light purple, Elbraith and her pastel blue, sapphire blue, dark and dove gray, and one desert tan—each set of color-complemented companions projected a different attitude.

For example, the flame-red partners, the Juvie a young lady and the Conductor, a wizened grand dame, raised angry voices at each other: *flaming tempers*, Yancey thought. *The silent, straw-pale yellow pair, both seeming in their mid twenties, appear timid and shy but promise blushing loveliness if one could but open them to plain view.*

Man, I'm cracking up, she thought. Then, *Well hey; I am a zombie or something. What should I expect?* The remembrance of Elbraith's and her little mirror-dance greeting, however, left her vaguely unsettled despite her attempt to laugh off her impressions. *What are we? Cagey blue pools of mystery reflect and reveal nothing past the surface.*

She resumed her outward inspections, which seemed far safer than her introspections. A grating voice interrupted her—the grating voice of unintelligible P.A. systems everywhere—from Paris airports to neighborhood schools. It announced something she could not understand. It made her chuckle—*snatch a person from death, rejuvenate her, and fly her to another planet—but your P.A. still gargles!*

A quick glance at Elbraith revealed his golden brown eyebrows elevated in childlike anticipation, his hazel eyes wide with excitement. Yancey stifled the question that rose to her lips when she noticed the Conductors moving their charges and themselves into neat, double-file. She could not repress visions of elementary children lined up in the hall.

Perhaps the announcement was recess. I could use a break.

She and Elbraith fell in behind the desert tans. The colors were not as pretty in rows.

Hydraulics sounded; a large door which would function as their exit ramp deployed from what had appeared a seamless silver wall opposite them. The two rows of oddly assorted partners filed down the ramp and into the outside. Looking back from the bottom of the ramp, her eyes were arrested by the sleek beauty of the black ellipse which she knew had been their ship.

O.K., so I'm the heroine in some weird sci-fi book... and *a zombie.*

Yancey's intellect had always been her weapon of choice. Now she let it attack her mounting sense of fear. To herself she recited nonsensically, *Jocelyn shook her wavy, chestnut-colored hair away from her face, lifted her chin, and determined that her captors would never break her.*

Yancey found flaws in her attempted satire. Here in front of a giant, alien ship, the old make-believe game did not work. Desperation intruded, and her flippant thought caught on a quickly stifled sob. *My hair is ratty gray, and that "lifting the chin bit" doesn't look* quite *the same with a saggy neck flopping below. Oh, yeah, AND I'M DEAD!*

I'm anchored here in weird science. I can't split myself off—create my own world and separate from unpleasant reality. It was the first time her imagination had failed. Her face scrunched. Tears betrayed her to her companion. It was truth without grace, though she didn't know it.

Yancey stared back at the alien ship in its alien berth. A brief glance upward revealed two suns. *I did not create this world.* Behind them the black bulk of the oval ship, around them the moving line of unknown others in this adventure—all mocked her.

Disappointed? Heart broken? Lonely? As an adult, I'd read a book and ease into some other person's imagination, experience some fictional character's pain, not my own; I could always close a book. I could control a book. Often, I'd read the end first to be sure the conflict reached some satisfactory resolution.

Circumstances might have controlled my body, but it had proved impossible to imprison my ideas without my consent. This much the Shrink had assured her. *Surviving, I found, required some control, or at least an illusion... or a self-*

induced numbness into which I could escape. I always escaped—until now.

I am not in control. The solidity of the hulking, black ship; the aliens in their matching robes; the Tank; her aged body, pathetic when stripped of science's interventions; the garbled P.A. like hundreds of others—all demanded some action she might be unable or unwilling to take. All these were boulders rolling over her, an avalanche calculated to crush her.

The next sob erupted without her consent.

Someone else is in control. I want to meet him or her. I could do better than this, have, in fact, for all my long life, except for the slight error of my death.

Her breathing rasped. Pains shot up her skinny, wrinkled legs and launched spasms of fear into her insides.

It was impossible that her companion, walking so closely by her side, had not heard the sob or noted her anguish. Elbraith offered his strong, young arm. She took it.

He whispered, "It may seem a long walk to the theater, but we are nearly there."

Grasping at his merciful diversion, she swiped at her tears and repeated, "Theater?"

"Standard Orientation Center for all Catch-candidates," Elbraith replied.

Then, smiling, he challenged her to smile with him, "Didn't you hear the announcement?"

Yancey's mouth wobbled, "Sure—it was Swahili, wasn't it?"

Then she continued, "Catch-candidate, is that what I am? I thought I was a Juvie."

Her comments amused her companion. "*Juvie* is ship slang for one rejuvenated in a Tank," he continued, then launched into a mini-lecture.

"The Catch-ship jockeys, mostly members of a race called Spacers, never interact directly with candidates and so do not speak of you as real people with lives which they know are precious to the Watcher. They appreciate how important you are to the Beloved, but the slang helps them keep emotional distance."

He continued, "On each Catch-trip, at least one Tank occupant seems to choose annihilation, or in rare cases the Tank will fail because of a split-second lapse in time."

Elbraith looked at her closely. Whatever he saw satisfied him.

"The work of mere seconds can determine the course of your entire life, as well as the outcome of your death."

Elbraith's level gaze physically hurt her heart. Experiencing incomprehensible love, Yancey guiltily skimmed over her suicide attempt in the Tank.

A twinge in her conscience mocked her decision. She wanted to whisper, "Sorry."

Wow, Yancey diverted herself by thinking; *I haven't allowed a twinge of conscience to register in years!*

Entering the theater, the first pair's approach to another seamless-appearing wall triggered the opening of double doors. The sudden opening did not compare to the surprise about to be revealed concerning the seats.

The red pair of figures happened to be the front of the double column.

When the Juvie of the pair—*Er, the Catch-candidate*— decided she wanted a seat glowing green in the back, her fiery Conductress yelled, "No! Up here—the red seats, see?"

The headstrong, young Red girl plopped defiantly into the green seat anyway. A visible compression wave immediately encased her suddenly shrinking body. Red girl yowled in shock and helplessness. The girl's hands with their fingers forcefully bending inward passed as clubs trying to clutch her head in agony, for her whole skull was compressing.

She screamed and screamed as her features mashed flatter. Her eyes grossly sank and her nose cartilage barely framed its two diagonal black slits. Bones audibly popping, she shrank two feet in stature before she could extricate herself from her predicament.

Looking like a caricature of her former self, Red girl surged from the seat and broke contact with the green upholstery. The Red Conductress sank with an exasperated sigh into one of the two glowing red seats.

With rocking footsteps both clumsy and heavy, her furious Red human stomped forward and crashed beside her into the other red seat. As when they compressed, Red girl's features and frame continued to look grotesque as they extruded themselves back to normalcy, the skin stretching and re-shaping with a repulsive elasticity.

All successive pairs carefully matched their robes with their designated seats without being told. First contact with the right color produced distinct notes weaving an unmistakable harmony.

Yancey and Elbraith sank into the middle of powder blue comfort in row two. Yancey's seat immediately began passing a softly humming set of sound waves through her body. *This is like the song in the Tank.*

She felt her tired muscles loosen, and she experimentally flexed her gnarled fingers and then her hurting feet and legs. Gradually elongated and caressed by harmonic waves, her body straightened and relaxed without pain. She was unhurt and suddenly invigorated, her mind sharper than it had been just moments before.

"Man," she quipped to Elbraith, "this is what I call a real tune-up!"

He tipped his head and grinned in acknowledgement of her pun. Then, with all pairs in place, the lights dimmed, and the Orientation began.

Later, Yancey realized a deeper significance of the color-coded harmony of the seating. Elbraith later confirmed her guess that while each pair received the same elemental information at the beginning, the Life-song and the particulars of the ending data pertained solely to the seat occupants in that color.

Chapter 6 –Show and Tell

After the lights dimmed, a harmonious blend of voices presented first the title of the presentation, "The Basics of Planet *X*, a Problem to be Solved in a Complex Equation."

It was not quite music, the sounds Yancey recognized as her life song, yet her pervasive impression was of a well directed concert replete with unison, counterpoint, and harmony. *This is some presentation.*

The humming field around her in her powder-blue chair suspended the presentation each time her mind wandered. After the fourth or fifth time, she grew embarrassed and began to concentrate.

Her Conductor's wise eyes penetrated hers with understanding. Apparently, his program and hers were interdependent; if hers stopped, so did his. Teacher Yancey blushed.

She learned she had been snatched from the very brink of death by *Catch-ship P-17.* She was Catch-candidate/Rejuvenate number Sixteen. Someone called The Watcher—Elbraith used that name before—had signaled the ship to save her life.

On Earth she now was considered dead. The flow of information paused…again…while she became distracted by consideration of her father and then by self-pity.

Self-consciously, she looked around. While Elbraith and she were not the last ones in their colorful seats, four pairs had already exited through a sliding door opposite their entrance. Impatiently, she dried her tears on the blue sleeve of her robe and re-focused on the presentation.

I wonder why—what good is it?

Yancey felt suddenly strapped in some bizarre rerun called "This is Your Life."

The pictures played behind her eyes where they had been safely locked up for a life sentence. Now, someone had not only turned the cell key, but was sharing each episode with Elbraith. Pride in her achievements, anger at this invasion, humiliation from the exposure—all warred within.

She felt like some dementia patient whose memories had been suddenly restored, syndicated, and displayed in a soap opera. *At least it seems to be a semi-private showing—just for Elbraith and me.* For this she was grateful.

I wonder what Elbraith thinks of me. His expression surprised Yancey. *I believe he already knows it all! What is all this about? How could he…?*

When Yancey became aware the pictures and music had abruptly ended, she wondered if she had interrupted the flow again. Just as if she had spoken, Elbraith replied to her embarrassed look, "That's all you need for now, Lady Yancey. Six inattentions stop the feed."

Teachers, she rationalized, *always make the rudest audiences.* The other pairs had left except for one couple, the tans, Pair Number Seventeen, snatched not long after her. They had brushed by her and Elbraith when Yancey had stopped at the portal to inspect the ship.

She and Elbraith had ended up following them in for this exhausting presentation. Yancey had seen them only from behind. Now they seemed to be emerging from their own experience at the same time as Elbraith and she from theirs.

Fury rose in Yancey as the pair's faces turned toward her and became clear. Throwing off Elbraith's hand, she wanted a gun, a knife, or, *YES, a palm laser*! The tan pair in front of her consisted of a short, youthful Conductor and… her murderer.

Chapter 7 – Event Number One

Jason Thomas, stone sober now—*too late*— in his tan tunic, stared at Yancey and turned brick red to the roots of his spiked brown hair. His weak, beardless chin quivered. His brown eyes appeared nearly black in his face under their dark eyebrows. He appeared frozen in shock or in shame.

Yancey had just re-experienced in slow-mo her own recent death at the hand of this drug-head punk. If thought could materialize into reality, this tall kid *would be dead meat NOW. I'd like to reach his neck and strangle him!*

Yancey looked at her fisted, impotent hands. *If only I had the strength of my thirty-seven-year-old hands, instead of these "Juvie" ones, maybe I could do it.* As she let her mind embellish the satisfying scene as she would like it to be, two sensations occurred simultaneously.

Through her ripped a subliminal sound so discordant that every molecule in her body felt disconnected from every other. Vibrations on the molecular level produced so profound a pain that she intuitively recognized that her body, though Yancey was not in a seat, was compressing as Red girl's had earlier.

Secondly, some kind of membranous shield, transparent and dull gray, rose around her and locked her in. The cellular prison concentrated the forces of gravity and her misery. Movement became nearly impossible.

I couldn't have reached the kid if I'd tried. Shockingly, her vengeful thought thickened the wall and added to the compressing vibration, and she knew it.

Jason, rejuvenated in all his fourteen-year-old glory, lifted his hand toward her, palm up and about waist high as to shield himself. Glimpsing her face, he recognized the lust for murder. Embarrassed, he broke eye contact with Yancey.

This is my teacher. She's not supposed to look at me like that. With a fleeting spasm of shame, Yancey thus correctly interpreted his facial expression.

Where does he come off with that "This is my teacher" routine? She hardened her heart even as her angry thought excited her molecules to accelerate their compression.

Jason, on his part, faced the fact that he had senselessly murdered this one who had mentored him. Like her, he had with great reluctance and tear-stained surprise relived it only moments ago in the Theater. Shame, now busy in this wordless exchange between aggressor and victim, dropped Jason's head.

He looked from his vengeful, dead-but-not-dead, fallen teacher to his youthful Conductor like a bewildered child about to cry. His mouth worked like a fish's trying to breathe in fiery air.

Disgusted, Yancey heard a sound curiously like an animal in pain rip from her executioner. Although it twisted uncomfortably in her compacted body like some giant maw worm, his scream arrested her vibrating compression. She figured she now stood about three and a half feet tall.

Yancey stood physically denser and smaller than she had been in life anywhere, even on this weird planet. Her eye level steadied at his waist—how humiliating! Furthermore, she was helpless, even more so than when Jason had pressed the trigger to end that other life.

Fuming, she thought, *I can't defend myself, and I have no more chance to escape than I did the last time I saw this lousy kid. Besides, what would I do? Pummel his kneecaps?*

She ground her teeth, which felt like heavy rocks grating each other.

His next scream pained her.

Yancey stood pressed in physical agony and hated Jason Thomas. Woefully obvious was the fact that wishing his immediate destruction prolonged the sound wave and increased her own suffering. She wished it anyway.

With his head hanging and his body bent down toward her, Jason slowly drew strength from his Conductor who now laid her hand on her miserable charge. Yancey knew that his Conductor offered him—*the murderer*— comfort and spared no such emotion for her, the victim.

Suddenly alerted by this understanding, Yancey turned her head, which was difficult considering she had nearly no neck and seemed to be fighting all the gravity this miserable planet could offer. Her bones popped in neck and spine as she gritted her rocklike teeth with the effort.

Elbraith! He can help me! Isn't he my Conductor?

Elbraith stood alongside her with his face contorted in agony. As a demonstration, he placed his powerful hand on the ugly gray membrane and pushed hard. It remained undisturbed around her and left her misery perfectly intact.

Resolutely, she muscled her flattened face back toward Jason. That creep had no ugly gray cell around him! *What's the Deal? I'm the victim here! Last time I checked I am the one who was murdered, and* el creepo *there pulled the trigger with no timeout for drool.*

The kid's bony body began to be racked with sobs. Despite her membranous prison, she heard him clearly. All by itself, Jason's sobbing resurrected the painful twisting sound which his voice had previously created in her.

Her anger blazed hotter. Causing more compression, Yancey nevertheless shouted, and her dissonant voice grated in the baritone range, Now *you're sorry! I'm the victim, here! Great! Just great! Too late, kid!*

Yancey relived the horror of the laser's contact and squatted there, albeit by force, hating this gangly boy who had ended her life and stolen her carefully engineered youth and landed her on this abysmal planet.

Jason cried to her in anguish, "Oh, Ms. Phillips! I'm so sorry! I was high. I didn't want to hurt you! I don't even know where I got the Las. Oh, please, Teacher, forgive me!"

His calling her *Teacher* struck one chord of sympathy, but Yancey refused to let it vibrate. She looked contemptuously at this pathetic, blubbering child who had wasted her life.

She yelled at him again, and her voice was deep and strangling, "I'm glad you're here! It means Dad got you!" Fresh pain ripped through her, but she experienced it as righteous indignation.

Having slumped to his knees to get down to her eye level, Jason wept. His bony, long fingers slipped down the face of her prison. His face crumpled at her words. He gasped quietly, "Yeah, but I don't blame him. I deserved it."

Boy-like, even in the midst of genuine anguish, his face perked up an instant. He leaned closer and exclaimed admiringly, "You should've seen how these guys"—Jason poked a thumb toward his Conductor— "zapped me out a split second before Rifer could take my head!"

Seeing she did not share his juvenile, scientific appreciation, Jason crumpled again. The kid's Conductor took his elbow. Her touch calmed him. He stood.

His Conductor was a child, in appearance perhaps ten years old. Her jet-black hair cascaded below her shoulders, and her silver-gray eyes momentarily pierced Yancey's gray prison. Reproachfully, she asked, "This is your decision, then?"

With dignity belying her childlike appearance, she urged, "Look at his heart. Jason is truly sorry."

Yancey glowered. It hurt. She held it.

Into the ensuing silence, his Conductor now spoke formally: "I declare my charge free in this matter."

Then in a gentler voice, she said to him, "Come, Jason, now is a time for celebration."

The two tans left. More sound of some comforting sort passed from his Conductor to Jason. Yancey could not understand the words, but even from behind her gray walls, she easily read the accompanying body language. It galled her.

The child's words restored him to harmony. She knew they did.

The tans left. Jason looked forward, not back.

Chapter 8 – Event Number Two

Yancey's head felt on fire. She fed the flames with added resentment.

That boy...that murderer...he has no gray wall...he left to celebrate! Celebrate what, she carped to herself, *what a terrific shot he is?*

The thoughts crushed her closer to the ground. She told herself, *Stop! I'll be as flat as the Catch-ship in a minute. All my bones feel broken.*

Although she did not really want to see Elbraith, she started the labor needed to turn her head again toward him. She stopped, however, after only the slightest movement. Some stirring in her membranous wall arrested her motion instead.

She shifted her eyes around —*sheesh! They're mere slits* —and formed the impression that an area of the transparent material of her cell had stretched somehow into a sort of face, just two bulges where cheeks might be, and a bump which she thought might be a nose.

The mouth of this apparition, if it really was there, was two smooth lines with blackness between. The eyes appeared as ovals of darkness; silver eyelids blinked under two softly undulating eyebrow-ridges. The dark ovals mesmerized her.

With her eyes squinched together from her compression, to see wide, dark orbs fastened understandingly on her face unnerved her considerably. Non-existent eyebrows wavered in sympathy and created a sense of concern rippling through the silvery face.

Strangely, the condolence she had just been demanding did not ease her.

Watching slightly glowing, transparent lip bulges speak to her from nothingness was terrible. The words, however, when they finally came, tried to soothe her as nothing had done since Elbraith's calm understanding during the picture show.

"It *doesn't* seem fair, does it?" the face oozed. The voice reminded Yancey of a "sell-you-a-lemon" used hovercraft salesman on Earth.

The thing continued, "That murderous, bumbling oaf goes merrily on his way while you, my dear victim, are, shall we say, weighed down with many cares?" Here the unbelievable face perked its brows and parodied a smile to see if Yancey had appreciated its humor.

"Weighed down, huh?" Yancey replied in her deepened tone, "Well, yes, you could say that about my current compression." Getting into the comic relief from the preceding scene, Yancey continued, "You know, where I come from, I've been *de*pressed before. It just never really brought me… down like this."

The face appreciated the feeble rejoinder. It said, "At least they haven't *crushed* your spirit."

"No," Yancey croaked, "that would be a real *downer*."

"You've every right to hate him, you know. Look at you. Even your already intolerable wrinkles are compressed. You look like an unhappy Sharpei with your skin all bunched up and baggy like that." The face registered false sympathy and mild distaste. "You're almost a puddle."

Yancey pictured the worried-looking Earth dogs with their deep wrinkles and agreed. Suddenly, Yancey remembered Elbraith. She cranked her head around and away from the face to see what had become of her Conductor. Looking for him took more effort than it did last time.

Just as she located the spot where he had been, the shiny face planted itself so that it once again was staring into her own. She supposed a membranous apparition would flow quite easily from one spot to another in such a medium, but Yancey resented having her view blocked and her great effort thwarted.

The face smiled at her and said conversationally, "What do you want him for? He hasn't been much help so far."

To Yancey this seemed miraculous: it was the very thought she'd had just before making this last turn.

A bit unnerved, she gritted out, "Move. I want to see Elbraith."

A huge sigh escaped the face. It said, "Oh, very well. I'll see you later." It disappeared as easily and mysteriously as it had come.

Her gray prison seemed darker for the loss of the ridiculous face, but peering closely finally produced a glimpse of Elbraith. He was kneeling, praying, and in obvious pain, but he had not deserted her.

Rising and coming toward her, he laid his hands on the areas where the face had been and remarked disapprovingly, "Do you notice the wall seems thicker where Fafnir appeared?"

Nervously, Yancey grated, "You mean that thing is real? I thought maybe my squinty eyes were deceiving me."

"Yes, that is one of his very successful tricks: convince his victim he is not there."

"Victim? What do you mean? All he did was make me laugh."

With a concerned expression, Elbraith said, "Really? Look back a moment."

Yancey did not know how Elbraith did it, but her recent words with the face, er, Fafnir, replayed on the inner surface of the wall. She reread them silently; he, angrily.

When it was over, Elbraith snapped, "Let's review; as a teacher you should appreciate that."

"For starters, your current treatment is unfair despite Jason's real anguish and your own hardness of heart. Fafnir encouraged you to believe you are right to hate the boy even for your present anguish, yet you were aware that your own emotions increased your pain. Remember your body's response to his scream?"

"In second place, Fafnir styled that child as a 'murderous oaf,' which sounds remarkably as though he *wanted* to kill you, which even you know he did not." Yancey winced as Elbraith's words scored a direct hit on her truncated body.

"According to Fafnir's third implication, you are a poor victim being tortured by unknown forces, not a responsible adult who first deserted and now denies her own creed."

Here, Yancey gasped, then protested. Elbraith spoke gently, "Your last, bitter thought on earth was 'her Father's daughter after all.'"

"You feared you had lived a sham in trying to do good to the students who had come through your classroom. You perished wondering if your dying demand for revenge wiped out a whole lifetime of sacrifice."

"Yet just now you refused to give one of those students a release from the anguish of his failure. What good did you do him during your second chance?"

Waspishly, she hissed, "He murdered me, you know. It wasn't exactly a final exam grade, this 'failure'."

If Elbraith's steady gaze had held anything but sorrow…if his look had condemned instead of loved…if he had just hated her meanness of spirit instead of encouraging her best, Yancey would have clung to Fafnir's approval, oily and unclean as it had seemed.

Receiving compassion even while she persisted in betraying her own standards, however, stirred what was left of her flattened heart. If Yancey had still possessed a lovely long neck, she would have bent it to break eye contact with her Conductor, who was squatting in order to maintain it.

Elbraith knows my dying bitterness, my own lust for revenge even now and still expects me to do better. I already know I did not die well.

Elbraith continued: "For his fourth and parting act, Fafnir praised you for becoming worse than Jason when he blasted you back on your planet."

Without trying to hide it, she shot compressed hatred at her Conductor from her eyes. Immediately relieved that looks could not kill, she nevertheless rasped, "How do
you figure that?"

It made his next words worse. "To hate in your heart is the same as murder. Do you now want to murder me, too, my Lady?" His truth combined with tenderness again disarmed her. She did not understand herself.

Seeing the slight softening, Elbraith tried persuasion, "Jason's act of murder occurred while under the influence of the rynlyn he hypo-sprayed himself with. He is sorry for his drug habit. He feels anguish for murdering you."

With a neat and convicting twist of logic, Elbraith stunned her with his next words: "Your act of murder, however, the one you are holding in your heart by unforgiveness and for which Fafnir commended you, is premeditated."

Finding his case compelling, Yancey jerked her flattened eyes from his again. Elbraith did not stop.

"You rejoiced that Duke Silva your father had killed him. You yourself wished to kill him again just now after the theatre. You wanted Jason dead…dead, Yancey—the very thing he inflicted on you. Whose guilt is greater as you persist in this? Yours or Jason's?"

Receiving no response, Elbraith spoke more intensely, "Yancey, to refuse to forgive Jason means you willfully part from me. It will mean you reject my influence and choose Fafnir's way, the way of hatred, murder, and deceit."

"He will use your choice, which he makes seem so right, to help you destroy, not Jason, but yourself. The pain in the membrane teaches you that you hold yourself captive, but Fafnir will finish you off."

"Good grief, Elbraith! I don't want that wavering nightmare. I want you! Where do you get off saying that?"

"But why are you taking that jerk-kid's side? How did that happen? The kid had his own Conductor to show him sympathy. You've got your wires crossed."

"And you're willing to desert me? To leave me to that...*thing*?"

Defying Elbraith and her hurt and fear, Yancey fired off, "That face-thing—Fafnir—understood me better, I think."

Elbraith replied solemnly, "Look at me through the two places where the face appeared."

Yancey did. From the first place she could not see him because of the angle but noted that everything was more indistinct to her eyes because the membrane had thickened in that spot.

From the second place Yancey admitted she could barely see Elbraith at all, yet she knew he knelt just at hand outside the wall. She had unconsciously looked at him around the edges of the lingering impression after the face disappeared.

Yancey fell silent. In a meek voice, she said, "But he seemed so friendly and harmless."

"Let us briefly conduct a second review."

Yancey groaned.

Elbraith questioned her briskly, "What have you learned about Fafnir?"

He answered his rhetorical question, "He wants you to believe he is not there. It is just your mind playing tricks on you."

Her Conductor became angrier with each point he made about Fafnir.

"He seems friendly and harmless, yet look where he urged your mind. He justified your lust to murder!"

"He pretends to be on your side, but why would he come to you and speak so? Think. You're a Teacher. Become a pupil again, and study the problem."

"Neither of us can change you, but both of us can influence you." Elbraith waited.

Yancey frowned, which pulled her compressed forehead down to her nose—neither of them laughed— and gargled, "He wants something. Everybody wants something, and he is willing to lie, and apparently, to murder to get it."

"You, on the other hand," she continued, "have a job to do as my Conductor, and seem willing to bludgeon me with the truth if that's what you believe it takes to do me good." Attempting to smile, her already flattened lips made a grotesque, elongated line across the vicinity where her neck should have been.

"I suppose I'd choose an honest critic over a thousand flatterers."

Perceiving no reaction, she continued thoughtfully, "You are correct in saying I am no victim. I alone am responsible for what I think and do and for how I handle my emotions. Often, my attitude toward an offense has damaged me more than the offense."

"I learned the hard way—emotions are excellent pointers to the truth but lousy guides for dealing with the situation. You remind me that it was my emotions I let betray me as I died. I will not make the same mistake twice. The picture show clarified that—I hadn't thought."

"Fafnir fanned my hatred and soothed my ego, and I...I liked it better than your approach; but I never felt settled while he was with me."

Elbraith nodded and said, "He is an excellent liar, if that is not too blatant an oxymoron."

Here, sensing her mind and will were beginning to subdue her sensibility, he narrowed his eyes and nearly smiled. This Teacher, already dear to his heart as he had studied her life to prepare to become her Conductor, would find a bit of normalcy in the familiar English term for a seeming contradiction: "excellent liar."

Because Elbraith now made an attempt at an English joke of sorts, Yancey saw she had pleased him in her reasoning over Fafnir. Her restricted breathing eased a fraction.

She proceeded, "Let me think a second about the thickened, blurry walls, O.K.?"

"Hmnnn, since he's not really on my side, but you are, he must blur the border between good and evil. *You* certainly did not take that approach."

Elbraith smiled sympathetically at his compressed, preposterously wrinkled charge. He said, "One last thing: the seeming miracle of echoing your last thought. Fafnir first placed the thought in your mind. Only then did he seem to bring your thought to reality."

"Now wait a minute! That was my own voice I heard in my head!"

Elbraith looked at her seriously. Then he bowed his beautiful head, closed his eyes, and said, "Dear Watcher, please convince Yancey of the truth."

Yancey suddenly had the impulse to run away. She would go back to the ship, let the Tank re-form her again. In her heart and mind, she leapt through the hateful gray membrane and tried to exit the equally hateful Theatre.

She attempted a violent withdrawal. *Ridiculous.* She fell smack on her face. *Good thing it's already flat and somewhat rubbery from all the wrinkles*, she thought as she ruefully worked to peel herself from the membrane and the floor. Her shortened arms and increased weight made for rough going. Elbraith rotated the ball and helped.

Jason suddenly came to mind as he had stood there just minutes ago, though it felt as if a slice of eternity had passed since then. Yancey thought of Jason and of Fafnir and of Elbraith and now of this mysterious "Watcher."

Jason's scream twisted in memory again deep within her short, squatty body. She remembered the hatred she held for him, but thinking this time how she might use it differently, she studied it.

She reached out her stumpy right hand, skin flapping along it and along her truncated arm, and touched the membranous wall she had apparently built around herself.

The compressing remained the painful result of her decisions. *Red girl and I could get along.* She remembered how Jason had walked off to celebrate. *What is the key?*

Then she thought of her heart, blasted on Earth by an unintentional child, and broken HERE by truth. The painful twisting tunneled through her.

Can unforgiveness really build a wall around you? Cut you off and torture you while the original guilty party walked off scot free? Apparently it can. Look at yourself, and then look at Jason.

That stinks! Even if Jason didn't feel sorry, I could still be imprisoned by my own unforgiveness. I wallow in my own misery way after the initial injury is history.

Yancey concentrated. She had experienced a momentary lapse from her life's work of blessing children, of embracing each student, of stirring them up and equipping them in her limited way to grow into their potential.

But, hey, she reasoned, *I thought I was a goner.*

The attempted distraction didn't work. Yancey sighed and resumed thinking. Elbraith's prayer to the Watcher seemed to be helping her. *Sure it is,* she thought cynically.

Her thoughts returned to Jason. He *had* called her the best magic word she knew: *Teacher.*

Again she could hear his sobs and plea for forgiveness. Again she heard his Conductor declare *him* free. She *wasn't.*

As she re-played the scene—*there seems to be a lot of that going around on this mysterious planet*—a remarkable phenomenon began. She tentatively let herself join his anguish, like putting just her toe into a bathtub whose water might be too hot for her to bear. She found, instead, that she could bear this. In fact, it did not hurt her as badly as her compression chamber.

Not to forgive him HERE would mean to make a deliberate denial, conscious this time, of all for which she had lived. *I see that now. Elbraith is right—premeditated.*

I am his Teacher. My words one day in class touched him. I remember. I sat with him after hours to help him master Beowulf. *He shuddered over Grindl's mother, and we talked— no wonder he uses rynlyn.*

The kid's remembered sobs vibrating through her did not hurt like his scream. She began sobbing with him this time and felt her own hard heart beginning to soften, like a glacier calving.

Her molecules, so painfully contracted, now began slowly to expand. Fat tears squeezed from her eyes and wet her face. She wondered frivolously if a Juvie ever drowned in a membrane.

Expansion waves rolled through her, and her sobs created new music with his remembered ones. These new sound waves replaced the burrowing twisting and healed as they went.

She mourned her dying failure of commitment and his waste of two lives, not just one. Yancey forgave Jason then. The ugly gray wall thinned and began to dissolve, the two face impressions lingering stubbornly till last. Even dissipating, they broadcast disapproval. She shrugged it off and reveled in her body returning to normal size with all the good space restored between its molecules.

Hmmph! I'll need to think this over again later. Forgiving Jason freed me; he has to deal with his own stuff. Luxuriously, Yancey rubbed her arms: the normal wrinkles of an octogenarian seemed nothing compared to the sagging curtains of flesh she had just straightened out.

For now I want to let it be enough to move without falling and to feel my gentle, honest Conductor's hand supporting my arm once again.

Elbraith smiled and escorted her from the Theatre. "Come. It is a time to celebrate."

Wow. I want to see Jason. I'd like to compare notes with him about how grudges and forgiveness work.

Once again, she was his Teacher.

I'll bet he can teach me something about that, too.

She huffed in amusement as Elbraith and she exited the Theatre.

Chapter 9 – Celebration and a Surprise

Yancey placed her wrinkled, gnarled hand on Elbraith's firm young one and rejoiced that her muscles were no longer compressing her body into a twisted brick about three feet off the ground. The sliding door sang its opening note, an A-flat, she thought, and Elbraith led her from the Theatre and into the adjoining room as if she were royalty.

The music of laughter and clinking glasses and utensils caressed her senses. Tantalizing smells of good food started her salivating. *I used to joke about attending my own wake.*

Entering this room, Yancey saw one long table covered with some dazzling cloth. Of thirty chairs, set with fifteen on a side, a dozen stood empty. Once again, the seating was color-coded. Still shuddering from her recent rebellion, Yancey refused even the thought of sitting anywhere but on powder blue. It proved a great choice.

Her seat stood next to Jason's. With Elbraith holding her chair, she seated herself silently. Only a fraction of a moment later, her former student, seated in tan splendor, threw down his napkin, half-rose with a cry, and hugged her neck. He repeated over and over, "Oh, I am so sorry, so sorry."

She put her wrinkled, old arms around his long neck and thin shoulders and comforted him in her best Teacher voice. Patting his back, Yancey murmured, "I know now. It's all right. I forgive you."

Again she felt some inexplicable stirring in her inmost being, this time like some synthesis of their two voices. This sound healed. *Man, this is nuts!* Looking in his eyes, however, Yancey knew he felt it, too. After a final eye contact enjoyed in harmony with Yancey, Jason leaned back toward his diminutive and now smiling Conductor and chowed down.

The food placed smoothly before Yancey by a willowy young girl who looked nothing like the competent Spacers was one of her favorites: French onion soup! She chuckled to herself, reflecting that she was past worrying about the cholesterol in all the melted cheese. *What's it gonna do, kill me?* She cracked herself up.

Elbraith looked at her again and caught the presence of humor. He smiled with the spare movement of lips which she already loved to see on his beautiful face.

Yancey dug in. Elbraith, whose soup was some green concoction with orange flecks, bowed his head and said grace.

Three courses followed. Each of Yancey's successive dishes was perfectly prepared to her taste. Elbraith, apparently, experienced the best of everything as well. She liked the looks of one lemon-yellow concoction that stood in a blue triangle of gravy or sauce and rose at least seven inches from his plate to form an old powder-horn shape.

When Elbraith and Yancey finished, perhaps four other pairs remained. She and her Conductor walked smoothly to the curved wall of the Celebration Room. The door slid open with its A-flat note vibrating and descending two octaves down from Middle-C this time. *A lock,* Yancey thought.

As the door closed behind them, Yancey jerked with an involuntary and unpleasant shock toward Elbraith. Outside was freezing! Gone was the idyllic perfection of one vibration ago. The portal they had just exited was immediately lost in madly swirling waves of snow pushed by a wind that numbed her bones. Whiteness engulfed them.

What came next unsettled Yancey even more than the cold. Elbraith's face showed distress. He stopped and blinked, in what looked remarkably like bewilderment, against the elements. Huge snowflakes gathered on his long lashes and blinded him. He seemed rooted to the spot.

That portal locked. Elbraith has apparently lost his script. He appears overwhelmed by the loss.

Man, he's the Conductor! Ten more minutes of this, and both of us might die. I've died enough for awhile.

These were Yancey's thoughts as she grabbed her bewildered Conductor, tugged his hand, and had the satisfaction of feeling him follow. *Where am I leading him? I don't know, but standing still in this bone-numbing cold is not an option.*

Given disorganization, Yancey naturally would seek to establish order. Facing an urgent need for guidance and seeing no better alternative, Yancey would take the lead. Thrown into a position requiring action, Yancey would risk a step, even if it were wrong; opportunities for revision or course correction in her world had abounded. She merely acted true to character in the present puzzle.

Drawing Elbraith with her into the mass of swirling whiteness, Yancey brushed aside the thought that they were no longer in her world. With her head bent into the unknown, she pressed into the wind and tugged her Conductor forward.

Chapter 10 – Going Somewhere

Strength coursed through her muscles. She no longer felt almost ninety! The wind picked up. Yancey and Elbraith now encircled each others' waists to help each other forge through the icy blasts.

Yancey was still leading. *Just great,* she thought. Despite her own lack of religion, she knew her allusions; there was definitely one about "if the blind lead the blind."

She feared what the next part of the quote, "they shall both fall into a ditch," might look like on this *X* Planet. This was not comforting.

The quote did, however, lead her quick mind to its source, the Bible, and this led, in turn, to a flashback of Elbraith calling on the "Watcher."

New place, new rules, Yancey thought. Bowing her head anyway to make progress against the fierce wind, she cried, "Watcher!" The icy wind gobbled the word. Nothing happened.

Together, she and Elbraith trudged another seven or eight steps. Then Yancey thought she heard a *G*-note playing insistently, as if some mad toddler bonged on a piano on earth.

Straining toward the sound, Elbraith and she after perhaps twelve more laborious steps reached the source of the G-note sound, which turned out to be yet another opening door, this one for entrance. Suddenly coming out of the wind's resistance, they fell sprawling into relative silence.

The smooth door glided shut, defaulted, bonged again, and then finally closed when Elbraith withdrew his numbed, sandaled foot from impeding the door's closing.

There was an immediate and definite lift-off. They had apparently stumbled into another craft; nevertheless, Yancey had more pressing items than a mere blast-off into space crying for her attention.

Shelter from the icy maelstrom did not guarantee immunity from the chills coursing through her body. She could not stop shaking. Even her insides trembled.

She shook her head like a dog freshly emerged from a bath, and Elbraith did the same. Snow and liquid ice flew around them and quickly puddled on the floor. Between slapping their arms with their clumsy hands, they rubbed their half-frozen fingers and toes. Clumped with snow and ice, their sandals looked ridiculous. So did their frosty toes—her Conductor had the same number she did, *funny I didn't think to count before!*

Elbraith helped her to her knees and then to her feet. His rocklike muscles comforted her irrationally.

Yancey chided herself even as she leaned into him for support. *Didn't he just lose it back there?*

Still adrenaline-charged, and never one to foster ambiguity, Yancey demanded, "What happened out there, Elbraith?" She crossed her arms and shivered, but not from the cold.

"Why, the Watcher had you conduct me," he replied with a quirk to his stiff lips.

"Are you kidding?"

Elbraith helped her to a seat attached to the wall. From the near end around to their right, Elbraith walked over and pressed a red-colored square, removed two warm cloaks from the closet thus revealed and walked back and placed one around a grateful Yancey.

She tucked her icy feet, sandals discarded, into the luxurious folds. Wrapping herself in the cloak made her look like a silvery pyramid, but she didn't notice. She eyed Elbraith warily. He looked the same in his own warming cocoon.

Then Elbraith joined her on the seat and gave a joyous huff. "Yancey Phillips, you conducted me!"

"The preparation books and my review in the Theatre state that the special relationship between Conductor and partner is one of mutual growth. Now I see that is not a mere platitude!"

"Thank you, Yancey Phillips. The catwalk over which we passed is a silver span roughly twelve feet wide and twenty feet long. The gorge below it lies 500 feet below."

Yancey spluttered, "But, but, I couldn't see! We could have died! Again!" This last was spoken with indignation.

Elbraith replied, "Thank the Watcher we did not! Instead, we entered the correct cutter-ship—if it weren't, we couldn't have launched."

Elbraith rose, walked to the end of the compartment to their left this time, and pressed his thumb to a powder-blue-colored square. Two steaming mugs of what smelled like hot cocoa appeared when a panel just below eye level opened. With their respective roles still slightly askew, Conductor and conductee sipped appreciatively for a few moments.

When her teeth stopped chattering for the most part, Yancey said, "Now, talk to me. What happened out there? What was all that about? Where are we going? What do you mean, I conducted you?"

Elbraith reflected, "When we walked out of the ship, it was supposed to be high summer: blue skies, balmy breezes, completed melodies, near tropical, in fact. The view from the catwalk is simply stunning. You can see the basalt mountain and crater in which the Catch ship landed. An aquamarine ocean laps at its great feet. Normally, there is amazing music, not the discordant blast of screeching winds."

Aloud she asked, "So, what happened?"

The little half-smile Yancey had grown to cherish played around Elbraith's mouth for a moment before he continued, "You might say I…froze."

Yancey grinned. Silently, she waggled her eyebrows above the steaming mug and demanded the rest of the story.

Elbraith continued, "Your prompt action short-circuited a certainly uncomfortable and potentially deadly 'wandering.'" He quoted, "Lack of resolution in either partner can result in most painful wandering and retard progress toward both immediate and long-term goals."

Yancey said seriously, "That's from your preparation book? A potentially deadly outcome can result from something as harmless sounding as a 'wandering'? What does it call a death? An 'unfortunate incident' as they do on Earth?"

Elbraith said, "Yes, the quote came from the manual. No, death is called death."

"It was probably a good thing I couldn't see. Knowing what we faced may be why you…"

"*Choked* is a good slang term, I'd say."

Yancey replied loyally, "Caution is more like it! If I'd known what lay around and below, I wouldn't have been so eager to move, either. Besides, you were expecting beauty but walked into danger. I went in blind and stayed blind, and it may have given me an advantage."

Elbraith replied, "Yancey, our mutual journey, if all goes well, has the potential to complete us both. I feel no shame over my failure."

"The manual asserts the Watcher prepares what is perfect for us. It does not demand we succeed, just that we try and continue to work for the outcome."

Yancey gaped. She thought, *not to succeed*?

Oblivious to her reaction, Elbraith proceeded, "We are currently journeying to the Latter Continent of Planet X, probably ahead of schedule, thanks to your quick action. You felt the cutter ship take off, didn't you?"

At Yancey's affirmative grunt, Elbraith continued, "You also asked what it means.   Do you remember how you extracted us from that snowstorm?"

"I...I heard a faint sound, the only marker in all the whiteness, and headed for it."

"Yes, you did that. What did you do just before?"

Yancey first widened, then narrowed her eyes and said, "I called on the Watcher, whatever that is, because you seemed earlier to believe it would listen to you, and it seemed to, because that oily Fafnir disappeared. I called aloud to the Watcher because of that and because I am in a strange place and did not know what else to do."

Elbraith's face registered approval and he asked, "What have you learned about the Watcher already, dear Student?"

"First, if it's real, it must watch everything and everyone all at once."

"Second, it seems to respond to anyone who sincerely calls on it. Frankly, I did not think the G-note bongs were an answer because nothing happened immediately. I see by your face, however, that you believe this Watcher caused the door sound to penetrate the wind. "

"Third, the Watcher seems to help and has, so far," she continued suspiciously, "asked nothing in return."

Then, mischievously, before Elbraith could comment, Teacher Yancey said, "Why, what have you learned?"

All the mischief drained from her immediately when she saw the awe-filled wonder in Elbraith's beautiful face as he answered, "Well, I guess I learned only the power called the Watcher determines what season a person or place is in, and the Watcher can change these as it pleases."

"You see, the landing place really is in full summer right now."

Elbraith stood as he said this and walked to the closet end of their cabin. He pressed a dark blue square and the silvery wall slid open its cover to reveal what reminded Yancey of a widescreen vid-panel.

What she saw was live-feed. The mountain and crater appeared Lilliputian in size already, but they looked exquisite in the aquamarine sea around them. Elbraith's fingers flew over the keys of a computer pad which appeared at the bottom of the dark blue square, and the picture zoomed in on the landing place from which they had just departed.

A chill, not from her recent exposure to sub-zero weather, frissoned its way down her spine. There, instead of their recent arctic passage, she saw a land in high summer replete with blue skies, balmy breezes, brightly colored flowers, and a near tropical stand of what reminded her of palm trees.

Eventually, Elbraith closed the viewer and they went to bed in separate rooms formerly concealed beyond the closet end of the bland, silvery cabin with all its recessed and hidden panels. The sleeping areas even offered individual bathrooms complete with showers, not as nice as those on the Catch ship, but with hot water from two jets.

The beds were amazingly comfortable. Both partners were exhausted.

Sleep came easily.

Chapter 11 – Pictures and Sound

Sleep came easily but did not remain so. This was torment.

She suffered Lady Macbeth's dilemma—sleep opened subconscious doors that let dreams escape into her defenseless mind. The Theatre experience had stirred up a hodge-podge of memories boiling out from the cells where she had locked them. The prisoners thus liberated demanded revenge for all their years languishing in the dungeon.

Dreams, people call them. Nightmares, she called them. In her nightly ritual for over fifty years on earth, she had posted the guards—one pink, one green pill—to suppress the nocturnal picture shows.

HERE, Jailbreak! Faces of her four children appeared in no particular order and held her hostage. One hated her. One prayed for her. The other two didn't care. Yancey thrashed and deformed all her nice bed.

Replacing their images, nausea became her new slave-master. Through a dream door her Grampa crept, sneaking into her bedroom as he had from the time she was ten. His ugly, yellow, horse-teeth shushing, "Sssh! don't tell! Your Dad will be jealous. Gramma will hate you because Grampa loves you."

Yancey wet her bottom sheet. Salt-sweat popped out from her pores like hot fat rendered from bacon. Her hair became damp and tangled from fat tears rolling.

Before she retched, the hated, crawling sensations shifted. She tossed and turned.

Terror assumed the position of head torturer. Incredibly, the final nightmare scene would be her worst. The memory first cracked and then oozed through the careful wall she and the doctors had sealed to keep it hidden.

Yancey felt again the million-pound weight of his head in her helpless hands. Garish blood ran from his ruined cranium. It formed an impossible sea in her shocked lap. Her own scream finally released her from prison: "Dan…nnnn."

The show at the Theatre had halted just before this picture now released in nightmare. *Who is that? What happened back on Earth? I don't remember! I have the name: Dan. But what…? Whoever it was, he's dead.*

She curled into the fetal position. No rescue came.

Now awake, Yancey remembered more of the blank: the private hospital, eighteen months halting between life and death in a coma, and herself emerging at the age of thirty-seven where she had chosen to "freeze" her outward appearance. *Pills, counseling, and new bio-treatments*—she remembered living the next fifty years. Sickness and a catatonic state beckoned her again, and Yancey let go, willing herself to slide down. On earth she had entered the catatonic state with its inviting blankness.

HERE, however, something new happened. A hand rested on her shoulder. It did not knead her flesh. It conveyed a wave of sound. For just a moment, stark terror of the unknown superseded all the remembered horrors of both the memories and the nightmare.

Then the wave of sound formed one Word: *PEACE. A word from the humming in the Tank,* she thought.

She whipped her head around for a look and saw no one. Her body uncurled. *How STUPID can I get? The word PEACE? That's it? That's all I need? After I survived all that?* So went her first shattered thoughts.

She wanted to despise the Word just as she had on Earth. She could not. Unbidden and unknown chords in her body trembled at the Word and began to resonate in tune with it, instead of with the horrors and sorrow which had been the stuff of her life and her dreams.

I'm not the one doing this. Who's giving me peace? How? ... I want it!

She did not slide. In this place, the trauma of the inexplicable Daniel remained but could not burn one centimeter past the boundary that sudden Word had established in her inner self.

What is happening? Who's HERE?

Yancey mourned for the first time.

Not one doctor explained the process to her as she now understood it in the light of this new experience. Busying herself with fresh linens, she thought it out.

It seems that to isolate from pain is to stop pleasure in equal measure. One spigot, not two. For one heady moment then, she knew the truth of a quote from Oswald Chambers, or was it Charles Spurgeon, *Oh, some book my son Patrick had me read*: "The valley is the measure of the mountain." *To the extent I refuse to experience pain, I render myself incapable of joy.*

I lived fifty years without real joy. I drugged myself into merely coping.

Her sensation of the hand stayed with her. The Word *Peace*, she understood, was a new spring intended to spread within her. It was alive and healing.

Let it dig me deep and wide and long, she thought. *I consent to feel my feelings.*

In the next room Elbraith pushed himself to his knees from his face-down position on the simple blue rug by his bed. He had hurt all over as he had called again on the force called the Watcher for his partner who thrashed and moaned and screamed yet could not wake up in the next compartment.

If not for his action of crying out to the Watcher, Elbraith thought sorrow might have broken his heart, *and that, he thought, is irrational. Whoever wrote the Conductor's Guide was a wiser being than I.*

Now, his tears and words turned to "Thank You," exactly as the *Conductor's Guide Book* proscribed. Elbraith snorted at how well the formula worked and at how well it predicted its subjects.

As soon as his peace returned, Elbraith went wearily back to bed. He did not question the phenomenon. It was enough that he had learned more about how to work it.

The sound of the shower running in Yancey's room pattered him to sleep.

Chapter 12 – Landfall

Hunger woke her. In a clean tunic, she went prowling for food and met her Conductor. He carried a full breakfast tray. "Hungry?" he asked.

"Either that or a bear's loose—hear the growling? My belly feels like my throat's been cut."

Elbraith got it. "An old western author's words, aren't they?" Yancey winked a "Yes" because her mouth was already full of food.

The meal was their only focus until Elbraith excused himself, walked to the far end of the cabin, and opened the ceiling-to-floor view port. An alien city circumscribed their now rapidly descending ship: as far as Yancey could see to left or right, and above and below, strangely colored towers and flattened rooftops filled the screen. She experienced the thrill of coming into an unknown port.

Some edifices looked like enormous jacks. Many rooftops seemed covered by beautiful, blue water. Multi colored skyscrapers reached far above the ship-pod, and Yancey glimpsed multi colored blocks of floors as they passed. She could not tear her eyes away.

It was not gaudy. It was not garish. It was not the chaos it would have been on Earth if such absence of uniformity had prevailed.

No, this city was form. It was symmetry composed of infinite variety. Even the colored towers presented different shapes: triangles, curved stair-steps, blocks, domes, and split edifices.

It was so clean, the colors glowed. Like the sounds back on the Catch-ship, they seemed actually to mean something, if only Yancey knew how to interpret them.

Elbraith said, "You might want to change and freshen up. You have an hour before we can disembark, and there is the formal gathering we must immediately attend."

Yancey vaguely remembered this from the Theatre's opening summary.

Upon entering her room, she faced a bigger problem than a formal gathering. As the ship's familiar G-note sounded behind her to signal the slide-door to her room had closed, her eyes lifted toward the left wall of her compartment. Yancey heard a slithering voice say, "Welcome to Plan-city of Planet *X*."

Perhaps Yancey's nightmares were not over after all. Barely ruffling the wall's smooth surface, Fafnir's slick face greeted her. Alarmed, yet both attracted and repulsed, she barely registered the multiplied, low humming as the pod ship sounded its note and successfully docked in its proper berth in the terminal's beacon-harmonic.

Chapter 13 – Ways and Means

Yancey snapped, "Fafnir, go away."

The shimmering face raised its faint eyebrows and looked contemplative. Innocently, Fafnir tilted his face so he looked inquisitive and harmless. "Mmmnn, I wonder what they've told you about me."

His faked innocent look made Yancey laugh. He looked like so many of her school children over the years. Against her better judgment, she felt slightly disarmed.

Yancey asked, "What is it you want?"

"Why, to help you, dear lady."

An unladylike snort of disbelief escaped her.

"Didn't they show you a bunch of disconcerting and quite painful experiences?"

At her silence, he continued, "You'll have to relive some of them, you know."

Yancey blurted, "But I just did!"

Fafnir's smile oozed sympathetic concern. His face slowly nodded and sent waves of comforting silence her way.

"Plan-city—get it? Here's where they'll mix you all up, shake you out, and make you PROVE yourself, according to THEIR plan, not yours."

Watching her carefully, Fafnir continued, "Poor lady. I'd have thought last night's ordeal was enough."

Remembering *PEACE*, Yancey kept her eyes down, but inside herself, quite distinctly, she recorded for future reference, "Fafnir is not omniscient." She did not know why she used just that word, but it fit. Maybe she could beat such a being at his own game!

He considered her sadly—she actually felt his momentary sorrow— then sighed, "Well, I can see you don't want my help with your journey."

After a pause during which neither of them spoke, Fafnir offered, "Well, I guess I'll leave now." His face actually turned as if to go. Then he looked at her with such compassion, Yancey suddenly felt churlish to doubt his sincerity.

Catching that reactive glimmer from Yancey's face, Fafnir turned back so she saw only his profile. He really was beautiful if one liked weird wall hangings.

Breathing peacefully as if he had reached some conclusion, Fafnir murmured, "O.K., I can see you're concerned about getting ready to disembark."

Then he turned full face toward Yancey, firmed his lips as if bearing some hidden wound nobly, and stated, "I'm going to leave you some help anyway, milady."

"Here." With this word there stretched from out of the wall on which his face mesmerizingly undulated a small, gray, smooth stone. It dropped onto the floor with a distinct thump, not a musical note, a good old Earth *thunk* which sounded harmless and produced a small despair in Yancey of ever returning to her home planet.

Careful to make no move, Yancey asked, "What's that?"

"It's a shortcut, a way of escape, should you need it, milady. If you ever find yourself in despair and believe you can bear no more, rubbing this small stone will return you to its place of origin."

As Fafnir intended, Yancey heard the words, "its place of origin" but understood them as "Earth" because that is what she wanted to believe. After all, it was an Earth sound the stone had made.

In a sudden guilty flurry, and disregarding the gray stone, Yancey said, "In the name of the Watcher, depart," which, she realized, was what she should have said to begin with.

With a lift of both eyebrows, practiced over centuries to mask pain at that name and hide anger at Yancey for using it, Fafnir's face disappeared. He left the impression of shock at her ingratitude.

Suddenly in a flurry, Yancey began rushing around to dress and tend to her hair. She looked everywhere, anywhere in the smooth room except at that innocent looking gray stone on the floor. *I don't want anything of his*!

Opening the slide-door closet, Yancey exclaimed over the beautiful powder blue body suit to fit under her clean tunic, boots, and soft outer robe with its subtle border of blue sparkles. She took extra time unplaiting and re-braiding her hair. It did not look quite as gray as it had.

In the mirror of her dressing table, yet another slide-out feature, she struggled vainly to keep her eyes from that innocuous stone. It reflected and stared at her with its innocent eye. It drew her gaze against her will.

It was like some "Wet Paint" sign on earth. If the sign said "Don't touch," that became all one's heart desired.

Yancey applied cosmetics to distract herself from the strangely inviting pebble. *I look a bit younger. Not a day over seventy-one or seventy-two,* she thought, trying to force a laugh to destroy the ridiculous drama she was making over the stone.

Elbraith knocked on her door. "Coming," she cried.

Determinedly, she stepped over the Earth-stone to leave the cabin. At the slide door, Yancey paused. Realization swept over her. *Why, THAT's why I can't keep my eyes off it: it's from HOME!*

Yancey turned around and closed her fist over the harmless gray friend. It was, she rationalized, *the single familiar thing, so far*.

She put the pebble into a small, Velcro receptacle on the belt at her waist. Sweeping the glorious cape around her, Yancey waited for the G-note exit sound from the door and smiled almost regally at Elbraith as she placed her hand on his arm. She commanded her conscience to silence.

Proud of his charge, Elbraith led her along the corridor and down the silvery gangplank.

Here the air was balmy, but Yancey had little time to savor it. Immediately inside the terminal doors waited a curious reception committee of one. With a deep dip, a mere girl in appearance swept them quite an accomplished curtsey.

She said, "Honored Conductor, Mizz Phillips." She introduced herself as Isabelle. Her laughter cascaded like pure water down a mountain fall and washed clean joy over Yancey.

Isabelle inquired with a friendly smile, "Does either of you have anything to declare for customs?"

Elbraith laughed lightly as if Isabelle had made some joke.

Yancey, however, suddenly wanted this girl to inspect her Earth pebble. Fingering her belt, Yancey waited. Then she thought, *How stupid am I going to look declaring a pebble? No, I'll just toss it away later when no one's looking.*

Isabelle came up only to Yancey's shoulder. As Yancey fingered her belt, their young escort looked up at Yancey with the penetrating eyes of innocent youth and found her wanting, Yancey thought. All Isabelle said, however, was "This way, please."

How could she know? Yancey reasoned to herself.

To Elbraith Isabelle now spoke in a language which really sounded like the tinkling of bells. If Elbraith's reply was like mellow golden bells, Isabelle's words complemented his like joyous silver bells with treble sounds in some delightful descant punctuating his melody line.

Did she tell him?

Elbraith's face did not change.

Expelling a long breath, *No.*

They turned to go. Elbraith made sure he was on one side of Yancey and Isabelle on the other. Yancey suspected this was not to protect her from the crowd: quite the contrary.

Their threesome emerged into golden sunlight that shimmered from and warmed the colored stones of every paved surface and building. Yancey's mind boggled. The colors overwhelmed her. She wanted to stand and gawk like a country bumpkin seeing his first skyscraper.

There was no time.

The dark interior of a small, gray cab engulfed them. With her face thus obscured, Yancey rebuked her guilty conscience: *I had no opportunity to throw it away without making it a big deal.*

Two fat tears slipped down her cheeks. The small gray stone secreted in her belt demanded her attention. Deliberately, she shifted her mind to the kaleidoscope of the city receding behind the cab.

Chapter 14 – G.A.L.A.

Signs of civilization thinned as the cab rocketed along. She settled back for a nap. When Yancey came to, Elbraith was looking through the window at a mansion lighting the mountaintop toward which the cab was hurtling. Yancey leaned nearer his tinted window and said, "Man, we really are out in the boonies." Nothing but a blur of sparse vegetation, rocky soil, and the blacker outline of other mountains framing the lone mansion's solitary hill could be seen, no matter which direction Yancey craned her neck.

Isabelle turned her patrician head toward Yancey but said nothing. Feeling at ease, Yancey answered her unspoken question. "'Out in the boonies' means away from civilization." Yancey's reward for her good deed was Isabelle's tinkling laughter.

Because the cab was a hovercraft, it did not zigzag up the side of the mountain to the imposing edifice. Straight up felt great if one liked roller coasters. She always had. The cab gently halted on the landing pad seven hundred feet above the canyon surface and on a level space below the building's front doors.

I sure like this planet's technology. If I ever return Earth side, I'll have to tell Dad. Yancey captured the "if" in her thought and mentally ejected it for the traitor it was.

The cab darted away and left them at the end of a short, broad slideway that conveyed them up toward palatial, wide stairs. A path of golden light spilled over them from subdued lighting suspended apparently in cobwebs, for all she could see, above the moving walkway. The fairy-dust lights held at bay the black darkness surrounding them.

From the slide-walk one could continue escalator-style up the stairs or step to right or left and ascend at one's own pace. The steps were grandly terraced. Leading Yancey onto solid, warm stone to walk up, Elbraith and Isabelle greeted a few acquaintances enroute. Her knees creaked a bit, but the familiarity of climbing stairs soothed Yancey.

When they reached the top, maroon-liveried footmen opened two great maroon doors outward. The inviting colors complemented the golden stone. *Tinkerbelle—no, Isabelle—* spied an acquaintance, thanked Yancey and Elbraith for the ride, and glided gracefully away.

Elbraith's attention was all forward, not on their former companion, so Yancey focused her inquisitive gaze on the other guests mingling on the grand stair landing. Numerous Beings like Elbraith and Isabelle conversed with others like themselves and with laughing youths and maidens. *Oldsters like me are rare in this assembly.* At least fifty double splashes of color identifying other Juvies and their Conductors brightened the crowd.

Strains of unearthly music caressed them. The music swelled as two more maroon-liveried footmen opened interior, fifteen-foot, ivory doors with panels and knobs chased with gold. Inside lay a grand ballroom the size of two football fields.

Yet another footman handed each of them a program which was really a small booklet. He then bowed and rapped an ivory staff three times on the floor. He announced "Sir Elbraith of Gimoire, Sanctioned Conductor, and Rejuvenate Yolanda Phillips."

A quick peek at the thick program's header revealed, "Guides' Assembled Lyceum Association is pleased to announce G.A.L.A., *IC,* circa 2376." Yancey had to dig mentally to come up with "lyceum: a hall for public lectures or discussions." The ballroom atmosphere didn't look like what the program promised.

Elbraith confirmed the "IC" signified "ninety-nine." *I sure miss my computer link implant,* she thought, *along with the hair implants, and ...*

As Yancey stood reflecting, a Very Important Person made his way through the crush and requested Elbraith to introduce him to his lovely companion. Without seeming to do so, Yancey took the gentleman's measure.

Elbraith announced, "Lady Yolanda, Colonel Ingress." As he stood with them and made small talk, Yancey understood that as Colonel Ingress saw it, he honored them by his notice of them. His figure looked handsome in a tailored military uniform of some sort. It was obvious he was accustomed to command. Discreet gemstone tabs on his ivory uniform's collar proclaimed him some great personage. He exuded charm and protection.

Ingress asked her to dance. Elbraith gave her hand with alacrity to the gentleman, who fortunately bent to place his lips on her gloved fingertips and thus missed the non-verbal communication transpiring between Yancey and her Conductor.

Her eyes flashed, "I don't want to dance with this pompous bag of wind!" Elbraith's intensity widened his eyes and conveyed, "This one is important. Do it!" She suppressed her reluctance.

As Ingress led her onto the floor, she suffered a surprising pang of loneliness. She wished suddenly for her Dad instead of this pompous stuffed uniform. Always a staunch advocate, Duke Silva would've made this popinjay squirm and leave, even if Elbraith would not. She smiled at the thought.

Looking down at his new partner, Ingress caught the smile and fielded the look of affection. *For whom could it be,* he reasoned, *but me? This Powder Blue will probably be an easy one to contract.*

Colonel Ingress drew himself up as he manuevered her masterfully through the dance. Ingress assured himself they made a stunning couple despite her advanced age in that bright throng; certainly, he thought his half did.

When the music ended, Ingress bowed, obviously a great honor for her. Yancey stifled a giggle. Then he stunned and confused her.

He boomed, "You know, my dear, if you select me as your Guide, we'll travel in style and comfort. My men will serve your every whim. I myself will be your ardent slave. The unit's equipment will make smooth, efficient work of the rough terrain and the crossing. Why, we'll have you up to Leapside in no time."

He paused, but receiving no response, continued, "You might tell Elbraith your selection now, you know, and save yourself some trouble. I can guarantee no more than eleven other Rejuvenates in the company and so can promise personalized service and top-drawer accommodations."

Yancey smiled politely and replied, "Oh, I believe I must take my time about it. Thank you for a stimulating interlude."

Yancey was thinking, *NO! I couldn't have missed this much! What does he mean? Guide? Rough terrain? Leapside? Trouble? I need to speak with Elbraith, pronto.*

The ball afforded no time for this, however. No sooner had Ingress restored her to Elbraith and pretentiously kissed her gloved hand in temporary farewell than her Conductor, who surely had gone mad, ignored her distress and said, "Yancey, you must meet Anthony Gael. Anthony, this is Lady Yancey."

After this abrupt introduction, Elbraith remarked, "Oh, excuse me. I think I see Isabelle."

When Yancey turned her startled eyes back to the new gentleman standing by her side, he said with an accent reminiscent of the British, "Well! The fellow certainly can move when he wants to!" Her thoughts were not so charitable.

Then Gael said, "I say, shall we get some punch?" He possessed her arm before she agreed. Despite her elbow-length gloves, Yancey felt a shiver of sexual discomfort when he touched her.

Currently, on *X* Planet, Yancey was about 75 years old as nearly as she could figure from her last look in the mirror. In the normal scheme of things, 42 year-olds did not hit on little old ladies. Still, a lifetime of experience had taught her not to ignore her "inner radar," as she liked to call it. She had done just that on many occasions and had come to grief for not trusting herself better. *Age has some perks.*

In his charming accent, Gael directed, "Now, let's make this a proper interview if we can, shall we?" He acquired two identical orange-frosted concoctions without consulting her preference. Then with a persistent lack of consideration for his companion, he settled them at a small table flanked by two elegant, carved wooden chairs.

Yancey scooted her chair away from his twice before he gave up and allowed her some knee space.

"I've made the crossing before, about four times, now. I know what bites, what stings, and what kills—and, how to avoid them. I'm an accomplished sailor, unlike that stuffed shirt you just left. I know three designated meditation spots where you'll want to stop. I can give you a list of provisions you'll need, and for the right price will even purchase and pack the gear and supplies. What do you say?"

Listening gave Yancey clues. She inquired, "How long has it taken you to make an average crossing?"

"That depends on the members of the expedition and the quality of equipment, but I normally expect to be across in five to six weeks."

"How many men in your outfit?"

"One dozen with a cap of twenty clients, and we supply the weapons and transportation."

Yancey thought, *Weapons?*

Making her voice sound confident, she demanded, "Describe the terrain and your selection of the route, please. How will you arrange for the boat?" This last question came to her from his sailor comment.

Gael's eyes caressed her and he replied in his smooth accent, "Ah, Ah, Ah, no trade secrets till you sign the contract. Would you care to review it just now?" He captured her gloved hand in his own.

When Yancey raised a protesting eyebrow and deliberately removed her hand, Gael masked a look of scorn and huffed, "Madam, I assure you I am simply the best. When you feel ready to come to terms, if I have not already engaged with my quota, you may have your Conductor contact me."

Still sure of his moves, Gael masterfully caught her hand again, turned it palm-up, and placed a lingering kiss before folding her fingers over it. His soft mustache brushed her glove suggestively. His fine, brown eyes promised more than that.

The whole action was at odds with the suppressed annoyance discernible in his body language. He released her fingers lingeringly, bowed and strode purposefully toward the mint-green partners standing some twenty feet down the room to Yancey's left.

Pervert!

Left thus alone, Yancey made a quick check of the room and saw Elbraith dancing with Isabelle. Before any other Being or would-be Guide claimed her attention, Yancey wanted time to consider what she had learned. She needed to scan that blasted program and see if the neglected guidebook mentioned all this leaping business and the dangerous journey.

What is this all about? She turned and walked toward the balcony doors about six feet from where she stood.

The air outside was as refreshing as cool water. Making sure no one followed, Yancey descended four broad steps into a subtly lit, formal garden. *Really, this is too much like a corny romance novel,* she thought, *the ball, the mysterious contacts, an impending journey, and now the structured garden. What's next? Oh, yes, Prince Charming.*

Actually, it was a relief no Romeo came. She noticed she was rubbing her gloved palm where the unctuous Gael's lips had touched. All she thought was, *Out, damned spot.* The reference from *Macbeth* calmed her, and she wiped her glove on a harmless looking, broad leaf, *poor leaf,* and chose a path to the right.

The garden was beautiful and extensive. Its loveliness far exceeded the glories of the ballroom. Ahead of her, two small clouds of phosphorescent insects like gnats back home swarmed in balls.

The plantings and flowers were other-worldly and lush. After numerous turns Yancey found an inviting bench looking like an oval-shaped mushroom on its pedestal. The niche where it stood was surrounded by a rare white garden with three or four clouds of blooms subtly silver in moonlight. She relaxed.

Where she sat, intermittent waves of aroma sweet as gardenias but not so heavy drifted to her. The seat in the niche was softly illumined from overhead, and she believed she could read in this place, like Scotland at midnight in a full moon.

Quiet prevailed except for the hinted sound of gentle water flowing off in the distance. Just breathing in this atmosphere became a great pleasure. That *Peace* Word she had heard spoken rose inside her.

She sat in this unfamiliar contentment for an indefinite time and then finally sighed and gave full attention to her "program." The guidebook seemed too ponderous for her delicate surroundings.

The small booklet contained a list of 108 Guides, those present tonight indicated by gold highlights and approved by the Lyceum Association, the people staging this ball. Each entry offered the person's name, a small picture often with equipment as the background, and stats. She skimmed entries like "42 Crossings of Outland, 7 treks in M'naouth (whatever/wherever that was), 79 Rejuvenates of 82 to Leapside. This last statistic became the one of most interest to her—what became of the other three? The information continued, birth-home: J'ruhn (*Yeah, that helps a bunch*); background: 20 years, Chief Administrative Assistant/Coram Technology; 10 years, Lyceum Guide Apprentice; 12 years, Licensed Lyceum Guide.

And so entry after entry went. Dutifully, she skimmed and scanned the booklet until somewhere around the "R's" her eyes tired. To rest them, she looked again at her beautiful surroundings.

Unexpectedly, Yancey found herself focused on a golden light she had failed to notice in the distance. She saw it now only because a vagrant breeze moved some obscuring branches. It winked at her.

Yancey smiled. Although reluctant to leave her alabaster sanctuary, she let curiosity win. She walked toward the place where she believed the light had been.

Soon she found a plain shed whose closest wall stood immediately outside the boundary of the garden; no fairytale cultivation graced its plank sides. Good windows on all sides emitted light. Rough, uncultivated land fell away from its far side in a slope that was obviously the backside of the mountain on which the chalet sat.

Low humming reached her from the shed and drew her beneath the generous overhang facing her. She walked under the slanting roof and on through the shed door to where a leanly muscled young man was sculpting.

Curious to see what he worked on, Yancey walked quietly around him and stopped about six feet from his left side. He acknowledged her with a friendly look and pushed his thumbs higher into the clay before him. The motion created eyebrow ridges in a most interesting clay face. She did not feel like an intruder.

As he continued to work, Yancey studied him as closely as he studied the art he was creating. He seemed much like his clay. Both were slightly reddish in coloring. Brown spots with lighter centers—exaggerated freckles, she thought—literally covered his strong face, arms, hands, legs and feet. (He wore sturdy sandals and a short, modest tunic that reminded her of a Roman laborer.) Both he and his clay seemed basic and honest.

When he finished the brows, sockets, and eyes which he'd been doing as she entered, he withdrew his hands from his work and turned to face her. All he said was "Hello," but Yancey felt as though she had won a prize.

She smiled. "I'm Yancey Phillips. I hope I'm not disturbing you. Your light and then your humming drew me here, and I felt so welcome, I'm afraid I've displayed a terrible lack of manners."

"I'm Trenell. You are most welcome in my studio. Not many come this way, and I delight in guests."

As they spoke, Trenell slipped his hands into some reddish-brown muck in a bucket standing on the floor beside his table. With a stubby brush he scrubbed most of the clay residue from his hands and from the ruddy hairs on his arms.

Yancey followed him as he walked over the dirt floor and out under the overhang to an oversized faucet and sink. Here he rubbed some more, this time with a used rag hanging there for the purpose, until the water ran clear. Grabbing a rough cloth from a second large hook, Trenell dried his hands and forearms.

"I would like a cup of tea. Care to join me?" he said.

Yancey replied, "Yes, please."

During the following modest preparations, Yancey walked around the inside of the shed and admired some of Trenell's completed works sitting on shelves or on the packed dirt floor. Perhaps ten of them stood or sat in no particular order. Most were of people. Only two were of natural scenes, one a clever tree and the other a single plant with a single, exquisite bloom.

Trenell led Yancey back outside and toward the left end under the overhang to a crude, high table with two elevated chairs. He had managed coarse bread with a chewy crust and a chunk of cheese beside it. As he asked Yancey to be "mother" and fill their handcrafted clay mugs, he used a sharp, curved knife to work on the bread and cheese, which he offered Yancey on a glossy, broad, green leaf. No cream or sugar appeared.

With both of them served, Yancey turned her head and frankly studied what she could see of the ground beyond the shed. As she did, he bowed his head and gave thanks, which she thought was rather quaint. It sounded nothing like the formal petitions she'd heard Elbraith offer.

Sipping the tea, which was surprisingly good, Yancey said, "So, what's it like out there?"

With a grave look, Trenell said, "The Outland is wilderness. Three terrains lie between here and Leapside: mountains, a desert plain, and a sea."

Pleased by his straightforward answer, Yancey asked, "Do you go to Leapside often?" Chewing, Trenell merely nodded.

"The Outland…it sounds scary."

"It is a testing or proving ground."

Yancey informed him, "At home they finally had to declare certain parts of the globe off-limits because it was so easy to die there from radiation pockets, chemicals, or new weaponry testing."

Trenell looked at her with an interested expression and understanding warmth that somehow made Yancey want to cry, but a beacon light broke the moment. The light rose into the air and cast the garden into a blue glare that seemed terribly harsh compared with the gentle golden light in which they sat.

Trenell said, "Your Conductor is seeking you."

With a sinking feeling, Yancey exclaimed, "How embarrassing!"

"Yes. He will be reprimanded for losing track of you. A beacon light means you have been out of his sight for more than sixty of your minutes. He will lose face and will suffer some merriment at the hands of his fellow Conductors when you safely return."

Elbraith had not been the one she thought would be embarrassed. Her heart went out to her unsuspecting Conductor. She rose, muttering, "One would think your technology could use something like a GPS locater instead of some big, blue light that announces the problem to the whole world."

Trenell was plainly amused. He said, "Yes. They may issue you a PL/Positional Locater for your upcoming trek, but most do not find them a necessity at a fancy dress ball." His mischievous smile made her feel better.

He pointed, saying, "Go down here to the silver column, and take the right-hand path and then a hard left. You'll be back safely in the fold in no time."

Within twenty feet, Yancey looked back and could no more see the light from the shed. Yellow and green foliage, ugly in the blinking blue searchlight, completely obscured it. She reached the column and took the right path.

The hard left appeared immediately. When she had hurried some five paces, Yancey ran into a tall, solidly built man of indeterminate age. His surprisingly strong arms caught her, and he cupped her elbows to steady her.

Yancey jerked herself from his grasp as if suddenly scalded and looked up some distance to his face, but with his back turned to the beacon, his face was in darkness. She yelped, "Oh! Please excuse me!"

He exclaimed, "Ah! I have the great pleasure of finding Elbraith's esteemed partner. Lady Yancey, allow me to escort you back to safety."

She did not like it that he knew her name, but even more, she disliked not seeing his face. This oversized Being with his obscured face gave her the sensation of increased gravity in his immediate location. As Yancey placed her hand on his proffered arm, she looked up and received a shocking, unpleasant jolt.

As they now faced the mansion, it had to be a trick of the garish blue light that touched his eyes with a look of covetousness so evil, Yancey knew what he wanted was herself. Unlike the exchange with the lascivious Gael, this was not sexual.

So, what is it?

Like the initial scalded feeling, the glimpse of his incomprehensible craving passed so quickly, she doubted her own perception. The gentle Being's harmlessness became obvious with further scrutiny.

What am I thinking? This man, on second glance, appears completely benign. From her peripheral vision she saw he smiled pleasantly with no hint of over-familiarity.

In a perfectly open and friendly manner, he asked, "Am I correct in believing that you need a Guide?"

Taking her silence for assent, he continued, "I take no more than three travelers at a time. I am an expert in every aspect of the Outland. My excellent contacts and twelve-man support crew provide comfort and safety. The crossing will take no more than five weeks, and the final patch over water will give us no trouble. I own a fast ship. Provisions are top quality, and" –he raised his eyebrows and quirked his head— "we offer a significant senior discount."

Why do I feel oily and heavy? The guy just made a joke, for crying out loud. Yancey scolded herself. *Snap out of it, girl! That blue light must be addling my brain.*

Watching her face, he chuckled, and Yancey made the mistake of looking directly up at him a second time. It was a mistake because the moment they made eye contact, Yancey felt an overwhelming urge to trust this man for her trek, with her life, or in whatever he might require.

It was his eyes. They drew her into depths she shrank from penetrating.

She was both repelled and attracted and could not break the contact. The idea of breaking that connection felt like losing a part of herself she had yet to discover. Walking with this stranger felt irresistibly alluring. She gave no thought to her footing.

All she wanted was to look and look at him. For such a large fellow, his face and body seemed perfectly proportioned. He was not overtly handsome, merely attracting. The whole gravity sensation influenced her to lean on his arm more heavily. He seemed unfazed and exuded massive strength.

Then Yancey stumbled. Afterwards, she marveled that such a thing as tripping could happen on such immaculately groomed paths. Of necessity, she jerked her eyes away from her fascinating companion. With easy grace he steadied her and prevented her fall.

With the mesmerizing eye contact broken, Yancey felt a panicky unwillingness to resume it. To restore some measure of normalcy to herself, for she thought surely the gentleman would think her daft if he knew what she was thinking, Yancey asked, "What is your name, Sir, that I may know whom to thank?" She kept her face down as if studying the path ahead of her for more inexplicable obstacles to her balance.

Her tall companion replied, "Pithom Eldritch, Madam." Then he continued, "Are you quite all right?"

It was a fair question. Fear that she might never reach Elbraith ambushed her. To avoid the normal eye contact such a question warranted, Yancey placed her hand above her eyes and began lightly massaging her temples. *If this stress keeps up, I'll probably develop a real headache.*

"That blinking blue light seems to be affecting me strangely. I'll be fine, thank you."

They walked on in this odd duet, or maybe it was a duel. Eldritch kept bending down as if to look in her face; at one point she even closed her eyes to avoid his light blue ones, lest they trap her again.

Elbraith's voice never sounded better to her as he called, "Thank the Watcher! There you are, Lady Yancey!"

Yancey felt sure Elbraith looked her escort right in the eyes before he inclined his head slightly and said, "Thank you, Sir Eldritch, for returning my charge safely."

Just to see if she really was crazy, when Yancey and her Conductor had walked some ten feet from Eldritch, Yancey turned deliberately around. She made eye contact with her rescuer and said, "Thank you." Nothing happened.

Man, she thought, *I am losing it.*

Sir Eldritch bowed, smiled, and said prosaically, "My pleasure."

Oooo...kay. Maybe that was some sort of ... "blue-light-special," Yancey quipped to herself. She certainly had no intention of mentioning her impressions to Elbraith.

That worthy Conductor clipped out, "Come. We're late for the selecting." He seemed flustered.

"I'm sorry I distressed you," Yancey offered.

As they hurried, Elbraith brushed off her apology and in a business-like tone offered one of his own, "Being gone has made you miss meeting many of the Guides personally. I regret that deeply for you, Yancey. I feel personally responsible for letting you wander off from the critical matter at hand."

They entered a ballroom in which no one now danced. Instead, there was "the old gang" with numerous other Juvies. They sat in chairs with their Conductors standing on a raised dais behind them. Creating a small disturbance, Yancey and Elbraith took their places. Elbraith assumed a parade-rest position behind and to the right of her powder-blue chair.

On a holo vid screen were pictures of various male and female Guides. Beside the Guides' 3-D pictures, Juvies could skim and scan data relevant to each one's experience in guiding treks. Then the highlighted Guide would come forward to stand by the proffered data.

An announcer suggested a final review of those being considered; the twenty-nine holo-vids and information bytes repeated. After about twenty minutes perhaps forty Juvies—of course, they were addressed as Rejuvenates—had formally selected a Guide.

The console on Yancey's chair allowed her to pull up any Guide's image and information. Years of necessity had made her a lightning-fast reader.

Running in a sidebar, the first selection tally surprised her.

Ingress was in the top three and had been selected ten times. *Hmmph*! He strutted in pseudo-military grandeur.

Next, she noted that Eldritch's eyes onscreen remained normal and somewhat attractive. He received two selections; only one vacancy remained.

Gael had thus far received eight. He inclined his head with false humility and moved to confer with each selecting pair. The canary yellow woman's Conductor seemed less than content with his human's choice.

Elbraith leaned down and whispered to Yancey, "I know it is all strange to you, but you must select. Without a Guide, we will perish. Anyone is better than no one. Your initial selection need not be final. Each Guide selected will come to speak to you personally, as you see Being Ingress doing with the lilac partners."

With her finger poised above an unknown, Yancey felt unsure. She faltered. *What if I chose an Eldritch or a Gael? No. I could not stand that.* Stoically, she folded her hands back in her lap.

By the fourteenth ballot, counting tiebreakers, all but two other of the Juvie pairs had matched with Guides. Pressure mounted to finish the business. It exuded from Guides, other already matched Juvies, guests, and from the three-member Selection Board.

The royal blue Juvie hastily keyed the pad for a military type with a cruel mouth. Yancey thought the blue partners might not have "all the comforts of home" for their journey.

The bright orange picked a man with a weak chin and watery eyes. Yancey suspected he would be a burden in the wilderness.

It seemed obvious the best Guides were the most frequently booked. Yancey wondered how, after all these selections, it could be that each of the candidates she'd met still had at least one open spot. The realization did not please her.

She wanted to see that "number of successes compared to attempts" listed for each candidate more closely, but it was apparently the Guide's choice to list this or not. Many chose to omit it.

After each selection, a Juvie's screen projected his or her choice into plain sight some twenty feet in front of the console. Beings in the ballroom acted like the audience on the *Price is Right* (now in its 1806th season on earth). Ignoring the public display and its accompanying shouts of encouragement or disapproval, Yancey sneaked a more thorough peak at Ingress, Gael, and Eldritch than she had managed in the garden.

With Gael she felt slimed. Ingress was a posturing steamroller. Eldritch was plain creepy. Their ratio numbers also were not stellar. Gael had three attempts unaccounted for; Ingress chose not to list these statistics; and Eldritch posted an even dozen. This last sent a chill down her spine: *what is the criterion for becoming a sanctioned Guide if it's not the number of safe passages?*

The Interlocutor and his two helpers had skillfully conducted the selections. They floated in chairs with rainbow-colored consoles on the far side of the dance floor. Yancey did not explore why she used a vaudeville term for the selection committee, but she felt pretty sure it had to do with "Who do these clowns think they are?"

The chairman directed, "You now need to choose, Lady Phillips."

Distinctly, Yancey stated, "I choose Trenell."

A murmur swept the assembly. Faces in various groupings showed a variety of reactions: anger, shock, disapproval, and thoughtful contemplation. No one smiled.

Sneaking a peek behind her, Yancey felt proud of Elbraith. Already publicly embarrassed by her in this assembly, not by a single breath or facial expression did he show his reaction. *He'd make a terrific poker player.*

The Board did not at first respond aloud as they had with all other selections. They conferred privately together.

Finally, the Head man declared, "Trenell is an outcast. He is an artist, and no longer a licensed Guide. We cannot guarantee success if you insist on choosing outside our sanction."

Yancey stated, "Statistics in the program do not seem to guarantee success, either. I waive your responsibility. Please ask him."

At a signal, she guessed, from Elbraith, for the Interlocutor aimed the barest of glances his way, the worthy Board Chair announced a three-minute conference period. Her Conductor hastened to her side.

"My Lady," Elbraith whispered, "I entreat you to reconsider your choice."

"What is wrong with Trenell?" Yancey countered.

"The Board revoked his license years ago after documenting that all of his charges simply disappeared," Elbraith rapidly responded. "Trenell maintained they had successfully solved their life puzzle and had leaped, but Leapside held no record of three of the parties ever even entering the city. The Board never proved foul play, and so they quietly disbarred him. He's a true mystery man."

Yancey's thoughts whirled. *All disappeared? Life Puzzle? Leaped? Trenell, disbarred? Trenell, lie?* All that was in her revolted at this final question. *The potter from the garden could not lie*—even as she thought it, she registered it as irrational: *all people lie sometime.*

What she whispered hastily, however, was, "Eldritch lists twelve unsuccessful attempts, and no one is banning him."

Elbraith hissed, "They all waived the leap and have become members of his Universal Church. People on the G.A.L.A. Board revere Eldritch as a holy man."

Now I really am creeped out, Yancey thought.

Elbraith withdrew to stand again respectfully behind her chair.

The Interlocutor said formally, "Lady Phillips, your three minutes have past. Does your choice stand?"

Yancey discerned this august being's disapproval, *almost a fear*, she thought. She weighed Elbraith's words. Although she deeply respected Elbraith, his words could not cancel her experience. She retained a sense of peace and cleanliness from her encounter with this strange, disapproved potter.

"Yes, Sir, it stands."

"Please be advised you may shortly require a second choice. After so many years of this Board's censure, the being in question will more than likely reject your selection of him."

Yancey did not believe this last prediction any more than she believed that Trenell had lied.

Not ten minutes later, after much activity on the respective consoles of the Board, the Chairman announced with a confounded look, "Trenell accepts."

Groups in the crowd snorted in disgust, whispered among themselves, or raised eyebrows in surprise; a few appeared fearful. *What is that fear-response all about with this mystery- man, anyway?* She asked herself but had no time to reflect.

She knew, of course, that she had refused Elbraith's counsel. A quick glance showed his expression did not by the slightest nuance betray his opinion that Trenell's acceptance was a bad thing. Yancey would never have dreamed her self-sacrificing Conductor choked on indignation as he stood impassively by her. Could she have guessed the truth, she would have admired his poker face even more.

She did manage, however, to catch a glimpse of Eldritch's face as he heard the news; *he could never play poker with Elbraith.* His face twisted with cold fury.

Yancey felt immediately better.

Chapter 15 – A New Day with a Pleasant Surprise

Planet X boasted two suns, the larger first one silver and the smaller second one gold. The very next morning, two or three hours after their departure before first-sunrise, as Yancey reckoned it, Trenell called a halt some fifty yards short of the edge of the inviting greenery she could see ahead. Taking a provision bar and a pouch of liquid from his pack, Trenell motioned for his companions to do likewise.

All morning they had passed silently through broken rock formations on faint trails Yancey would never have seen if left to herself. They now halted in the shade of a last great boulder. They sat for awhile in grateful silence comtemplating the vegetation of a green meadow. It led into brush and trees on the clearing's far side from them. The stop provided Yancey time to think.

Just last night, perhaps an hour after her choice of Trenell, the fancy ball had begun to break up. Juvies and Conductors all over the ballroom had become groups of three or more as they joined their respective Guides in conference regarding immediate plans.

Eldritch conferred with a party of eight Juvies and eight Conductors, a fact which recalled her unpleasant jolt while speaking with this Being—*he told me three in a party. Either he lied, or he changed plans after I refused.* The creepy Guide and Head of the Church Universal, or whatever they called themselves, sent one penetrating stare Yancey's way and turned his back toward her.

Yancey shivered. She read the look as "I'm not through with you yet."

Jason and his young Tan companion stood with "Colonel" Ingress and his group. Like a little Napoleon, Ingress paraded in front of the ten pairs he had garnered. His initial remarks, overheard in passing, expressed pity toward those foolish enough to have chosen anyone but him to guide them. Yancey kept the "Colonel" in quotes in her mind and silently wished Jason the best.

Gael, his sliminess, now addressed six female Juvies with their Conductors; the Conductors looked none too happy. Gael was too busy oozing charm over the Juvies to spare a look to anyone outside his influence. As Yancey and Elbraith passed his group, Gael was saying his party would be enjoying the mansion's pleasures for four days before leaving in their luxury vehicle to begin the first stage. Yancey's skin crawled.

On the far edge of the great stone patio just outside the ballroom, Trenell had met them just after his announced acceptance. Yancey had instinctively led Elbraith there. Her humble Guide in his plain tunic, she reasoned, would not fit in with the resplendent Beings still present inside. Elbraith had followed her stiffly.

Her new Guide had begun with, "Thank you for your trust, Lady Yancey. Conductor Elbraith, a privilege." Fascinated, Yancey had watched her faithful Conductor send a non-verbal, purely male-to-male challenge toward Trenell. The Guide—she didn't know how—disarmed the veiled hostility and began prosaically to outline their upcoming trip.

They would start the very next morning one hour before first-rise, as he called the silver sun's initial appearance. Silver, all-weather jumpsuits and footgear would await them in his studio, which would be the mustering place. He would have all packs and equipment ready.

Elbraith's face had flushed. "Tomorrow morning before first-rise? Why so soon?"

Trenell had gravely replied, "Departing immediately will take advantage of the best weather conditions available for the next two weeks." Having done his research weeks before, he had already planned tomorrow to leave on a private trip for some clay.

Secondly, the travel plans for his own proposed trip would prove the best for Yancey and Elbraith as well. "Lacy Yancey will not profit from delay in the palatial estate."

Trenell's third reason produced a frown of flat disbelief on her Conductor's handsome face. For Yancey, however, it merely validated a growing unease. Trenell said, "Our early, unannounced departure will help us avoid undue interest in Lady Yancey's movements. Our chosen path crosses no conventional travel routes open to curious eyes."

Her Conductor shot a hard look at Trenell. He spoke intensely, "Aren't you being a bit melodramatic? You cannot suppose Lady Yancey to be in danger from any in this assembly?"

Yancey had interrupted the rigid Elbraith by laying her blue-veined hand on his arm. Flashing through her mind came Ingress's pompous over-confidence, Eldritch's menace and Gael's plans for his small group. She said, "Trenell is our Guide. We will follow his lead."

Tight-lipped, Elbraith had snapped, "Yes, milady."

Trenell quietly nodded his approval and took his leave.

Briefly, as Elbraith stiffly turned and offered her his rigid arm to support her to her sleep-chamber, Yancey had wondered if her Conductor had made private plans to visit his friends, like Tinkerbelle, for instance. Leaving immediately would rob him of that.

One last look at Trenell as he departed into the surrounding garden quickly reassured her. She thought perhaps it had been some quality in his eyes. The Guide seemed respectfully sympathetic to Elbraith and at the same time determined to do her good.

"What an odd thought," Yancey whispered to herself. "It must be this wacko planet warping my mind, but I feel as though I've known Trenell somehow forever."

This she muttered to herself as they parted to seek their beds. Elbraith stalked along by her side and muttered a few words of his own.

Yancey's thoughts suddenly snapped back to the present. With their meal in the shade of the boulder mostly gone, Trenell suddenly disappeared from sight: he sat eating, and then he was not! Or so it seemed to Yancey, who was drowsing over the last of her snack.

A split second later, adrenaline banished her sleepiness. A giant blur of reddish-brown speed rocketed down from the formation directly above their heads. A terrifying animal larger than a bull elephant switched its long, silky tale in annoyance at having missed its prey.

A successful landing on Trenell would surely have killed him. Instead, he had impossibly exceeded the great beast's swiftness and evaded the predator before she or Elbraith had sensed any danger.

Looking like some prehistoric, saber-toothed tiger, the giant beast stood where Trenell had sat, lifted its whiskered muzzle to the golden sky, and roared in frustration. The rocks forming their small shelter seemed to shake.

Elbraith jerked Yancey behind him: outrunning this beast was clearly out of the question, and the packs Trenell had provided them contained no weapons. Later, Yancey's heart would be stunned by her Conductor's immediate devotion. Now, however, she was shaking too hard and scrabbling around for a decent rock to throw at this behemoth.

Incredibly, Trenell materialized from the boulder right beside the roaring beast—Yancey later decided his silvery jumpsuit, like hers and Elbraith's, perfectly blended with its surroundings and had rendered the Guide "invisible." More astonishing still, Trenell in an enthralling baritone launched a line of song with unintelligible words aimed straight up at the beast now towering over him.

The roaring ceased. The gigantic head with curving fangs and the powerful shoulders with packed muscles rippling lowered to the ground in a bow. In a less terrifying beast the crouching posture would have appeared an invitation to play. Yancey believed, however, that Trenell faced imminent death.

The melodic line Trenell sang rumbled at its beginning like the deepest bass notes on a piano. It rose through the octaves with incredibly beautiful words to shape the ascending sounds. With no understanding, Yancey felt a shock as she caught the peace and a sort of delighted joy in the simple, musical line. Elbraith stood ready to fight.

When Trenell's voice reached and floated on a pure, high *F* above the staff, a word accompanied it: Ta—aa—ax. It sounded an exuberant joy.

The next second, the animal leapt back onto the boulder twenty feet above, turned on a dime, and raced out into the green field that lay before them. Still with no verbal explanation, Yancey began to shake again, but this time she did not cower but laughed from some place deep within her.

The crazy beast flashed through the meadow beyond and zoomed in joyous circles back over the rocks, and so on. Watching these unbelievably fast, gargantuan antics, Elbraith opened his mouth in a bemused smile.

Trenell threw back his head and laughed and finally called, "Tax!"

Yancey formed the impression of a red-brown hillock suddenly sprung up just in front of the delightedly laughing Guide and doing its best to wriggle the south end of its formidable mass for pure joy. The silky tail undulated with a life of its own.

In the manner of cats everywhere and some dogs, Tax's head, saber teeth and all, butted against Trenell and rubbed against him so affectionately, Yancey could not see how he remained standing. It was probably released hysteria, but Yancey began to giggle.

For a split second, she thought she'd made a fatal mistake. Her mirth attracted the enormous, impossible feline's attention to her own relatively small self still hidden behind her Conductor.

Tax bounded lithely right over Elbraith's head and landed behind them. Turning, Yancey suddenly stared into deep, golden brown eyes, fringed in glorious, thick brown lashes. The majestic cat regarded her with deep intelligence. The huge, glorious eyes seemed pleased with her still giggling, new person of interest.

Then a rough, brown and pink tongue that looked half as large as a queen-sized mattress suddenly traveled over Yancey's bare knuckles and on up her silver-covered arm. The grating sound of the animal's rough tongue over cloth made Yancey shiver.

Yancey sing-songed, "This better not be a taste-test."

Tax ignored the Conductor, ready to spring between his charge and this red-brown monster, play-bowed to Yancey as she had to Trenell, but then thumped down and rubbed her head sideways on the ground. Yancey reached over the black lip bulging over a curving fang and managed to touch and rub the sweet spot behind the great cat's ear.

Yancey laughed out loud and with great fun spoke into that furry ear, "Your purr sounds like thunder rumbling!" The rumbling increased. Tax's pink and black-spotted tongue lolled with pleasure as Yancey continued to scratch and fondle the wonderful softness.

Looking at his charge's proximity to the great fangs and serrated teeth within the huge mouth, Elbraith informed her with remarkable steadiness, "Lady Yancey, that's a *wild Endi*."

Yancey looked into the nearest great golden eye with its lid half closed in the bliss of her rubbing and replied, "Not to me, Elbraith. I don't think she is, to me."

Into the lazily flicking ear, she nevertheless whispered, "O.K., Girl, that's all for now."

Tax stretched luxuriously and yawned straight toward Elbraith—Yancey thought it was deliberate—and curled her powerful tongue in an upward arc that gave the Conductor a perfect, head-on view of razor-sharp teeth. Elbraith did not flinch. By this Tax seemed satisfied.

She padded over to Trenell and lay down contentedly. He sang four words or syllables for her ears alone. Tax briefly leaned into his hand on her shoulder and then stretched out on her side to rest.

Yancey gurgled, "You certainly have tremendous friends, Trenell!"

Her Guide merely slid his eyes drolly her way to acknowledge the double entendre. He gathered them back into the shade of the overhanging boulder and said, "We must talk. Her coming is no accident."

Chapter 16 – Valley People

Trenell began speaking earnestly then as they finished their interrupted lunch. Tax ambled away and nosed around the meadow and the edge of the broken rock area where they sat.

"Before we enter the valley, I must give you some instructions. Valley people are robbers and scavengers."

"Their culture admires those who are the greatest thieves and liars. Both sexes gain prestige, power, and mating privileges in their individual villages by acquiring the most contraband and by fabricating the biggest lies around the quarterly Gathering Fires held Valley-wide."

"Some of the more harmless to travelers would rather lie successfully and then brag convincingly to their village than to commit an actual theft. Others, however, are soldiers willing to kill in order to score a big or prestigious heist."

"All are masters of subtlety because to be caught in the act of robbery or of lying makes them lose face. Usually, they use a 'hook' to set one up for the theft or the scam: some beg or appear diseased and dying."

"Separating a traveling party with lies often prepares their would-be victims to come totally under their power. They might, for example, use covetousness to split a traveling group by offering some great gain, falsely to be sure, but skillfully."

"Other times, they employ children or their animals. Children themselves must succeed in a lie or a theft in order to gain a name among their people. There is no age limit."

"Fortunately, Valley People hate Endis, and the feeling is mutual. Tax will assure us a speedy passage unless one of us stops to hear or to take action. She will even shepherd us if an assailant comes too close or seeks to accost us violently."

"You need to zip your packs inside the front of your coveralls. Place the zipper tab at the top of the collar, and button the protective cloth over the tab, inside and out. Some of the women and a few among the children have developed so delicate a touch that travelers have emerged from the wood with articles of clothing missing, not to mention possessions vulnerable in pockets."

"If anyone approaches you close enough to touch you, and you become alarmed, whistle this note"—here Trenell demonstrated, and Tax, who had wandered off to scent the wind, appeared so quickly that Yancey and Elbraith could not tell from whence she came.

They practiced. The huge Endi moved with such speed, she blurred as she had the first time when she and Trenell played their pouncing game.

"Finally," Trenell continued, "you must steadfastly hold to my belt, both of you beside each other and in step behind me. At some point, you will be convinced you have been robbed and/or deceived, and the temptation to let go of me to check will be nearly overwhelming. I tell you now, before we begin, that if you maintain personal contact with me, the sensation of loss will be a skilled lie."

"I never lose anything that is mine. If you stay in touch with me, you can lose nothing, either."

Elbraith looked at him sharply but said nothing.

Trenell stood and all three began shifting their backpacks to rest under their jumpsuits in front of them. If Yancey had not been so frightened, she might have laughed at their suddenly big bellies.

Trenell looked them over and said, "Questions?"

Looking across the meadow with her far-sighted eyes, Yancey thought she saw a face. It appeared in the brushy greenery and as quickly disappeared between two trees growing where the forest began. Tax's lip curled and bared her teeth but made no sound. Yancey thought, *They're getting ready for us.*

Elbraith exploded, "Is there no better way? I know some of the Guides avoid this area, and many of them, like Ingress, roll through in huge, sealed machines."

Trenell calmly replied, "What you say is true, yet this is the best way for Yancey."

Both Beings, Conductor and Guide, looked at her. Trenell's gaze unsettled her because it hit her like an X-ray probe—*how does he do that?* Yancey shrugged off the uncomfortable sensation of the escape-stone suddenly revealed by said X-ray vision and burning in its hiding place at her waist. Elbraith's narrowed eyes and thinned lips launched hard doubt straight at her.

He'd turn back in a New York minute if I show the least hesitation.

For answer to the unspoken question of her trust in Trenell, she rolled and stuffed pieces of a disposable handkerchief in her ears. Determinedly, Yancey hooked her fingers in Trenell's waistband. Eyes clouded for once, Elbraith hardened his jaw and came alongside her.

The big Endi trotted closely and alertly ahead of Trenell. Despite her innate sleekness, all Tax's fur stood out in a worthy display of battle-readiness. Her tail stood straight up with its tip twitching like some aberrant periscope ploughing, not through water, but through the charged atmosphere.

They passed from the meadow and entered the valley. Yancey involuntarily turned frightened eyes to left and to right as her peripheral vision caught traces of movement in the beginnings of the green border through which they passed.

The first being she saw was a small child, perhaps eight years old. The pathetic small girl, undernourished and displaying a crippled left arm and leg, held out her hands, palms up, begging for Yancey's help. Yancey tightened her grip on Trenell's belt.

Perhaps fifty feet later, the same girl appeared by the wayside. At first Yancey thought, *not twins, not both so afflicted!* As Trenell's belt pressed harder into the flesh of her hand and the poor waif appeared a third time some hundred feet ahead, however, Yancey realized it was the same girl. The child actually was so spry, she was passing them through the undergrowth to station herself repeatedly ahead of their party.

The makeshift earplugs muted the piteous cries and other sounds assailing Yancey from all sides. She had the distinct sensation of being touched all over her coverall and looked to check that it was still there.

It was unnerving, like being in the Metroplex subway at rush hour but submerged in a sea of pickpockets. She perceived all these other frantic beings rushing: only Trenell and Elbraith and she seemed doomed to move in slow motion, as under water. She and her two companions were cumbersome deep sea divers out of their true element and being preyed upon by sleekly mobile sharks.

At the "crippled" child's fourth appearance, Yancey over-corrected her line of vision and glanced away to her right. A rather plump fellow made lewd gestures to her and then pulled what she knew was a weapon. He pointed the business end of it directly toward her.

In panic, Yancey looked at the back of Trenell's head. He trotted unconcernedly along behind Tax at the same pace he had struck when they entered the green valley. Apparently moving to protect her from the same brigand, however, Elbraith stumbled.

Before she knew what she was doing, Yancey reached with both hands to help her falling Conductor to right himself. The confusing thing was that as she bent to help him, Yancey suddenly became aware that Trenell and Elbraith, who had not stumbled at all, were rapidly drawing away from her. Panicked, Yancey whistled. She was aware of hands touching her, this time, roughly.

One moment later, she knew what they had taken. The blue velvet pouch containing the earth stone, her stone of escape, no longer rested behind her belt. That same moment later, Tax swept down upon her.

The Endi's great mouth simply scooped her up by the coverall at her waist. The huge beast restored her effortlessly to her contact with Trenell. Trenell, however, and thus, Yancey and Elbraith also, did not immediately resume their trotting.

Yancey followed Trenell's gaze to the fat man who was dancing up and down because he had scored. He held his prize from Yancey's waistband aloft.

What happened next occurred in another split second.

The thief's filthy knee bent in mid air as he shuffled in a taunting victory hop. His head and body moved in time with the whooping, sort of "Hai, hai, hai" sounds he made. He closed his hands above his head and rubbed the blue bag so all could see it. The smooth gray pebble thus rubbed inside the bag exploded with a loud BANG, and the hapless thief combusted!

Screaming and writhing on the ground, he burned instantly and viciously. His body produced a nauseating, hissing sizzle. Too soon, his blackened, dead body curled piteously into a grotesque fetal lump connected by tar strings. His charred body smoldered with putrid black smoke coiling upward. So hot was the flame, the green sward around him caught fire. Like him, it burned quickly out.

Elbraith stared at Yancey with his mouth twisted in horror and his eyes demanding an explanation.

Trenell, however, seemed again to bore holes in her that reached down into her soul. He had no question. Yancey wanted to drop her eyes away from his; instead, tears of sorrow spilled down her face.

She wept softly, "I'm so sorry."

If I do not break eye contact with Trenell immediately, my heart will break. I as good as killed that man!

Standing in shame, yet perforce in such close proximity, Yancey pushed her head alongside her Guide's chin and rested her forehead on his collar bone. She did not let go of his belt. She sobbed there. Then Trenell spoke.

"We'd better move out. Even Endis wear out eventually." His tone was kind.

Yancey glanced up to see the brindled, red-brown blur around the three of them as Tax circled them at amazing speed. She sheltered them as a protective wall roundabout.

They resumed their ground-consuming trot that Yancey had formerly thought so slow. After perhaps twenty paces, Elbraith figured it out. He spat out the word, "Fafnir!"

Yancey's tears fell down again. Her crying blotted out her Conductor along with the rest of the beings trying to attract her attention. Though they trotted in forced nearness, it seemed she had isolated herself from friend and foe alike.

Momentarily, Yancey considered letting go again and letting these fiends end her sorry life. Not until much later did she realize even this was some of their subtlety. Such an action would have left the whole group vulnerable as they tried to save her beleaguered self.

Elbraith broke the temptation. He carefully shifted hands on Trenell's belt and placed his freed hand at Yancey's waist. Knowing by his tenderness that Elbraith had forgiven her, too, Yancey cried it all out and hung on grimly as they trotted unrelentingly along.

I have caused enough trouble, and they have forgiven me.

After another half hour, Elbraith pointed his finger at a sight not to be missed. A village appeared in a clearing just past the outer edge of the valley. The exit through the green outer border was now, thankfully, visible on *their* side of the charming little town.

It appeared the determined trio had made it, and this fortunate village rested just outside the outskirts of the forest, beyond the reach of their lying, thieving neighbors. It beckoned them to celebrate so perilous a journey successfully navigated.

Happy, laughing people walked around eating and gawking and pausing to take turns on carnival rides or to try their luck at carnie games along the midway. Familiar smells came supercharged to the travelers' nostrils. Hot dogs, barbeque, popcorn, funnel cakes—carnival food can be some of the most tantalizing in the world.

How cool we hit a day when the circus is in town! Still grieving her part in the fat thief's shocking death, Yancey drank in the familiar, happy sights.

The rides she could see as they trotted along included most of Yancey's favorites. The big, super-coaster twisted and dropped its occupants impossible distances and whirled them upside-down to the tune of delighted screams of mock or real horror. The Ferris wheel's paint was new, and it shone in the now golden light. Small children's laughter and squeals permeated the air. Friendly hawkers carried signs inviting them to the little circus under the big tent: ONLY TWO MORE DAYS!

Trenell did not break stride, and Yancey, yearning toward the joyous release the little village offered, almost stumbled. Elbraith supported her by the elbow.

The bobbing rump of the great beast that went before them continued to shift up and down in its mile-eating stride. Tax did not slow down. The view of the town and its little circus as they trotted past seemed much more inviting than the big Endi's departing posterior, despite the long, now gliding tail.

Yancey wanted more than anything else at the moment, to stop. She wanted to relax and do the rides. She wanted to eat that tantalizing food. She might even win a stuffed animal at the shooting booth. It felt great to look at something besides Tax's rump, charming though that was; and it would be wonderful to meet some friendly, fun-loving people who did not want to kill or rob her. She needed to erase or, at least, balance internally the events of their recent passage.

She yelled to Trenell, "Can we stop?"

He shook his head and continued moving past the little hamlet and its tantalizing fun.

They crossed the true green border, this time. The charming town and circus sat inside the valley boundary, not outside as it had appeared. Yancey's heart dropped all desire for the carnival and its enticing pleasures. It had been the last trap!

Now, Trenell did stop. Tax thudded on the ground and her spotted tongue lolled out. Her Guide instructed, "Yancey, look back."

When she did, she saw, not a carnival in a picturesque town, but a clapped together, filthy, mud-and-stick travesty of a village, a starving place. The truth revealed no carnival, no happy people, and no food.

The throng of "happy citizens" shouted curses and shook weapons at them and leapt around bashing into each other in their fury and frustration. Yancey gasped. The scheming Valley People had faked not just the illusion of the town and circus but also the place's position of "safety" outside the pernicious valley's boundary.

Great teacher that he was, Trenell asked, "What are two great lessons you have learned?"

Yancey replied, "Don't believe everything you see and hear."

Then her eyes glinted and she said, "And, Fafnir wants to murder me!"

Chapter 17 – More

They moved their packs from beneath their clothes and into normal position between their shoulder blades. When they had rested for perhaps fifteen minutes, Tax loped back into the Valley Forest. Yancey shot a quick glance at Trenell.

Answering her unspoken question, Trenell said, "Mature Endis can be owned by no one. Tax goes and comes at her will. There is much game there, and she will be safe anywhere in the valley. Only in the heights are there predators that she must fear."

"You mean there're carnivores bigger than Tax on X Planet?"

"Yes, and some smaller that work in teams."

"Speaking of that," Trenell continued, "what do you think of the Green Valley?"

Yancey shuddered. "Thank God the thieves and liars and murderers like them are confined to one area."

Trenell studied her solemnly. Elbraith's eyebrows formed a slight pucker.

Yancey sighed morosely. "Ah, man... Beings like them are out here, too, aren't they? Of course they are," Yancey continued, "I met some of them at the GALA, didn't I?"

Trenell seemed pleased. Elbraith's pucker deepened. He still believed their mysterious Guide had hustled them on foot through darkness and virtually impossible terrain for his own reasons. The idea that any Being from the GALA wished them harm and had to be eluded was, to him, preposterous.

The trio rose and began to climb the hillside before them. The rust-red boulders resumed, and huge black rocks began to contrast with the golden clay on which they traipsed.

Trenell asked, "What more is there to learn from the fat thief who combusted?"

Yancey did not want this topic. She looked at Elbraith, who frowned over his own thoughts and offered no diversion. She changed the subject.

"I wonder not just about predators large enough to prey on Tax but also about game big enough to feed her."

Trenell refused the bait and switch.

Elbraith seemed still to be thinking his own unpleasant thoughts.

Eventually, Yancey realized until she answered Trenell's last question, she would walk in silence. *Very well, I can handle silence.*

After perhaps forty-five minutes of upward progress, Elbraith's brow cleared. Yancey's mind did not.

She felt awful. Fafnir had tried to kill her. He had lied to her and promised a way of escape.

A stranger died in my place. Stomachs, she found, literally could turn. Yancey tasted bile.

If I hadn't taken Fafnir's small stone, that ruffian back there would be alive right now. Although that thief's death was his own fault, I guess no one ever sins alone.

Man, what an archaic concept: sin. Earth's scientists, philosophers and poets long ago disproved God.

Yancey knew the drill: *no God means no external standard. That means no sin, no judgment.*

I didn't sin. I made a mistake.

One step later, she thought, *Still, that thief's dead.*

What are the odds? She smiled internally at her Dad's favorite expression. She re-shuffled the facts: *I made a private transaction aboard a transport pod hurtling through the atmosphere of a mystery planet. This decision contributed to the death of some poor, totally unsuspected thief in a green valley I had never known.*

I made a MISTAKE. It was not some innocent who died back there! That poor schlemiel took what wasn't his. He offed himself and got what he deserved. Deep inside she slammed the door on the thought that she was glad *his* death spared *her* life.

I am not guilty! I didn't ask him to rob me!

Carefully, she renewed her unofficial vow of silence and focused ahead and around her on a dirt incline littered with rocks much as one saw in some sections of Mars. Although this side of the mountain was half in shadow, Trenell led them steadily, and silently, upward on a path like the others, hard for her to see.

Problems of logic demand honesty if one wishes to make progress. Her mind was such that those problems usually nagged her until she wrestled them to some reasonable conclusion.

Unbidden, she pictured the fat robber as he had danced around with her little treasure. She visualized his filthy rags as he joined his hands above his head and rolled the stone between them to show he had beaten her. The BANG had pierced her makeshift earplugs. Then the exultant thief had burst into flames.

That poor crook back there offed himself, all right, but he got what **I** *deserved.* That thought rattled her. Suddenly, Yancey remembered Trenell's words to Elbraith: something like, "This is the best path for Yancey."

Trenell couldn't have meant that to save my life, someone else had to die.

Suddenly short of breath, Yancey broke her vow of silence and wheezed, "Could we take a break?"

Trenell headed for a large boulder's shade.

Elbraith offered her his canteen. She drank sparingly. With her tongue and throat thus lubricated, Yancey figured she'd had enough silence with Trenell. She missed him, and it had only been about an hour and a half. When she walked over to speak with the Guide, Elbraith looked at her curiously.

To Trenell she whispered, "I'm sorry I helped cause that guy's death," and wondered in herself why she should apologize to Trenell in such a manner.

Trenell rose from where he squatted and offered Yancey his hand. "Come," he said to her, and Yancey felt more refreshed by his voice than she had by the water. "We need to make camp at the top."

With a shamefaced look at Elbraith, Yancey paused in the process of reseating her backpack and said, "Sorry, Elbraith. Aside from almost losing your charge, which I expect would be very bad news for a Conductor, I...I failed to trust you and took Fafnir's word instead."

In a small voice Yancey added, "I don't know how I could've been so stupid."

He had already forgiven her. Yancey watched him put the episode behind him. Elbraith made eye contact with her, nodded twice, and accepted her into his good graces.

He reached to help her shift her pack to a better position, and the two of them wearily followed Trenell. Trenell led easily along the path still indiscernible to them and still, apparently, winding upward. Elbraith and Yancey, laden with their private thoughts as well as their backpacks, trudged heavily behind.

Chapter 18 – Prepare for the Test

Joyous thunder that was really Tax's deep roaring greeted the trio as they neared the top. The big Endi peaked at them over the rim. Foolishly glad to see the huge beast, Yancey said, "Wow! If Tax were a stereo, her woofer would beat any speaker I've ever seen."

Good thing I laughed at my own lame joke. A quick glimpse back at Elbraith showed he had skipped "Stereo 101." Trenell, at least, turned his face back toward her so she could hear his snort at her humorous sally. Tax's "yoww—oww—oww" of a truly big cat grew louder the closer they got.

They crested the final ridge and found themselves overlooking a shallow green bowl of vegetation misted by a stream rushing down the opposite side. It was an Eden. Sapphire ponds of hot springs, silvery grass plumes, floods of flowers, a lifting breeze—all made music. Yancey thought, *Whispering Valley.*

Trenell and Elbraith made camp. Yancey went down to a smaller pool for the first bath, but Tax, the big moose, jostled Yancey, probably for fun, as she sinuously passed her up.

Yancey yelled, "Hey!" and rushed down the short incline after the Endi. The pursuit ended with a Tax-sized "SPLASH!" which made Yancey laugh as she arrived with perfect timing to be the waterlogged victim of the Endi's cannon-ball. They played for an hour.

Eventually following the food smell back to camp, Yancey found her Conductor and her Guide engrossed in deep-voiced conversation. They barely spared her a glance. It sounded serious, but she shrugged off her misgiving.

The two Beings rose, kept talking in low tones—it seemed Elbraith leaned toward Trenell to catch every word—and moved on down toward the pools. Trenell said to her over his shoulder, "Please eat. First sun will come early in the morning, and you must be on your way."

Yancey heard the pronoun, but the two Beings were striding toward the pools with great anticipation. *What does Trenell mean, "You"?*

At first-sun the next morning, Yancey found out. Fully rested, she launched herself on a quest for hot tea. Just outside her zip-door, Elbraith smiled his welcome and hefted the steaming pot.

Settled thankfully with her fresh brew, Yancey finally noticed the most upsetting circumstance she could imagine: Trenell's tent was gone. She spluttered, "Where's Trenell? He can't leave like this. He's our Guide!" Her unease dismissed from the night before developed teeth and bit hard.

Elbraith answered, "He has some potter business to attend to but continues to function as our Guide: last night he gave me minute instructions for the next leg of our journey." Elbraith's attitude expressed satisfaction at the new development.

Yancey's mouth moved, she thought, *something like a fish out of water*. Resolutely, she closed it.

Summoning coherency, she asked, "Care to share?" The enormity of what she saw as Trenell's desertion of them tuned her voice down to a forlorn, small sound.

She felt disgusted for being so gullible. *How did I become so dependent so fast?* She fed her sudden feeling of vulnerability to her anger and reasserted self-control.

It's good for Trenell he didn't tell me *he was leaving!*

Giving herself a mental shake, Yancey focused on Elbraith, who seemed to know her turmoil; he waited to gain her attention before answering. She sighed, squared her shoulders, and made eye contact. With a tight smile he began.

"I must conduct you down there." Elbraith led her to the edge of the Eden-like bowl where they had camped. Staring ahead and down made her heart and stomach both revolt.

The steep, sloping sides of their mountain looked for all the world as if some giant child had dumped sand buckets in descending, inverted "V's" down to a beach of red, tan and black that simply did not end.

It's a beach with no water. The barren desert extended as far as she could see. *Welcome to Namibia! Come see the Rocky Mountains of sand dunes!* She looked at Elbraith; tears welled up unbidden. He took both her hands. "We will find our way across, Yancey. Come."

Elbraith is happy to be back on the job!

They finished a meager breakfast and loaded up on liquids. They broke camp quickly—fitting sleeping bags, tents, and gear back into their packs.

The Endi had decided to stay with them. Trotting up when they were ready, Tax trailed water from her latest morning's swim. The beast proceeded to a notch in the rim, and her great hindquarters simply disappeared. Elbraith and Yancey followed.

The notch brought them to the top of an inverted "V." A dirt and gravel track led along and down from the top to where the next "V's" side intersected. The sides falling from the tracks of each one sloped steeply.

There was no compromise. Sculpted dune faces folded into light or dark shadows. From the bladelike division of each top, blackness obscured dark crevices between the folds of the V's. *Harsh, forbidding beauty that could kill.*

The big Endi trotted unconcernedly with each big paw sliding and leaving a soft, deep print. Downward progress simply meant switching to the next intersecting track when the next "V" met the one they traveled.

Yancey's and Elbraith's lighter weights meant they sank only ankle or knee-deep with each step. The sand was already warm. At first it was rather pleasant.

They zigzagged down the mountainside. With Tax's rump bobbing downhill in front of her, Yancey's fear evaporated.

The playful Endi from time to time started galloping and several times used the "runaway truck ramp" technique to curtail her momentum. Yancey laughed at the tank-sized holes the crazy cat left to mar the beige and black symmetry of the dunes. A couple of times, Yancey giant-leaped down the big dune after her for the fun of it.

By second sunrise, unlike Tax, Yancey lost pleasure in the game. Elbraith settled down to an occasional glower in her direction.

Her Conductor wasn't talking; Yancey's mouth felt too dry anyhow.

This desert's too BIG! *Nobody said I had to be cheerful about it!* Yancey's world, cooked by two suns and floored with interminable, V-shaped ridges of gritty sand, shrank down to *one foot in front of the other; slide; is there no bottom?*

But they finally emerged into a band of twenty to two-hundred-foot-high stacked rocks which Yancey had watched for the last third of the descent. At first they had looked like aberrant Tinker-toys.

Now among them, she saw they were obelisks, many with seemingly impossible boulders perched on top. Others featured caves, high or low. A few made arches. All were swirled and carved by wind and, inexplicably to Yancey, by water action.

Like a stone river of soldiers, they marched as far to her left and right as she could see. The towering platoon was perhaps half a mile wide and stopped as abruptly as it began.

Behind Yancey some twenty feet, Elbraith stopped to look up at a smooth, tall column with a cave about fifteen feet below its cap. Two small boulders perched atop the cap. Two other, smaller rocks peaked up from the cave bottom.

Yancey looked at Elbraith's slightly curving lips and moved to view it from his angle. It formed a comical face more froglike than human. The two smallest boulders were goofy looking bottom "teeth" in the cave-mouth. The two boulders on the cap formed the "eyes."

"Too bad it's not green," Yancey croaked.

"It is the first of the trail markers Trenell described." Here Elbraith turned his back squarely to the face-tower. The second sun's light shone through the "mouth." The light pointed into the far distance where a pyramidal bump seemed to float on the impossibly remote horizon of the sand.

Yancey blinked rapidly. "Is it real?"

"Yes. It is our next destination. Let's break here for lunch and discuss the next leg."

"'El Sole' is what Trenell called it." Here Elbraith sketched a map in the sandy soil at their feet. The desert seemed to stretch about thirty miles between the band of rock towers and the pyramidal bump.

"It takes three to five days' walking to cross El Sole," he continued.

"Three predators can be problems: first, the small banji—one-foot tall is a large one—are land creatures that look like red and black-striped boulders partially concealed in the sand, but they move on four swift legs. For big game like ourselves, they assemble in packs if you fail to kill the first one or two that find you."

"Used to cut through the hardest surfaces on the planet, banji fangs are coveted prizes; as many as two dozen teeth have been extracted from the largest ones."

"The beasts give a high-pitched screech signaling their hunting mates to come help. Four screeches are required before others will join the attack, and each screech depletes the animal for minutes; thus, if you haven't stumbled into a colony where four different beasts may screech at once, and if you make your kill within the first fifteen seconds, give or take, no others will generally assemble."

Yancey grimaced. "You mean I have a weapon?"

Elbraith grinned. "You say to them, 'In the Watcher's name, die!'"

"Huh?" was all the comment she could manage. "You're kidding, right?"

He regarded her stoically. Yancey asked, "Does that work with all predators?"

When he replied, "No," Yancey continued, "What if I'm too scared to speak?"

Elbraith said, "Even forming the words with your lips with no sound will work. The screech is quite terrifying, by the way. Once roused, they're fast. They screech, subside, and the colony shreds their victims. No physical weapon works quickly enough to drop one."

Yancey sighed and asked, "Predator Number Two?"

"Strictly an air attack—stinging insects called Runja. They cannot see you clothed in silver—our suits will camouflage us—unless we walk right up on a hive or one flies into you by accident and wants to call its swarm. They fly solo, but a hundred stings can kill any bi-ped."

"If attacked, fold into a ball so only silver material shows, and any swarm mates will pass over you. Safety requires about five minutes of immobility."

Elbraith continued, "Predator Number Three is the largest, a sort of ill-tempered little bear about the size of a large badger. Tunlers, as their name suggests, are subterranean dwellers; they surface only when seeking food or when it rains. We're food, but they are very near-sighted and won't attack an erect human. The suits mask our scent from them."

"In your pack you'll find a silver walking staff. Touch a Tunler with it, and the thing will run. Tunlers are not fast, but lumbering. Our problem will be avoiding stepping on and sinking into a Tunler cave. The brutes have six-inch claws that can break through most rock."

"Fortunately, they leave a dark track like a small tank tread on the surface wherever they burrow, and they do not like the crests of hills or dunes. We'll take the 'high road'."

"And we have to cross this desert because...?"

"It is your designated path to Leapside, Yancey. There is no way back."

Through all this briefing, Tax had been determinedly digging: the size of the initial hole at the base of the rock tower where she worked would have swallowed two elephants. Tax lengthened and deepened it. Pulling massively on something that remained hidden in the depths from their view, the giant cat bunched her muscles and wounded the ground with her steely claws as she played her side of tug of war against whatever resisted in the hole.

From time to time, Tax ceased tugging and pounced, slung her giant head up, and with just a few crunches swallowed a small animal or a piece of some vine whole. Her work was not in vain. Her tail twitched in enjoyment.

Now she came trotting proudly to Yancey. From her jaws hung a large, twisted, black vine perhaps three inches in diameter and trailing fifty or so feet on each side of her mouth. Repulsive, pulpy, orange spines protruded from the black exterior. Both severed ends dribbled orange goo onto the ground as Tax pranced on her way toward her new friend.

When Tax reached Yancey, she dropped the vine proudly at her feet. Yancey felt relieved to see the mess was vegetable, not animal.

Elbraith said, "Stroke her, Yancey. She has brought you an invaluable prize."

The Endi lowered her muzzle to Yancey's reach. Yancey dug her gloved fingers in behind the ears and stroked.

Knowing that sharing her hunt with Yancey meant Tax loved her in some way brought tears to Yancey's dry eyes despite the questionable nature of the gift.

Tax's muzzle was dirty. Crooning softly, Yancey rubbed and patted till Tax gave a pleasurable yawn which startled Yancey. Then Tax nosed the vine toward her, ran her rough tongue with a scraping sound over the leg of the silver jumpsuit, turned and loped off.

Shaking off the shivers the sound of tongue over fabric always produced, Yancey fondly watched Tax disappear into the trackless distance. Sand filled in the evidence of her going. Yancey and Elbraith stood alone in silence.

Yancey shook off the grand sight of Endi and desert and refocused on Tax's parting gift. At her puzzled look, Elbraith moved toward her and her present.

He tied off and then trimmed the two dribbling ends and tied more knots side by side at twenty-foot intervals. Then he slashed between each set of knots to form five ropes that bled slightly at the cut but did not dribble more because each twenty-foot length now had a knot at its ends.

"These are Y'min vines. They are very light-weight. The orange pulp and juice provide perfect food and drink. Rubbed on a wound and used as a poultice, they will disinfect and spur healing. The vine itself is a rope virtually impossible to break—Tax had to chew the two ends to sever them."

"Endi prefer the taste above all others and will chew on bits of the vines for hours. For her to give you her prize is a mark of extreme affection."

Elbraith twined the ropes around each of them like bandoliers. With a twinkle in his eyes, he said, "All three predators hate the smell and taste! The orange liquid so good for Endi and bi-peds repels and poisons many other life-forms."

Yancey exclaimed, "Did I tell you I love that Endi?"

Elbraith grinned and said, "It's mutual. Let's go."

Chapter 19 – Take the Test

Breaking out of the band of rock towers, Elbraith and Yancey faced a basin of dried mud plates cracked and crazed in dizzying patterns for perhaps a mile.

Walking on them made them crack and crumble into soft, clay dust, like pottery that had been improperly fired. Larger pieces disturbingly touched their legs and ankles as their feet stirred them up.

Elbraith in front of Yancey led single-file. He used his silver staff to prod the ground as he walked. It reduced the ankle and leg contact for Yancey. He would not take turns trail-breaking.

Once he led far to the right of an area littered with a dozen red and black-striped boulders. *I'm so dull right now— wonder if I'd've seen it. Thanks, Elbraith.*

They left a trail a blind man could follow. Yancey forced her thoughts away from Trenell's comments about possible pursuit and plodded on. *This whole mess is for my sake.*

Yancey thought what good clay Trenell could probably find but shut that idea off. *I'm mad at Trenell. He deserted us.* This she felt in spite of the fact that he'd warned them he'd pursue his business need.

Perhaps half-way across the dried plate region, two parallel tracks like tread marks from a large tank began to run alongside their path toward their goal.

Yancey pressed the throat mike in her helmet. "Elbraith, are those tracks from Tunlers?"

"No.   Tunler tracks leave only one tread-like impression."

Then he looked back with an unreadable expression and commented, "These are probably from Ingress's crossing party."

Yancey groused, "Tell me again why we're trudging along in 100-degree heat without our guide while Ingress and his clients are riding in a climate-controlled tank."

She heard the mild but approving humor in Elbraith's voice as he said, "Builds character! You picked Trenell, didn't you?"

Yancey ignored the jab and remarked, "Say, Jason and his tan young Conductor should be with Ingress. Going in style!" Elbraith spoke not a word.

Finally they trudged across the end of the mud flats. Yancey found herself watching in the distance a puzzling black tower that seemed to waver in the heat. She thought, *Mirage*.

It would turn out, instead, to be a living nightmare.

Chapter 20 — Restitution

The mud flats they'd just exited fed into a series of dried gulleys averaging five to ten feet deep by twelve to twenty feet wide. Laboriously slipping and sliding in the gritty sand, the two travelers navigated several of these.

Yancey lost sight of the odd black column except on the crests of the waving terrain. The sheer physical strain of trudging and keeping her footing quickly dulled her interest in the enigma. Breaking through the scrub brush at the top of the eighth or ninth rim, however, settled her curiosity but shattered her lethargy with the dreadful sight opposite them.

A swirling red and black, fifty-foot-tall, ten-foot wide, living tower of six-inch-long insects was systematically circling, diving and re-forming around their large target stalled in the sand at the bottom of the depression. Elbraith and Yancey could see roughly half of the frenzied insects' target. The back half remained camouflaged and thus of no interest to the swarm, but the whirling, nightmarish column nearly blotted out the front half of what clearly was an armored vehicle under siege.

Yancey cried, "Oh, no! Jason! Will they be all right?"

Elbraith replied, "Their engines have stalled. Ingress cannot open the air intakes, or the Runja will enter, too. The motors cannot fire without oxygen."

Already moving forward, Yancey yelled, "What can we do?"

Running alongside her, Elbraith answered, "He must have driven over a water seep where they were busy, and they signaled for help! The Runja he disturbed must've inadvertently clogged the camouflage mechanism as Ingress roared across. See how only the back half is silver and unmolested? Perhaps a small amount of oxygen for breathing is being admitted through the silver back, but he dare not re-fire the engines, whose intakes are in the front."

"Sooner or later, one Runja will randomly bumble into the interior through the silver back side if an oxygen access actually is open there. The rest will follow, and all the travelers will die."

As he spoke, Yancey was fingering the bumpy Y'min vines wrapped around her body. "If we can place the vines on the tank and slash them open, will it be enough to repel the swarm?"

Elbraith shouted, "We can try! Then pray the engines can fire up. You understand, we may die with them?"

Yancey yelled, "Not this time! Come on! We've got to save that boy!" They ran clumsily, slipping and sliding down the gulley's side.

Elbraith commanded, "You, climb up the silver back. From the top throw the vine lengths around the turret down to me. I know the vehicle and will shield the intakes. We must slash the vines open without severing them."

Elbraith charged around the tank's side. Yancey pulled herself aboard by the back ladder protruding from Ingress's "foolproof" stalled vehicle. Shakily, she plunged toward the boundary of silvery camouflage still working on the tank and uncoiled a precious Y'min from her body.

Charging into the edge of the insane swarm was like reversing a magnetic field in the midst of a million iron filings; the winged terrors sheered away from her silvery suit. Random collisions nevertheless panicked Yancey as swirling, six-inch insects dashed blindly into her suit and face mask. Although the bumpy, orange bristles on each black vine wrapped around her also repelled the turbulent black tornado, neither her hairy and repulsive drapery, nor her suit camouflage could prevent literally hundreds of hits from the wavering, constantly reforming swarm.

The Runja's vast numbers roiling slammed her as rubber bullets might punch into a target. The Runja buzzed and reshaped their orbit. Despair called her name loudly: to toss the Y'min forward over the front, she had to penetrate the horrifying tornado.

Crawling seemed her only option. Vine in hand, Yancey threw herself down. Repulsive carapaces crunched under her. She wriggled forward into the swirl. The world went black.

Madness beckoned her. *So many hitting me! Camouflage must've failed. THUD, THUDTHUDTHUD, THUD! O GOD, DON'T LET THEM GET ME!*

Six-inch, purple-black, flying missiles smashed her savagely. Her gloved hand found the turret. Gripping a top-mounted, protruding barrel, she pulled herself forward.

Below the exposed front, Elbraith groped for the thick end of the first vine. Runja swerved to avoid their black-orange nemesis. In the thick of the whirling mass, carefully, Elbraith slashed the vine.

Whipping the Y'min in tugs smeared it on the first of four screened air-intakes too high for him to reach from the ground. Sensing their prey just inside this frustrating barrier, Runja battered each screen.

Topside, visibility betrayed her. Like a pilot losing orientation in a black storm cloud, Yancey battled vertigo— *and I'm lying down! How will Elbraith stand up?*

A solid tug on the first vine still in her hand broke her panic. *Thank you, Conductor, for that!* With the blade of her silver staff, Yancey slashed the Y'min from her end. In the black, whirling Runja, the process played in slow-motion.

From the opened vine, orange goo seeped like bizarre blood. It stank like noxious sulfa, even through her mask filter. She choked and gagged.

Runja lifted angrily away from the toxic orange stuff. Insects, even armored as they were, died as their oblivious swarm-mates pressed them into even the slightest contact. The swirling mass formed avoidance tunnels shaped like miniature, demented croquet wickets wherever the Y'min blood ran.

Time to cover the left corner. Yancey crabbed herself sideways from the turret. She butted into two blades like the sharp edges of ice skates—*state-of-the-art antennae if you can believe anything Ingress bragged about*—that might have severed her silvery camouflage suit. Yancey shuddered.

The vine in my hands is safety. Lose it, and Jason dies. All her instincts screamed "No!" She inched herself away into solid liquidity.

She cast the second vine between the antennae blades. *Wait for Elbraith's tug. Slash, don't sever, the Y'min.*

Move! Keep moving. The partners in this death dance sliced open the next and next sections. Some of the cleared spaces overlapped. A two-inch layer of immunity hugged the tank's now orange-gooey top. Orange spread as if on a mission.

I HATE bugs! Crawl through, cast the vine—it did not usually go true the first time—*then wait for the tug.*

I CAN'T DO THIS!

The goo's slick. THE BUGS WILL GET ME! Don't jostle a vine.

I CAN'T BEAR ONE MORE HIT... SWARMING DARKNESS...THE NOISE...THE STENCH...THE FEAR... ANOTHER SECOND!

With her arms and legs themselves now coated in orange juice, *MY SUIT WILL NOT TEAR. THE BUGS WILL NOT GET ME.*

"DO NOT FEAR, FOR I AM WITH YOU."

In a stupor and ready to give up as she labored her way toward the right front corner, Yancey jerked alert at the last message. *That thought— it was Trenell's voice, not Elbraith's in my helmet.* Anger coursed through her and revitalized her.

RIGHT! Trenell's always with me. Look around, Cupcake. You're alone the same as you've always been. Only, Elbraith tugged just then on the vine, and she knew she lied.

The adrenaline rush woke her. She re-focused. The crazy chain-saw buzzes from innumerable hordes concentrated over this last, uncoated section.

I CAN DO THIS! SLASH THE VINE! The last I have. She slashed it.

She wallowed in orange goo. She dripped orange goo. It was her only plus. The stink caused her eyes and nose to run, but the THUDTHUDTHUD on her suit decreased as the swarm moved backward and away from the vines and from her sticky self.

Seeing the bleeding vine between the two right antennae, Yancey directed a tension-breaker Ingress's way— *hope it messes up your surround-sound, Bucko!*

Elbraith's voice boomed in her helmet: *Catch hold of the antennae blades, Yancey!*

Elbraith scraped the last intake, charged to the back and scrambled up alongside her. The mad Runja withdrew from before them

Together, they clung to the antennae and waited. Yancey wondered why. Elbraith's arm sheltered her body, muscles now painfully jerking and cramping, close to his.

The camouflaged screens in the silvery back section had kept the tank's passengers and crew alive. The slippery, orange semi-liquid she and Elbraith had applied now freed the four engine intakes forward.

The buzzing, angry, withdrawing horde still wanted to circle and destroy. The swarm sound remained phenomenal.

Suddenly, a more welcome sound erupted. The powerful engines below them coughed to life.

Dead bugs blasted like torpedoes out of the exhaust tubes on the undercarriage behind them. Resuming power, the tank accomplished its transformation to silver. Thousands more of the flying enemies swarmed off searching, no doubt, for their vanished target.

Elbraith and Yancey barnacled themselves as the tank lurched forward and roared almost vertically up the far side of the gulley. *Enough of this black, buzzing plague.*

Bolts like lightning shot from the short cannons mounted on the turret above and beside them. Fire penetrated the black, swarming horde searching for its escaped prey. Several blasts followed. *Sheer ill humor, eh, Ingress?* But she did not mourn the thousand buzzing horrors that plunged to the ground. On perhaps the eighth shot, the swarm catapulted to a flying wedge formation and rushed away into the desert.

Yancey turned toward Elbraith for an explanation. Elbraith keyed his mike and said, "Most likely, the queen died. Runja queens, unlike those in most hives on earth, lead and coordinate battle. The swarm will find water and plunge to its corporate death. Not one of the hive must outlive its queen for long."

She shouted, "Hooray for the code of the hive!"

Beneath them, the tank roared up and down sand hills scraggly with intermittent grasses and sedges. Elbraith held them aboard through the violent bouncing. Yancey's worn-out body felt spineless.

The machine moved with ground-covering speed. They traversed two days' walk in an hour. The hills racing past turned to complete sand with no more scrub growth.

It was becoming increasingly perilous to hang onto this silver juggernaut. Passengers and crew inside, no doubt, never knew of her and Elbraith's intervention. Whatever the reason, the fat cats inside had no plans to stop to rescue their rescuers.

Too bad. An iced glass of anything wouldn't hurt my feelings.

The tank veered away from their pyramidal rock's direction. Yancey caught Elbraith's glance and followed his lead. Leaning into his arm for the task of turning their jouncing bodies seat-downward, they shifted to face the back of their bruising steed. Yancey gulped, realizing they must propel themselves over the back to evade the caterpillar treads churning at each side.

Genuinely weary, Yancey struggled to place the soles of her feet on the tank. It was not a normal task for an octagenarian to demand of already stressed muscles.

Oh, like fighting insect torpedoes with hairy, orange vines is. What am I thinking? But she smiled inside her helmet: *Jason is safe. Farewell!*

Looking at Elbraith assured her they would die or be crippled together if she could not make the move. Her Conductor would not leave her.

With the silver staff she maneuvered her bruised body to a rough, sitting position facing backward. *Orange goo,* she found afresh, *is slick.*

With Elbraith on the count of three, Yancey thrust with painful knees and feet; she slid and then vaulted off the back. Unlike her, Elbraith flowed with an athlete's grace.

Who knew sand could be so hard? She rolled over and over down the slope their oblivious steed was climbing. Yancey lay still, the wind knocked from her, wondering how many of her old bones she had broken. *Maybe if it's my leg, Elbraith will just shoot me. It'd be a kindness.*

The snorting juggernaut that owed them its escape churned indifferently on and disappeared over the next ridge of sand. Silence settled with amazing speed. Just a moment ago the world's song had throbbed to the pulse of the huge engine. Ears tingling, Yancey could not yet hear if the sand on this planet sang its own song the way everything else seemed to.

Surprised, she found a sort of singing within herself. *Jason's safe! I'm glad he's not dead!* A rest ensued. The singing resumed, *I don't want him dead anymore! Say, can forgiveness make that much difference? Life and death?* She tucked the thought away; *it's a happy song.*

Buoyed by her new thought, Yancey started moving, taking another skeletal inventory as she flexed body parts. Nothing seemed broken. Individual bruises and sore spots were only beginning to call for her attention. For now, her body ached everywhere. Elbraith reached to help her up, but she waved him off and initiated her own slow progress toward vertical.

As she continued to stretch kinks and to massage serious cramps from her back and shoulders, she consoled herself by muttering, "I don't feel a day over sixty, errr, sixty-five—what do I know? I'm used to thirty-seven!" Every joint ached, and all her back and neck muscles popped and cracked like Rice Krispies.

She removed her headgear when she saw Elbraith take his off. First sunset had passed, and the second sun hung like an impossibly large balloon just above the horizon. The sand softened into reflections not as vibrant as the sky but incredibly lovely. *I think I do hear a whispering!*

Ingress had carried them to new land. Nothing but mountains of sand showing gold, black, or blood red surrounded them. Symmetrical ripples marched in ascending curves of light and shadow toward the top of the low dune immediately ahead. The effect looked like old rivers with waves of knife-sharp edges where dark met light.

They slip-slid their way to the dune's top in the tank's ruts, the only flaws in nature's symmetry. From the ridge Elbraith took a sighting for the black pyramid.

Only one black object appeared briefly on a far sand ridge. It was too small to be the pyramid, and it was moving their way. Yancey wanted to whimper.

Elbraith replaced his headgear, so she did, too. Running down the side of the stately dune would have been fun if only Yancey could have felt their lives did not depend on escaping the oncoming black thing.

Elbraith angled toward a sort of cup about six feet below the top of the next ridge, and Yancey followed. The shallow bowl shape was perhaps twelve feet deep and twice as wide. The lowest point lay in blackness.

When they reached the darkness, Elbraith motioned for Yancey to lie down on her side and began to cover her with sand. He joined her with his back to hers and the two of them finished pulling sand over themselves. She heard him whisper, "Staff ready. Perhaps fifteen more minutes till we see if whatever that is, missed us."

Subjectively, the wait lasted hours. Holding still was beginning to re-cramp her already savaged muscles.

A roared blast of joy shattered the agony.

Yancey screamed, "Tax!"

Surging from their flimsy hideout, Yancey decided she hadn't seen joy until she witnessed an elephant-sized, great, saber-toothed tiger thingy with a head like a lion lower its shaggy face between its massive paws and roar a barking invitation to play.

Tears surged from her eyes. *Avoiding sudden death can do that to a girl,* she thought.

Elbraith relaxed his death-grip on his staff. He and Yancey rose with their new sand cascading from them like umbrellas opening and with their old sand still stuck in orange goo which even the silvery suits could not entirely shed.

The Endi bounded madly around the crater perimeter and splatted yet more sand over them. Tax cavorted hilariously.

When she calmed down, Tax approached and flopped on her belly at their feet. Turning her massive head toward them, she barked another thunderous roar and tugged Elbraith's sleeve toward herself but became distracted by residues of her favorite food. Tax licked the messy patches of Y'min goo, stuck sand and all.

Wincing from the tongue-on-cloth sound now amplified by sand, Yancey said, "Try to climb on her back."

Her Conductor's face split into a grin. Elbraith buried his gloved hands in Tax's magnificent mane and climbed aboard. The Endi looked expectantly at Yancey, who cooed, "You darling girl!" and climbed aboard behind Elbraith without further ado.

Tax rose effortlessly. Elbraith leaned forward and dug his hands into her mane. Yancey held his waist for dear life. The Endi bounded back in the direction from which she had come.

Her speed up, over, and down the mountains of sliding sand surpassed Ingress's. Her webbed feet, so effective in the hotsprings, now gave her an equally sure purchase in the sand.

Elbraith's and Yancey's legs strained to grip Tax, but this was a joyous ride. This was no snorting, stinking machine, but a brindled lover whose smooth lope was punctuated by brief breathers and tawny eye-checks as if to tease her passengers to share the fun. Tax's broad, muscled back trumped unyielding metal any day.

Second sunset passed and stars appeared. Their tireless steed hit firmer ground and made even faster speed as the sand gave way to shale and then sandstone outcroppings. The landscape and their ride firmed up, but the terrain began to tilt.

Ahead a low star began winking in and out between rock outcroppings. As Tax wound up some trail visible only to her, her riders felt even her formidable muscles begin to tremble with the strain. Still, she wove up and between arches and sweeps of wind-sculpted rock. Eventually, Tax scrambled up one last stone facing—to Yancey the ascent had seemed impossible— and the star resolved itself into a campfire.

The big Endi moved straight to the solitary figure forming a black silhouette against the fire. The figure turned and opened its arms. Tax padded over and laid her great head over Trenell's shoulder.

Her sides heaved. Trenell—Yancey recognized the music that was sometimes his voice—crooned to the big beast. Tax's answering rumble was somewhere between a purr and a satisfied whine. If tiredness were visible, Yancey felt sure it would be dropping off Tax in great, fluffy heaps like wool at a sheep-shearing.

The sound of his voice—*it has to do with the sound of his voice.* Then she thought, *Girl, you've been too long in the desert.* She softly laughed, thinking, *I thought I heard it among the buzzing Runja!*

Because she and Elbraith sat on Tax's back, Yancey and her Conductor were invited as silent partners into this adoring love-fest. For a few moments, Yancey thought that under Trenell's influence, she too might be able to run joyously around in these mountains. Her muscles unkinked.

Tax backed from Trenell's embrace and crouched. Trenell approached, cupping his hands for Yancey's foot. Trenell eased her to the ground.

Some sort of exchange passed between Elbraith and Trenell as the latter offered his cupped hands for her Conductor's foot. Yancey wished it had been light so she could see well. Elbraith's foot barely touched Trenell's hands; he leapt nimbly down as if reluctant to receive a favor from the Guide's hands.

Tax stretched herself luxuriously, butted Yancey gently in the side, and bounded in absolute silence away into the darkness.

Trenell then said some of the most glorious words she'd heard lately: "You two must be hungry. Come."

It was hot, wonderful tea. Whatever the food was— she laughed—it tasted like chicken and the best dumplings Yancey had ever eaten. *Where he got anything that tastes like chicken in this place, I'll never know,* she thought. *No way am I asking!*

By the time she was sipping another perfect cuppa and letting a dark chocolate melt on her tongue for dessert, Yancey forgot to wonder about where Trenell got anything. The dishes were disposable and made the fire flare up beautifully. They rinsed their own cups in boiling water, hung them to dry, and rose to follow their Guide.

A cave became visible. The fire held back the blackness enough to see it stood perhaps fifteen feet high and stretched perhaps nine feet across. Yancey would never have believed a cave could feel palatial.

Some six feet into the cave lay a bed that smelled like lavender. Under her own silvery blanket stretched over the source of the wonderful lavender smell, Yancey felt she snuggled in a feather comforter— Yancey mused, *maybe he found more than one chicken; hence, the feathers.*

Elbraith bedded down to the left and she to the right of the entrance. For the few minutes spent nuzzling into the softness to find just the right position, Yancey thought she saw swift movements outside the cave at the far edge of the fire. Whistles and low grunts reached her ears.

Each movement and sound prompted an unsettled shift of her body; she tried to see or to hear into the dark and understand what seemed to threaten. She listened hard for the reassuring sound of Trenell and heard him moving around, seemingly unfazed.

Hearing her Guide's steady movements, Yancey let her poor muscles relax and stopped lifting her head in futile attempts to penetrate the secrets of darkness.

When Trenell entered and stretched himself on his sleeping bag across the cave entrance, Yancey marveled. *I never felt so safe in my life.* Sleep claimed her.

Chapter 21 – Really, Students, Testing is Good!

Yancey slept like some untroubled infant safe in its mother's arms. When Elbraith shook her awake the next morning, he and Trenell had already removed their own beds. Not a sound had disturbed her.

The only sound she heard now was the pleasant chuckling of the small stream flowing on the right side into the cave and on into its recesses. Peeking from her bedroll, Yancey saw a crackling fire inviting her out of the cave. Water steamed. The smells of coffee, biscuits, and bacon teased her nose. It was enough.

Yancey stretched and emerged from her cocoon. The coolness of the cave urged her out into the sunshine and toward the fire, but she had fallen behind the others and so stayed to deal with her pallet. After folding her bedroll and refitting it into its niche in her silver jumpsuit's backpack, she dragged her "mattress" outside to burn with the others.

She made her way past the camp to some boulders. Despite the enticing food smell, Yancey climbed higher and out to the edge of the rocks to look through a large opening.

Below her as far as she could see lay desert. Studying what had to be the section she and Elbraith had traversed for the last two days, Yancey saw they had crossed only a narrow sand peninsula protruding like a broad thumb from the vast hand of the main body they had avoided.

Remembering the endlessness of that relatively narrow peninsula taught her the vast scope of the desert proper. She wondered how much of it Ingress and his party had crossed—the tracks had seemed to come from the desert that formed the "hand" of their sandy peninsula. Again she questioned who might be tracking her and why; *Trenell certainly led us off the "beaten path" if the desert even has one.*

Tax had carried them across on the diagonal to their current position, which seemed an isolated monument with perhaps two others cropping up from the sand to her right. First sun's angle and the rock faces enclosing her crevice obscured visibility in that direction. She wondered if sand and more sand would greet her view from the opposite side of their rocky tower.

Yancey suddenly needed company. Braid completed and tucked once again inside her silvery suit, she followed her nose back to camp.

Taking the food Trenell offered with a "Thanks," she was searching out her folded pack to serve as a rough seat when Trenell asked, "What is your assessment of our current situation?"

Yancey plopped down. She pulled her eyebrows together, narrowed her eyes in a facial expression that had warned generations of recalcitrant high-schoolers they were in trouble, and cocked her head toward Trenell.

"Let's see. Do you mean the part about, hmnnn, I died on earth and now find myself alive—I think—on some *Survivor* nightmare on an alien planet named X because the whole experience is incomprehensible?"

She rushed on, "Or the fact that my 'current situation' represents such a puzzle that I don't even get the *question*, so how can I find a *solution*? Planet X—yeah."

"No," she hurried on when Elbraith looked as though he might interrupt her. To Trenell she continued, "You mean the part about facing and forgiving my killer, an event that depressed me into an unsightly blob."

"Of course, a blob was kind of fitting, seeing as how I schlepped out of some oozing tank with all of my eighty-plus years painfully in evidence—I'm wearing orthopedic boots, for crying out loud!"

Sneaking a peak at Trenell revealed amused affection on his rugged face and encouraged her.

Thus accepted, and honestly becoming indignant, Yancey proceeded with, "No, what am I thinking? You mean three weirdoes trying to seduce me at a ball which wasn't really a ball, but some forum for hiring a professional Guide to take me to some bungee-jumping appointment"—here she paused to see if Elbraith clicked with the town of Leapside, for it was obvious Trenell was vastly enjoying her little summary— "which everybody else on this weird world seems convinced I must attend."

Encouraged further despite her momentary pique by a slight twitch now of Elbraith's mouth—he got the Leapside pun—she said, "Or do you mean being grateful for escaping swarms of lethal insects built functionally as torpedoes?"

Trenell's approving look diverted her for a moment into admitting, "Or maybe it's the very real pleasure of a good night's sleep and a ride on an Endi?" Parenthetically, she added, "Now that really WAS fun!" She gathered her sarcasm again before it could escape.

Yancey continued, "Ah, hold on! You were, no doubt, referring to some wavering, malevolent phantom-thingy which appears and disappears at will and who staged an actual murder plot against me. He continues, I assume, to seek my demise?"

Trenell nodded silently but then locked eyes with her. Yancey remembered that her own lust for control over *something* in this crazy world had made Fafnir's plot viable. Then she remembered that another being had died instead of her and that she had jeopardized her whole party. She blushed deeply as shame broke loose inside her.

She whispered, "I'm so sorry."

When Trenell spoke her name, Yancey looked into his eyes again. *Forgiven—he's forgiven me.* She revisited forgiving and rescuing Jason. She remembered that word, "Peace."

Both Beings gave her time to grieve. She hadn't known she needed it. Even giving up something bad like her shame could demand mourning.

Eventually, Trenell said softly, "Yesterday you risked your life to save Jason and the others."

She flicked tear-stained eyes to meet his and then shrugged.

Rallying herself, she picked up her interrupted narrative. She was about to surprise herself again.

"How do I assess our current situation?" She paused to see if her companions were ready. They were.

"Oh. I know what part you mean. You mean the parts where unknown parties may be following me to do me harm, but my Conductor and I set off into the desert alone and could've died while our Guide went shopping for clay!"

Her own bitterness shocked her. *I've always guarded my tongue better than this*! Speaking her mind had always produced what she feared she was about to experience: abandonment.

In her peripheral vision, like some horrible prophecy about to be fulfilled, Yancey saw Elbraith stiffen. Worse yet, Yancey thought she saw across his face a momentary hardening; *how awful if Elbraith resents Trenell for that as much as I do! Oh, I wish I'd shut up.*

But, no, I accuse Trenell and stir dissension between these two on whom my inexplicable existence depends.

Trenell is here now; forget the past. Never mind that I don't know if I can ever trust him. I need him.

His food's in my stomach. His body like a kind of gate protected me last night. His messenger, the big Endi, has twice given me the only fun I've had on this miserable planet.

One fleeting moment before she spoke, Trenell was her safety. If her resentment drove him away...*well, look what Elbraith and I got into yesterday.*

I don't know these aliens. I don't know the rules. I'm an ungrateful, bumbling **idiot***.*

When Trenell stood without a word, Yancey feared he might abandon them—this time for good. Terror crawled under her skin.

It rose within her with panic from some hidden place deeper than her fear of her "current situation," no matter what that turned into. It was deeper than her fear of her presence on this mysterious planet, no matter what that was about.

I do not understand.

Her stomach clenched and her breakfast rose with black bile up toward her teeth. Finding her mouth clamped shut, it burned its way through her nose. She retched. Hot tears gushed to join the vomit. Her nose ran. Mortified, she knew it was a huge over-reaction. All Trenell did was stand up.

Elbraith handed her a cloth he'd moistened in the campfire's steaming water.

Yancey wiped her face. She cleaned a couple of spots on her pant leg for as long as she could. It let her keep her eyes down—anything to avoid the sight of Trenell picking up his pack and leaving. *Stop crying!*

Trenell broke through her misery, "Yancey. I found *very* good clay."

He was still here! He had made a joke! Yancey looked up and saw his steady eyes, *inviting me to humor.*

She could not maintain eye contact. *What am I? Nuts? This guy is a hired hand, and I don't even know what payment he'll demand.* So went her thoughts. *Besides, I almost puked on him.* The last reflection restored her to reality.

Trenell said, "Elbraith, please break camp. Yancey, please come with me."

Yancey could not avoid the sinking feeling of "being taken out behind the woodshed." It was an old saying in her family. Her Dad as a boy received multiple paddlings for whatever trouble he was in at the time. It became one of those specialized phrases (gerund, she had joked with him after she became an English teacher) that families use for "shorthand" communication. Dad would say, "I'm thinking 'woodshed,'" and she would know she'd better shape up.

Now, here she went. Yancey squared her shoulders and followed Trenell.

He led her out through the sun-warmed rocks with bands of ochre, dark brown, and gray and under one spectacular arch to the cliff face opposite her earlier exploration.

Holding her arm, Trenell motioned for her to step out on a boulder visibly upheld by nothing; it was a natural outcropping that jutted out into the air. With no woodshed in her immediate future, just a possible crash down the cliff face into nothingness, she did not wish to risk disappointing Trenell again. *Let's see: death...or disappoint Trenell? Death...*

Despite her fear of heights, and a rogue thought that Trenell might push her off and be done with her, Yancey stepped out to stand virtually in open space. She was breathing hard.

Water? As far as I can see in any direction? Where's the desert?

Shock combined with vertigo almost toppled her. Trenell's steadying hand on her upper arm along with the rock beneath her feet was all that sustained the world in its proper orientation.

He said, "The place where we camped is an enormously high, natural tower."

She nodded.

Trenell continued, "On the other side there is one tenuous trail upward. Our friend Tax zigzagged your way up that last night. This rock chimney is miles high and many more miles around at the base. On your world, three sides of it would be a climber's dream."

"About half way around the tower's huge base and out of sight to your left, the sea meets the desert spit you crossed. Straight down you see the beach or shoreline along the tower's base." Yancey did not look down. *Think I'll take his word for it.*

"To your right, of course, the cliff curves around and you see the shoreline, but the tower is surrounded by water each night for six hours before first sunrise; then the desert reasserts itself. On the other side of this sea toward the horizon lies Leapside."

"Besides rappelling, there are two ways down to sea level. One is Tax's route from last night, as long as one avoids the tide before First Rise. The other is down through the cave."

Trenell guided her back to a convenient boulder where they sat facing the blue water spread before them. Yancey wanted to embrace the big rock. She grinned at her own squeamishness.

"I brought you over here because our friend Elbraith has a problem of which he is unaware. To descend through the cave is, for him, certain death."

Yancey cared for Elbraith. She took a sharp, short breath and then said, "Then we must return the way we came."

"The cave is, unfortunately, not his whole problem. He faces a 58% probability of death if he accompanies you back down the trail."

Yancey frowned and her lips tightened to a straight line. She averted her face and closed her eyes to process his words.

The lines in her brow deepened. *How could Trenell know all that?* Two big tears crowded up behind her eyelids and sneaked out when she wasn't looking.

The trouble is, on this wacko planet, I believe him! Elbraith dies if he does his job as my Conductor. That's what Trenell means. Her earlier mistrust over her Guide's trip for clay had evaporated.

Trenell continued, "If, however, I accompany your courageous Conductor down the trail, he will experience danger but will merely grow thereby."

She did not care about the tears now flowing through her fingers and down her cheeks and neck. Opening her eyes again, she swallowed and asked meekly, "What can we do? Do I stay here and you come back for me?"

Trenell's dark brown eyes looked into her own. She did not know how he did it, but she knew he was feeling along with her. There was one more thing: Trenell seemed pleased with her answer.

"To stay here on the tower even one night without my protection will bring grisly death to you."

The night rustlings outside the cave entrance replayed in her mind. Remembering the whistles and menacing growls that had been almost grunts popped Goosebumps out on her arms and legs. She wrapped her arms around herself and rubbed up and down.

She had no further need to ask the question of how she was to descend. *Alone!* Darkness was her greatest fear, unless it was dying alone. *Great! I can do both at once—sort of an economy package.*

She reviewed, "We do not have the rope to rappel down, even if I could do it. For me to go on the trail with Elbraith leads him to better than one in two chance of death. You must go with him. For him to live, I must descend through the cave alone."

"Trene-ell," she wailed, "I ha-a-ate caves!" She hiccupped a sob. "And darkness. I can't..." Her breath caught again. Mentally, she slapped herself.

Then fiercely, Yancey hissed to herself, *save a beautiful young man with his life still before him, or a wrinkled, old Educator who has already lived* and *died?*

She closed her eyes and witnessed horrific visions of dark, dank tunnels that sprawled all directions and wound down to death...*my death, all alone, in the dark. Yeah, yeah.*

She pursued the thoughts to their sorry end. Death from a Las in a tubular hallway, in the midst of a busy school, back on good old Earth, suddenly seemed a mere blip on a radar screen.

Yancey exhaled and gathered her tattered fears. She tucked them away in a dark place and locked the door. It was her method: *think* through a reality and find a way to *live* through it—*if possible.*

She looked into Trenell's steady eyes and felt him feeling her terror: *he has no fear of his own for me.*

What? Man, I'm weirding myself out.

Weird or not, she accepted the new idea: *he believes in me.* Hope shivered alive. It sliced through the glum horror of darkness and oblivion she had just visited. She would either prove him right or die trying. She straightened her shoulders and stood.

Trenell said, "I will prepare you for your journey. Come."

He says that to me often, she thought. *I like it.*

He can prepare me? Right.

On their way back to camp, Yancey could not look enough at the colored stones, the occasional scrub growth, and, especially, the clear sky. She breathed as if believing she could store up oxygen. Her ears soaked in the sweet singing that seemed ready everywhere on this planet if one had ears to hear.

As if her finger tips could store up sensations, she touched clean, warm stone as often as she could. She stopped and drank in the beauty of the stone arch once again above them as they passed back to camp.

The colors, as they had been in the city, seemed three-dimensional. *The wind, I guess, accounts for the soft, singing sound.*

She willed herself to store sight and touch and melody and smells in her heart. *I'm like some miser who has learned he cannot visit his treasure for a fortnight and so takes pictures of his wealth to insulate his heart from the coming separation.*

Elbraith waited unsuspecting by the deadened campfire. His and her backpacks stood on the ground behind where he sat on a smooth stone. He looked up. His dear golden locks of hair gleamed in the sunlight. His incredible eyes caught hers with concern. He shifted his gaze sharply to Trenell.

The Guide spoke with authority, "Yancey must go alone to the bottom through the cave, Elbraith. You and I must take the rock path Tax used to bring you here."

The stalwart Conductor leapt to his feet with a flat denial: "No, Trenell. I'll not leave Yancey. She is in my charge." His hazel eyes dared anyone to contradict him.
He looked from one of them to the other. His jaws tensed. His hands curled into fists.

To Yancey he growled, "You can't be considering this."

Yancey caught his blazing eyes and held them, "Remember the Green Valley? Trenell is our Guide, Elbraith. He was right then. We must trust him now."

Skipping over the Green Valley, for Elbraith felt partly responsible—Yancey had been in his charge when Fafnir got to her—he rapped out, "You nearly died in the desert. Where was he then?"

"I have pledged years of my life in preparation to conduct you on your pilgrimage. Him you chose because of some moonlit tea party. Who is *he*, anyway? You need *me*, Yancey. I cannot allow you to go alone into *that*." Here he gestured toward the cave.

Yancey's traitorous heart wanted for one moment to grasp Elbraith's offer and to keep both Guide and Conductor with herself. The moment passed. Here Elbraith stood, ready to offer his life for her. *He would insist even if he knew all the circumstances. How can I do less?*

Yancey wrinkled her brow at her Conductor. "Is it true that though I am the Juvie, you are duty-bound to allow me free will?" Elbraith glowered back.

She had deduced this from the cage-encounter with Fafnir and from how Elbraith had followed her lead to rescue Ingress and his conductees. Additionally, the Conductor had not been, as he had just confirmed, happy with her choice of Trenell; yet he had given a curt, if astonished, nod when she chose her Guide and had schooled himself to support her choice.

Mad clear through, Elbraith's face turned brick red; blue veins stood out on his neck and forehead. His hands clenched and unclenched. He appeared presently to want to sabotage his first duty and strangle her himself.

He glared at Trenell. "Why would you endanger her through such a preposterous course?"

They were two strong Beings in an unpleasant face-off. Trenell spoke, "Yancey has chosen. We must prepare her and depart."

"She must be well into the cavern before second sunrise. I have cleared the cavern of ground grunts, but they will emerge from their hiding places when darkness comes and re-enter their cave. They cannot cross the water barrier the Ubus River forms about a mile and a half past the entrance, so Yancey must be safely on the other side before second sunset this night."

Elbraith snorted in disgust and unbelief, unclenched his fists, and unconsciously posed as a soldier ready to receive his instructions.

Trenell walked over to his own pack. From a tightly secured side pouch he handed Yancey a lamp woven into a silver-mesh headband.

"This," he said, "is a light that will not fail. It shines continually and adjusts to the light level, whatever it is. Once you put it on, it will conform solely to your own DNA signature and ride securely, no matter what."

Yancey slipped the mesh onto her head like some silvery laurel wreath; it settled so naturally and lightly, Yancey had to feel with her hands to be sure she had it on.

From his pack Trenell next extracted and thumbed open a glowing, holo vid map complete with sound; it intoned in a calm computer voice, "Ubus Cave Schematic, 8:17.33. You are here." A glowing red dot blinked above the numbers 10.75 feet, displayed in green letters, to indicate the distance from the cave entrance.

When Trenell recompressed the map between his palms, he had her focus her mesh light on a silver band spanning the palm-sized packet. Although the light was invisible out under the workaday sun, the holo sprang open in her hand. She re-closed it for herself by lightly pressing the top of the image down toward the base. It formed a booklet, and Yancey nervously thought, *So far, so good.*

She had to fight thinking *Ground grunts, ground grunts, grisly death.* She managed with unsteady fingers to place the map in the front pocket of her silvery suit.

Trenell said, "The booklet will highlight the path and tell you, 'This is the way. Walk ye in it.' It will warn you of pitfalls and answer questions you ask it as you trek through the cave."

Next, Trenell gave her a water bottle and a flat packet of bread. She knelt and placed these into her backpack. When she looked up at him, he explained, "The Ubus River, which is this small trickle here, is too acidic for the first third of your journey to drink without a filter."

"When you leave the cave, you will actually have been following the Ubus River both above and underground for four miles or so. Some of the terrain is vertical. The river disappears and re-emerges several times. It widens into a respectable river at the end where hidden springs join to feed it."

"At the lower cave mouth will be a stone dock with a power boat. This launch will respond, as does your map, only to the light on your forehead to start it; you'll see on the panel where to shine it. The craft will bring you to our beacon."

He said, "Elbraith and I must go if we are to avoid First Rise tide before we reach the desert and the safety of a highpoint. Since our way is longer, you should not have to hurry once you first cross Ubus River. If you have used your map well, you will proceed at your own pace and arrive in a timely manner."

"If not, we will wait three days at Beacon Point and then come looking for you. Your map will function outside the cave, also, and will prove a reliable time piece."

"Questions?"

Yancey looked at him sarcastically. Trenell looked briefly approving that her sense of humor had resurrected. She tucked the look away for encouragement later and turned with a sobered face to look at her unsmiling Conductor.

Elbraith unbent from his disapproving parade rest of silence. He handed her the silver staff and her backpack. "Prosper, Yancey. Since you have chosen Trenell's way, follow it with your whole heart."

Elbraith looked her up and down as if memorizing her. Yancey thought of her miser analogy from earlier. He raised his hand briefly to her, palm out, broke eye contact, and then marched, still in a temper, to the edge of the small clearing to await Trenell.

Trenell, standing close to her said, "You've made the right choice. Trust me, Yancey."

Trenell moved away and added, more publicly, "We will see you at the bottom. Fare well."

Then Trenell spoke her favorite word to Elbraith, and she felt jealous: "Come."

Yancey stood there, silent, and watched them disappear on the path into the rocks. She checked to assure herself plenty of daylight remained. Then she turned toward the cave and shuddered. Her stomach was going to get used to turning upside down if this kept up.

Yancey thought, *Trust him? Mr. Vanishing Guide? O.K., I believe him about Elbraith, but trust him when grunty things could come after me?*

How am I supposed to cross some water barrier for crying out loud? Oh and what about that small caveat he brushed over: 'some of the terrain is vertical? What did that mean? How do I get down? It doesn't quite sound like a gently descending path. Questions? Yes, I have questions.

What could "Trust me" possibly mean when I AM ALONE IN A DARK CAVE EITHER FALLING OVER A CLIFF OR DROWNING OR BEING EATEN ALIVE AND HE IS NOWHERE IN SIGHT?

Trenell will have to earn the rest of my trust if I live to see him again.

Yancey nevertheless was walking while grumbling to herself in a bit of a temper. It helped suppress her fear. *My decision will save Elbraith. Let's see if I can do the same for myself.*

I've gotta get a move on. How long before second sunset, and how far to the river barrier?

She arrived at the entrance. From just inside, Yancey took one last, long look at dirt and rocks and vegetation and sky, and sorrowed that she could not really memorize them. Then she thought she heard a slight scrabbling on the other side of the clearing from the cave entrance. With an irrepressible shudder, she turned her back on the surface world and plunged through the opening into the cave.

Chapter 22—"Come."

When Trenell said to me, "Come," I wanted to demolish him and charge after Yancey.

I did not mistake the authority in his voice. He trusted in his superior rank and in my superior training to save him from assault!

Fuming, Elbraith watched Trenell shoulder his pack and turn with a military economy of movement. The subtle implication of duty helped Elbraith clamp down his urge to mutiny, but he boiled: *He knew I would follow his command. Who does he think he is?*

Jaw locked, Elbraith answered his own question: *Both of us know the Guide/Conductor bylaws: The Guide has unmistakable pre-eminence over the Conductor—except I know the Guide Association dropped Trenell's sanction eight years ago. To my mind, that makes the chain of command not quite so clear as he assumes.*

As he force-marched, Elbraith seethed, I know it's a technicality. Right now the Lady Yancey, my charge, walks into danger without my protection. Honor the code, or save my charge? The book...I go by the book.

Why would she believe Trenell's word and cut out on her own? I am bound by her word, NOT HIS! Elbraith would have believed it if someone had told him his hair was on fire.

Successful Conductors established personal relationships with their charges. Part of his training was to do so swiftly and surely. To that end, they studied their to-be charges for years before the actual link occurred at Rejuvenation.

Elbraith's sandy hair would have crackled with lightning bolts if his body could have translated his outrage into visible electricity. All his being screamed, "Follow Yancey!" Yet all forty years of his special training commanded he uphold the code.

The only reality that keeps me following Trenell is Yancey's own choice. I made my decision when I pledged to conduct her.

Even in his rage marching behind Trenell he admired her. *She discerned early on that I am duty-bound to respect her wishes, not the other way around.*

Elbraith's mind turned over the immediate events that had him marching AWAY from his charge. He searched for a loophole that would free him from the Conductor's pledge of compliance with her will, a loophole that would free him to run back, take her hand, shelter her life and her progress.

Finding none, Conductor Elbraith marched sullenly downward behind the erect, graceful form he now resented above all others.

Chapter 23 – Who Set Up these Tests, Anyway?

Natural light illumined the first twenty feet or so as Yancey descended into the cave. *Depending on the angle of either of the suns, portions of the cave must receive more*; the result was moss-like vegetation with small pink flowers peeking from the green on the walls. The patches shrank as the cavernous tunnel sloped downward.

The Ubus hugged the left side. Although she saw no stalactites from the heightening ceiling, boulders and rocks jutted from the walls and cave floor. Only one path led down, winding between them. It appeared to be the former stream bed for the river. The Ubus ducked underground about a hundred feet from the cavern entrance.

Her mesh light glowed more obviously as she left the sunlight. It illumined a pie-shaped swath before her perhaps five feet to the right and left of center. *Good light*, she thought and walked on with a gratifyingly athletic stride. *Not bad for an old lady.* She grinned to herself.

She was a moving spot of light and life in the midst of a dark, still, damp void. Shuddering, she hoped she might continue her status as the only thing moving. Her suit's boots gripped the rock path well, but she proceeded with caution. The staff further promoted a sense of secure footing.

She negotiated small drops in the path, two where she sat down, scooted, and then slid to her feet on the next level.

Her silvery jumper was all that kept her seat dry, for moisture increased as she pressed forward and down.

After negotiating the second drop, ahead of her on the path she heard a definite scrabbling noise. "Trenell drove all grunts from the cave. They cannot re-enter till second sunset," she said aloud in a small voice immediately absorbed along with her confidence by the vast nothingness around her.

All the blood in her body plummeted to her feet, and she could not have taken a step if her life depended on it. Although light-headed with dread, she tilted her head so her mesh light more particularly illumined the path beyond her.

Now, Yancey had not laid eyes on a single ground grunt, but she felt quite certain that if the animal caught and confused by her light beam ahead had been one of those nasty beasts, it would not have been rushing *away* from her. Momentarily arrested by the unaccustomed light, a small, pale yellow rodent with webbed, blue feet and a single blue stripe down its back turned around to face her, scrabbled to its right where it bumped into a boulder, and, with an indignant squeak, sat down rather hard on its yellow, furry rump.

Yancey giggled at the comic relief, then cooed, "You poor little thing, I won't hurt you!" The animal seemed dazed from its encounters, first with the light and then with the immovable rock, and turned its unique little face toward the sound of her voice.

Above its cute, pointed snout, its eyes were enormous, pale-blue orbs that stuck up on stalks and currently rotated independently of each other like two crazed periscopes. Through two small incisors, it whiffled with a rising end-note that sounded so much like a question, Yancey laughed out loud.

Delighted with finding some life other than her solitary self, and it not bent on eating her, Yancey followed her fancy and answered the pretend questions. "Yes. I'll tilt my light elsewhere, and, yes, you are quite free to go." Blue-toes scampered off.

Back on earth as a little girl, Yancey had collected rare Popeye cartoon books. Bluto had been the big, bad guy who always fought the spinach-eating hero for Olive Oyl, the stick-like, lady heart-throb. Yancey called, "Bye, Bluto!" and felt not quite so alone for just a moment. She smirked at her pun.

She walked on thinking about Popeye and a couple of her favorite comic books. It helped prolong the pleasantness of the brief contact.

The sound of the suddenly tinkling and re-emerging Ubus halted her musings. She heard splashing far below the level where she walked. Yancey pulled up cautiously at the fat edge of the boulder before her and looked around it. Immediately past where she stood, her light revealed nothingness.

Tapping with her silver walking staff confirmed there was no floor beyond the fat stone in the middle of her path. Carefully, she rested the staff alongside her body, for its catch-strap would not allow her to lay it down.

With both hands, Yancey grasped a knob on the boulder and leaned over a bit. Tilting her head down let her light reveal two huge shelves of rock protruding like gigantic tree mushrooms from the suddenly vertical shaft of the cave. She could see these two, and the truly serious drop between where she stood and the next one down.

Beyond the edge of the top shelf she saw a tall, narrow stalagmite's tip. The cave's floor lay far below; she could not see the base of the tall finger of rock. The cavern had enlarged, and her light could not discover the far wall or the floor.

To her left the small, re-emerged Ubus fell twenty feet or so to the next rim below her in a beautiful waterfall that looked like a diaphanous curtain sparkling in her light. It hit the top of the lower shelf and splashed loudly in the silence of the cave before disappearing over that rim in another fall only dimly illumined below it.

She pulled herself back fighting a touch of vertigo and sat down shaken but in relative safety. From her pocket she pulled the map. A frisson of fear rippled through her.

Why didn't I pull this out before? I could've walked right over the edge! What was I thinking? I must have missed the real path. How am I going to get down from here? Oh, is it getting close to dark outside? She shivered, this time not from damp or the cold or the path's sudden drop.

Yancey shined her light on the band on the map packet. The green-glowing holo vid sprang to life in her hands. Its very first words encouraged her: it sounded like Trenell's voice, an impression which had escaped her when they had opened it together on the surface.

It said, "Good afternoon, Yancey. You are here": the red light blinked. Trenell's voice continued, "and right on schedule."

"The water barrier collects in a very deep, vast natural bowl in the cave's floor approximately sixty feet below you. It spans the entire width of the cavern.   You have roughly two hours before second sunset on the surface and perhaps another half hour after that before you could possibly have unwelcome visitors."

Yancey chuffed out a blast of relief. The warning, however, was not lost upon her.

Trenell's voice continued, "You are facing a series of four shelves with drops varying from four to twenty-five feet."

"This first drop is twenty-two feet, seven inches. Depart from the old river bed you have followed and veer to your left around the near side of the boulder in front of you. You will find a sort of slide area to follow down to the next shelf. It runs along the wall of the cavern. Hold close to the water's right side but walk through the Ubus whenever you see the path crosses under it. Despite its acidity, it's cold but harmless. The path, nevertheless, is wet shale and is slippery. Proceed cautiously. Remember to watch your head when near the walls."

For good measure, an orange path blinked in sequenced segments to form a moving arrow on the handheld display. This was the way: *O.K., I will walk in it.*

In order to use both hands and her staff to climb down, Yancey compressed and pocketed the map. She looked up and saw a U-shaped cavity replete with small stalactites forming the cathedral ceiling over the gigantic, descending stair-shelves.

Bluto, or one of his cousins, flicked across the path and around the front of the big boulder. He bobbed his duck-shaped tail at her as he passed and proceeded in the direction she must go.

"O.K.," Yancey responded to the obvious invitation, "I'm coming."

Rounding the boulder to the other side revealed the path Trenell had described. Her heart lightened at this and at the glimpse of a cheeky, flipping yellow tail above blue feet. A Bluto swam effortlessly downstream and across the swift Ubus's current in water as high as her mid-calf.

She led with her staff tapping the ground before her. Perhaps six feet down, she crossed the Ubus the first time and found the wondrous jumpsuit really repelled water as well as insulated against the cold. Crossing over had her walking close to the cavern wall. She ducked outcroppings and pendulant rocks that would have brained her if she hadn't stayed alert.

She scooted down on her seat for the final four feet and easily dropped the last two onto the next of the four gigantic shelves. The splashing Ubus dropped in close proximity and managed to insert two cold water drops down the back of her neck. They chilled her to her waist. *Go figure*, she thought, and moved over to a flatter, drier part of the massive platelet.

The movement cast Yancey's mesh light onto the surface behind the falling water. She gasped. The rock face there was not the dull slate color which formed the monochromatic world through which she had trudged and contorted herself for what already seemed to her like days, not the hour or so it had really been.

Instead, fascinating her eyes was a wonderland of color like some giant's kaleidoscope shifting with the movements of her light. She oohed and ahed and touched stone after stone and admired the play of light and shadow. The cold water ran off her suit, and only her hands—she had removed her gloves—grew cold.

She lost track of how long she played the mesh light over the emerald greens, ruby reds, sapphire blues and gleaming golds. Her deprived senses grasped the shifting colors with the desperate love a drunkard shows for his booze.

With her staff, she pried one glorious stone loose and gained two for the price of one. A ruby and an emerald the size of jawbreakers glowed in her hand. They were mesmerizing. She wanted more.

Inexplicably, while she dug more and more stones and heaped them almost drunkenly at her feet, images of herself and her father on one particular day began to play on her mind. Desperately, she began to shut off the memory as she always had. Like her digging, it played out of control.

She was a little girl.

Her grandmother's funeral—she knew with desperate clarity which day it was. Digging harder amid the bright stones did not change the gray scene in her mind's eye. As the image sharpened, the stones dropped unheeded from her hand.

Yancey, her Dad, and her grandpa had been on their way home from the funeral. She had turned twelve just two months before.

Her lecherous grandfather had told her for weeks before her twelfth birthday that she must be especially quiet during his loathsome visits, for grandmother was ill and must not be disturbed.

Yancey both loved and scorned her grandmother. Grandma tried to break through Yancey's reticence and defiance. She never was to understand the child who suffered to protect her and who hated her because she had to do so.

Grandma finally died. Yancey traveled from the cemetery with a guilty rejoicing. Her grandma's funeral was to bring liberation from slavery. Nothing more could hurt grandma. In the airbus on the way home with just Yancey, her Dad and her frightful grandfather, Yancey grasped her freedom.

When her grieving father heard her hate-filled story and saw his own father's eyes, he knew this was no lie gleaned by his pre-pubescent daughter from who knew where. Her details tumbled out in gutter talk that broke his heart; she shouldn't even know such words, let alone have experienced what the words meant.

His baby girl.

His dad!

Deucalion Silva had the driver remove his father from the vehicle after slicing right down through traffic and onto the filthy street below. With loathing, he told him, "From this day, you are no longer related to me. I will cancel all your accounts maintained by me. For Mother's sake, I will settle all outstanding debts, but you will never receive another penny. If you ever so much as try to contact my daughter again, I will kill you myself. Get out."

Yancey had thought, *Now I can be a good girl. I don't ever have to be afraid again. Now Dad will love me and won't leave me alone again.*

That day she made her Dad cry. Her mother's death years earlier and her confession—the two times he had ever cried. She hated it that she made him cry. There in the airbus, Dad had rocked her and sobbed, "Oh, Yance,' I'm so sorry, so sorry." She felt dirtier now that he knew.

Instead of gaining her liberty, Yancey entered solitary confinement. When they got home, like some mad man he stormed upstairs. He broke up her bed, tore down her clothes from their hangers and ripped everything from her dresser. He hauled them outside and burned them while she silently watched. Yancey worried he would get rid of her, too. She had broken up their family just the way grandpa had warned her she would if she told.

Dad took them to a fancy hotel and put the hated mansion up for sale. He had her shower and wash her hair, and he called LaVant, an exclusive clothier. They delivered new clothing.

He hired a private tutor and a personal attendant who took her everywhere. Down the years he bought and bought and gifted her with all that his princely fortune could supply.

He gave her all new things, but for the next critical years he could never give her a hug. He sent her to therapy, the finest, but he could never again listen to her story. The episode of the funeral homecoming sent him into therapy, too.

It was all my fault. Nothing my counselor said could change the facts. Grandfather ruined me, and my own father could not love me. I ruined my Dad.

He tried. If hired companions reported I cried, Dad sent a new gift. I hated each present because it was not him, *but I pretended the gifts were enough and the attendants were not spies Dad paid to stay with me. Money was the only reason they stayed.*

Yancey snapped back to her current reality. She had long since stopped her furious digging. She stood ankle-deep in fabulous gems. *Why such a flashback now?* She was about to find out.

In the shimmering sheet of water that cascaded down and down, she saw a familiar face forming: Fafnir glimmered and looked like the iridescent jewels on the wall. He said nothing. He merely glided in and out of her vision. Yancey pretended she wasn't sure he was there while she cautiously stepped sideways over the gemstones she had just mined.

Fafnir's expression became invitingly iridescent with the colors of emerald and ruby and sapphire at her feet. He appeared softly to love her. It was a gross miscalculation.

A small Tiffany lamp in her little-girl bedroom had always stained her grandfather's face just so. She had blocked out that detail until this moment. Looking at Fafnir brought it screaming into her consciousness.

I'm an adult now, not a helpless child!

Fast on the heels of this grotesque, stained-glass memory came a sudden flash back of the explosion of the Green Valley thief. Yancey looked at the spoiled pile of muddy jewels and looked squarely at Fafnir's undulating, multi-colored image.

She remembered her grandfather's jewel-colored face, and she remembered the last stone Fafnir had given her. All her horror and shame and outrage coalesced into the glowing colors of the malignancy she now faced.

Disgusted with herself as she really always was on the deep level she had just visited, she kicked the jewels away as if they burned her; and maybe they did. Yancey wanted to destroy all the empty, beautiful substitutes for companionship, value and love.

Fafnir is a substitute, too.

With a primal scream that hurt her throat, Yancey hurled herself into the falling water to break the counterfeits. She screamed and screamed and the cold water choked her and still she screamed. She wept great, cleansing sobs that she had never released before. There was no one here for whom to pretend, no one to protect.

Eventually, the cold water brought her back to the reality of her isolation. It was fitting. *I was in isolation long before I landed in this cave.* She let all the memories wash away and then stepped out of the flow.

If I live, and ever get back to see Dad, I'll tell him I forgive him. I'll give him a real hug. Maybe we'll heal—my kids, too.

Fafnir was gone. Isolation suddenly didn't look as uninviting as it had. *I feel new.*

Her amazing jumpsuit wicked the water away from her skin and dried and warmed her.   Wearily, she pulled the map from her pocket. She might have been at work for hours, as tired as she felt.

When the map constructed its light show, Yancey asked, "Trenell, why am I here?"

She wasn't thinking of the gizmo as "Trenell's voice." She wasn't talking just about the cave. Yancey leaned back onto the hard rock and covered her eyes with her free arm. *I am talking to a **map**, for crying out loud, in a dark cave on an alien planet and am actually hoping for an answer. Man!*

She straightened up. The holo vid responded, "You are here because The Watcher wants you."

The red dot glowed, and Yancey stood there stunned. Warmth spread through her again, but it was not generated by her coverall. This warmth penetrated down into the shame she had not known how to live without and never could wash away even if she tried.

I broke up my family. (The Shrink said it wasn't my fault, but I knew better.) The Watcher wants me anyway.

My own Dad couldn't love me. My kids sure didn't. (We shut each other out to pretend away the pain.) The Watcher wants me. Apparently he has a new life plan.

I want someone to love me. I need to see Trenell and find out who this Watcher is. I don't think it's some impersonal power the way Elbraith said.

Some remote noise suddenly alarmed her. She thought, *probably just a cute yellow Bluto.*

Her heart slammed against her ribs and beat out the truth. No more pretending. That was no Bluto. *Dad, my kids, Trenell, Elbraith—I will never talk to anyone if I do not pass the water barrier in time.*

The map blinked and urged, "This way. Hurry. You have perhaps fifteen minutes to descend unmolested, Yancey."

"Why did you say it that way?" she screamed at Trenell, but she had snapped the map closed. Yancey rushed in the direction the orange arrow had indicated.

The next two shelves were only four feet apart. Terror stabbed her and hastened her through the two easy drops. Yancey hung from her hand and hooked her staff on the ledges and landed on her feet both times.

With terror her wild companion, Yancey checked her map. It showed in closer detail an under ledge that jutted fifteen feet out and led down to what the map identified as the water barrier.

Twenty feet below her current shelf, the ground level and the barrier along with the last of the drop remained shrouded in mist. Her mesh light showed only swirling water drops hurled upwards from the waterfall that plunged into the mystery below. She pulled her hood on.

The orange arrow had directed her to the extreme right edge of the shelf on which she stood. She had to climb through a notch, find the under-ledge, and descend on a series of natural foot and handholds, like rock-climbing in reverse. She shoved the map into her pocket and raced to the shelf's edge.

Yancey was waist deep into the notch when she heard keening, grunting whistles. The sounds were remote no longer.

The first night on the tower, the sounds had turned her guts into water. Then Trenell had laid himself down like a door shut between the ground grunts and her.

Now the grunting sounds approached swiftly. To produce that much sound from that broad a span, there had to be a pack of them, and there was no door to shut. Terror tried to immobilize her again.

Yancey wriggled. The first beasts were on the upper four-foot drop. Their grunts were not soft. They squealed with dissonance in the low bass range; then the tone ascended to end with a high shriek growing in discord that pierced her brain like tines of a fork.

No Trenell challenged them here: they had no need to tread softly. The slobbering beasts made short work of the two drops that had slowed her down.

Yancey's backpack stuck on some irregularity on the side of the notch. She struggled violently to dislodge it.

Two nightmare shapes landed on all fours about twenty feet from where she thrashed. Her light showed coarse, filthy fur on an animal that for size and head shape appeared much like a compressed Komodo dragon. Their forked, slithering tongues darted out and raked through the air between three rows of serrated, dagger-sharp teeth that would make a Great White jealous.

Despite the dragon-like heads, their bodies resembled heavily muscled wild boars with bunched, overdeveloped hindquarters pushing their rumps into the air. Their stumpy, spear-head shaped tails were ridged like their backbones with triangular plates as hard and lethal as sharpened axe-heads.

Solid thumps as they landed punctuated the swelling cacophony of their hunting squeals. They were multiplying on the shelf as their pack mates made a mockery of the last drop and landed indiscriminately on those already on the shelf. The beasts bit and snapped at each other as they jostled for firm footing under their pack mates thumping onto their backs.

They tossed their heads furiously, forked tongues flicking, and charged her from all sides as if on cue. She appeared to be a prized *hors d oeuvres* about to be ripped to bloody shreds by their hungry fangs.

Yancey screamed, "WATCHER!" The name came from that newly cleaned part of her where the awful memories had washed away.

The three front beasts stumbled as a large, new arrival crashed down from above; the quartet fell in the path of those behind them. With brute strength the six behind their fallen pack mates ripped the four new dinner guests to twitching pieces and swallowed them in savage contests with each other for the largest shares. The three unfortunate leaders and the drop-in died in rage with squeals, whistles and grunts that threatened but could not deliver them from destruction.

Yancey strained and twisted herself, and the backpack jerked free. With a swing that blotted out the bloody scene too close to her, she levered herself onto the ledge below the last shelf's rim. Which way was the descent? These animals could not follow down the cliff face. She had to believe that.

In her panic, Yancey rushed the wrong way. Two grunts scrabbled with their curved front claws and thudded, one falling haunch-first as if it had been pushed over the upper shelf's rim, onto the under ledge with her. It twisted upright in a blur of movement and stood with its stumpy tail rigid and twitching in challenge to any ideas its not-so-clumsy pack mate might have. Both grunts landed between her and the way she needed to go to correct her error.

Above them on the shelf, war had broken out. Heavy bodies whammed to the ground and vibrated dust and rock fragments down to their ledge.

Ripping sounds flowed down and filled their small space with dying squeals and whistled challenges from a sudden, cannibalistic feeding frenzy erupting on the levels above them.

The two grunts on the under ledge with her showed red, panicked eyes. Their gaze, however, steadied with renewed bloodlust as they re-focused on her, their weak and easy prey so close before them. Their ceaseless, obscene tongues flicked and reached. Pushing their rumps higher into the air, the beasts crouched and stalked her.

She faced them. Her mesh light seemed to disturb the grunts in these closer quarters. The under-ledge where they stood shivered as the two boar-dragons began to rear and then thump down in stiff-legged menace. They thrashed their nightmare heads up and down and twisted them laterally. Saliva flew. Yancey hoped it was non-toxic.

Each beast wanted Yancey but also watched for an attack from its unwelcome partner in this terrifying death dance. Each thrashing step brought them nearer to her. If not for their mutual distrust, Yancey would already have been grunt kibble. *Or maybe grunt gravy.*

Her light did not sweep a large enough arc to cover both grunts at once. The clever grunts moved apart and decided to work as a team. *Terrific.*

The one to her left made a giant leap to finish her. When she rolled in the opposite direction, its partner in the relative darkness grasped her ankle with its muscular, sticky tongue to drag her into its serrated maw and finish her for itself.

What saved her life was the grunts' uneasy truce. Recovered instantly from its great leap, her captor's partner caught her other leg with its own nauseous tongue. The partner would force her first captor to share. They would rip her apart and settle for a mere appetizer instead of a tasty *entrée*.

Yancey whipped her staff and cut off a two-foot length from the forked tongue of the first beast. The severed portion fell away. A shower of black blood hemorrhaged onto her leg. The stench was like a thousand sewers overflowing at once.

Partner number two liked it. It let go of her leg long enough to gobble the abandoned organ of the first beast. It seemed fresh grunt was the prime delicacy in pack life. Plenty of time remained to resume interest in her helpless, small self.

The wounded grunt squealed its bass to treble distress, coiling its body and bashing its head on the ground from pain. Yancey guessed lost sensors in the severed member left it greatly disadvantaged in the dark. The imperious stump of a tail gouged the rock of the ledge and cave wall brutally but with little effect on the impervious stone.

The uninjured beast leapt once again in a macabre sort of dance with its reluctant partner. This time its quest was two-fold: to avoid injury from the nightmare fury of its former partner and to score a larger meal than the odd prey with the blinding, hateful light.

With one calculated and successful leap, the ravenous second beast overbalanced and flipped its tongueless partner. The terrific back claws ripped partner number one's leathery belly open. The ledge swam in black gore. The predator's black, flicking tongue swabbed the delicacy in ecstatic abandon.

It proved a nearly fatal mistake as the dying beast's nightmare jaws nearly locked onto its killer's throat. The successful, larger predator avoided disaster by parrying and pinning its gutted challenger.

Avoiding the sticky, thrashing pair, Yancey saw all this as she scrambled back toward the edge. She tried to pass to the other side where the access down toward the water lay.

The maddened beasts might kill her in their death throes, but she would not wait for another grunt to re-categorize and kill her for dessert. Before she could reach her goal, however, two new problems presented themselves.

The death squeals and the stench of blood from the under ledge drew two young grunts from the shelf above. The carnage up there had calmed to feeding challenges. Apparently these two were not large enough to gain an initial share in the rampant cannibalism topside. They dropped catlike onto Yancey's ledge to investigate the menu chances there.

Wisely, they avoided the larger diner and its victim twitching to their left. Their long, sinuous tongues flicked toward Yancey. *Great!*

To remain facing her two new enemies and to keep the light shining on them as much as possible, she retreated backward toward the edge, a most dangerous game. They began closing in on her from two sides.

Yancey doubted she would survive the two new predators. They were younger and quicker even than the incredible speed the older ones had shown. The access down was too far away.

Flickering movements passed between the three-foot youngsters' already massive legs. Her momentary panic that yet another grunt had joined its comrades changed to bewilderment; from unseen holes in the cliff face swarmed hundreds of Blutos.

The hungry brutes began trying to scoop up great mouthfuls of the pale yellow rodents who eluded them with lightning speed in crazy paths that had the squealing animals doubling in on themselves trying to catch *something*.

Sticky black tongues fielded the small rodents. Blutos disappeared into the grunts' fetid maws, but not as many as she expected.

The two new grunts seemed to prefer the taste of blue stripes over the flavor of an unknown quantity whose light hurt their eyes; or perhaps they liked the familiarity of this hunt better than any game they might play with her. *My light disturbs them more than the older ones.*

Additionally, they did not have to share rodents with a partner. Whatever the reason, the youthful grunt to Yancey's right stopped pursuing Yancey and began bobbing and weaving to scoop up what it could from this new buffet. *Teenagers can be so fickle.*

Yancey moved toward her goal. She turned away from her brave small army none too soon.

A high-pitched squeal rasped from the mouth of Yancey's left-side attacker. One moment he was catching Blutos like his partner. The next, he was heading straight toward her in mid air and with fantastic speed.

The airborne grunt, propelled by his powerful hind quarters, crashed down toward her. Her turning mesh light caught him squarely in his fierce, yellow-red eyes. Black loose skin with repulsive warts beneath each eye stretched as he leapt. Jerking his juvenile eyes away from her direct light canted his trajectory and saved her life again.

Yancey hurled herself to the opposite side away from his projected landing. The foul grunt recovered and leapt so swiftly, she hadn't even begun to scramble upright.

The powerful beast thudded onto her. Front claws curved under her collar bone and over the top and down into her shoulder in back, like pinchers spearing a side of beef.

Yancey jerked her hooded head away from its fangs. The hood deflected them, but the foul, sticky tongue forked around her air passage and its two prongs met behind her neck.

Her jumpsuit acted like a super Kevlar vest against the front claws and the scraping fangs, but it was not rigid, and Yancey felt her collar bones and shoulder blades threatening to collapse from the weight. The grunt's back legs dug and clawed. The jumpsuit split.

Yancey screamed in agony as the curving blades pierced her legs and thighs. Her muscles ripped away from her bones. Sinews and cartilage popped and broke.

Her puny, clawing hands could not prevent the tightening of the grunt's horrible tongue around her throat. *My staff—where is it? Helpless without it.*

Warm blood gushed from her legs. *I hope it's a major artery. I don't want to stay conscious while it eats me alive.*

Ready to black out from asphyxiation, Yancey suddenly visualized the catch-strap from the jumpsuit to her staff. The creature's grasping claws trying to crush her upper body failed because of the rock surface where it pinned her shoulders. She fought a desperate, one-handed battle to prevent the sticky tongue from crushing her windpipe. With her free hand she groped for her silvery last hope.

She rammed the staff's blade-end up, under and into the monster's chin. He screamed in rage and jerked back, breaking the catch-strap. It dislocated her bloody right shoulder and broke her wrist on the hand guiding the staff but freed her upper body, *for what that's worth!*

The great news was that his lethal tongue jerked back with him. Glorious, sweet air entered her lungs. *I may bleed to death, but I won't suffocate.*

He thudded sideways and off her to the ground, scraping his dragon chin spurting black blood. The silvery staff stuck. He swiped at it with his front paws but couldn't reach.

Scrambling Blutos suddenly swarmed over the outraged beast's eyes and snout. The heroic small rodents sank sharp teeth into these vulnerable organs. One red eye winked out and gushed purple. Grainy goo from its emptying eye socket spurted onto a hundred swarming yellow bodies.

The powerful grunt, maddened from the staff blade and now from the converging yellow threats to its remaining eye reared onto its powerful back legs. The pain-maddened young grunt commenced a series of thundering bucks for all the world like a wild bronco. Blutos flew off in all directions.

In its wild gyrations, the bucking grunt thrashed into the older, still feeding grunt. Yancey held her breath, hoping for a hard response. The adult slung its head and raised its dagger-encased stump of a tail in warning. Junior hopped away unscathed. The adult turned back to the carcass, tore off another slab of gore and ignored the clumsy juvenile delinquent.

The second young grunt eyed the flying rodents its injured pack-mate was flinging. Those stunned or broken by hard landings fell easy prey to its speed. Some landed in blue-striped, yellow balls of fur and scurried *en masse* back into their holes. Its bucking hunting pal was on the outer part of the ledge and so remained ignored.

The under ledge was thin and brittle on this edge where the young grunt's attack had landed her. As the heavy animal continued to buck, Yancey heard a deep, thundering *CRACK!* But no cave-in followed.

The grunt's violent, stiff-legged bucking continued shaking their fragile perch. The tenacious, wounded grunt turned its attention back toward Yancey. *It gets an* **A** *for effort. Terrific.*

Its fickle juvenile partner scrabbled its way back up and off the crackling under-ledge to the shelf where the war had ceased. Its combatants, sated on the spoils, had called a truce.

Except for a few late diners now gorging themselves on the leavings of their stronger and faster pack mates, the grunts had withdrawn with no remembrance of their original prey. The Bluto-sated second juvenile loped off after its vanished mates.

The wounded young one, though, studied Yancey with its one good eye as if questioning why she was still among the living. Brutish fury erupted in battle squeals.

The enticing smell of her blood mingled with grunt-blood was not to be ignored, either. Here lay a wounded victim about to yield him his hard-fought dinner. Bloodlust eclipsed pain from the staff.

It leaped for her again. The wily grunt skewed its good eye away as it catapulted to the kill.

She could not move her shredded and hemorrhaging legs. *I must be three quarts low already.* Weakness pinned her where the grunt would land. Yancey braced herself. The bitter knowledge that she had failed Trenell and Elbraith as well as herself pounded through her brain with her dying heartbeats.

The delicate edge beneath them gave way like some graceful stone waterfall cascading from the grunt's terrific leap to become airborne. Yancey fell with it.

The enraged animal shot over the place where she had lain. The two older grunts, one a quarter consumed and the other still eating, fell with them.

Squeals from the two living grunts now changed to a terror pitch such as she had never heard. Wet mist obscured their prospective landing place.

My mutilated body, escaped from being ripped apart, will burst open on jagged rocks instead. So what?

She hit the surface of the water with a *Thwack*! No rocks greeted her. She sank down and down. *I think I broke my neck. Nope, my head turns.*

The grunts left massive trails of bubbles as they continued their ponderous plunge along with her.

It doesn't matter. Mutilated beyond repair, lungs bursting for oxygen, Yancey surrendered. She gulped water, expecting to get this over with.

Her battered, bruised lungs and internal organs seemed suddenly to ignite, the water seared them so badly. *Volcanic action somewhere.* Liquid fire worked its way into her bone marrow, muscles and sinews. A million cuts, abrasions and bruises ignited as the water boiled its way into her cells and nervous system. Screaming with pain became a norm.

Blood from her wounds released a black cloud of pollution as she swooshed downward.

What is this…acid? Trenell said the Ubus was acidic, but this? Sulphuric, at least.

The waters around their plummeting bodies boiled like peroxide on a fresh cut—a furious, underwater geyser. What floated up from her foes' descending bodies, however, was more than foaming bubbles.

The grunts' flesh disintegrated. Pieces floated upward.

The red-gold, rapacious eye of her juvenile, would-be killer turned away even in its death throes from her light. Yancey averted her own eyes and closed out her last sight of the horrors' carcasses disappearing as if eaten by molecular-sized piranha. The beasts' dying squeals disarranged the water.

Her silvery staff, no longer encumbered with a half-ton of thrashing grunt, floated silently up to the surface. Still descending, Yancey watched its upward progress dispassionately and breathed in burning water as comfortable as iodine on an open wound.

She flashed her light down her body. Yancey looked for skin cells sloughing off or, maybe, her own body parts disengaging and floating upward, gruesomely independent of her torso.

No parts floated up. No patches of skin decamped for parts north. Despite swallowing what felt like half the pond, she remained conscious.

Instead of cooking her, the fiery waters that dissolved the grunts began to regenerate Yancey. Her thighs, legs, wrist and shoulders felt intimate with fumaroles and geothermic activities everywhere; nevertheless, she lived.

Finally beginning to rise, Yancey twisted her eyes downward. Peering through the foaming boil she witnessed her body regrowing bones, muscles, skin. Reaching the surface, she gulped a great, shuddering breath, this time, of air.

A sense of forgotten well-being invaded her consciousness. The fiery pain in her inner organs, thighs, shoulders and wrist began backing down to a warm, soothing glow.

I'm grateful to be alive, even here, alone— if I am alone. I remember calling the Watcher!

The feeding frenzy, the Blutos, the rescue from the nightmare animals, re-growth—to believe all is coincidence seems irrational. I did not make it unmolested, but I am now healed.

She gulped. *I forgive Dad, my grandpa and grandma, too. That doesn't take them off the hook. That takes me off the hook.* Sobs shook her: bitterness dissolved like the grunts in the barrier water.

By paddling and shining her mesh light around, she located and retrieved her staff. It felt cool to her touch, and she wanted to embrace it like a lost lover suddenly restored.

Wearily, and awkwardly because of the staff in her hand and a still uncooperative right shoulder, she began paddling opposite the sound of the waterfall. This produced one more huge, burning agony and a loud POP! Her shoulder socket burned as her bone followed its own path back into place. When she found the pool's edge, she gingerly eased herself out, exhausted.

The basin of healing waters did not work on cloth. The ragged, shredded tatters of pants now so short they ended no more than six inches below her pockets showed her what her legs looked like before the pool. Miraculously, boots still covered her feet. She groaned. At the pool's edge she finished crying.

The stones are cold. Yancey shucked out of the remains of her suit, laid the staff on it, and slipped back into the water.

Once again the boiling was like peroxide around her skin, but this time everything tingled pleasantly —scalp, eyes, sinuses, and even her tummy when she opened her mouth and drank deeply. The warm bubble action massaged her muscles; only tiredness remained.

Yancey's mesh light caught an impression of something dark in the clear water. It tumbled around caught where the fall of the Ubus River churned into contact with the pool. After an unpleasant moment, she realized it could not be a grunt, not even a dead one.

She swam toward it and was thrilled to find her backpack. Like the silver staff, it was buoyant. She dragged it thankfully to shore.

Back in the remains of her jumpsuit and wrapped in the warm thermal blanket from her pack, Yancey ate the bread and drank the water Trenell had provided. After refilling the water bottle from the pool, she stretched out with her head on the backpack and slept before she could so much as roll over onto her side.

Chapter 24—Elbraith Avoids Some Lessons

Elbraith followed Trenell silently and grudgingly between boulders that sometimes blotted out the sky. At no time did the path down appear obvious to Elbraith, yet Trenell led without hesitation. In this, Elbraith acknowledged Trenell's expertise but flatly grumbled to himself that he would choose a different route if Trenell would show him the map.

Too proud to ask for a look or for inclusion in travel decisions, Elbraith contented himself with economy of movement and continued lithely to descend behind the equally tireless Guide. The two made fast progress that Yancey could not have matched. Elbraith thought *Score one for Trenell* and then quickly dismissed this idea that ran contrary to his sense of grievance.

The silvery jumpsuits controlled their inside climate to a degree, but both beings perspired as they wound steadily downward through switchbacks along an obscure path that often appeared to end in thin air, only to double around through openings invisible until the last possible turn.

Brushy growth bristling with thorns scratched the Conductor's sleeves and gloved hands and tried in vain to draw blood through the impervious, silvery coverings. Both suns shone in their strength and by midmorning made the rock surfaces too hot to touch bare-handed.

We have left the path along which Tax brought Yancey and me to the camp. Elbraith ignored the niggling memory that he had enjoyed that trip engineered by Trenell and settled instead upon a determined resentment of the one currently underway.

Elbraith heard Trenell's soft singing when the path leveled out and sound could float back instead of dissipating into the heavens. His cheer grated on Elbraith's surliness.

After two hours of this pointed non-relational progress, Trenell called a halt. They doffed their packs and stretched, and Trenell gathered moss and lichens and lighted a hand-sized fire to brew some coffee.

During this process, Elbraith glowered silently at him and offered no help. Trenell looked at him once with a bland face and continued his annoying humming. When the coffee smelled ready, Trenell said, "Help yourself, Elbraith."

Elbraith gritted his teeth and said, "No thanks."

Trenell sipped his brew, looked at his still companion, and said mildly, "Let's hear it, Elbraith."

The Conductor recognized permission to speak. He erupted.

"How can you sit and drink coffee when Yancey needs us? I am her Conductor. I can't help her when you send her off alone into who knows what."

"And I know you sent her. She was scared of that cave. No way would she have chosen to go that route! Let alone without me!"

Elbraith continued to spew. "Her history indicates her greatest terror is being alone—or didn't you study her life before you sent her off maybe to die just that way, without either of the two whose job it is to protect her?"

"What's with you, Trenell? Why do we two who know the rules on Planet X find ourselves in this oven maze with each other for company while Yancey proceeds alone and no doubt into danger?"

Receiving no answer but a steady look full of compassion, Elbraith gritted out in frustration, "It's no wonder the Association barred you from guiding if you care no more than this for those who trust you."

Elbraith waited three beats for Trenell to answer him. The Conductor's already red face flushed more deeply under the Guide's steady regard, for Elbraith realized he had just passed from accusation to condemnation of and possible slander to a Guide, disbarred or not.

A charge of slander put the Guide within his legal rights to call a Conduct Board on Elbraith. Depending on the Board's verdict, Elbraith could be removed from Yancey's case and dismissed from Conductor status.

Trenell finally replied, but his eyes spoke first and acted on Elbraith like some super solvent: they peeled layers of indignation off the frustrated, reluctant Conductor. With just that one, evanescent glimpse, Trenell left the Conductor feeling blistered by his own accusations. Trenell's eyes broadcast no malice toward the surly Conductor. No responding hate clouded the expression Elbraith saw there.

The look provided a blitzing flash into Trenell's own devotion for Yancey. It revealed a shocking depth Elbraith could not fathom. Later, Elbraith would question whether he had seen it at all.

The Guide's tone when he spoke was pointed and strong. "I believe I have demonstrated knowledge of Yancey superior even to yours. I assure you that I am dedicated to Yancey's progress toward wholeness and a successful leap."

Elbraith's mouth thinned to a tight line, and his neck and jaw muscles worked as he suppressed further comments. Several leapt to mind.

Receiving no reply, Trenell continued, "The passion you show for the well-being of your charge commends you as the proper Conductor for her. Go for a short walk, Conductor. Decide to cool off. We will speak of this again later."

Elbraith suddenly, reluctantly, regained some respect for this man. He tasted his own blood inside his cheek. He turned with military precision and stalked with unmilitary mien off around a boulder. It hid the tiny campfire and this Being who was undeniably his superior officer in the current situation.

An argument with himself ensued. *I know my attitude is in error. The Conductor's manual clearly subordinates me to the wishes of my charge. Trenell is Yancey's wish.*

Not so clear, however is why *he thinks he knows my charge better than I do.* Elbraith elected to count that unnerving glimpse into Trenell's devotion to Yancey as a simple impossibility.

Equally nebulous is how to explain Yancey's choice. Trenell must've played on his idea that someone may be following us to do her harm. The subterranean route hides her from prying eyes and allows us to make more rapid progress.

Does someone intend her harm? We have only Trenell's word to justify these obscure measures. Perhaps he deceives himself and us as well.

Elbraith's pride hardened into obstinacy. *No matter what he thinks, leaving Yancey alone could never be the correct solution to her journey toward wholeness. I was chosen to remain at her side. Yet here I am, bound to obey a rogue Guide with visions of grandeur: "dedicated solely to Yancey's progress toward wholeness." Right!*

Returning to the cave now to ensure her safety would justify charges of treason before the Conductors' Board. They would remove her permanently from my charge; I could never help her again. I am trapped.

He reboarded his former train of thought. Aloud he seethed, "I studied her files, memorized every event and person, joined myself with her feelings and interpretations as far as I am able. When did he ever demonstrate 'superior knowledge'? I suppose he means the Green Valley crossing."

Elbraith turned his face away from the view over the cliff and faced the boulder by which he stood. Heat waves shimmered over its surface. He fancied he could almost see his own reflection through some trick of the two suns' exact positions.

Into his pseudo image he finally breathed the jealous questions: "How could anyone love her more? How could any Being know better than I what might benefit her in her journey to wholeness? Trenell believes his knowledge superior to mine. That does not make it so."

Then with a sigh he whispered to his pseudo-face, "Yancey has chosen against my will. I am bound by Conduct code to obey. I hope, little Yancey, that you fare well in this."

Unbidden, Elbraith again recalled that brief look into Trenell's eyes. Could the Guide really hold such devotion to Yancey? Or did Trenell hide some personal agenda? *Trenell looked sincere to the core, but don't con-men always appear so? People following us! I have seen no one.* Here he deliberately squashed the idea that their obscure route might have accomplished this success.

I hate Trenell for separating me from Yancey.

This shocked him. Conductors schooled themselves to love.

He nearly recognized then that his love for Yancey was somehow twisted and self-absorbed. This truth, however, promised too much pain, so he stoked his resentment instead.

Yancey needs me more than she needs Trenell. The Guide has possibly sent her to her death. ***All of my four decades of work might end with this shattered dream.***

Elbraith resumed studying his ghostly reflection in the shimmering heat waves. He thought of Trenell with deliberate calm and refused yet another breakthrough.

"What motivates me is care for my charge," he said gently and firmly.

Guides are experts on terrain, weather, and inhabitants both animal and humanoid indigenous to certain areas. Theirs is a privileged niche like no other on the planet. Guides take jobs for pay and prestige, and sometimes just because they are odd ducks who do not fit in civilized society. No one ever called on them for devotion.

Conductors, on the other hand, volunteer and undergo rigorous weeding out. Character is key. Self-sacrifice is another. The desire for deeper personal development is another. After years of training and military discipline, we are matched with a human. Then we devote many more years of study to the one life which we are to join.

Elbraith quoted his handbook: "On Planet *X*, one begins conscious life in extreme old age. Learning to understand life, to master one's lower nature and then relational realities like love and respect, and to acquire erudite knowledge with which to help others grow both corporately and individually determines one's own rate of growth. One works one's way from extreme old age back to youth."

He reflected as he always had, "Failure to learn life lessons or to experience personal growth arrests one at the age reached until the lesson is learned. Most beings work conscientiously back to some point in middle age. Progress is optional. Some beings live hundreds of years and simply die in whatever state they have reached. Performance determines outcome."

Reviewing the familiar steadied him. Elbraith continued.

On Earth one might, for example, be wrinkled yet no wiser for having lived. Here, however, transformation does not take place unless the lesson was laid to heart and resonates with the desired behavioral change. True inner change is the only means to trigger outer transformation--youth coupled with wisdom, in fact.

He rattled on from his memorized credo: "As on Earth, with which Planet *X* is dimensionally linked, one might follow a practically infinite number of vocations: truck drivers, seamstresses, surgeons—all benefited others while supporting themselves.   In hundreds of years of excellent health and mental challenge here, many beings choose to work in multiple careers during their lifetimes. One profession gives no merit above another; that is, except for two: Conductor and Guide."

Becoming a Conductor puts many beings on a seeming fast track to transformation. He recited again: "Life as a Conductor demands heart change nearly every day. Visible progression back toward youth offers an infallible measure of one's success in personal growth."

With proper training, a successful Conductor could apply to become a Guide. No one questioned a Guide's appearance or maturity, ever.

Elbraith tried to look again at the semblance of himself in the shimmering, reflective surface, but the suns seemed to have passed to another angle. He would have been astonished if he had seen three of the shiny facets reflect disturbingly like two slits for eyes and a malevolent, smiling mouth. All he saw was the boulder and his duty.

Elbraith squared his shoulders to return to Trenell. Elbraith skipped over the guilty truth that his dream for Yancey's success had bled over into his dream for his own success. Yancey's choice of another above him coupled with Trenell's assertion of confidence had started a crack in Elbraith's heart: for the first time in four decades, Elbraith felt his own good might be divided from the good of his charge. He felt unsettled.

The Conductor did not know he had been in a battle for control of his mind, let alone that he had just lost the opening skirmishes. Instead, he left nursing one thought to explain his current outrage and discomfort.

This is all Trenell's fault.

Chapter 25 – Cave Test, Part II

Yancey did not know how long she slept, but she knew what woke her. She jerked awake from a dream in which Trenell and Elbraith sat stranded on a high rock tower surrounded by rising water.

Omigosh! Trenell and Elbraith!

Yancey drank from the barrier water and washed her face. She fashioned a sari from the blanket to protect her legs. With a torn section of the jumpsuit she rigged another catch-cord to her staff.

Moving away from the swirling mist of the pool, she found the Ubus River disappeared from view as it exited the bowl; she now stood on solid rock above it. The ground felt warm beneath her feet despite the battered silvery boots which had stayed on through battle and triage.

She keyed her map with the mesh light and waited. Relief flooded her when it sprang to life.

"Good morrow, Yancey," Trenell's voice greeted. "It is mid-afternoon of your second day. You are here." The red dot blinked. The orange line sections began to sequence.

When she began walking, the going was fairly smooth. For company, Yancey kept the map on in one hand. She tapped along with her staff in the other.

The blackness of the cavern surrounded but could not swallow her small light. The bleakness of her situation, however, despite the open map, began to eat away her morale.

She became aware of chambers leading off on the sides. Above her, the ceiling, often invisible because of its great height, in some places began to crowd so close to her path that she had to walk bent over like some scuttling crab to navigate the stretches.

The cave's sounds since she left the noisy basin and falls behind were now muted water sounds falling in drips that made soft thuds if close by. This began to wear on her like, *Oh, 10,000 leaky faucets.*

Keeping a steady eye on her footing with brief checks on the orange line and red dot, Yancey said, "Talk to me."

No doubt programmed to cue from the last conversational exchange, "Why am I here?" and from his startling answer about the Watcher and herself, Trenell's voice began by quoting, "Genesis One: '*Barasheet bara Elohim, et ha Salayim, et ha Eretz,*' Hebrew for 'In the beginning God created the heaven and the earth.'"

She had asked why she was here. He had answered. Now, he would demonstrate. Yancey felt very surprised to hear Trenell quote from Earth's Holy Bible. *I'd think Planet X would have some inexplicable holy book of its own. It's O.K., though... the Bible's inexplicable enough to fit both puzzling planets.*

On Earth, and now here, religion seemed to pursue her. *I've always been a good runner.* Just hearing the words had her on red alert to start a sprint; however, *it might prove a really short race if I bong my head on a place where the ceiling closes in.* She kept walking.

Trenell's voice continued, "The Hebrew word *Bara* means to create out of nothing. Thus, it is a verb that can be applied only to God. Other verbs, like *yasar* or *asah,* which mean "to create from something," can be used for God or for men in whom He put the creative spark like His Own.

"From the first verse, God is the only God, the Creator of all matter and all life. He introduces Himself as having no beginning and no end."

"He employs the Hebrew word *Elohim*, a word that means *God* but, interestingly, can be either singular or plural in form. It appears again in Genesis 1: 26—27 where *Elohim* creates humans."

"English translations read, 'Let Us make man in Our image, after Our likeness...'' Scripture uses plural pronouns to refer to God in both the Hebrew and in the English translation."

Yancey could not help herself. The grammar lesson and more importantly the meaning hooked her. For just a few minutes, she would desist from her itch to run; here in the dark, she would really listen. *It's the word study that's intriguing.*

"Did you ever ask yourself why God created *two* visible personas—male and female— to represent Him? The two come from one. It becomes an interesting question when viewed in the light of the word *Elohim*'s possible plurality."

"Some Scriptures that shed light on this "One that is plural" are Genesis 1:2 and John 1: 1—3 and 14 and 18."

"Genesis 1:2b says, 'And the Spirit of God moved upon the face of the waters.' Elohim reveals His entity called the 'Spirit of God.'"

"John 1: 1 says, 'In the beginning was the Word, and the Word was with God, and the Word was God.' The 'Word' used in the Greek is *Logos*, which means 'something **said**.'"

"John 1: 2 and 3 reveal 'The same was in the beginning with God,' and 'All things were made by Him; and without Him was not anything made that was made.'"

"You probably know God *spoke* everything into existence."

"John 1: 14 and 18 identify the second and third entities of *Elohim*: Father and Son. 'And the Word, the *Logos,* was made flesh ... the only begotten Son, which is in the bosom of the Father.'"

"Three entities, one God, still a mystery until the Father sends the Son to reveal Himself through the Holy Spirit (an idea found in John 17 and Luke 1:35 as well as in numerous other passages)," Trenell summarized.

Yancey found a rock and sat down hard. She asked her Trenell-map to repeat all that slowly.

When he finished the second time, she questioned, "Man, who could see that from just those few verses?"

Then she asked, "'The Word made flesh' and the 'only begotten Son of the Father' is Jesus, isn't it?"

Trenell replied, "Yes."

Yancey mulled it over, "That's tough to believe."

Trenell surprised her with a seemingly unrelated topic, "Describe the essences of any person you know."

Yancey snorted inelegantly, "Huh?"

Trenell clarified, "What are the three parts of any person?"

"Oh, uh, you mean body, soul, and spirit? That's what Mom taught me."

"Yes," Trenell replied. "What distinguishes them? You studied psychology."

Yancey was suddenly enjoying herself. She did not feel alone in the least. The stimulating mental exercise and the physical rest from walking both felt good.

"Hmnnn, the physical body is what we see and is how we interact with the world and others around us."

"The soul basically is our will, mind, and emotions—personality, I'd call it."

"The spirit is a tough one to define. It's our life force, I guess. I know when it departs from the body, it snuffs out both soul and the body, as far as we can see, and we die. It's our one supernatural part, if you like to put it that way, the one scholars debate and Christian fundamentalists say must be 'born again.'"

"I've seen people die. *Something* sure leaves."

Trenell now surprised her again. Instead of commending her definitions as she expected, he said, "It is so easy for you to believe you have three parts that are all equally you. Why is it so hard to believe the One God is really triune in nature?"

A very long silence ensued. At the end of it, Yancey said, "O.K."

Rising hastily, she resumed walking. She pocketed the map hurriedly and picked up her pace—it was as close as she could get to running without breaking her neck. The path wound downward. If she'd been willing to risk another Bible lesson, Yancey would like to have known how deep she was, and how close to the exit.

The cave's sounds reasserted themselves.

The numbers of stalactites and stalagmites increased to legions as she rounded curve after curve in the path. Often, they joined each other to form massive pillars that made her feel like some Lilliputian mistakenly thrust into the giants' world of Brobdingnag.

Yancey's sense of isolation and complete irrelevance grew as steadily as the numbers and scope of the rock formations around her. Consciously, she refused to allow her recent lesson to have a part in her thinking, but her rebellious mind, or something, kept going back.

What finally succeeded in blockingTrenell's words was the unvarying, total blackness outside the radius of her puny light. A sense of claustrophobia took root. She breathed in blackness. Panic blossomed.

Trenell must've been crazy to believe I could reach him and Elbraith. Find them on some unspecified rock sticking up in the vast reach of an irresistible tide? I'll never make it out of this cave, let alone find the rendezvous point.

Yancey forgot she was running away from Trenell's religion lesson. She commenced doubting she was moving toward any goal.

Her black claustrophobia tuned up with growing panic to sing along her nerve endings her deepest fear: *I am alone. Abandoned. Isolated. Forgotten. Defeated.* She tried to squelch it. She even tried humming out loud, but her puny noise in the cacophony of *drip, drip, drips* mocked her attempts to distract and cheer herself.

Her troubled path curved to reveal a chamber filled with stone draperies. What she could see in the radius of her trusty small light was curtains of wavy stone with bands of mineral deposits. Out of the solemn gloom rose these giants' sculpted walls as far as her light could show her. Mineral deposits gleamed in magical bands of colors: burgundy and chocolate and black and tans with greens thrown in for good measure.

They curved away to form passages roughly diagonal from where she stood bewildered with the glorious beauty breaking the monotony. Then anxiety rose: not one straight path presented itself to view.

I'm going to have to risk another Bible lesson. My life depends on it. Resolutely, Yancey reached for her map.

Chapter 26—Elbraith Gets His Way

Elbraith trudged heavily after Trenell until just before second sunset when the Guide turned aside to make camp in a shallow hollow in the rock face.

With no words exchanged, the two beings functioned efficiently to start a small fire, clear the ground of debris, spread their sleeping bags, and start their simple dinner from their pack staples. Elbraith did not know where Trenell found the water, but there it was, sizzling in a collapsible pot with coffee grounds producing smells dark and aromatic.

As they sat sipping coffee and eating, Trenell broke the unnatural silence between them with, "The coffee is perhaps the only thing you have received readily from me."

Nonplussed at Trenell's blunt but low-keyed challenge, Elbraith puzzled over how to respond. Trenell's patient eyes focusing on him made the Conductor feel ashamed of his own surly conduct during their first day's trek.

Elbraith tried a little humor to break the moment. "No, actually, I felt very grateful for the purple berries and water-bearing vine you shared at the mid-afternoon break."

Trenell's eyes creasing with humor were visible even in the flickering light. They ate in a slightly more companionable silence after that.

After a fast after-dinner cleanup, they banked the fire. Trenell arranged his silver blanket over himself, turned onto his side and fell asleep. Elbraith stretched out opposite the fire from the Guide and blinked owlishly at stars reflected in black water that had crept up unseen to surround their mountain peak. The glorious show coaxed him into the sleep of exhaustion.

Trenell woke him to the sight of the same stars, shifted over the course of only about six hours as nearly as Elbraith could reckon. The Conductor was not a happy camper.

Coffee was on again, and hot cereal. As the two finished, Elbraith could not fail to notice Trenell's urgency, the first he'd shown.

The Guide leaned toward Elbraith and unfolded a flat, silvery map with glowing points on it. Carefully but with no wasted motion, Trenell began to trace lines of travel with his finger as he spoke.

"We camped tonight just above tide-line. We must make the third peak, here, before second tide tomorrow night. It is necessary both to begin and to end in dense starlight. The distance is farther but not all mountainous as it was today."

"We will chase the receding tide down the mountain and climb the second peak ahead of its return. The tide will reach fullness some four hours after second sunset."

"Three paths we'll call *A*, *B*, and *C* all lead to Smoke Mountain. I will take *Path A*, which is the longest distance and so requires the fastest time. It is the safest of the three but demands almost unreasonable endurance which pushes travelers past the edge of what they believe they can bear. You are invited to accompany me but are free to choose your own way if that does not suit you."

"*Path B* covers the medium distance of the three but involves the haunt of predators called Saumjin. They are hippo-like creatures for temperament, size and speed but are omnivores who graze and hunt in pairs. Although freshwater otters are their favorite fare, they would find meat as big and slow as a human to be a favorable substitute."

"You may cross the Reuben River, which is very deep and wide here"—Trenell tapped his finger on a glowing point—"at the only safe place to swim across, without ever encountering them. If, however, they happen to be on this cycle of the river, rest assured you will face grave danger. In the water they are fast and deadly. The only sure way to kill them is to penetrate their eye. It is a difficult target on beasts so huge and fast."

"If the herd or even one pair is present, you will drown trying to cross elsewhere, or you may drown later from your delay while they pass because you will fail to beat the tide."

"*Path C* lies along by far the shortest route but is the most terrifying and can take the longest to traverse. Although the terrain can be challenging in places, your main obstacles there arise from yourself."

Elbraith's head snapped up at this. "What?"

Trenell's eyes looked into his with great compassion. This irked Elbraith.

"Why would I put obstacles in my own way?" Elbraith asked with an unbelieving smirk.

Trenell moved his bottom lip so his mouth formed the beginning of a wry smile. A brief, unwelcome review of his time beside the boulder and of his ungracious trek behind Trenell all day stalked through Elbraith's mind. Inwardly, he squirmed.

Trenell only stated, "Choose. Time is fleeting."

Emphasizing his point, Trenell packed up his share of their camp. Elbraith did likewise.

When they finished, Elbraith and Trenell headed down the mountain. The trail was freshly wet. Their chosen paths would not diverge until they reached the valley floor. Elbraith noticed the tide receded quickly. *Woe betides anyone caught when it comes in*, he thought, then grimaced at his poor pun. *Yancey's habits are rubbing off on me. Yancey! Is she safe?*

At the bottom Elbraith said, "*B* is for me."

Trenell said, "The map is yours. I know the routes. Fare you well." He resettled his pack and jogged off at a fast clip.

Elbraith felt a surge of satisfaction and jogged off at a fast pace himself. He might need extra time when he reached the river. It felt sweet to travel on his own without the smug, irksome Guide.

Path B rolled up and down sandy terrain packed smooth by the tide. It pulled at his muscles but cushioned his footfalls. He thought as he ran, *I could maintain this pace indefinitely.*

Path C at first seemed the most alluring. Challenging terrain would have offered more interest than this boring topography. This time with no reality check, he wondered again *how could anyone be stupid enough to provide his own worst obstacles?*

For awhile as he jogged at his ground-eating pace, he imagined conquering Path C, *and putting that pompous Trenell in his place.* He visualized climbing rocky formations where he would hang by his fingertips, or crossing hanging bridges suspended thousands of feet in the air, or shooting through whitewater, or leaping over chasms. *Such physical rigors might prove to be challenging obstacles.* Abruptly, Elbraith remembered his somewhat unpleasant self-encounter at the boulder and turned off his fantasizing.

Shrugging the memory off, Elbraith hit a long, straight patch that strung out for a half mile. It felt great to let go and run.

The Reuben looked on the map as though it lay roughly two-thirds of the way along the path. I'll have only a third of the journey to finish after I cross, but most of it's uphill. No problem. Elbraith pulled in his pace.

At mid-day Elbraith arrived at the last knoll before he could see the river. Instinctively, he dropped down behind the shielding ridge to study the water where he must cross. He groaned, seeing the three bulky beasts grazing near the river's edge. *The fourth must be submerged and feeding nearby.*

The big question is whether these four represent the beginning or ending of the herd. From his pack he removed powerful, long-distance viewers and put them on like sunglasses over his eyes. Systematically, in quadrants from far to near, Elbraith examined the river.

Mystery-beast Number Four still did not appear. Over twenty minutes passed while Elbraith searched. The three Saumjin topside grazed their bulging way to thirty yards from their original positions. Careful scanning revealed most of the herd far upstream, so these four were stragglers out for a picnic on this sunny day.

Great was all he thought. He settled in to wait.

Elbraith expected that at this rate these four would pass in plenty of time for him to cross the river and run the last third of his trip. From his point of view, however, disaster suddenly struck.

Number Four announced its imminent surfacing with a six-foot-tall plume of water which jetted from the river surface about fifty feet behind its grazing companions. They ignored their newly surfaced pal until it emitted a high, two-blast, shrill whistle followed by a pause and then a repeat. This sound coming like a shrill fife's huffing from such a behemoth sounded downright undignified, like a pressure-cooker gone *AWOL*. The results, however, were immediate and far from comical.

To his great dismay, Grazers One, Two, and Three lumbered to the river, entered with gigantic splashes, and swam back beneath the surface to Number Four with such amazing speed, Elbraith would not have believed they could have reached their whistling companion if he had not seen their three gigantic heads bob up. What followed was unnerving.

Elbraith watched Number Four the Whistler jerk up its massive head and fling into the air a large creature which it plucked effortlessly from beneath the roiling water. One of the other beasts, presumably Number Four's partner, bounced the helpless prey off its wicked snout over to another of the four.

Elbraith watched in horror as the Saumjin played with their still living food. The pitiable dinner of this gruesome team trumpeted in hoarse shrieks that seemed to excite its torturers. Bright blood began to stain the Saumjins' heads and snouts and spread unsightly dark fingers on the river's surface. The Saumjins' high-pitched squeals sounded increasingly indecent as the game continued.

The macabre volleyball was horrible, but Elbraith averted his eyes to the rest of the herd when they began tug-of-war. He glimpsed what was still worse, from his perspective. The original foursome was attracting attention, or perhaps it was the blood floating down to where the tail-ends of the herd were feeding.

The animals, so clumsy on the riverbanks, moved like streaks in the water. Another dozen joined their sporting companions and three plucked likewise unfortunate "balls" of their own. Elbraith surmised it was a family of the unfortunate prey who proved too slow to reverse direction and escape.

The returning herd of Saumjin proved as disgustingly playful as the original four stragglers. The games and feeding frenzy would not stop in time for him to cross and still reach the safety of high ground before high tide overtook him. *I have lost over an hour and a half.*

Elbraith took a last look at the map which he had begun minutes before to study in earnest. Two choices presented themselves. *One, I could just make it back to the peak where Trenell and I stayed last night. Two, I could try Path C.* His finger traced a cross-trail with a natural bridge. It seemed an easy choice.

Elbraith eased off the ridge. It seemed hard to detach from the horror still playing out down below him, yet when he broke eye-contact, relief flooded him.

Stretching, Elbraith worked out the kinks from his enforced inactivity and raced off with a sense of urgency lending speed to his pace. Although the cross-over path roughly followed the river, he often lost sight of the water.

Where he did glimpse it, the Reuben's wildness shocked him. Now he understood first-hand why only one ford had been marked as safe.

After an hour of steady running, Elbraith veered left onto what he believed was *Path C*. After another hour of a mile-eating jog, however, he began to wonder if he had taken the correct fork. *By my calculations, I should have crossed the Reuben by a natural bridge a quarter of an hour ago.*

Stopping to catch his breath and take a drink from the water in his pack, Elbraith re-opened the map. The locater blinked a comforting pinpoint that indicated he was, indeed, well along *Path C*, actually way farther along than he had hoped. As he began to put the map away, however, another doubt assailed him.

Tracing his finger over the route the map indicated he'd traveled showed he had crossed the Reuben some forty-five minutes ago—just fifteen minutes, not forty-five, after the split in the path. He grunted, "The distances seem inverted."

"Besides, I saw no river." *How could I have crossed in broad daylight without seeing or, at least hearing, such a huge body of water? Which is right? Do I trust the map or my gut feeling?*

My own worst obstacle, he thought. *Do I trust my perception and retrace my steps or trust the map and go on?* Another disturbing thought piled onto the last. *How can the map be correct when it indicates my progress is so much farther than seems reasonable?*

Well, if I'm the obstacle, I guess I'd better stick to the map. Once again, he stretched his muscles and set out. As his feet pounded the soil, which was becoming rockier, he puzzled, *If I'm the obstacle, how can I trust my own reasoning? Maybe I should have gone back.*

The path dipped down a sizeable hill. Ahead of him he saw the peak that was his destination. The terrain between rose and fell despite his trail's generally upward climb. Some sections disappeared beneath vegetation, and ahead he occasionally glimpsed one stretch of trees whose golden foliage glowed even through his viewers like some amazing, giant nugget burnished by the suns.

Mentally allotting time for twists and turns, Elbraith calculated, *It looks like a good, three-hour run, barring, well... obstacles.* This he thought to himself and grinned. He began to think the Guide had mistaken the perils of this path, or *maybe Trenell never tried this way because he was unwilling to face its demands.* Elbraith's feeling of satisfaction in this thought settled into a tidy place in his ego.

When Elbraith had run for an hour that felt more like two, what with his pride growing and slowing him down, he rounded a bend and arrived in the glory of the golden forest. He slowed down to try to take in what he saw and heard on every side.

Bird song—one incredible type of warbler with a twelve-note song repeated and received answer at irregular intervals that made Elbraith impatient for the next sally. Other birds formed what he thought of as the choral counterpoint for the sweet soloists.

Accompaniment for this Hallelujah Chorus was rustling. Millions of leaves whispered secrets too precious for mortals. Occasional whirlwinds added brief fortissimos. *Planet X always resonates with sound, but this is beyond my experience.*

Additionally, his eyes began devouring an evolving feast. White tree trunks as far as his eyes could see in all directions reached up with tapering arms to an impossibly blue sky. Golden leaves fluttered and shivered like bright coins scattered carelessly upward from some giant's treasure chest. The forest floor and his path lay littered with the same gold pieces. Elbraith grieved to step on such beauty.

The thudding of his feet on the path seemed a desecration. Running would produce disrespectful bruising on the fragile golden carpet.

Turning around to hear a fleeting song or to absorb a 360 degree view of his surroundings slowed Elbraith to a walk. The place evoked an awareness of what he thought the Watcher might be like if it were not just a power to harness as described in the Conductors' manual.

The splashing sound of water falling lured him off the path to investigate. Elbraith's throat tightened with the sound. *I could use a drink.*

Not seeing the source required him to press through the golden wood just a bit farther. A few minutes' search revealed a pleasant looking cascade ending in a six-foot drop to a pond whose surface, as blue as the sky above, floated golden leaves downstream like miniature treasure ships running before the current.

The scene so extravagantly unnecessary amid the glory of the forest arrested his progress completely. Elbraith felt he must stand and stare at such beauty until it included him.

When he finally breathed in and breathed out the fresh scents of water and washed earth without seeming to disturb the scene, Elbraith made his way to the pool and lying on his stomach drank and drank from the cold freshet which must be the headwaters of the Reuben. He rolled over and looked up through the white and golden riot of color, and then the first feeling of alarm passed through him.

The gold of the leaves seemed to tint the blue of the sky. Elbraith knew better. First sunset had occurred while he had dreamed his dream of perfection. Urgently, Elbraith fumbled the map from his pocket.

I'm way off course.

Progress back to the path was not nearly as pleasant as his deliberate detour had been. If one were hurrying, even wayward limbs of beautiful white tree trunks could poke one in the eye and gouge one's scalp and grasp one's clothes with bony branch-fingers. Pockets that could wrench one's ankle hid in the earth beneath beautiful golden leaves. Having learned this last principle firsthand, Elbraith limped along to the spot where the map showed the path.

It was hard to believe all this golden glory flooded nightly. When he broke through to the path, however, a new sound arrested his ears. Thousands of birds, no longer singing, flew through the tree tops and above the canopy of the forest. Elbraith understood that they were making their nightly departure to nests wisely built above tide level.

The grim understanding lent his own heels wings. Elbraith ran.

Each time his left foot touched the ground, he gritted his teeth as pain shot up his leg. His former smug visions of navigating whitewater and hanging bridges or of crossing chasms returned to mock him. *It will take a miracle for me to avoid drowning.* Elbraith ran limping for an hour.

One more hour's travel should lie before me. Hastily consulted, the map showed the path winding around the approach to Smoke Mountain and steadily upward. Elbraith tried to calculate the speed of the tide and the distance he must travel uphill before he could reach safety.

At my current rate, and this last was not even uphill all the way, I will drown. Not so far below, the tide began to come in.

His ankle and his leg above the silver boot stretched the once loose jumpsuit until even its resilient surface looked ready to split. *If I die, the swelling will take care of itself,* he grimly reasoned. Through all these observations and speculations Elbraith continued doggedly moving.

Making as much speed as he could, and he sensed how he tended to slow and then pushed himself in increasingly harder spurts, Elbraith began to wrestle with another problem. *My own worst enemy, Trenell said.*

Now in the pain of running and of believing he would soon die, Elbraith faced himself. *I wanted Trenell out of my face. Well, I got what I wanted and went my own way.*

I hated him and, yes, hated that Yancey chose his way over mine. No way does Trenell know Yancey better than I do, but both of them thought that.

Here the suffering Conductor paused but then plunged with no mercy to the next thought: *I have barely thought of my Yancey all day.* He continued ruthlessly to himself. *You have failed as a Conductor. It is the primary rule: love your charge, but I loved myself more.*

Trenell has chosen wisely. Perhaps he knew how much was pride for me.

His jaw set. *Watcher, please forgive me!* Then he chided himself for falling so easily into a ritualistic pattern meant for Conductors to soothe and redirect their charges.

Below him Elbraith heard the susurration of small waves pushed by a huge ocean. He kept plodding, waiting irrationally for the inner release the Watcher's formulas always brought.

Long ago Elbraith had decided the soothing effect was a form of self-hypnosis. He continued quoting to himself. *Even for failures, the Watcher has mercy.* It became the new cadence of his footfalls. Hope was good even if self-induced, but he experienced only pain.

A new problem arose: *I did not reckon on fog.* Smoke Mountain, it seemed, was properly named. Gray tendrils of earthbound cloud covered its mass and obscured its top. Elbraith began to weave his way in and out of its clammy grasp. Visibility became more demanding but not yet impossible.

He held stubbornly to his course.

If I live to see Trenell, I will tell him he was right. If I live to see Yancey, I will tell her I failed her.

With sudden clarity he understood the Conductors' book, *7.13, Section B-7*: "the Conductor's prime function: help your charge solve the puzzle." He had always believed it said, "Solve the puzzle for your charge." It broke on him in clear simplicity.

Page 1.1, Section A-1/Beginnings: "Love does not take captives, does not re-create the charge in the Conductor's own image, and does not accept the loved one only when the Rejuvenate does what the Conductor desires. Love loves."

Elbraith stifled the mocking self-commentary that rose with these thoughts and surrendered instead to the words of the training manual. Hope stirred.

On the heels of this epiphany, a new, horrifying sensation sent chills to his brain. For one moment the cold water reaching for him actually felt good on his swollen ankle. Then Elbraith realized what it meant.

I will not live, then, to tell Trenell or Yancey anything. In the now fairly dense fog, Elbraith let out a frustrated yell. *I will die trying.*

Elbraith slogged uphill. The incoming tide, in the way of tides everywhere, began to pull earth from below his feet. The water sucked him backward. He began to use his hands to climb upward and to hold the ground he thus gained.

Then, through a hole in the swirling fog, Elbraith thought he saw a light wink from above him. Elbraith bellowed, "Trenell! Help!"

In what seemed the very next moment, a rope slapped down beside him. Trenell yelled, "Grab on! We'll get you up!"

It was the most welcome voice Elbraith thought he had ever heard.

Elbraith fumbled to form a loop around his waist. The water was up that high and fought his efforts. In addition, his hands were clumsy with fatigue and bleeding from finding hand-holds. The dense fog determined to swallow him and closed in again. Elbraith decided *wet is down, and dry is up,* to keep him oriented properly.

He yelled, "Go!"

Elbraith formed a "V" between his torso and the rope and walked up the mountain's side as well as he could. His efforts helped preserve him from injury. He rose up the side as surely as if he rode an elevator, despite the rope's drag against his weight on the rocks.

Reaching Trenell solved that mystery. Tax, with her great tail swishing against the tree into which she had backed, pulled the rope behind the Guide, who smiled an equally unrestrained welcome to the bedraggled Conductor as he slithered onto dry ground with them.

Trenell smeared his sprained and throbbing calf, ankle, and foot with a mint-smelling poultice that eased the pain and relaxed the strained muscles. Wrapping it also helped.

After two cups of strong coffee and a good meal, Elbraith had much to say to the Guide. The conversation lasted well into the starlight hours despite their need for an early rising the next morning.

When talk ceased, peace reigned between the three on Smoke Mountain and they slept well.

Chapter 27 – Cave Exam: Part III

As her mesh light keyed Yancey's map to life, three things happened simultaneously: first, she thought she heard a sound out of place among the *drip, drip, drips* and coming from one of the ribbon-wall corridors; second, she snapped the map shut in the midst of Trenell's voice saying, "Good day" in order to listen better. Third, a bolt of fear ripped down her nervous system.

Yancey listened another few seconds. Someone was whistling. This unknown whistler was headed toward her.

Stepping out of view behind a neighboring stalagmite, she placed her hand over her mesh light. It glowed red through the blood in her hand.

The sound she heard more and more clearly was aimless whistling such as one might do when alone—a snatch of melody here or there, a silence, a run where the whistle bottomed out or couldn't reach a high note.

A shimmering, iridescent light began to waver in and out of her sight with the bends in one of the rock draperies. When the glow emerged from the corridor, it played around her position. *Mr. Whistler must've covered his own light with his hand.*

What'd he cover it with to produce such blackness? The rosy glow of her mesh light impacted the darkness with the punch of a lighthouse beacon. *No mistaking my location.*

Whoever or whatever this was, it did not move. Only Yancey's breathing sounds mingled with the drip-drip-drips.

She remained hidden until curiosity became more urgent than fear. Exposing herself as little to view as possible, she peaked around her pillar.

A faint, green glow, totally invisible from behind her sheltering rock, illumined two hands black in the darkness and cupped in an attempt not quite as vain as hers to shield the visitor's own light. Not until later did Yancey register the contrast between those black covering hands and her own.

With her body still hidden from full sight, Yancey called, "Who's there?"

A rich masculine voice replied, "Ian. Who's there? Is that you, Roxy? You about scared me out of a year's growth!"

Yancey stepped quickly out to face the stranger and removed her hand from her light. Its brightness blinded the being thus illuminated. She stepped quickly to her right, turning her light to stay in focus on him but shielding her position just in case.

He held his hands up to block the light but did not offer to move or to escape. "O.K., then. We had no lights like this. Mind telling me who you are?" The voice was deep, and the accent was faintly British; hearing it stirred pleasure in her.

"My name is Yancey. How'd you get here?"

"A bunch of us walked in from the Emerald Grotto. I got lost from the others and then saw a gorgeous gypsum flower. That one led to several others, kind of like chain-smoking." The voice invited her into amusement with him at his own silliness.

"To save my wrist battery, I scooped up a thousand or so illuminati, the small phosphorescent worms you see in my ersatz lantern here, and kept walking." His substitute lantern, again unhindered, glowed green. Yancey's stomach protested as she got a closer look at his glass bottle. Its shut lid imprisoned innumerable glowing worms crawling to nowhere inside the greenish glass.

She never liked looking at worms. *They turn my stomach.*

Her visitor continued, "From there I caught a glimpse of a really spectacular helictite chamber. Still not seeing or hearing any of our party, I pressed on a ways and found the other end of these draperies—great colors. Did you know that on Earth they grow only from the ceiling?"

"Really, from there I HAD to walk through them, like Alice in Wonderland, I suppose, to admire them and find the other end."

Yancey said, "What?" She supposed her face looked as confused as Jerry Whitson's had the first day she read his class some lines from *Beowulf* in old English. The thought made her lips twitch, but Ian did not look amused.

Pedantically, Ian responded, "Here, look at this." Without thinking she stepped nearer as he pressed the holo-vid on his arm to life. On Earth she would've avoided such an abrupt teacher.

In his delightfully cultured accent, Ian proceeded to describe with deep pleasure the pictures he had taken. First came a study of fragile crystalline spirals sprouting from reddish-brown, porous rock. The pictures were beautiful. Ian narrated, "Gypsum flowers."

Twenty other pictures showed weirdly twisted cylinders crowded and growing from every available space—ceiling, floor, boulders, stalagmites—it didn't seem to matter. It looked like a beautiful storage warehouse gone mad. It was almost comical from some angles. Ian looked puzzled at her amusement but only remarked, "Those are helictites."

Yancey supposed she must feel giddy from such a huge break in her solitary trek. She busied herself more with studying him than she did with viewing every shot in his show and tell.

He was, quite obviously, from Earth. His speech, his allusions, even his garments which looked like smart, twenty-fourth century casual, all shouted "Home!" to her starved perception.

Her sharp intake of breath just at the end of the 3-D helictite pictures captured his interest.

"Yes," he said, deadpan, "I thought that last shot quite breath-taking, myself."

Then he laughed out loud. He looked at Yancey expectantly and asked, "What is it? I could've skipped all but four of those pictures, and you never would have noticed."

Grateful for his humorous acceptance of her disinterest in his hobby, Yancey replied, "I've just realized you remind me of someone I used to know."

Ian quipped, "If it's someone you disliked, I don't want to know."

His eyes let her know he wanted an answer to his unspoken question, but he said, "Sorry about droning on about my pet hobby."

She obliged him by replying, "No, you remind me of someone very dear to me." Unexpectedly her mind had screamed, *Daniel*!

On this planet, the beloved, hopeless name had twice bored through the impregnable wall closing it off from her waking life. As she had aged on Earth, only infrequent dreams tried to pass the barriers she maintained; then his dear face might briefly be seen again in sleep, playing on the wall of her mind like some old movie, rarely in color.

I'm awake now. Still, the name and the departed face came roaring out of prison through a breach made by a stranger. His appearance, the rich male tone of voice, and an accent never forgotten—all evoked memories of Daniel.

Ian tilted his head and lifted his eyebrows at her in a mannerism so reminiscent of Daniel that Yancey's world tilted with it. Her rebel heart reached out and embraced the memory with the fervor of a snake-bitten man for the antidote. With a move that nearly overset her, she jerked back and away from this confusing stranger.

Ian reached out and caught her wrist to steady her. Arresting her progress, he looked at her with penetrating eyes but apparently found it difficult to see her expression because of the mesh light. He squinted and said, "I say, would you take that light off so I can see your face? It's like looking at one of those antique silent movies. I'm obviously missing some dialogue, and the brightness of your torch makes the picture dim, to boot."

This time Yancey ignored his question. "Let go, please. I tripped, I guess. Thanks for the hand."

Ian frowned into the mesh light and shifted gears. "How'd you get here, anyway? You know how I did." He moved more to her side to avoid the brightness and study her profile.

Yancey did some shifting of her own and mentally backed away from him. Remembering the last parties who disliked her mesh light unsettled her. *And he is,* she reminded herself, *a stranger.*

Despite the weird coincidences, this is not Daniel. How, she wondered as she allowed herself to think his name and to remember even this much, *can pain from decades ago feel so fresh?*

That's an easy one. I buried the memories alive when Daniel died. This guy inadvertently, she reasoned, *cracked the door of the tomb.* Confusion beckoned: *how did Daniel die?*

Sorely distracted, she replied, "Trenell guided me, and I walked, same as you."

She rushed on, "I need to get out of here. My friends are waiting for me."

Ian said, "I'm ready to call it a day, myself. My friends are probably wondering about me, too. Let's go." He turned and started back down the waving corridor from which he had emerged.

A feeling of dread sank through her, seeped through the soles of her feet, and rooted them where she stood. She felt foolish when Ian turned around, stopped, and headed back toward her.

"Anything wrong?"

"Just wanted to check to see if that's the shortest path down."

Yancey was in the act of pulling out her map when Ian stumbled into her. The map clattered to the cave floor. He apologized in his charming accent, "Oh, I AM sorry!"

As he stooped to retrieve it for her, Yancey amazed herself by placing her staff as a barrier in his way and said, watching him, "No thanks. I can get it."

Knowing what she did was rude and seemingly uncalled for, Yancey chalked the look of displeasure on his face to embarrassment from his stumble and then awkwardness due to her response. She knelt with the silver staff, its honed blade on top, between them. Mainly, she kept her eyes on Ian.

When he backed away, obviously offended and with palms toward her in a gesture of peace, he showed a puzzled frown on his face. She risked a look downward and scooped up the map.

She keyed the map with her light. Trenell's voice said, "You are here." The red light blinked steadily. "Count four passages to your left and proceed with caution. You will have to maneuver to fit through some of the bends." The orange sequence displayed.

Ian broke in, "I'm not going that way. The way I came I didn't have to stoop or bend for anything. The scenery was breathtaking, as you saw; the pictures didn't do it justice."

Yancey felt an inexplicable, fresh wind of relief blow through her soul. Immediately, almost smothering that fleeting sensation came a tidal wave of regret at losing contact with one so reminiscent of her lost love.

When she didn't move, Ian stomped off down his preferred corridor of entry with a terse, "So long, then." He mumbled to himself as he went.

Wounded ego, she thought.

It is the staff that freed me. It felt so right between me and him. He is not Daniel. With long practice, Yancey restored her memories to their walled tomb, closed the door, and re-locked her heart. It required slow breathing and four attempts.

Yancey counted carefully and entered the fourth passage. The red dot intersected the orange display and marked her progress along the correct path. Without the map she would be hopelessly lost. Twice she took steps into a side configuration, saw the dot and sequence diverge, backed out, and resumed her course.

Often she had to wedge her way through. She turned sideways, bent her head down or stuck her derriere out. Her contortions amused her.

After perhaps an hour of this maze, she appeared to be about half-way through. The draperies were not one, continuous flow. New passages formed at irregular intervals as new up-croppings intersected the one where she might find herself. As she pretzeled herself out of a beautiful, sweeping set of curves that bent so deeply it had twice appeared a dead end, ahead she noticed a faint, green glow.

Her heart sank.

I don't understand. These feelings are illogical. I've been alone in here for two days, for crying out loud. Now company becomes available, and I'm not grateful.

*Maybe it's the worms. Maybe it's because he reminds me...*she shut off the thought eagerly. *Pain avoidance—that's the reason. There's my logical explanation for my negative reaction to Ian's company.*

Ian's cultured voice greeted her with, "I thought I noticed a light from that seemingly impossible bend. I might have passed by thinking it was solid rock if not for seeing it. I say, how DID you come through it? I'm glad my way has required no such herculean feats."

Ian had apparently decided to let bygones be bygones but could not refrain from assuring her his way had been superior. Yancey wished it had also been faster so they might have missed this meeting.

If it was so easy, why did it take you as long as it did me? She grumbled to herself. *He reminds me less and less of Daniel.*

With this traitorous thought, a despair of loneliness which had been building in darkness for decades tore through her. She wondered why she heard no tearing and rending as she had when the grunt broke her wrist and shoulder: surely her soul was coming apart under this equally violent onslaught.

Ian remarked, "Our way seems to lie together for awhile. Care to join me, Lady Yancey?"

It was what Elbraith had called her. Sudden urgency to break company with this disturbing Ian and to see Elbraith and Trenell helped a little to settle the pieces that had broken loose inside her.

She would not understand until later that stones carefully laid to build a wall around Daniel and her pain were being shaken to be removed, not re-set. For now, remembering her goal re-focused her for her task and freed her to function.

More scraps from her past thrust their way up through the new cracks in her mental armor. *Still, I do not remember Daniel's actual death.*

Ian's next words disturbed her memories, "So, did you say that thing is a guide-map?"

Yancey replied, "Yes, you could call it that."

Ian rattled on, "Guide...did you say *Trephell*, or some such as that?"

Reluctant to speak to Ian of any personal matter, Yancey hedged, "Something like that." Yancey's lackluster, non-committal reply did not discourage the talkative Ian.

"Oh, I just wondered. One hears many preposterous stories if one stays on this crazy planet long."

Ian waited, received no encouragement, and proceeded anyway, "I've never met a guide personally, but there's a story of one chap with a tank that goes on land or sea."

He'd caught Yancey's attention. She asked, "What about him?"

Ian replied, "Oh, just that he charges tribute at the end of each crossing."

This time Ian did not wait in vain for Yancey to respond. "What sort of tribute?"

"Oh, it's just tales of the desert and sea, but they say this fellow Ingress takes a passenger of his choice at the end of each passage and makes him or her virtually his slave. Of course, rumor has it that he selects the most crooked, amoral traveler of each bunch; these slaves remain under passage contract for five years. Fine print, don'tcha know. After that, he frees them."

"Lots of them stay for a cut of the action. One thing for sure, most of his partners in Ingress Enterprises are filthy rich."

Yancey thought, *Jason's Conductress won't stand for that. Besides, Jason does not fit the profile.*

Ian continued, "Whether the rumors are true or not, it's a fact that he has built up a little kingdom of trade and commerce along both coasts. He's quite a respected business man, except for the occasional gossip. Thousands of people hire into his companies each year, but the passage slaves are reputed to be his elite recruits, hand-picked and personally trained. No one knows if the tank or the story is real or not."

Receiving no reply, Ian bored on, "Some other guide named Eldritch is supposed to be in the religion business. He has established temples on nine of the eleven continents. Supposedly, he recruits his priesthood from clients on the guide trips. That part's speculative."

"His priests, they say, are scary. When they curse someone, that person dies. When they cure someone or bless someone, that person heals or prospers. Their services require payment. Slaves, whole populations, huge sums of money, a house, a boat, a goat, or a child—whatever the client, er, devotee, is willing or able to deliver—provided the holy men say they'll accept it for payment." Ian's tone sounded frankly admiring.

Yancey spluttered, "That sounds like lots of religions back home. Parents dedicate their babies to churches which take them as young children and train them. People make out wills to them. Some towns have voted ninety percent of their income to the local house of worship, but they really worship their leaders. The Church of All-knowing is the largest single business in the New-Boston Metroplex. Even Dad cannot infiltrate their local commerce: the church's workers are too fanatical. "

Ian snorted with laughter.

After a short silence while they climbed a temporary rise before heading downward again, Ian offered, "The worst of them, though, to get back to guides, is some guy who calls himself *Trenell,* or *Trephel,* or some name that sounds like that one you said earlier, I forget."

Yancey refused to ask. Coldness wrapped itself around her despite her thermal coverings and her exertions.

Again waiting in vain for Yancey to respond, Ian sniggered, "This *Trephel* character proclaims himself to be some Messiah figure or something. He says he can lead you into a whole new life. Rumors fly about his kingdom, which is supposed to be hidden. Fairly convenient, if you ask me."

"Thing is, not one person he's ever guided has returned alive. His kingdom's like a graveyard: people are dying to get in."

Ian chortled at the lame and in this case derogatory old joke and waited, ostensibly for her to join him in laughter. Yancey, however, felt her heart constrict. Her breathing became labored. Hot tears cascaded down her cheeks, and she averted her head to avoid Ian's curious glance.

She clutched and checked the map for something to do.

Apparently oblivious, Ian continued, "The tales say even some Conductors who get mixed up with this *Trephel* guy never come out alive. No one's ever seen even one of his clients on the planet again. That's what you call a really elite group, don't you know?"

"At least half a dozen researchers investigated the fate of this guy's clients, but not one has ever either seen the client or, conversely, been able to prove foul play. Leapside has no records of them. That was the final reason the Board gave for finally banning the guy."

"Unofficially, people say he appeared on their summons and actually expected the Board to take his word. Then two of the Board's own trained researchers came back brainwashed and stood up to testify for him despite the lack of evidence. That probably shook the Board as much as anything."

"It's a cult, I guess. Clients who trust him have a way of vanishing. The two brainwashed researchers quit their jobs and relocated. Other people never see him—maybe they never took an initiation oath." Here he chortled at his second unfunny attempt at humor.

"He's quite a mystery man."

"Since the union banned him, he isn't allowed to attend the fancy election ball for newbies trying to reach Leapside."

Yancey pulled back and stopped walking as Ian made this last statement. Still holding the map in one hand, she reached down with the other and pretended to fiddle with her boot to buy time to think.

I wondered why the name of someone who seems so imminently qualified as Trenell had not appeared at that G.A.L.A. True, I did not ask. Equally true, he did not volunteer the information. She resumed walking.

Ian and she emerged from the draperies area and walked into a narrow connecting tunnel. The map showed it leading to the second-to-last chamber in this vast underground complex.

Her breathing constricted with the space. Fatigue crashed down on her muscles. Stones of doubt avalanched into her mind. Her strength sank from sight as if covered by irresistible forces. Her frame trembled involuntarily. Weakness engulfed her.

Ian caught her by the arms. He helped support her as she fought to stand up against the onslaught.

Ian said, "Look into my eyes, Yancey."

She looked.

She seemed to see not Ian's, but Daniel's eyes looking back at her. How had she not noticed the similarity immediately?

I always trusted Daniel's eyes. He could never fool me if I looked into his beautiful eyes.

Ian's hands constricted her arms, and looking into his eyes seemed to force more thoughts of Daniel. Both circumstances irritated her. Inside, her overwhelmed self began faintly to stir.

These are NOT Daniel's eyes, she hissed to herself. The hissing was weak but, like a curl of wood poked onto a spark, it fed the small fire of anger she had started.

Ian inquired gently, "Yancey, is this bloke your guide?"

A great sob surprised her and escaped. She nodded. *Way to quench hope*, she prodded herself, *drown it in stupid tears.*

Ian coaxed, "Come, love, I'll get you out of here."

It was exactly the wrong word to use. Daniel's nickname for her from the lips of this stranger lanced her crushing fatigue and her anguish of doubt. They drained like a boil relieved.

Who is this guy, anyway? Here I am on another planet, and he's walking around with Daniel's eyes and using our special name? And sliming Trenell? She looked hard at Ian and tried to see if any part of him wavered to show Fafnir, her nemesis. *I bet they know each other.*

Yancey pulled back from him. She snapped the map closed and slid it in her pocket.

Yancey looked at Ian's eyes and once again pierced herself, this time deliberately, with the fact: *these are NOT Daniel's eyes. They look shockingly like his.* She let the fact feed her anger at having Daniel's sacred tomb in her heart thus bizarrely excavated. It provided clarity.

Whoever, or whatever he was, she did not know this Ian with his hands that did not show red like a human's when placed over a light. Suddenly, she remembered that.

I do not know this Ian who traps worms and trashes reputations of those unable to defend themselves. I do know Trenell.

She shook off his black hands. She closed her eyes and tried to picture Trenell. She could not do it, but something better rose in her.

She FELT in her inmost being the peace she had felt with Trenell. She tapped into it as surely as one might put one's hand under water running from a faucet. She remembered the strange occurrence on this planet of the word *PEACE* and knew it had changed her, *so HERE it is a word with power. Watcher is another one, just as Elbraith said.*

Her strength revived. With wonder, she let *PEACE* mingle with her newly surfacing memories of the real Daniel. *I shall have to study that later.*

Trenell's words returned to her: "Trust me, Yancey." She heard it like a song bringing harmony to this discordant place.

"Ian," Yancey said, "please leave me alone. I need time to think."

It rattled her growing peace when after just a split second he said, "Say, I think I hear my crew calling me. Listen!"

It was true. Yancey heard voices.

With a growing sense of urgency, Yancey scrambled the map from her pocket and snapped it back open.

Ian looked at her with incredulity and at the map with quickly disguised displeasure.

He yelled, "Over here, fellows! Over here!"

The disembodied voices headed their way. Yancey hated it that she thought of them that way. Fear tried again to immobilize her.

Trenell's map voice said, again without preamble, "Hurry, Yancey! Don't walk. Run, Yancey! Run!" The last of the fatigue released her muscles.

Yancey had played basketball with her classes for over seven decades. She feinted right toward Ian, pivoted, and charged left. With the agility of a twenty-year-old, she whipped by him as if shot from a pistol. Fear proved a powerful launching pad.

Only thirty feet remained in the connecting tunnel to the second-to-last chamber which she must enter.

Ian charged behind her calling, "Yancey, are you nuts?" The accent and the idioms disappeared simultaneously: a Brit would have said, "Crackers," or, "round the bend."

Ian suddenly appeared right alongside her. That he caught up so quickly disconcerted her.

He said, and his phony Daniel accent was back in place, "Yancey, you can't be seriously thinking of believing that bloke?"

When he grasped her arm, she reached across and smacked him on his hand with her staff. He let out a howl and let go and fell behind.

With ten feet to go, Yancey saw circumstances take a hard turn toward the weird, as if all this other had been mere preliminaries.

First, the map showed her passing through solid rock to reach the next chamber.

The tunnel she now exited ended three feet from a solid rock face. At the bottom, it appeared to offer one six-inch opening, just enough room for the re-emerged Ubus River to pass through, not enough for anything else. Yancey skidded to a stop.

This is gonna hurt, and Ian, or whoever he is, is gonna divide me up with his friends.

Second, Ian, or whatever he was, now appeared between Yancey and the rock face at the tunnel's end. His thin body nearly touched hers in the tight quarters.

He gestured to her right to direct her to the opposite side from where the map pointed her. As it had been in the draperies, an angle hidden from view when farther away now appeared to offer a passage right where Ian pointed. It certainly appeared more feasible than the map's course.

Third, Ian yelled, "Fool! Time is up! You're ours!"

Behind her the voices ululated like a pack of wolves ravening for the final spring at their victim. They seemed closing in from the tunnel behind her.

Fourth, the map said, "Leap!"

Ian screamed, "My way, and live!"

Yancey, not to be outdone, also screamed: "I'd rather die with Trenell than live with you!"

She leapt at the rock face, which meant she had to plough through Ian. It didn't happen. Instead, a shimmering black THING with glossy black hair to its chic collar appeared where Ian had been. It was horrible yet somehow beautiful.

It was well she was in mid-leap. The beauty of the thing connected with her emotions. Her impression, again, was of Daniel, but the vision repulsed as much as it attracted. She screamed, "Noooooo" as it seemed to welcome her flying body.

Fifth, and thankfully, it seemed there were rules. At her "No" the black wraith jerked aside and she caught a glimpse of eyes that still showed a trace of their borrowed likeness to Daniel's.

The wraith's last deception presented itself with a mute appeal of "Pity me. Don't leave me alone." The tone excavated long-buried ruins of her shattered hopes.

If she had not been air born, she would have lingered. As it was, she sailed past the still haunting eyes. The thing's deceptive appeal broke. *Talk about a leap of faith!*

Just when she thought she was going to splat against solid rock and suffer a massive physical trauma which would *put me on oxygen during my new coma and then require major plastic surgery if I ever recover*, her mesh light shone on a tooled rectangle invisible except from the zenith of her leap. When her light hit the area, a stone door dropped into its pocket on the floor concealed by the Ubus, and Yancey sailed through the opening it created.

Adrenaline-powered, she sailed over four or five feet of water where the river bent left. She landed on her feet on the far bank and proceeded to slide in some shin-deep, soft material which obviously was very thick.

When she hit a bump hidden by the slick stuff, she fell and caught herself on her hands. At that point, with her nose just inches from the foot-deep, greenish-gray matter, Yancey discovered with fair accuracy what it was had cushioned her fall.

She yelled, "Guano!" At least, she said something that meant about the same as that. Then in earnest, she started cussing like a sailor. The horrid, smelly stuff oozed in unsightly, greenish-brown clumps down her sleeves and legs.

Not in vain had she hung around teenagers and learned every swear-word they'd sent her way. *Ah, education!* She cussed in foreign languages, too. Yancey called her new discovery every bad word she could muster, and it took a minute and a half before she began repeating herself. It broke off the creepiness she had just experienced.

She tried wiping excrement from her hands and forearms and from her knees and legs where the improvised skirt had ridden up to her shorts' bottom. She pulled up her hair from where the long braid had flopped over her shoulder and plopped its three-foot length alongside her appendages. The guano smeared.

She stood carefully. She shook herself like a dog to remove it, lost her footing, and sat down hard with a revolting squish.

When she yanked to free her malodorous braid, it slapped her in the face. Yancey started to giggle. She knew the laughter was probably hysterical but preferred it to crying. *Take that! That'll teach me not to have a potty mouth!*

Her wonderful jumpsuit, or the parts left of it, succumbed to the clinging, lumpy mess. *Really, the stuff's like glue.* She smelled like all the chicken coops and pig sties and malfunctioning septic tanks she had ever had the misfortune to experience back on sweet planet Earth.

Yancey cautiously rose to all fours and then stood again. The door through which she'd sailed had closed and looked as much like solid rock from this side as it had from the other. Carefully, she again began removing as much of the mess as she could.

Although sure she was without Ian and his crew on this side of the rock, Yancey had the uneasy feeling that the noise of her arrival had created a disturbance.

She began to hear rustlings and susurrations from overhead. Gradually, she could hear breathing multiplied by millions of lungs. *Is that dry leather scraping on itself?*

Not really wanting to, Yancey shined her light toward the cave ceiling. Black bodies shifted and stirred, jostling their neighbors. Yancey took a careful look and then re-focused the light on the horizontal. *Big suckers!*

They weren't exactly bats, but that was as close as she could come to describing them. She remembered dimly that vampire bats were the exception, not the rule, and determinedly made her way onto what she thought was the path.

With a quick map check, she quietly slogged forward. *No use to disturb the neighbors any further. I am going to be so-o-o glad to get out of this place!*

The chamber where she walked narrowed down to what she thought of as a classic "fat-man's squeeze," a place so confining that a fat person could not pass through it. This was no problem.

Above her about twenty feet, the cave broadened out like an hourglass top to a huge ceiling. All of it teemed with the bat-like creatures.

Those plop, plop, plops I'm hearing in the thousands are not water. How could I have complained about water drops in the last section? She donned her gloves and snugged up her hood over her malodrous braid and plodded carefully on, for the footing became increasingly slippery.

Is it I, or is it getting awfully warm in here? After perhaps fifteen minutes, the walls ended and Yancey emerged into a scene straight from her nightmares of hell.

Chapter 28 – Cave Exam: Conclusion

Yancey overlooked a huge, active, volcanic world. A vast band of black, ropy lava showed veins with fiery blood coursing below its skin. Cooled on the surface, the lava field lay before her in some terrifying, beautiful crazy quilt made by cracks and fissures glowing ominously red from magma flowing down below the surface where she must walk.

This may be the final chamber in more than one way. As always, the floor of the chamber slanted down. She shuddered, thinking what this would mean. *I'll be walking downward in the same direction of the living flow moving below me. The black surface will grow thinner.*

The hardened lava is sharp and brittle and can appear solid where it is not. Sudden holes can hide in level looking folds. Sections can cave in without warning.

If unseen pressure mounted up, the magma would erupt, melt and deposit a new path for itself to flow down to the sea. Anything alive on the surface will liquefy along with the rock.

Among the living red seams where the surface lava thinned, deadly hollows breathed out sulfuric acid through steam vents. Invisible in the darkness except where tinged red by volcanic activity below, the clouds of steam hovered randomly, appearing and disappearing like unstable wraiths against the blackness. *If I'm caught in a bowl when it vents, I'll asphyxiate.*

Exhaling this poisonous breath, the river of burning death ate its way through tubes it gnawed out below; the red, glowing seams threatened death to anything foolish enough to try to cross.

Yancey sat down hard. She looked up and saw bat creatures above her but not above the lava field. They jostled and scraped against each other to avoid being on the outside fringe above the actual bed which would slowly cook them.

Occasionally, disgruntled bats shoved to the edge by their peers would detach. Snapping massive, flapping, leathery wings open, they would relocate farther away from the heat source.

Once in motion, they glided soundlessly above the bed, then back to safety. Their flight, once begun, seemed effortless.

How am I supposed to cross this? I can't stay here. I can't go back.

Careful to use her gloved hands, she chewed some bread from her pack and drank some of the water from the barrier pool so far behind her in time and space. Again, as the water progressed down her throat and hit her middle, tiredness and discouragement left her body and soul. *It's like the water is living.*

Yancey munched and took out her map. Keying it open with her mesh light, Yancey thought, *This better be good.*

Trenell's voice said, "Good Morrow, Yancey. You are here. Your safe path down to the Emerald Grotto lies along the Ubus River, which here is mostly on the surface. Barely visible to the left of the volcanic field, you can see..."

Disaster interrupted. The map jerked out of her hand with a force that nearly broke her thumb and fingers. Apparently attracted in mid-flight by her light or the food, a great bat creature swooped off with all it could grab: the map, and her hope.

The creature must have begun a relocation glide and decided on a detour. She heard no wings flap until it snatched the map from her hands and had to regain altitude as it bore its prize away in bony talons. Even in victory, the creature remained silent except for the motion of flapping, leathery wings.

Yancey's scream broke the sound barrier. "No-ooo!"

Undeterred, the creature's flight path curved out over the edge of the lava beds. About thirty feet out from where she was unraveling, the creature discovered the map was inedible. It released her only hope of survival into reddish air and returned, probably disgusted, to rejoin its disturbed mates.

The map twisted as it fell and shattered with a muffled crash like the shutting of a coffin lid clumsily dropped by indifferent fingers.

Yancey feared being alone and dying alone more than she feared death. She dropped her head in her hands and wailed. This new sound close on the heels of her screams and the map's shattering stirred her repulsive neighbors hanging overhead. She plugged her mouth with her gloved knuckles.

She rinsed out her mouth with the barrier water. Trenell's words returned to her. "The Ubus River." A sob of hope escaped her lips.

Resolutely, before the overhead community roused to trouble her further, Yancey moved onto the lava field. Testing each place for her foot before putting her weight on it, Yancey tapped and poked with her staff like some blind woman in a new darkness. Fearfully, she stepped over red seams reflecting up through black cracks. Heat assailed her.

Once only, she stopped and really looked down. A murderous red flow perhaps thirty feet below her at this point pushed its hot way alarmingly near to the soles of her feet. Occasional bundles of fiery, liquid rock snagged in the channel bed below. The magma behind the more amber colored laggards bullied them from shore and swept them on downstream.

Irrationally, she breathed shallow breaths.

Yancey moved on. *The Ubus River veered left the last time I saw it. Trenell, I think, said, "left."*

Hopefully, the Ubus has not crossed underground where I couldn't see it. It seems unlikely. Such a crossover would steam the entire cavern. Trenell said the river of water here was mostly above ground.

She believed it, clung to believing *him*.

Navigating around steam vents and frail pockets and black rock surfaces glowing too redly near the surface, Yancey threaded her way left. Her own voice erupted in hoarse, relieved sobs when she heard the sound of water running. She angled more sharply toward the sound.

After perhaps twenty feet of progress toward her slender hope, she stopped as her searching staff helped her avoid yet another brittle spot. She rolled her head and neck and worked her shoulders in circles. Some fifteen feet later, Yancey topped, or rather, dropped, over an obscuring mound and found the Ubus.

The Ubus was a busy little river; hugging the wall of the cavern, it had carved its own channel around the edge of the lava flow. Light steam hovered above it as far down its length as she could see: even the stubborn little river could not pass without paying some form of tribute to its gigantic, volcanic neighbor.

She knelt, tested the temperature, and began to splash herself like some desert-mad pilgrim. Finding hot, flowing water, which here was perhaps nine inches across but two to three feet deep, Yancey stopped her splashing, disrobed, and began a systematic wash job.

Yancey did not believe her chances of surviving to meet her friends were very good. *If I have to die, I'll die clean.*

She washed her jury-rigged skirt and the remains of her jumpsuit. Yancey unbraided her hair, washed it free of dung, and re-braided it; she coiled and tucked the sopping mass into the newly cleansed jumpsuit hood.

She felt better. *Cave women's needs are...,* she told herself and shook her head at her own lame humor, *simple;* she finished her whimsy by hitting her chest and grunting "UH, UH."

Walking alongside the persevering little stream felt better than crossing the lava bed even though she still had to test before each step because the bank's lip was petrified lava. Yancey had descended for a careful half mile when the Ubus again went underground, a fact concealed by a swirling gout of perpetual steam until she unhappily arrived at the spot.

She strained her light into the darkness but could not see a place where it re-emerged. Resolving to stay as close to the left of the field as possible, she proceeded on her best guess at the way to go.

Fifteen minutes later, she tapped the tilted side of a bowl-shaped hollow that butted up against the cave's left wall. She saw no trace of acidic steam waiting to smother her if she walked across instead of around.

Seams of flowing magma below the bowl's right surface sent a red glow up to meet her. It was hot. *I want out!*

She looked for options to avoid entering the hollow yet stay where she believed the river must be flowing out of sight. *I can walk the next fifty feet near the top, go ten feet down inside the bowl, and save a detour as long as a football field.*

Playing her mesh light around, Yancey sighed. *The longer path looks safer.*

Making a snap decision, Yancey entered the shortcut. Her conscience screamed, *Don't do it!* She stifled it. *No steam's coming up! I'll be O.K.*

Yancey was twenty-five feet out and ten feet down below the rim when a red-gray cloud began rising around her ankles. Red seams showed to her right as they had everywhere on this hellish walk. *Maybe I can still make it back to the rim.*

She took a deep breath and held it so as not to inhale the deadly vapor. *Man, I better pick up the pace. No turning back.*

Flooding her torso as she progressed, the cloud thickened. She sipped the merest breath because she had to. It burned her nostrils and throat, but it was that or no breath at all.

Yancey's limbs grew heavy. Her eyes blurred. Her light wavered as she weaved her head aimlessly. *Which way's out? Must go forward.*

Some malignant hand weighing tons pressed her body down onto the unforgiving black roughness of the lava. It shredded the remains of her makeshift skirt to cobwebs along her shins and cut her knees and hands as she fought not to sink down and end it.

She tried for balance. She reached one gloved hand to the surface to make her body a tripod and give her some leverage. Vainly she struggled to stand upright again. Crouching brought her nose into the thickest of the steam.

Gotta breathe; some air has to be better than none. Her lungs burned. The acidic air leached her strength. Her body bumbled her brain's demand to move faster. Sluggishly, she crawled. Greedy haze claimed her face.

Oppression made her limbs heavy and useless. To move one hand forward took the effort of climbing a mountain. Her brain flashed a picture of herself dead and cooled into black rock to match her dark grave. She was barely sure she cared.

I'm going to die in here. After all this.

Her head drooped. She let go and breathed in desperately. *Might as well.* The chemical burning of the air was, at least, sensation; she clung to it.

With her head swimming in some darkening soup, and with her vision dulled like a camera out of focus, Yancey discerned one last, alarming reality. *How bitter.*

She had felt herself past pain, but this sighting penetrated her understanding with the unwelcome force of a blade slashing across her dying synapses: *I am not alone after all.*

She wasn't. Not only that, but the unwanted intruder's face wavered undulating and gloated silently in the acid cloud of steam. *Fafnir has come to collect me.* Yancey's eyes could not see him smile, but she knew he smiled.

He came to enjoy watching me die because he's won.

This was a creeping terror. One death had already shown itself as a portal to a life beyond. This time, the decision would be final. *I never intended to choose* **FAFNIR***!*

Oh, where is the true Watcher? Yancey understood for the first time that not to choose the One meant tacitly to choose the other.

Trenell, save me, or I die!

In that moment, with her worst enemy her only companion, she grasped the truth. *On my planet, Trenell's Name is Jesus.* She had run from Him while on earth.

He brought me HERE! Trenell said He would never leave me alone.

This is not what He wants for me—this creeping death that seals me to Fafnir!

He isn't a religion, or some impersonal power, either. Dying this time, Yancey met Truth.

He is a Lover Who loved His creation enough to die for me. He wants me—Trenell said so. Until now I refused. My biggest sin—yes, sin—was not to believe in You. Forgive me, Lord.

What a waste. I could've been with Him always.

In that moment, with her body already a loss, Yancey's soul stopped its flight.

It's a great, last coherent thought, a finding of self, not a betrayal like when I died on earth. Save me, Jesus. I'm so sorry. This time she did not plead for Him to save her from red death and her implacable enemy. She asked for eternity with Him Who loved her.

This is the right way to end. I wish I hadn't waited!

Crying to Jesus to save her, Yancey now met truth's companion wherever Christ is involved: she met grace. *What's next?* Something within her had changed again, and she knew that even now there would *be* something next.

It was His voice.

"When Jason shot you, the lights went out and you awakened in a puzzling world, Planet *X*, which is always the unknown quantity for which humans must solve, no matter what world they inhabit."

"You tried to solve the puzzle alone and taught others so. HERE, you learned truth: you cannot figure life's mystery out by yourself."

"God is the quantity people dismiss from life's equation there and here."

Yancey didn't know the foolishness of God brought to nothing the wisdom of men, but if she had, she would have grasped the concept immediately.

Because she had no breath except what burned, Yancey thought back, *Fafnir, the devil, is real...and that Ian-thing...*

Now, I get it. On Earth, just like here, we're all in a battle, but we think it's bad luck or other people or bad decisions; and some of it is, but not all. What kept me restless, un-whole, and alone even when I grasped for relationship was that I chose to stay separate from the only One Who could offer me life.

Lord, I don't want to be separate from You ever again.

In a windless cave, a current of air blew the red haze from her. Her vision cleared. Fafnir disappeared.

Her white mesh light illumined black lava laced with red seams—the rim! She breathed painfully because of her raw throat and lungs. *This is not God's time for me to die—same as before!*

This time, whatever life brings, I'll live it differently. Jesus has entered my life's equation. He saved me! This time I am different and I am not alone. Thank You, Lord.

Yancey scrabbled her way up the rim by virtue of the staff Trenell had provided and on which she now leaned.

Chapter 29 –Endure Hardship like a Good Soldier

Tax surprised Elbraith by rooting him out of his blankets before Trenell was stirring.

"Thanks, Tax. It's about time I made myself useful."

Elbraith rolled out of the sack, stirred and fed the fire, put on coffee and then grease in a pan for fry bread.

Every move tested and pained sore muscles and grated on abrasions declaring themselves. Elbraith stoically accepted this as his due. He limped despite the ointment and wrappings on his ankle.

The big Endi, who had watched hopefully for a handout, gulped the piece of bread Elbraith tossed her and whirled away into the mist. A huge splash a few minutes later revealed the crazy animal was off for a morning swim in the already receding tide.

Trenell a few minutes later inhaled the boiling coffee smell appreciatively as he approached the small fire. Elbraith offered him a cup and was ready to start frying more bread when the unmistakable sound of Tax's return distracted him.

What broke the mist first, however, was the wriggling, black and green body of a four-foot-long fish. Its tail still flipping disconcertingly enhanced the impression that it swam in the fog. Tax's huge snout and jaw dispelled the comical illusion as the big animal dropped its catch at Elbraith's shocked feet.

Trenell sat grinning. "If you don't tell her thank you, you'll hurt her feelings." Elbraith's mouth quirked. He leaned forward and rubbed the three-hand span of forehead between the animal's massive ears. Tax crouched as if to bow and bounded away.

Trenell observed, "You two seem to have revised your opinions of each other."

As Elbraith gutted and filleted the fresh fish, he replied, "I may have quite a bit of that to do." He made eye-contact with the Guide then. He found only acceptance.

The fish fry and clean-up, which Elbraith insisted on doing alone, took an hour. Trenell assured him their timing for the tide would be fine.

Tax returned to assist with all things fish-related. Elbraith remarked to her, "I see now. You prefer cooked fish. I have merely been duped into becoming your slave."

Trenell sat enjoying the trivial, one-sided banter. He offered no help and no comment as Elbraith, stretching sore muscles, rolled both their beds and prepared both their packs and broke camp.

Full of breakfast, the big Endi plunged away into the mist and did not return.

When all was ready, Trenell spread the map he requested Elbraith to provide from yesterday. "The third mountain is Beacon Point," he said as he tapped his finger on their destination.

"There is only one route to reach it. The path lies exposed only in daylight while the greedy tide waits on both sides to reclaim the ground in the darkness." He traced the route with his finger and said, "Take point."

An hour later as Elbraith jogged with only minimal discomfort ahead of Trenell, he admired the man's savvy. There was hardly a better way to restore a military man's self-esteem than to demand in a matter-of-fact way that he do his duty.

The path was a no-brainer: water lay on each side and gulped away mouthfuls of earth when it could muster a wave with greedy lips. If one stayed in the middle of the narrow way, the miniature cave-ins posed no threats.

Thirty minutes later as the path began slightly to rise, Elbraith began wielding his silver staff to clear away vines. The glossy green plants had started as low, incidental ornaments to be jogged over but had grown thicker so that now many were the size of a man's neck.

Soon the Conductor was hacking a tunnel through greenery that reached tangled heights of twenty feet above them and extended as far as one could see through the foliage to either side. No water lay in sight.

After thirty minutes of hacking and with his body objecting against his new demands, Elbraith gratefully complied when Trenell ordered, "Fall back."

Elbraith, who was sweating profusely inside his silver suit, nevertheless shot Trenell a questioning look as they traded places and he began clearing the way. Trenell had not merely spelled him. The Guide was looking for something.

After chopping their way for some twenty feet, Trenell stopped and studied the vines immediately before him. He cut and then brushed aside green leaves the size of elephant ears and made his way to the side and over to a low brown trunk about six feet in circumference; tangled roots, Elbraith could now see, jutted from the surrounding ground, and vines the size of his waist twisted at all angles from it in snarled profusion.

Trenell jabbed his staff blade straight down into the heart of the trunk. Elbraith distinctly heard the plant's soft tissue liquefy as the invasion progressed. The wound required mighty strength to administer. The trunk thus attacked bled green fluid.

If Elbraith had not witnessed the results for himself, he would never have believed it. On the path immediately ahead of them, seventy or eighty feet of clogging, elephant-eared vines withdrew. Perhaps a third of the gigantic leaves and stems fell to form a jumbled sort of pavement. The result was a narrow path easy for one being at a time to pass over.

It was well Tax had deserted them after her cooked feast. She would never have fit through the strange green tunnel.

Trenell motioned for Elbraith to follow. Trenell hacked their way another ten or twelve feet past the end of the cleared corridor, found another main trunk and repeated the process, but this time Elbraith joined him unbidden and helped with the cutting blows.

They emerged from the green mess with hours saved because of Trenell. Left to himself, Elbraith knew he would have again missed the tide and drowned. As it was, a half hour after the verdant tunnels, the path began to wind more sharply upward on the beginning slopes of Beacon Point.

They stopped to rest and eat.

Tax, her shaggy belly still wet with the fur dripping from darker points, rejoined them. Elbraith's eyes widened at the thought: the Endi had journeyed by water all the way around the long path they had traveled. Only hours and hours of swimming could have landed her back with them. Although panting visibly, Tax seemed no worse for wear.

The massive, lolling tongue seemed to make laughter from the exertion. Elbraith tossed her one of his rations. The sight of her tail twitching and her huge frame twisting in a happy dance cheered him irrationally.

After another half hour's respite, the three of them began climbing to Beacon Point.

Chapter 30 – New Lives for Old

Intellectually, Yancey knew as she stumped her way out of the bowl on numbed feet and legs that there was no breeze in this cave, let alone a brisk wind. But here it was, the fresh wind of the Spirit.

Yancey sucked in great gouts of clean, warm air that hurt her lungs in a good way. She coughed and her eyes and nose watered. *Pain,* she reminded herself, *is an attribute, not of death, but of life. Didn't birth occur only with pain? Yes.*

From the store in her water bottle, she drank barrier water that burned its way down and healed her throat. Her lungs mended, also. She splashed the water on her skin where she felt like a grilled wiener with its casing about to split. Her epidermis sizzled and healed. Everything hurt where her drinking water percolated.

Yancey grinned and felt drunk with JOY. She looked around her. *Still a dark cavern laced with seams of what looks like hell, so that's not it. The scenery has not changed.*

Still, her face creased with her grin. *Jesus is with me and will stay as He, my Guide, promised. He touched me before and spoke that word PEACE, but I didn't understand. PEACE is a PERSON.*

Tap-tapping, and step-stepping over an active volcanic field, her feet and limbs now coursed with thousands of needles. *Peace, then, is not the absence of trouble, but the presence of my Lord.*

That isn't all. My whole life that I lived out in the daylight suddenly looks as dark as this cave. He sent me into this cavern with just one light. Here, without all the competition, the true light did not blend in or become lost among all the other wannabe's. For the first time in all my long life, I feel complete.

She stretched. Laughter began as an unexpected bubble down in the core of her being, erupted painlessly up her recently tortured respiratory system and blasted out against the darkness.

She threw her head back and laughed and laughed until she cried and could not separate the two. Waves that were at once tears and laughter convulsed her torso, radiated from her whole heart, huffed through her breathing, and energized every molecule in her whole body. The diaphragm workout did wonders for expelling deeply inhaled noxious fumes, too.

She recognized the Spirit of God. She experienced life from above, *and it is in me.* She thought of the living *barrier* water.

She knew her heavenly Father's love, then; *He is the Watcher I needed.* She loved Him back in a delirium of joy and thanksgiving.

While she did not know this definition of holiness, she embraced Someone radically OTHER than herself. She felt suddenly multi-dimensional, as if blind eyes of her heart had suddenly awakened and pierced through spiritual cataracts, like the physical ones back at the Rejuvenation Tank, and let her see into a new reality. *Planet X*, she thought.

He had been waiting patiently through eternity for her to show up at this exact spot and for her to want to hug Him back. She tried and laughed out loud at her arms wrapped around herself.

It's O.K. He got the hug. If anyone had tried to tell her she was crazy, that this was after-effects from near-asphyxiation, or religious hallucination, she would have laughed in his face.

Her gyrating mesh light continued to conquer the darkness, and Yancey sobered up as she again focused on her current black and red circumstances. *I'm not afraid anymore, but sooner or later, I've gotta get back onto the path.*

For the third time in this black testing place, He did not let me die. She chuckled ruefully.

Finally, I get ready, but, Noooooo, she thought. With exuberance she felt His pleasure in her silliness. Her impression was, *I created your sense of humor.* It energized her beyond belief. She looked around as she continued to struggle back to the river's bed.

Black lava, check; red glow from underground magma, too close for comfort, check. Then, *OH! Is that a sound of water running just ahead?*

She sped up. With the agility of a forty-year old, she left behind the crater where she had not died but had received life. She swiped sweat from her face and cleared grit from her eyes.

Yes! That's water ahead and to the left!

Her silvery garments flapped in their worst shape so far. They left her skin more accessible to the unrelenting heat. Tapping industriously with her staff, Yancey trudged forward. *I hope my bottle of barrier water holds out!*

She shouted when the Ubus became visible, now four feet wide by about nine inches deep. Yancey stuck a hand in and found the water somewhat cooler than when she washed off her bat-dung.

Either that or my hand is more cooked than it was then. The cloud of steam still hung above the length of the water's exposed path.

Continuing to test with her staff, Yancey stepped into the river. She didn't plan to stay but changed her mind when she discovered the absence of slick plant life one would find out in the sunlight. The river's bed was solid rock and the current not overpowering.

Splashing along with the Lord's presence strong and fresh with her banished the eeriness of her surroundings. She spoke aloud to Him as she tapped and walked.

No audible answers came. Still, she knew He listened and forgave, for much of it was repentance for the sins of her former life. She felt comfort, and He delivered her from shame. It swept away from her with the steady current.

Yancey felt amazed He forgave what she had done; she must pass it along. She named names, relived scenes, and asked for healing for herself and for the others. She cried buckets.

The next thing she knew, her staff failed to hit bottom. Her foot slipped. Her bottom hit the river's bottom with a jar cushioned by the suddenly rushing water. Down she went. With her feet out in front of her, Yancey whooshed along.

The Ubus River, or more likely, her Lord Who created it, now showed an hilarious sense of humor. The Ubus entered a cooled lava tube that formed a water slide, a flume. A now raging torrent swept her uproariously downstream.

Yancey gushed through a long, twisting patch where the current's force had her screaming with delight and spluttering with water. A veteran of such rides, Yancey folded her arms across her torso and kept her feet and legs together. Plummeting feet-first, she mimicked a torpedo.

All the long way down, the tone in her spirit was merry. She forgot fear. She was on a surprise joyride with the One Who had watched her for her whole life, had seen everything, and had loved her anyway. She and her new Best Friend were playing together.

Why, Tax was like that, too! Thank You, Lord!

When she burst from the tube, she joined the Ubus's last waterfall and arced twelve feet out to splash with a great Ker-whoosh into a deep, broad pool. Yancey came up spluttering with exhilaration.

"Lord! That was fun!" she yelled. "Thanks!" She felt His laughter. She thought she always might.

A new set of wonders burst on her sight as she swam out of the mist dancing where the falls hit the pool.

"LIGHT!" she shouted.

"DEAR GOD! IT'S LIGHT!"

That's the most beautiful light I ever saw! Yancey pulled herself out of the pool.

Starved for the sight, she stared at vegetation growing on the cave's walls and ceiling. She patted clumps of violet flowers waving majestically on fuzzy green stalks. Vegetation grew on all surfaces leading down to the cave's mouth and into the light as if to make up for the endless blackness she had endured.

Blue river, blue sea beyond, blue ferns, blue flowers among the greenery—all these competed for her delighted attention. Yancey had not realized she had missed the planet's song until the flowers and vegetation whispered in the gentle breeze flowing through the cave opening—His song!

I have a new Father, too!

She gloried in the flower song beside the Ubus, now a respectable looking river on a mission to help fill the sea. Boulders with vegetation peeking out from cracks and crannies marked the channel where the boat would exit.

"THE BOAT!"

"YACHT is more like it," she said when she caught first sight of it. Some fifty yards long, the beckoning luxury craft rode sedately moored to a beautiful stone dock reaching out into the Ubus perhaps a hundred yards before the river joined the sea.

With the silvery tatters of her suit dripping, she slogged her way down to the dock. *Sunbird* was painted in white on a broad, blue band running around the exterior a foot below its deck.

Yancey's mesh light focused on a blue circle with a picture of a gangplank. A section of the side smoothly lowered to meet the dock. She walked aboard. As the gangplank closed silently behind her, machinery recessed the mooring posts. *Sunbird's* lines reeled into her side.

Yancey spotted the bridge forward and sheltered behind a wraparound set of windows. Two passages fore and aft led below to a cabin area which would have made Croesus jealous.

Where she entered aft, white, built-in couches followed the contours of the ship's hull. A clever screen hid the doors to three sleeping cabins, right, left, and toward the stern. All was guest-ready. She promised herself a closer look—as in, from a prone position on one of the inviting beds—later.

Making her way forward, Yancey hurried down a short corridor.

Thoughts of Elbraith and Trenell, especially Trenell, hastened her steps.

Elbraith should be all right. This whole cave journey started as a mission to save my Conductor. Trenell, she thought, *did you want to save him as you did me? If Conductors can get saved, that is.*

Yancey re-focused on the beautiful yacht. Millionaire's lairs fall short of this opulence.

How many days, and more importantly, nights, have my two companions waited?

She charged onto the bridge. Her mesh light sparked the yacht's engines to life with a purring rumble. Just like that, *Sunbird* weighed anchor.

Chapter 31—Reunion

The Sunbird follows some sort of homing beacon. The luxury yacht glided down the Ubus River and into the ocean— *oh, glory!*

Her faithful mesh light fell off into her hand and she laid it carefully on a ledge above the control panel. *I'm out of that blasted cave!*

Thank You God! I'm alive!

Yancey lingered on deck to watch the self-propelled, self-guided *Sunbird* turn left, *er, to port,* alongside the cliffs that included the lookout where she had stood with Trenell before entering the cave a lifetime ago. With unbelieving eyes, Yancey studied the up-thrusting enormity of the tower whose innards she had traversed. The sleek yacht glided through open water at a safe distance from the rocks.

Comfortingly useless up here on deck, Yancey thought back to that bed she wanted to befriend. As they had before, motion sensors turned on lights as she walked the corridor.

Yancey reached the bathroom before the cabin with the bed and turned aside. Gleefully, she peeled off the poor remnants of her gear. The hot shower water steamed up the small bathroom most satisfactorily. Soap and shampoo with a girly, lilac fragrance purged her hair and body of any lingering grime the flume ride had left.

Like the hot water, weariness enveloped her. Toweling herself dry required an effort. She wrapped her hair in a high, thick towel-tower that listed from side to side as she turned to the closet opposite the bathroom.

Here she found another silvery jumpsuit complete to the boots, pristine in condition and a perfect fit. She donned the suit thankfully and unwrapped her precariously swaying hair. The new suit began to wick away the moisture. A convenient bin audibly disposed of her rags.

Yancey needed the handrails on both sides of the corridor back to the cabins. She turned right. Pulling back the covers instead of flopping onto the blessed bed took willpower. The bed was a puffy cloud. She passed out when her head hit the pillow.

An exuberant Tax pranced off-path ahead of the two beings. Elbraith waited respectfully for the Guide to indicate whether he wished to lead behind Tax, now out of sight, or come along behind Elbraith. Trenell signaled Elbraith to point as he had yesterday.

The Conductor started off at a brisk pace that was not quite a jog. After new salve and re-wrapping, his ankle felt good.

The trail corkscrewed up the mountain—Elbraith sometimes glimpsed Tax romping above them, in and out of sight.

After twenty minutes' progress Trenell shouted, "Conductor! Sing loudly to the Watcher!" The Guide's tone made it a command.

Resisting the urge to turn his head to see if Trenell's mind had snapped, Elbraith responded, "Yes, Sir!" and began to sing in his pure baritone.

Trenell said, "Loud, Conductor!"

Elbraith increased his volume. For one less in shape than Elbraith the task would have been impossible. The pace of the climb strained breathing. Singing, and loudly at that, demanded breath support.

Elbraith's song, memorized from the Conductors' manual, continued for ten trying minutes. *This is nuts* warred in his being with *obey your superior officer*. He sang.

Singing doggedly thirteen minutes later, Elbraith witnessed two feet ahead of him an innocent looking patch of sandy surface in the path suddenly vibrate away; an odd, spiraling circle about nine inches in circumference emerged. The spirals looked like some repulsive pile of fuzzy intestines.

Elbraith halted and watched the creature rise to form a mound about nine inches above the cavity it occupied in the trail. Lethal tendrils thus exposed writhed, testing the air and searching for moving heat sources.

Instinctively, Elbraith shied away from it. With a loud voice, Trenell picked up the chorus the Conductor had momentarily dropped.

The repulsive thing shuddered as the renewed waves of song hit it. Its movements became exaggerated. Exposed now, the thing could not spring its trap on Elbraith as he passed by. With its repugnant pink bands of muscles quivering and convulsing, the thing collapsed and violently sank back into its hole.

Shuddering, Elbraith joined his voice with Trenell's. From around the next bend, they saw Tax emerge in the distance. Seeming drawn by the singing, the friendly Endi loped toward them down the path.

With his eyes flicking in a wild scan of the trail ahead, Elbraith spotted a large vibration in the sand fifteen feet ahead of his and Trenell's position as they jogged and sang. Perhaps a hundred feet lay between the approaching Endi and the danger zone.

Tax is fast. She closed the distance with nightmare speed.

Reason told him an animal as huge as Tax would not be threatened by these trolling muscle spirals. Reason fled as Elbraith began to discern the true circumference and threat of the circle emerging from the trail ahead.

Particles of sand were shaking away from a seven-foot area. At five feet of distance, what had appeared as fuzz on its smaller cousin glinted like needles on this overgrown menace. The enlarged muscle bands showed a rusty color with white, repulsive warts serving as follicles for the silvered, wire-like hairs.

At three feet, with Tax lumbering ten feet away from disaster, Elbraith suddenly realized the truth of those searching, silvery needles. In the sunlight each bristle bulged with viscous, clear venom. Some dripped, appropriately—glands salivating before the kill.

Enough poison, I'll bet, to kill an Endi.

He and Trenell increased their volume with great shouts.

The spiral quivered. It would collapse too late.

Elbraith leapt the three remaining feet and landed in the circle's center, rising rapidly but not yet arrived at its full ten feet of height. He landed on a muscled ring where the center had been; it now formed the third tier below the rising top. It was enough.

He stabbed downward into its ravening heart with all the power that adrenaline, his strength, and momentum could give him and hung on by blade penetration and will power.

The seven-foot cylinder writhed and bucked trying to rid itself of him. A million poisoned darts thrust at him. Elbraith figured if the thing could poison an Endi, a being a third that size, like him, was history. He accepted the fact.

If his boots and suit proved impervious, he would walk away. If not, he would die a warrior's death, not alone, but taking the foe with him.

Again and again, as he struggled for balance, for the wounded thing now jerked in agony from blade and sound—

Trenell sang on lustily—Elbraith hacked the contracting, pure muscle beneath him.

Trenell stopped at the edge of the contorting circle with his companion on this trip finally where he belonged, fighting unreservedly to save the life of another. Trenell's hand, palm out, shot into the air to halt the bounding Tax.

Trenell never left off producing a pure blast of sound like the roar of a king. His voice acted as it does on evil, and the murderous rings of poisonous muscle began to die.

Silvery, crystalline needles began to shatter. Deadly poison sacs that formed their bases ruptured. The predator's own poison burned and scalded its skin. It writhed in agony from a thousand acrid wounds rotting to death.

On the other side of the retracting bands of corruption, Tax had executed an unbelievable stop in response to Trenell's hand signal. Arrested short of the thrashing menace trying to kill Elbraith, Tax added her considerable roar.

Elbraith leapt out of the collapsing, dying bands. This spiraled troller would never rise again. With its fleshy skin blackening, the muscular spirals of the circle shriveled as they receded.

More alarming was the depth of the hole into which the flaccid, ropy corpse sank: at eight feet it finally grounded. Sand began to trickle in on it. Elbraith caved the rest of the earth in, its former camouflage becoming the thing's grave cover.

Elbraith exchanged steady eye-contact with Trenell. He knew he had pleased his superior officer. It felt good.

Tax's rough, mattress-sized tongue scoured him briefly. Pushing the big nose and fangs away, Elbraith grinned at Trenell.

Singing lustily, Elbraith resumed point. When the Guide joined in from behind him, he sang counter-point. The harmony was good, but Tax's big, bass howl joining their efforts dissolved both beings into rumbling laughter.

Trenell said, "The spirals cannot exist above high-tide level. Tax must endure our serenade, and we hers, for another half-mile."

Tax did better than that. Two more spirals, each under two feet wide, exposed themselves in response to the vibrations. When they did, the two beings' large companion started at the edge and swallowed the pink, muscular spirals up like a kid slurping spaghetti. Unlike mature venom, fledgling poison from needles still in the fuzzy stage provided an excellent substitute for marinara.

Elbraith felt hoarse but pleased when they reached the high-tide level, demonstrated by the lack of mud deposits on plant leaves, almost as if Beacon Point had emerged victorious from a serious bout with "ring around the collar." *Well, it was "rings," but I'm glad they're behind us.*

Surprisingly, the trail grew dimmer. After a brief rest stop, Trenell took point.

They arrived at their destination two hours before high tide. An unknowing land traveler would never discover the spot to which they climbed, but Trenell led them unerringly to a shallow overhang unworthy of being called a cave. Its craggy ceiling and up-thrust floor protected a mechanical, circular device measuring four feet in diameter and imbedded in the cliff's vertical wall under the sheltering rocks.

Elbraith only saw Trenell pass his hand over the silvery, curved surface, but the Guide activated it, for the device began emitting light and sound. For only a moment, Elbraith searched for what memory the device triggered in him.

He relaxed into it when it came: the mesh light Trenell had provided for Yancey. What had he called it? "The light that never fails." *Trenell remains a mystery.*

Thoughts of Yancey pushed the puzzle from his mind. With questions about himself at least temporarily resolved, Elbraith felt more capable than before of conducting her to a successful leap-off—if she survived the cavern. Elbraith briefly wished the Watcher was not an impersonal force applied by a focusing method and taught in the manual to help Rejuvenates and Conductors center themselves.

Each silent with his own thoughts, the two beings climbed back down the rock face and camped in a level spot where between boulders they stretched their blankets to form a rough windbreak. Tax prowled off exploring again.

That night, Elbraith dreamed pleasantly of Yancey. Trenell had proved more than once that he knew his business. Not once in his dreams did Elbraith witness Yancey failing to emerge and rejoin them.

Yancey woke a refreshing ten hours later. Rolling from the incredible bed, she performed her morning rituals—she needed no mirror and barely noticed the luxury yacht offered none. Hunger drove her forward to make tea and snag some breakfast.

Somewhere in the middle of her second cup, along with a rasher of bacon beside a modest mound of French toast, she felt the yacht dip and right itself. When she emerged on deck, a joyous Tax slurped her right off her feet.

Yancey shouted with joy. Throwing her arms around the Endi's dripping neck, she felt every bit as jubilant as her unexpected friend, whose body wriggled with twitching tail.

"I made it! Oh, Tax!" *An animal who doesn't want to eat me or steal from me and who won't have to die for me—and beings who are true!*

And one of them is Trenell! *How will that be?*

Disengaging from Tax, Yancey ran for the port side rail to search the side of the mountain next to which the *Sunbird* had anchored. Tax would not allow it.

"Hey, you big lummox!" she exclaimed as the Endi began herding and nudging her away from her search-attempt and toward the control console. She got a clue.

Playing the carefully laid-aside mesh light over the console produced a mechanized hum which she recognized as *Sunbird's* engine lowering a boat. Tax leapt over the side. The yacht rode the swell from Tax's splash. The cabin was all that kept Yancey from becoming drenched. She did not care.

She caught sight of the dinghy as it hit the water. Yancey wanted to jump in after the big Endi and climb into the small boat, but that animal grabbed a rope hanging from its prow and swam off with a speed that would have left Yancey bobbing alone with water slapping her face.

Tax's course focused Yancey's attention on a patch of shoreline where two beings stood looking her way. Yancey flailed her arms and found more tears than she had with Tax. Both her Conductor and her Guide waved back. She settled in to watch their progress.

When the trio—both passengers and their "motor"—boarded the *Sunbird*, the reunion was loud and unreserved. Yancey experienced their absence as years, not days. The Endi roared for joy.

Trenell's fantastic eyes showed Yancey love, compassion, and understanding that felt like oil poured forth. Yancey wanted to fall down—kiss his feet and worship, but he held her upright in their threesome with his hands on her arms and with the power of his eyes.

She knew it was for her Conductor's sake.

Yancey hugged Elbraith. "I'm so glad you're safe!" She did not want to let go of him until over his shouder she again caught sight of Trenell.

She missed the puzzled frown marring Elbraith's face.

Meeting Trenell now that she knew who he was surprised her by feeling natural. *Well, except for a hilarious, better-than-intoxicated joy and a sense of freedom that's got me wanting to explode to catch up the rest of creation, especially Elbraith, so he could somehow feel the same way!*

Trenell wrapped her in his arms afresh but greeted her as the Guide he was. She leaned back and looked into his eyes and thought her heart might burst with love, but she followed his lead and blurted nothing.

Flashing a quick glance at Elbraith, Yancey suddenly saw that spreading joy to the rest of creation, namely him, might be trickier than she first thought. As a matter of fact, Yancey's immediate, Conductor-aimed project of joy-spreading hit a snag as soon as she saw his altering expression. *What...?*

Dark blood flooding Elbraith's face made his cuts and contusions contrast sharply with his skin. His mouth thinned to a straight line. His eyes narrowed.

Briefly, her resentment stirred. *Way to spoil a reunion! It's so perfect for the three of us to be together again. What's up with you, Elbraith? Hasn't Trenell ordered our trip and saved both our lives? Are you still mad we split up?*

I'm confused here. Elbraith was supposed to live and to grow. Thank You, God, that he lived, but how can he act so distant if he has grown?

What she said was, "Thinking of you alive helped get me through the cave."

The Conductor shot a hard look at Trenell. Focusing back on her, Elbraith demanded, "What did he tell you?"

"W-why, that you would die if you accompanied me. Didn't he tell *you*?"

Elbraith's face puckered with rage. Speech exploded from him.

"I **knew** you would never go into a cave on your own!"

He pivoted and closed on Trenell. "Why do that to her?"

Elbraith launched a powerful fist that failed to land. Evading the blow with a fluid movement, Trenell grabbed Elbraith's forearm and forced it behind him. Pushing upward, the Guide strong-armed the fuming Conductor until Elbraith's shoulders dropped.

It took some time. Trenell released him and stepped away, again facing him.

Elbraith hissed, "Why tell her a thing like that? A thing you couldn't possibly know?"

Looking calmly at Elbraith, Trenell asked, "Would both of you have made it through the way we went? Think, Conductor."

Elbraith dismissed him by whirling toward Yancey, "And you! Why would you believe such garbage? Charges do not risk their lives for Conductors, Lady Yancey. It is our privilege to protect you." Elbraith pushed down the memory of his failure and maintained his indignation.

Taking her cue from Trenell sapped her anger at Elbraith's behavior. Instead of the blistering reply that burned at such ingratitude, Yancey asked, "What happened to you, Elbraith? Trenell said you would grow if we split up for a season. What did you learn?"

Her compassion shamed him. Elbraith's shoulders slumped.

Believing Trenell's words, she offered her life to save mine while I also worked toward that end. I grew, all right. I betrayed my charge. It was a moment of revelation that he wished he could skip.

Despising himself, Elbraith turned away and crashed his way below deck.

Yancey was crying. *What just happened?* Mutely, she looked at Trenell. He opened his arms and she walked into them.

Peace returned.

Backing up, she searched Trenell's eyes. "Trenell, did Elbraith grow?"

Trenell replied, "Yes, Little One, he did."

"Then why…?"

The Guide smiled at her with the wisdom of the ages and answered, "Do you remember what it took to bring *you* to me?"

Her eyes grew large. Her mouth formed a small, comprehending *O*. Silence with thanksgiving passed from her heart to his. Hope sprang from his words. Trenell had waited for her. *I will wait with him for Elbraith.*

Yancey nodded slightly, but what she unsteadily whispered was, "Oh-h, but Trenell, I liked him better before."

Chapter 32—Altercation

Later that afternoon the two suns produced more diamond sparkles across the water than anyone could reasonably expect. Despite Trenell's, Yancey's and the weather's sunny attempts, however, the climate in Elbraith's immediate vicinity remained dark and cloudy.

Standing with her arms crossed in front of her and looking over the *Sunbird's* stern, she, who had languished for light and air, failed to appreciate the sparkling water.

Something terrible happened out on the trail. What was it? Elbraith was with Trenell. I wish one of them would tell me.

Trenell disembarked around two and rowed ashore. For the next hour of the afternoon aboard the *Sunbird*, Yancey's Conductor performed a stilted dance of avoidance with her. When their paths crossed, Elbraith politely pretended a normalcy which they could not find in reality.

Elbraith wore shame like a cloak and wondered if Yancey knew he had failed her. His forced politeness with Yancey cracked a little each time he caught her troubled eyes.

She went into that horror in the cavern believing it would save my life. Meanwhile, I believed she betrayed me. While she faced her horror of darkness for me, I thought only of myself. She deserves better. In his heart he knew—and somehow Trenell knew, too—that he had broken the oath and code of Conductors and had put himself first.

The Manual demands I tell her, to my everlasting shame. There is no recourse: the matter of failure to put the welfare of one's charge above all else stands clear in the bylaws: Yancey will then choose to retain me or to cast me off.

Trenell knows. I must tell her before he does.

Elbraith stalled. Pride and self-hatred, two sides of one coin, tossed his resolve spinning round and round to land one side up and then the other.

Wiping imaginary spots from the white seats, he let bitterness eat him. *Trenell's know-it-all attitude parted me from my charge and landed me in the role of villain.* Finding this easier to deal with than his gnawing admission of total failure, he fed his rage to starve his guilt.

I need to protect her from his influence for her own good, Elbraith steamed. *I need to hear her story so I can confront Trenell. He handled Yancey's life irresponsibly.*

It felt right. He would show Yancey again who her true advocate was. With such reasoning, he locked shame and guilt away and put them on bread and water. Resentment flared: *I must have this over before Trenell returns.*

During the next long hour of the afternoon, the misunderstood non-conversation raged, marked by tense body language on her part, and on his in vigorous, misdirected action. Hardest for each was the strain of studiously avoiding eye contact while nevertheless looking for some avenue of approach. Each made a dozen false starts.

I have GOT to break through and see what's wrong, Yancey fretted. *Watcher, help me, please!*

Resolutely then, she turned to Elbraith, whose eyes in this moment of contact seemed to burn into her own. Yancey blurted, "Elbraith!" The Conductor said forcefully, "Yancey!" They exchanged a genuine smile, the first one today.

After mutual "You firsts," they asked to hear each other's story. *I trust the Watcher,* Yancey thought. *Wait till I tell Elbraith the glorious truth about Trenell. Surely, this will help Elbraith with his own story.*

The *Sunbird* bobbed and strained at her anchor as if impatient. Yancey felt the same.

Her Conductor suppressed his fear that the confession of his failure might scuttle their relationship beyond recovery. He squared his shoulders. *I will tell her the truth nevertheless. It is the foundational rule between charges and their Conductors; our lives are forfeit for theirs.*

Looking at her shining, great eyes peppered the truth into his tortured soul: *In this matter it is not Yancey who needs correcting. I am sorry I blamed you, my Yancey*—sanity and a resigned, gallows sort of peace returned to Elbraith.

I call on the Watcher to heal us! Elbraith hadn't thought of the benign force called the Watcher for many days. *Of course! Reliance on the Watcher is also a fundamental principle—how could I have forgotten?* Elbraith's tension relaxed a few degrees.

They talked and listened to each other the rest of the day and far into the night. Yancey began. Neither Trenell nor Tax showed up to interrupt their memory fest.

When Elbraith heard of the colored stones and her flooding memories, he reminded her he knew her history, and she need not hesitate to tell him the truth as she experienced it. He held her gaze with tender respect and comforted her as her own father had failed to do.

He marveled at the changes he saw and heard in his charge and commended her courage a dozen times. He saw that bringing the horrors of her grandfather's abuse to the light healed her in that dark place, but he refused crediting Trenell's plan. *The Guide could not have known this.*

Elbraith's heart contracted as Yancey described her near death from the grunts. It was good to laugh over her fear of dissolving in the living waters of the barrier pool.

Yancey praised the Watcher but stopped her tale at this point. Telling the last two parts and revealing Trenell's true identity seemed prohibited. *I'm sure it's not time—the rest of the story can wait.*

Yancey studied Elbraith. The Watcher's intervention, the mesh light, and Trenell's companionship through the map all were producing agonized discomfort that Yancey discerned was not a response to her story. "Something else is going on with you, Conductor."

Greatly agitated, Elbraith leapt to his feet and strode back and forth in the small space. His face twisted, he took a slow breath, then sat down and took her hands in his large ones. Not understanding, Yancey feared what he would say.

Intuitively, she knew what she would hear from him would explain both his attempt to punch Trenell and his estrangement all day. Silently, she resumed praying.

"Yancey," Elbraith started, "I failed you while you risked your life for me in the cave."

Mutely studying his dear face, she invited him to continue.

With true misery in his eyes, Elbraith continued woodenly, "I felt betrayed by what I saw as your defection from me. I refused to accept the idea that your Guide might know the course for your journey better than I did."

"I was furious at you both. I bordered on insubordination and in my heart broke several principles to which Conductors must swear."

"Trenell forgave me, but I had not finished my defection. I proceeded to break the fundamental base of trust between Conductor and Charge. After you hear this, Lady Yancey, you must, by the terms of the Conductor-Rejuvenate relationship formally retain me or dismiss me from my position as your Conductor."

Yancey jerked herself upright to stare at him. Elbraith stopped her spluttering protest with a stern look. Muscles in his handsome face and strong neck worked themselves into pained cords. "It is the rule by which we must live, Yancey."

Frowning, she waited.

"Mentally and emotionally, I abandoned you, Yancey. If Trenell and his word were all you cared for, then, fine, I thought. You were free to die following his lead."

"The most shame, however, comes from this: when I retaliated by releasing you to a senseless death, I went one step farther. I thought how I might save my own reputation and salvage my years of wasted training if you died."

"I am worse, my Lady, than Ingress or whatever faction Trenell insists may be pursuing you for its own ends. You understand, Lady Yancey, while you risked your life to save mine, as you understood it, I worked to save my own reputation and calling?"

Elbraith passed his large hand over his face. He stood. She knew he awaited her decision.

"So," she probed, "it is a moral violation of Conductor code of which you stand self-accused?"

Elbraith assumed the position of parade rest and answered, "Yes, my Lady."

"And you, who know so much about me—you remember my dying thoughts as the Las blew my heart apart back on Earth before I found myself snatched to Here?"

Interested in his beloved charge again and no longer self-focused, Elbraith replied with puzzlement, "You know I do."

With her face twisted by regret, Yancey said, "You know my dying thoughts betrayed all for which my life had stood. You know that, don't you Elbraith? Have you wanted secretly to abandon me because I am such a colossal failure?"

Elbraith's eyes filled with pain now for her. All he said was, "I never wanted to abandon you."

Yancey continued as if he had not spoken, "The Watcher knew all that, too, and rescued me from the death I deserved, Elbraith. First on Earth and then in the cave He forgave and healed me."

Then she asked, "How can I not forgive you?"

A ripple of hope crossed his face.

"Don't you see? We really are perfectly matched, dear Conductor. Didn't you risk your life for me when I rushed into the Runja? How about when I risked your life with the escape pebble—do you think the explosion would have destroyed only me?"

Standing, she formally stated, "My dear Conductor, you are both forgiven and retained!"

Elbraith wrapped her in a joyous bear hug.

With her face smushed up against his chest, Yancey gargled, "You know, Elbraith, I really wouldn't like having to take up with the likes of Ingress if he's a sample of my alternative. We're all out of Y'min vines; really, it just wouldn't work."

Elbraith's beautiful eyes snapped to focus sharply on her and he released her to arm's length. Yancey pursed her mouth playfully and tilted her head slightly. She grinned. Elbraith's heart flooded anew with love for this gallant Rejuvenate of his.

Although Elbraith now smiled, he did not break contact until Yancey thoughtfully offered, "I wasn't exactly focused on you and Trenell while I was in that cave, believe me. I was scared stiff most of the time. You say you violated the Conductors' Guide, but Rules in a manual can't change what we are inside—real...beings."

Elbraith replied solemnly, "The code is my life, Yancey. To abandon it means I become nothing."

Yancey looked at him and waited for the opening to lead him to the truth about Trenell. It did not come.

Instead, they sat down to fresh cups of coffee, and she asked him about his journey. Fitting his confession into the tale, he began to recount his adventures from the time they parted outside the cave.

Soon they were starving. They worked together again while Elbraith finished his story. Yancey filled him in on other parts of her adventures. They crammed their mouths with food and their hearts with renewed joy in each other.

Elbraith pointed out the healing she experienced by facing her fears. Her courage and willingness to risk her life for him humbled him, but Elbraith continued obstinately to view their separation as unnecessary. "Surely," he reasoned, "the two of us could have spared you much of your travail, whether above or beneath the ground."

As if granting her a great favor, Elbraith forgave her for believing Trenell's bizarre prediction and reversing roles to try to protect her Conductor.

Yancey's eyes flashed angrily at this, but she felt constrained not to speak. *This sort of muzzle I feel whenever I start to speak of Trenell's true identity is getting annoying.*

Frustrated, she began firing words back at him, "You just said how much healing I gained. Don't you think I might have missed some if I hadn't been alone?"

"What about the Watcher?" Although she shuddered when she continued with the next thought, Yancey stated, "I cannot calculate what experience I would change if it meant not knowing him as I do now."

Elbraith's brows drew together. He shook his head with disbelief.

Beginning cautiously to recount her own last day in the cavern, Yancey was about to discover why the ban on Trenell's identity had been necessary.

Internally, she felt it lift. When she told Elbraith she now knew Trenell was the Christian Jesus, Elbraith's face registered surprise, unbelief, and then outrage.

Yancey's face glowed with love as she recounted the moment of her salvation; Elbraith's face grew dark with hot blood. Challenging her Conductor's reaction, she said, "Well, a stiff wind rose in a cave where there was no wind and blew the gas away. How would you explain it?"

Another look at him changed her mind about hearing his opinion. She rushed to change the subject before Elbraith could reply. "Then there was a hilarious water ride for a shortcut. The Blue Grotto was like coming into another world, and then I found the *Sunbird*. I shall never view darkness and light the same again."

He brushed aside the change of subject. *I'm about to hear what he thinks, and I'm not going to like it.* In a hard voice through thinned lips, he sneered, "I see your hardships left you vulnerable to suggestion."

"Let me see the new map, Lady Yancey."

His manner, his tone and his use of her title warned her to beware. Skeptically, she fished in her pocket and found the map. Before handing it to him, Yancey instructed, and her voice was not friendly, either, "I remind you, Conductor Elbraith, the map is my property, and I will want it back."

Wordlessly, Elbraith keyed in a name and number. John 3:16 from the Bible sprang holographically from the map. Trenell's voice read the words: "For God so loved the world that He gave His only begotten Son, that whosoever believes in Him might have eternal life."

Elbraith returned the map to Yancey and said condescendingly and with great amazement, "I did not think that you, with your tremendous background in literature, would emotionally adopt and seek to apply as truth a fictional experience from Earth's mythology."

He continued although she burned him up with her eyes, "Then, to believe Trenell, a potter and disbarred Guide on *Planet X,* is one and the same as the epic madman your planet's Bible calls Jesus, God's Son—well..."

One more look at her face, and Elbraith stopped.

Yancey fumed, "'Epic madman? You...'"

He interrupted formally, "You were under terrific stress and reached for comfort. I am sorry, my Lady. I did not mean to offend you."

Furiously refusing to let the subject drop, Yancey ground her teeth and gritted out, "Why do *you* believe, then, in the Watcher? You prayed to him and he answered, remember? I was there. Did you not tell me he's a force described in your Conductor's book?"

Elbraith reddened and finally replied, "Conductors do not generally share all the secrets of the manual with their charges, Yancey."

She cocked her head and raised her eyebrows demandingly.

Sighing, Elbraith quoted, "'The Watcher is no god but is a fundamental energy everywhere on *Planet X*. One finds it present in all creation. Living beings can, by harmonics, by light, and by certain formulas revealed to the wise, focus this force to effect change.'"

Seeing her fuming, Elbraith continued, "My dear Yancey, did you not notice the sounds of the planet? The colors? Have you not felt them as 'other dimensional'? They possess virtue which the wise can release."

Aghast, Yancey spluttered, "Sure, but you think *I* like mythology? At no time have I thought your skies or your sound systems were gods! Or that I could manipulate circumstances if I prayed the right **formula**. Besides, where does the *energy* come from to gather and apply at just the right time?"

She ranted on, "And, by the way, I don't know how you define the word *god*, but if you pray to it, you're asking some outside force either to help you avoid evil or to bless you with good."

"That's religion. The least honest pagan on Earth would readily identify what he treated this way as his god. A being educated as highly as yourself might admit at least as much."

"Harmonics and focused lights—I should take you back home and introduce you to my stereo! You two would hit it off—you could press the right panels, harness the **energy**, and become your own god."

"Besides," she continued, provoked by Elbraith's expression of pained superiority, "what about the *good* and *evil* for which you undeniably pray? I know you recognized Fafnir as evil and the Watcher you prayed to as good! Don't try to tell me you didn't."

Pityingly, Elbraith quoted as if reciting from a tome, which he was, "Only the enlightened know the formulas to access the power called the Watcher."

"Is Fafnir enlightened? He has power. You mean he prays to the same power you access with your *prayer*? Or that the Watcher does *evil*? BALONEY!"

"Elbraith, God is not some power for faulty humans to harness for their own ends. God is a Person Who wants to buy us out of death and slavery and fit us for life and freedom."

Condescension dripped from Elbraith's reply, "Yancey, on our planet, only fringe lunatics and the highest order of the truly enlightened ever try to debate what you call 'religion'."

He continued formally with tone, voice, and face geared to end the conversation but determined to end it amicably, "I am grateful you survived your ordeal and I my trials. Thank you for sharing your heart with me, as I with you."

She looked at him aghast at this retreat into the cold structures of intellectualism.

"*Some* of your insights were quite edifying," Elbraith said. "Good night, Yancey. I am glad we are again friends."

When he extended his hand to shake hers, she gripped it too hard and gave it one passionate shake to fling it away. His lips quirked at her peevishness.

As he turned to walk away, he had an afterthought and turned back to face her. With amusement playing around his lips Elbraith said, "Despite your rather astonishing *revelation*, I know you are too wise to let Trenell make a complete fool of you again."

"Meanwhile, we should watch him carefully to see if he begins to walk on water. So far, I have observed him rowing around in a boat just like the rest of us."

She stood there open-mouthed and speechless at this disrespectful humor. *I failed with Elbraith. I am sure I got the "go-ahead" to tell him. How'd it end so badly?*

Frustration birthed a traitorous thought: *Trenell so far does not seem to be behaving... well, supernaturally.*

Maybe Elbraith got to me more than I did to him! NO! I trust Trenell. He was enough for me in the cave. He is enough for Elbraith in the sea.

Fat tears slid down her face. Yancey angrily swiped them off with her hand. *The Watcher, who is not some weird energy, is the Heavenly Father of the Bible. Trenell is the real Thing, who he says he is, my Lord and Savior Jesus Christ. On this I stake my life, do or die.*

Elbraith will see. His rule book won't save him! Trenell, hurry back! Then she remembered he promised to be with her always, whether she could see him, or not. *Lord, I need to talk to you about Elbraith.*

On her knees back in her cabin, she began, *If I'm forced to choose between Trenell and my Conductor, well, I know You're the only way to salvation. Losing Elbraith will break my heart—how did I come to love both of you as deeply as I do?*

She rubbed her forehead irritably and changed directions in her thinking. *Perhaps nothing is as it seems.* "Great thinking, Yance'," she muttered to herself. "Did you happen to forget you're still on a mystery planet **named** *X*? Oh, and your Guide is Jesus Christ Himself but He won't reveal Himself to Elbraith who just a few days ago was my personal choice for 'Being of the Year' but now qualifies better as 'Pain in the Rear'." The rhyme coaxed a flicker of a smile.

She resumed thinking. *After I risked my life for him, Elbraith grew in some mysterious way—I do not doubt Trenell in this matter. For this growth I risked my life? No, not for just this growth: I risked my life to spare his. So far, I don't like what he's doing with it.*

I find Jesus, and what happens? Elbraith, my first ally on this inexplicable planet, grows apart from me.

That hurts. I had no warning. Tears flooded her face. She sobbed but resumed praying. She hadn't yet read the part where Jesus promised persecution to all who believe.

Chapter 33 – Departure

The next morning, with Trenell and Tax both back on board, they weighed anchor. The wind blowing off the mountains joined the receding tide and hurried the *Sunbird* out to sea.

Within two days, Yancey and Elbraith settled into an uneasy truce and worked together under Trenell's guidance with fair efficiency on sails, engine maintenance, and navigation. Within a mere six days, life aboard ship eased into a shared routine.

The duties and activity required for sailing together created a rhythm that restored Yancey and her Conductor to fellowship. Eventually, he apologized to Trenell for swinging at him.

Yancey's hopes perked up. Trenell, however, warned, "Do not believe everything you see." Just that morning Yancey had read in I Samuel "God looks on the heart." She reigned in her optimism.

Trenell had organized the three of them into designated watches, by day and night. He always returned from his mysterious excursions in time for first watch beginning at first sunrise. Yancey's watch followed, and then Elbraith's.

They watched for weather changes and natural hazards in the water.

They watched for other crafts: not all, Trenell warned, would be friendly.

They watched and steered clear of mists that rolled like clouds low across the water: some might prove deadly.

These precautions jolted Yancey and pressed her to take her shift on watch seriously.

From time to time, Trenell and Tax would notify Elbraith as he stood night watch and would disappear over the side, Trenell always in the small skiff, much to Yancey's frustration, and return the next morning.

Her seventh day standing watch, Yancey spotted what looked like a boat emerging from a gray, misty cloud a half mile from their position. She caught a flash of light, a glimpse of dark sails, and a curved silhouette. She screamed, "Elbraith! Trenell! Quick!"

They came swiftly but saw nothing but a distant fog bank. The spy-craft had disappeared. Yancey gleaned a sense of foreboding as both beings exchanged a hard glance and then left her without comment.

Fear of this voyage took root and grew like some sickly weed inside Yancey. A very real and unwelcome sense of dread about the end of the journey planted uneasiness in her mind. Yancey asked first Elbraith and then Trenell, "What are Leaping and Leapside all about, anyway?"

Neither being thought it time to go into detail. Yancey ground her teeth. Loud enough for first one and then the other to hear, she mumbled to herself, "I suppose whatever IT is, it'll be time to explain just as it comes upon me! Hmmph!"

The two males shared a look showing they had finally reached consensus on something. *Yeah, this is the bond I wanted between my Conductor and Guide. Way to work together for my good! Keep the Juvie in the dark.*

Then, more soberly, Yancey thought, *Apparently, there is more to my life equation than I have yet found. Most people think of "finding God" as an end. Perhaps it is only a new beginning.* She hugged her salvation and Trenell's presence to her as the two unchangeable pieces of her life's puzzle.

Her early morning times with Trenell became the highlights of each day. On a normal day, Yancey would study the Word from the map and then discuss with Trenell what she learned.

No one opened the question of Trenell's true identity, but trying occasionally to involve Elbraith in their discussions paid off. Trenell, obviously, was one of the fanatics Elbraith had mentioned: Trenell asserted "the Watcher is real."

Yancey chortled. *This ought' ta be good: try debating Jesus Christ about God and His Word! And Elbraith isn't even a scribe or Pharisee!*

The Conductor's knowledge of Scripture from the manual was vast. He set out to trip Trenell up with seeming inconsistencies. Yancey stifled her giggles when the Conductor tried to argue some point with Trenell. *I always appreciated comic relief.*

Once or twice, even Elbraith had the grace to feel amused at how he had lost the argument *this* time. To Elbraith, the possibility of winning a Scriptural argument with Trenell became a hotly pursued goal.

Privately, the Conductor dismissed Yancey's revelation of the Guide as Jesus as hysteria. Trenell certainly made no attempt to identify himself as such.

On one such day when Elbraith entered the Scriptural discussion between Yancey and the Guide, Trenell laughed out loud, long and hard, when Elbraith voiced his "Watcher-as-energy-that-men-controlled" theory.

Yancey prayed silently, expecting a fight.

Yancey, however, did not understand what happened next. Spontaneously, Elbraith began to laugh aloud with Trenell at his own, carefully evolved, "according-to-the-book" theory that had seemed to him to make sense of the "Watcher."

Elbraith did not understand it, either: *when Trenell laughed, I felt a heavy burden jiggle loose from within me and slide off my shoulders. I remember looking around at Trenell laughing and then at the sea and the sky.*

I felt the wind on my face and simply knew that the Watcher is a personal Being, the way I used to believe in my earliest days before I became so... "enlightened." The irony sent me off into gales of laughter. The realization strengthened and refreshed me as years of philosophy have never done.

Throwing his head back , Elbraith shouted, "Lady Yancey! You are correct! The Watcher is not sound and lights manipulated by a formula. My apologies!"

Later, however, discussing the incident with Yancey, Elbraith added, "The rules and principles nevertheless remain true. These are given as working equations for guiding one's choices and for controlling what otherwise are events beyond our reach."

Back to the rule book, she thought sourly. *Trenell gives him a revelation and still he wants to be in control!*

Yancey felt an unexpected fury and asked tersely, "Do you think at the Theatre you used an equation superior to Fafnir's and so lined up the 'positive energy of the Watcher' to rescue me? Is that what you think?"

Elbraith smiled. "Why, my dear Yancey, we just established the Watcher as a persona. We'll just have to let him be responsible for the break-through you experienced!"

Then, in his favorite way to end a disagreement, Elbraith walked away from her before she could reply to his clever exit line.

It took real effort to stop grinding her teeth.

Yancey sought out Trenell. She asked, "That was a huge break-through, wasn't it?"

Trenell replied, "It was a break-through for our friend, but even the demons believe and tremble in fear. Elbraith will need to realize his own need for a savior and make a personal surrender. He does not see his own need yet."

Studying his dear face a moment, Yancey asked, "Trenell, may I go with you and Tax some night when you leave?" She had wanted to for a long time but had feared to ask.

Trenell said, "Yes. We leave tonight six hours before first sunrise. I will wake you."

Elbraith did not take the news well when Yancey appeared on deck during his watch. The Conductor wanted to keep Yancey aboard and under his protection.

Yancey simply replied, "See you at first rise, Elbraith," and slipped over the side into the small boat. Tax's splash shortly after rocked the yacht and made Elbraith scramble for a hand hold on the ship's railing.

Elbraith yelled, "You're all nuts! Why go paddle around in the dark?"

They signaled Elbraith an "all clear" and slipped out of sight into the night.

With wide eyes Yancey watched what came next. One moment they were in total darkness with the waves slapping the little boat's sides. Then Trenell slipped his oars into the water, and Yancey heard sandy shore swishing under their prow. Since it was perfectly obvious they had been near no land for days, her mouth formed a perfect "O" as Trenell helped her disembark. Yancey's thought was, *Ooh, I wish Elbraith had seen that!*

A small group wearing mesh lights like her own, which Trenell had her bring, conducted them to a land vehicle which whisked them up onto a high mountain. Yancey's jaw dropped open. A crowd of 10,000 or more people waited for them as they crested the ridge.

When Trenell became visible to them, every able individual within the natural valley bowed their knees and worshiped him. Thousands of mesh lights illumined the scene, but Trenell's whole body shone so brightly, they were eclipsed. They began singing, and Yancey flung herself onto her knees and joined in.

It went on and on. She wished it would never end.

Eager hands passed pallets bearing sick people through the crowd toward Trenell. He healed them all. People touched the hem of his garment, which was the potter's robe Yancey had first seen him wear, but longer and now whiter than snow.

When he spoke, his voice, she knew, carried to every being present, even on the utmost fringes of the crowd. He taught them from the Word, and he smiled each time he healed. He loved every single one of them, and every soul present knew it and loved him back.

Yancey felt she had been there only a few minutes when Trenell motioned, and they found themselves back in the boat and approaching the *Sunbird*. Yancey discerned no progress until they arrived back at their wave-tossed home.

Tax, who had gone off hunting on her own when they had first landed back there, had rejoined them and now hauled herself contentedly aboard. Trenell and Yancey followed.
Elbraith grumbled, "Well, I hope you're happy! Let's see how watch goes after you've been out all night rowing around in the dark! Glad you're back! I'm sleepy." With this, he stomped below deck.

Yancey stayed topside with Trenell and slept during his watch shift. As it turned out, Yancey never had been more alert when her own watch shift came. She had to school herself, however, to assure she saw what was needed rather than reliving the glory of the night before.

She could not help playing and replaying the night's events over in her mind. Cameos of faces and healings that she had not known she even saw delighted her as they rose to her conscious mind and stirred worship, awe and love all over again.

Trenell went below to his cabin.

To Yancey's great joy, he invited her company two more times in the next weeks. Each time was different. *I can't choose which visit I love best—the second trip, we visited just one, lonely person down on his knees praying; Trenell just sat down and talked with him. The third was three older ladies praising God whole-heartedly, and Trenell didn't even show himself to them.* She smiled, "But they knew he was there! What fun!"

Life aboard the *Sunbird* progressed much as it had except for their occasional excursions. Yancey could not comprehend how Elbraith could rub shoulders with Trenell each day without really seeing him.

The Conductor would occasionally catch her looking at him with sorrow and misconstrue what he saw. He would at these times scold, "You really need to catch up on your sleep— all this studying and these night excursions are catching up with you!"

On the twenty-second day of their voyage, Yancey again accompanied Trenell on a trip. This one differed vastly from the others despite its similar beginning.

Again, Trenell molded creation so they arrived in a matter of moments on land that had not been in range of the *Sunbird*. Privately, Yancey wondered how far they had really gone. The answer didn't matter. What did was their surprising destination.

After a short walk from the beach, they arrived in a small bedroom where one young woman sat in a rocker praying. Even in the soft candlelight, Yancey could see tears streaming down the woman's already wet cheeks. When the woman saw Trenell, her tears stopped and her face lit with joy.

She fell to the ground before him. Her tears now dripped on his feet. With her rich chestnut hair, she began to wipe his feet and kiss them. Yancey thought, *I just read this yesterday,* and waited for the Lord to pronounce forgiveness.

From there, however, both the woman and Trenell went "off-script." He raised her to her feet, and she looked straight at Yancey and exclaimed with gladness, "Oh, you have brought her!"

The woman embraced Yancey with the tenderness of a mother for her only daughter. The hug was firm but so light it would not have crushed, it seemed to Yancey, a fragile soap bubble. *That ended*, Yancey shocked herself by feeling, *too soon*.

The woman invited them both, "Come have tea!"

"Tea" was a repast fit for the king Trenell was. In-between delicacies and more solid courses, they laughed and even sang little snatches of song. The woman's name was Miranda. When she said it, Yancey's eyes, which had been blinded to the recognition till then, discerned the identity of the seeming stranger.

Tears jetting from her own eyes now, Yancey gasped with bewilderment, "Mom?"

Yancey's mother had died decades ago. One look at Trenell settled her doubts. This was a holy reunion.

It made perfect sense that Trenell who bent and sustained creation molded time to suit himself also. He alone possesses the keys to death and hell, too—*I just read that!* ***That's*** *how come I didn't die on earth! And Mom! ... I need time to catch up with all this.*

When Trenell rose, Yancey realized painfully that they must leave. Trenell's voice, however, broke in on her thoughts now weighted with sorrow over parting from her mother.

He smiled. "Not so, my Yancey. You must stay for a time with your mother. It is she who will tell you of leaping and of Leapside and of many other of your life's puzzle parts."

At Yancey's look, flooded at once with both hope and doubt, Trenell continued, "Your Conductor and I also have important business to do. It will be well, Yancey." He finished with tender amusement, "Trust me, Yancey."

Peace spread through her heart.

When Trenell opened the door, light flooded the darkness which still, incredibly, surrounded the small bungalow where they stood. Tax bounded into view and play bowed to Trenell, who chuckled and said, "No, dear Tax. This is not a time to play. You are to stay with Yancey and Miranda."

Trenell turned to Yancey and explained, "Tax will escort you from this place when the time is full." Saying this, he smiled tenderly upon her and her mother. Yancey teared up. No one ever loved her as this One did.

Tax tore away beside Trenell, but Yancey knew she would come back.

Miranda—*how weird to be older than my mother*—closed the door, and the two walked into the cozy parlor and settled in to talk. Both were much too excited to sleep.

His usual punctual self, Trenell arrived just before first sunrise. Intermittent, violent squalls of heavy rain twice engulfed the surging *Sunbird* and then disappeared as Trenell explained Yancey's wonderful surprise. Elbraith's curiosity was deeply stirred when he heard the news. *Miranda* was a familiar name from Yancey's beginning files.

"What island? I was aware of no land."

"We passed it at the end of Yancey's watch today. The beginnings of the storm we're running alongside obscured it from her view. I knew where it lay, though, and had been waiting for it. I have waited eagerly to rejoin our charge with her mother. Miranda will join Lady Yancey when she goes to Leapside. She will prove a great comfort."

Elbraith faced over Trenell's shoulder as they spoke but did not get to ask any more of his questions, for in the distance visible over the Guide's shoulder despite the approaching storm, Elbraith spied a ship as *Sunbird* was pitched up to the crest of a wave.

The Conductor cried out, "Sail, Ho!"

Chapter 34—Dark Craft

Pithom Eldritch's fast ship, the *Hoham*, employed a dull, blue-gray paint as camouflage. Dark at the *Hoham's* sleek hull, it refracted light as it ranged upward to obscure the surfaces rising above the waterline. The effect was to render the craft virtually invisible when underway and easy to overlook when it sullenly sloughed and pulled on the heavy chain that held it when anchored.

Except for sightings of its sails—and these were what Elbraith had momentarily glimpsed—it distorted the air around it as it passed. It was a useful trick for a slaver.

Unlike its exterior, no mere paint job could lighten the darkness inside the *Hoham*. The dispirited lights that allowed functionality below deck had themselves succumbed to dim gloom. They provided just enough contrast to cast uncompanionable shadows and allow movement for sailors whose routines forced them below deck.

At the heart of this cultivated aura of darkness, Pithom Eldritch reigned. He no longer appeared the benign Guide and humble servant Yancey met at the G.A.L.A. where his eyes had nearly captured her.

Wherever he went on the *Hoham*, there spread a creeping feeling of dis-ease. Even his hand-selected crew felt this, and they were an assortment of brutes too bestial to serve Eldritch on land. Pithom ruled his crew of sociopaths with a raw, immediate brutality he masked when ashore.

Pithom slithered between several personas as naturally as serpents shed their skins. One was the brutal *Hoham's* captain. Another was the astute CEO of Eldritch Enterprises. Commanding supreme loyalty, he also presided before the world of Planet *X* as the wise, spiritual father and guide of his Church Universal. His considerable network of informers from this last avenue alerted him to potential "converts" of particular interest, like Lady Yancey.

Seven weeks ago, Eldritch and his devilish crew re-provisioned the *Hoham* after delivering a cargo of 150 slaves to Ektan, a little-known coastal town 200 miles east of Leapside. Eldritch's management enforced by a thriving Secret Police maintained Ektan as the closed, company town of Eldritch Mining, Pithom Eldritch, Proprietor.

In Ektan the *Hoham's* crew mingled unnoticed and recreated unreproved. In Ektan, the crew's shore leaves generated, not revulsion, but avarice. Ektan provided anything-goes-for-a- price pleasures that were the corrupt town's specialties. Pithom Eldritch was the law.

Twenty-one days ago the *Sunbird* was sighted. Informants from all branches of Eldritch's empire had scoured sea and land for news of a mysterious Guide called Trenell, a Conductor called Elbraith, or a Rejuvenate called Lady Yancey. The small black craft that brought the report received a considerable reward.

Savoring the news, Eldritch had stood on his gleaming balcony in Ektan and overlooked his town. The familiar sights and smells helped him think.

Degradation belched the stench of human misery and slavery from all quarters; they tainted the air like the sulphur from his mine. As a smoker inhales the aroma of a fine cigar, Eldritch absorbed the atmosphere of the town *he* created and controlled. He exulted that the elusive Lady Yancey should soon be likewise in his power.

He turned and entered his office. He depressed one small square on his console and activated the skin implants required of the *Hoham's* crew. He spared a brief moment relishing the thought of electric shocks growing at fifteen minute intervals if crewmen unwisely ignored the call to quarters.

Such a loyal crew, Eldritch sneered with amusement as he hurried down to the dock where *Hoham* waited. *We'll be underway in forty-five minutes.* Sailors who missed the deadline died from the third shock: only scanning one's chip onboard could stop the agony. *It's an inspired incentive plan,* Eldritch commended himself.

Today, the *Hoham's* twenty-second at sea, the sought-after cry of "Sail Ho!" greeted his eager ears. Eldritch furled his sails and fired the *Hoham's* engines. His ship was three times the size of the *Sunbird. We'll charge straight into them and sink her.*

His goals were simple.

Kill Trenell. *The sea kills her own so frequently; no one will question Trenell's unfortunate demise— if anyone misses him at all. The Guide has robbed me for the last time. Stealing away Lady Yancey—and at the G.A.L.A., when I might have taken her easily—has created an expensive delay. That upstart has had luck and has eluded all pursuit.* Imagining Trenell dead, Eldritch reveled.

Capture Conductor Elbraith. *A Conductor should fetch a king's ransom when sold at auction. Beings trained so highly can be drugged or broken and exploited for so many purposes. Elbraith is handsome, too. Perhaps a highborn lady might be moved to covet such a prize. I'll think on that.* Pithom smiled slightly, and seeing it caused one of his monstrous crewmen to scuttle like a crab away from his captain's vicinity.

Secure Lady Yancey. *She promises astronomical profit.* Pithom schemed as *Hoham* made all speed.

Elderly Juvies' cells were, like all on the Planet, programmed genetically with the ability to grow younger as exposure to the planet increased; however, folks receiving Juvie infusions, like Eldritch himself, would never have to bother with the positive, personal growth required as the catalyst. Specimens like Lady Yancey, whose organs and tissues would grace Petri dishes and special laboratories all over the planet, eliminated worry about such trivialities.

Lady Yancey's cells offered two other incalculable bonuses. Juvies who arrived in an elderly state, past the age of eighty, in fact, were universal donors.

Additionally, while cells transplanted from younger Juvies suffered up to a sixty percent failure rate, cells from a Juvie above eighty grafted successfully one hundred percent of the time. Healing every disease, even growing new limbs and organs—all was absolutely guaranteed success.

Smiling, Pithom remembered his first such find. *Harold remains my most closely guarded secret.*

The scientific world thought Eldritch had discovered a formula for genetic manipulation and cell stimulation. The mystic world, the masses at least, believed they had found their holy man. The truth, however, was that the underworld had found its genius.

Centuries ago, when Eldritch had founded Ektan and launched his empire, he had generated the cash from a single, old Juvie named Harold. At that time, the recently arrived Harold had fallen for Eldritch's fledgling church endeavors and subsequently *"gave his all for the universal good,"* as Pithom describe it. Pithom liked his private joke.

Vastly enjoying the irony, Eldritch had named Harold a patron saint of his now blooming Universal Church. The phenomenon of Saint Harold was one part of history that Eldritch determined to repeat.

Inordinately proud of his own youthful vitality that let him masquerade as good and growing, Pithom owed all his unwrinkled skin and healthy organs and limbs to dear old Harold's cells. After a few centuries, however, the artificially reproduced cells of the naïve old man had degenerated to the point of producing unwanted mutations.

"Going flat," Eldritch called it. In his black heart he feared the day his own treatments would fail. *I do not intend to die.*

I think I'll immortalize Lady Yancey—we haven't named a new patron saint in decades—wouldn't want to miss opportunities for miracles!

That, of course, is how I'll spin it to the world. With the technology I command, Lady Yancey could appear to the whole planet to say anything we lip-sync. Sacrificing herself to Mother Church will be a sensation sure to catapult her to sainthood with the eager affirmation of my bishops.

Won't Lady Yancey be glad to know she'll be providing hope to the hopeless through what a genius from her own planet dubbed the "opiate of the people"? Oh, my, yes—tithes will rise. We'll have to make sure one or two of the miraculous recoveries in the church group aren't rich.

The simple faithful donate so much more when they see even one miraculous healing, which Yancey's cells will provide in answers to selected prayers. The mystique around learning—and the fun for my priests of creating—acceptable methods to worship a new saint will also generate new converts in droves. It livens up the faith.

Yes, my dear, you are about to attain sainthood! Priests who brokered healings garnered tremendous followings and generated enormous revenues. *Now to what faithful ones shall I distribute those privileges? I must check my service records and judge wisely.*

Along with the long arm of his Universal Church, Eldritch controlled vast networks in the black market for obscenely rich clients whom religion did not reach.

It took exactly one dozen cells of any sort to rejuvenate its corresponding cells in ANY BEING ON THE PLANET. "Suffering from blindness? Have we got a deal for you! Pancreatic cancer? Eczema? Sexual or reproductive woes? Need a youthful appearance to interact with your world? Baldness, indigestion—you name it! We can help!"

So ran the black market hypes.   As Eldritch stood anticipating his upcoming personal and financial rejuvenations, his eyes narrowed in on the unarmed *Sunbird*, which they were approaching on the starboard side.

Crashing the waves and leaving them broken behind, the *Hoham* at its present velocity would ram the hapless *Sunbird* in seventeen minutes and thirty-five seconds.   That was the estimate Pithom's grotesquely scarred helmsman croaked to him as he manned the bridge.   For the sheer joy of the hunt, Pithom shouted, "Full speed ahead!"

Chapter 35—Encounter

Aboard the *Sunbird,* Elbraith was startled by Trenell's instantaneous response to his sighting of a ship. The Guide leapt to the navigation console—Elbraith did not register that Trenell used his fingertips to activate the board without using the mesh light until days later when he had time to think many new thoughts—and tapped in new coordinates that turned the racy little yacht so hard starboard in the growing waves that Elbraith staggered and grabbed for support.

On this new course, *Sunbird* pressed at considerable speed *toward* the bank of the massive, black storm they had been trying to outrun for forty-five minutes. Roiling clouds dropping heavy rain blotted out the southern horizon for miles and merged with the dark, troubled waters. Growing turbulence pitched the sleek yacht like some white bobber warning of a bite.

Peals of crashing thunder rolled over *Sunbird's* deck. Lightning arced within the front like some giant's welding tool.

The predatory juggernaut that was the *Hoham* charged its sleek prey the *Sunbird* to intersect on a right angle. *Hoham's* reflective paint job only partially obscured her bruising progress.

With half of his concentration focused on the *Hoham* closing fast, Elbraith with the other half watched Trenell steer them with all speed into the maw of the killer storm. Waves as tall as a two-story building mocked *Sunbird's* progress.

It was impossible to yell for identification of their pursuer. Elbraith did not really need the name. A horror-filled weight of dread poured through his system like liquid iron. He felt no wave could have moved his solidity. If such a storm beckoned them as to shelter, what must the relentless ship behind them offer of danger?

The *Hoham* tearing headlong into the towering waves ceased punching through them and began a terrifying two-step: race up the front to the twenty-foot crest and crash down into the trough. Her metal shrieked like demoniacs in pain. Her powerful propellers chugged in naked air and then surged as they again met water. She muscled her way forward like some enraged brute oblivious to its own possible destruction.

Finally in range, the *Hoham*'s cannons were frustratingly useless in such a sea. Eldritch tasted the smoky flavor of a tooth broken from grinding his jaw. He spat, muscles straining over near victory, near loss.

When *Sunbird* slid down a last massive wave and entered the storm's edge with the grace of a surfer riding a big one home, Pithom Eldritch's scream of rage penetrated below deck all the way to the engine room. "All speed! Follow them in!"

The sweating troglodytes who labored there obeyed. *Hoham* crashed down into the black cloud bank like some steam locomotive cut loose on a downgrade.

Inside the dark cloud bank, *Sunbird* entered a ten to twelve-foot chop. It was as if they emerged from the gauntlet of its true power focused in the twenty-foot waves they had survived out in front. Puzzled, Elbraith watched Trenell maneuver as surely inside the boiling motion of the dark clouds as he had in clear daylight from the moment of sighting the other ship.

He now told Elbraith it was the *Hoham*. Elbraith shouted, "Thank the Watcher Yancey is safe with her mother!"

Elbraith felt, rather than saw Trenell looking at him. Pausing a beat, Elbraith said as if responding to an unspoken question, "Yes, thank the Watcher, a Person who cares if we live or die."

Trenell, after a while, continued the strange conversation, "Even the demons believe, Elbraith, and tremble. You do not tremble, Conductor Elbraith."

Despite the tossing of the waves and their determined pursuer, Elbraith considered Trenell's words, realizing below his conscious level, that this shouted conversation was somehow pivotal.

"I have no need, Guide Trenell. I wish not to over-rate myself, but my credentials and personal life experiences suggest no need to fear the Watcher."

"Being head of your class, being the Conductor who made the most personal gains toward relational maturity, possessing the highest IQ recorded in 150 years—none of these things recommend you to the Watcher. The IQ—indeed, all your other personal attributes—are his gifts to you. All your kind acts and good deeds performed by the rules—all the rest of your accomplishments—mean no more to him than a pile of dirty rags might mean to you."

Elbraith, too enraged to form a reply to this casual dismissal of his life, listened with gritted teeth to his superior officer.

"Study more deeply and learn that you compare your merits with other planetary beings like yourself. A moment's honest reflection must show you that such a mighty being as the Watcher who created all these things and counts the nations as a drop in a bucket will use a far higher standard by which to judge."

"You are about to meet yourself, Conductor Elbraith."

Where does this guy get off? What's with these cryptic pronouncements? He must be loony.

"As I once promised Lady Yancey, so now I promise you: if you will believe in and cry out to me, I will be always with you. If you refuse, I am who I am."

"You have wanted to control your own life and to exert influence over the lives of others. Come here and take the wheel, Elbraith."

A chill not from the moisture-laden clouds about him coursed through Elbraith as he labored his way forward. He accepted the ship's wheel with conflicting emotions: elation warred with indignation.

Elation surged because like James E. Henley, an Earth poet, Elbraith asserted, "I am the captain of my soul." Exultant power quickened every muscle.

Indignation rose because Elbraith knew Earth's Bible well: *Trenell just claimed to be Jesus Christ. That means he thinks he's the standard the Watcher will use to judge. That's preposterous! Sounds as though he fooled himself along with Lady Yancey.*

He thought simultaneously, *well, now I know for sure the answer to two of my oft-posed questions, "Who does he think he is?" and "Is he nuts?"*

Another question popped up: *I wonder what the Watcher thinks of that?* A moment later Elbraith believed he had his answer.

A mighty lightning bolt split the darkness and struck Trenell as true as an arrow directed to its target. One moment he saw Trenell looking at him with compassion; the next moment the Guide vanished. Elbraith's chill grew to a shaking as his mind fought to sort what he witnessed.

In the darkness made blacker by the withdrawal of the lightning, Elbraith assured himself that Trenell's charred body couldn't be lying on the deck: *the waves won't permit it.* Despite his reasoning, not locating the Guide's body disturbed him.

Terror mixed with awed satisfaction. *I see the Watcher deals swiftly with blasphemy.* Swift trouble of his own, however, interrupted his appalled inspection.

As he clutched *Sunbird's* wheel, the roaring sound of full-throttle engines burst from the starboard blackness. It dwarfed the howling of the storm. *Hoham's* shape blacker than the writhing clouds charged the yacht's railing. Its steel prow crashed through the sides of his smaller craft as effortlessly as one might open a soft-boiled egg with a spoon.

Elbraith's hands were wrenched away from controlling the wheel by an overwhelmingly superior force. Instincts of self-preservation plunged him overboard to save his life. The black water was cold.

Rain and waves beat down on him when he surfaced. As he dragged in a breath, his lungs suddenly felt seared by acrid smoke blanketing the choppy water. The funeral pyre of the *Sunbird* sent red tongues licking up the clouds around him.

A powerful searchlight caught him in its beam. He dove. Three times he evaded the small crafts hunting him. The fourth time when he surfaced, lungs screaming for air, an earsplitting *CRACK*! sent him immediately back under.

A weighted, black net tangled him then, and Elbraith felt sure he would die. He knew he was not ready. It was the first time he had ever thought that.

When, net and all, an irresistible force yanked him from the water as easily as popping a champagne cork, Elbraith dangled from a hoist like any fish ripped shockingly from its element. The *Hoham's* exulting crew hauled him like that to where rough hands jerked him aboard the mother ship.

Dropped from the net, he hit the deck hard to the accompaniment of raucous laughter. Hands jerked him upright. In high and unholy glee, powerful crewmen pushed, jerked and pounded hard blows on his torso. He had caused them a great deal of trouble. One mallet-fist connected squarely with his stomach. He retched seawater.

"Hey, Darvo, ya might'a' just saved his life!" one sailor croaked at his fellow assailant and then landed a double-fisted blow to Elbraith's kidneys. It laid Elbraith out on his face.

They clamped iron shackles that bruised his wrists and ankles. Pulling him up with a combined force that threatened to burst his sinews, two of his tormentors hauled him to his feet. Dashing him to his hands and knees or tripping him as they propelled him, staggering along in his new impediments, seemed to be great sport.

The storm raging around the ship became suddenly personal at the hands of these gloating sadists. They hissed, "Conductor, hey?"

"Ooh, pretty boy. Don't hurt his face!"

"Captain has plans for you! Heh, heh, heh."

The *Hoham's* searching crafts still played probing lights over the water. Dully at first, and then deliberately tuning out the pain and degradation, Elbraith tried without much success to focus on that.

One dim thought surfaced: *I hope they find Trenell's body.*

The three repulsive brutes who escorted him stopped their abuse as their party reached the circle of dim light surrounding the Captain's Bridge. One with sloping, muscular arms knocked with two, sharp raps and propelled Elbraith in at a sharply barked order to "Enter!"

Only gorilla-man (apologies to gorillas everywhere) entered with me. With true grit, the Conductor assessed his odds.

Elbraith did not recognize his host until the being spoke. The oily voice was unmistakable.

Pithom Eldritch is the Captain of this hell-ship? Trenell had it right—someone was chasing Yancey.

"Ah, welcome aboard, Conductor Elbraith! You cannot, perhaps, imagine how I have hoped for just such a reunion!"

All Conductors trained first to be soldiers. Silently ignoring his chains along with his screaming muscles, bruises, and contusions, Elbraith straightened and remained silent.

"No polite conversation, Elbraith?"

"Very well, let's stick to business. I would find it devastating to think your two charming companions from the *Sunbird* might have come to harm. Where are the Guide and Lady Yancey?"

Elbraith looked away to the left and schooled his features to impassivity. A slight smile played around Eldritch's lips.

He motioned to a cadaverous, tall crewman in dress whites, and the impossibly concave man shambled forward from the gloomy corner where he had stood unnoticed. In his hand he held a compressed-air syringe.

Pithom's eyes burned into Elbraith's, which once again focused on his captor. With a curt nod to the medico, for that is what the emaciated man was, Eldritch turned back to his captive, who stood as tall as he, and purred, "In a few minutes, I will know everything you know."

The next thing Elbraith knew after that, he awoke in blackness with a headache that could split trees. His stomach, which he would have sworn contained nothing, heaved. Every muscle in his body screamed in protest with each ripple and lodged their complaints in his pounding head.

He fell back gasping. That hurt, too. Unconsciousness reclaimed him.

Elbraith woke to profanity and dull light but pretended he was still out of it. "How much blinkin' stuff did Saucer give him?"

"If he dies, Captain'll kill us."

"Get Saucer down here. He's gotta do something. Pretty Boy ain't wakin' up the way he oughtta."

"Captain's already fried because the ol' woman and the other guy got away."

"S'all right. We're goin' fer the lady now. She's the main one, Darvo says."

"Man, I'm just glad we got outta that blasted storm. I never seen such a thing. We were lucky it wasn't *all* poisonous clouds, on toppa ever'thin' else. Ensile's search crew comin' back with their skin sorta peelin' off and what was left, all green like that... " here the growling speaker broke off with a shudder.

"That could' a' happened to any of us in them boats."

"Shh, here comes Saucer."

"Hey, Saucy, yer guy ain't wakin' up."

The concave medico thus addressed couldn't possibly spare the flesh to form a decent scowl, but there it was, creating deep creases in his taut skin.

"You guys better not be messing with me," he said menacingly. "You remember Tragur, the last guy who tried that?"

Both gruff conversationalists shut down. The chilling admission made sense.

Lots of crewmen picked on Saucer. They now removed themselves from that number. Maybe it would pay to make a new best friend. The medico could get you through your air, your skin, your food—the possibilities seemed suddenly endless.

The talkative jailer pointed his grimy, stubby finger at Elbraith and said with sudden respect, "No, we're straight up. Look at him."

Medico Saucer growled, "Open the cage."

Laying one long, bony finger below Elbraith's ear, Saucer counted till satisfied. Elbraith stirred and opened his eyes.

Saucer harrumphed and ordered curtly over his shoulder, "Get him lots of water and some good food. If he loses much weight, Captain will kill you."

He backed out of Elbraith's metal box and banged both elbows on the entrance. The loquacious sailor left to follow his orders. The crewman standing watch did not snigger at Saucer's awkwardness; just fifteen minutes earlier, it would have generated snorts and catcalls.

Relocking the cage, the remaining guard exchanged a thoughtful look with Saucer. The medico peeled back his thin lips in a grimace of understanding and strode off, arms and legs splaying akimbo with minds of their own.

When the talkative sailor returned, it was the water Elbraith reached for. He poured the coolness down in measured sips until his throat reopened and his tongue could move from its glue-spot on the roof of his mouth.

I have not been so thirsty since the desert when I was with Yancey. Then he clanked his shackles and closed his eyes in impotent fury. *They are going after her!*

Chapter 36—Help

Yancey's mother Miranda laid her soft cheek against her only daughter's and cherished her with a hug. Yancey felt she might never get enough and returned her mom's hug with interest.

"Worry will gain you nothing but wrinkles. Try prayer," Miranda advised with a warm smile. "I'll be glad to pray with you if you'd like."

They migrated to the irregular kitchen island and joined hands. "Dear Father," Yancey began, and suddenly she was praying with deep sobs for Elbraith. She ended, "in Jesus' Wonderful Name, Amen."

Her mother added nothing verbally until she joined the "Amen." Handing Yancey a hot cup of tea, she looked at her daughter with deep affection and said, "You loved him in that other world, too, my Yancey."

"Who? Jesus? I never really knew Him, Mom."

Miranda tilted her head and smiling, said softly, "No, you loved Elbraith."

Yancey dipped her head and clattered her teacup. "You're kidding. If Earth had had an Elbraith, don't you think I'd remember? I would've latched onto him in a heartbeat and never let go!"

"Memories should never be forced. You'll remember him when the time is right."

Yancey looked at her skeptically but chose a sip of tea over confrontation. She already had enough thinking to do.

When did I come to love my Conductor? Slowly, she breathed to herself, "I love my Conductor." She waited, but the Lord's peace settled into her heart, not the denial or outright revolt she had half feared, half expected.

Looking at her mom, Yancey whispered, "But I can't love him. I'm at least fifty years older than he is. Even if I weren't, he makes me madder than anyone else I've met on this whole planet! He's condescending…critical…bullheaded…he doesn't even fight fair."

"Besides, he doesn't love me, except as 'his charge.' He's jealous of Trenell, but it's just professional…Oh."

"Mom! Elbraith feels *jealous* of Trenell! Hah! Elbraith feels jealous!" Tears spurted from Yancey's eyes. She got up from her stool, hugged her mom exuberantly, and began pacing the kitchen while blowing her nose.

"Let's go down and walk the beach. I can't stay inside just now."

Her mother grinned, got up to go with her, and said, "Meanwhile, tell me what you *do* remember."

"Well, I have four kids, each by a different partner, and most of them hate me."

Her Mom frowned. "What do you mean, 'four different partners'? You'd better explain yourself, Young Lady."

Yancey smirked and said, "Watch it there, Mom. I'm older than you!" Her mother's look was indescribably comical; they broke into gales of laughter with showers of tears following.

Yancey's mom was serious about listening to her life experience, including her four contracts, her four children, and their hatreds for her. Before her first nervous account, Yancey nearly balked and refused to start. Her mother's arm encircled her waist, and Miranda said understandingly, "That's O.K., Honey. If it's too painful, you don't have to."

That loving acceptance freed her to begin. Listening closely over the next few days, her mom comforted, held, and even rocked her and said things like, "that must have hurt terribly."

Miranda did not tire of hearing of her daughter's life. She offered no direct advice.

The closest she came was, "Stop. Could we pray about that a minute? What do you believe the Lord thinks about that?" Or, "Wow. That makes me angry. I'm going to need to stop a minute and forgive him/her/them for that. Did you? Do you think you could now with Jesus' help?"

Yancey forgave the others involved, whether she felt like it, or not, in the power of Jesus' Name. Her Mom explained, "Obey by forgiving, and God will make your emotions catch up with your decision." Smiling, once she added, "That way, you accept Jesus as Who He is—the Righteous Judge; you leave the people to deal with Him and stop trying to 'fix things' yourself, and you 'get outta jail free!'"

Yancey erupted in laughter and told her Mom about her crushing experience in the membranous prison, her forgiveness of Jason, and her own 'get outta jail free.'"

Miranda prayed for God to heal her daughter and the others involved.

Last would come thanksgiving and praise. Her mom played the piano and guitar. Sometimes they sang acapella.

During this process her mom often cried as much as she did. It helped.

Between sessions, they cooked and shared recipes. They swam and lazed on the beach. They played rummy and Monopoly and all the games Yancey had missed since her mother had died back on earth. They played with Tax, who excelled, as they giggled, at leftover clean-up, no matter how it tasted.

Twice, Trenell joined them for dinner. The second time, he led them in deep intercession for Elbraith.

Onboard the *Hoham* for what seemed an eternity, Elbraith nevertheless knew his caged existence had lasted, so far, a matter of sixteen days. Thirty-two meals, two per day, assured his crude count. Eating like an animal with no utensils and in close, forced proximity to the corner he had designated his own latrine helped force the Conductor's thoughts inward.

He tried to say a formula prayer that had worked before with the Watcher, but his misery made his words stumble. He knew he harnessed no harmonics and released no power.

Failing in prayer, he began an orderly review of his most recent experiences before captivity: life aboard the *Sunbird. Trenell saved Yancey. I'm grateful.*

Trenell fascinates me. This surprised him at first. Then, the Conductor snorted to himself: *I actually never before met anyone who seemed sane and yet claimed to be God. Yes, surprise is in order.*

He repeatedly revisited the last few seconds before the collision. Perhaps his current wretchedness was warping him toward hallucination.

Reviewing the last scene repetitively produced in his mind a supremely unpalatable question: did that lightning bolt **KILL** the Guide, or did Trenell **ASCEND** in it? The first scenario befitted a blasphemer. The second *...doesn't bear thinking...* but Elbraith's mind stubbornly refused to let it go.

His day guard was Lynch. The short, squatty fellow sat or paced while endlessly manipulating pieces of rope, twine, and string—anything, in fact, that he could weave with his blunt fingers. His hands seemed too massively clumsy to pick up his medium of choice, let alone produce such useful objects from his compulsive habit.

Elbraith nevertheless saw knots, so many he lost track. Two hammocks emerged and "fetched a good price, I'll tell ye." Nets, belts, string bags—all took shape under Lynch's ministrations; his favorite items, which he restlessly formed and unraveled, were nooses and had spawned his nickname.

The night guard was Frog. His bulging, ugly eyes told his name's story. He carved things with blades from a kit he carried in a sagging pocket over his heart. His most sickening medium was his own flesh; his tattoos were rampant and threaded with scar tissue—*mute witnesses to a learning curve,* Elbraith figured. Finding him at last proficient, the crew came to him for their own fleshly artwork. Frog bragged endlessly of So-in-so's back or another's bicep.

When time came to change the guard on their seventeenth day, Frog launched a blistering attack on the more muscular Lynch. Without appearing to, Elbraith followed the exchange with interest.

Frog liked carving people up, even uninvited. Lynch's demeanor was too cautious for it to be otherwise. The nature of the complaint Frog made was "we'uns got watch over this here Conductor fer the rest of the voyage, but all them banks of poisonous fogs has cost us hundreds of detours on our way to the island where thet infernal woman done went."

"We're s'posed to deliver that pris'ner in excellent condition. But look at 'im. His muscles is fallin' off ever' day. And stink? I don't smell like no posy, but I'm not settin' another night anywhere near him. Nope. He's gonta do somethin' about it and yer gonta keep mum. Get it?"

His face contorted, Lynch protested, "If he escapes, it's our lives, and it won't be pretty." He backed cautiously away from his cohort and tried to disappear, but Frog stopped him.

"You get a chem crapper down 'ere, and fetch three buckets o' water. If *you* do it, everyone will think it's just more o' that blasted string 'o yers in the buckets."

Lynch snarled. In Frog's hand appeared a throwing knife. He said, "Take this here blade, now. I could put it in yer wuthless neck afore ye could get to the ladder, and…"

Lynch interrupted, "I'll be back in a bit."

Frog's plan offered them all some relief. One of Lynch's custom rope collars around his neck attached to Frog's ankle by an equally thick rope allowed Elbraith to clean his own cage and the surrounding area and stretch his muscles.

The porta-toilet was shared by all. Chemicals and Elbraith's efforts kept it empty and odorless. The Conductor washed not just his own clothes in one of the buckets, but also those of his jailors. They chortled as a "high and mighty feller" like him performed these menial tasks for them, and pulling his rope tether to bring him hard to his knees or his face into a bucket became a rich source of laughter.

He bathed. Frog and Lynch hooted at such a preposterous idea and said he went too far. Lynch gave him just enough twine to tie his growing hair at the nape of his neck and out of his face.

Knife in hand, Frog made him exercise an hour each night after he did the cleaning and before being locked up again. Elbraith welcomed both the exertion and the distractions from his disturbing thoughts.

He tried to pray for Yancey but still could not get the formula or the harmonics right. Then he remembered: the Watcher is personal.

For the first time, Elbraith trembled. *Judging by my present circumstances, the Watcher is none too pleased with me.* Elbraith learned to fear Him. It was the beginning of wisdom. Abandoning the grand phrases and the beautiful cadences he had always followed from the Conductors' manual, Elbraith found one acceptable prayer: he thanked the Watcher Yancey was safe and requested she remain so.

That he felt in great disfavor with the Watcher rocked him: *how can the Watcher be angry at me? I have followed all the rules with only one lapse, and Yancey forgave me for that.*

His mind, not just his body, felt taken captive and betrayed. Finding himself in disfavor with a Watcher who is personal forced him to reconsider all he believed. He had, he reasoned, done virtually everything right; yet calamity had still overtaken him.

Yancey is safe through no intervention of my own. Trenell saved her.

The Guide's preposterous last words haunted and angered him. *The Watcher killed Trenell personally. Or, did he?*

In sync with his sit-ups and push-ups, Elbraith's questions repeated. Running in place described his progress in answering. Frog and Lynch's petty sadism gave some respite from the angry torture of his mind.

I remember my last night on the Sunbird. I prayed to the Watcher that I was ready to die but discovered I wasn't. Apparently, the Watcher agreed.

This angered Elbraith. *The Watcher is personal. I keep coming back to that.* Elbraith groused to Him, "What do you want?" The only answer he got was another mental replay of Trenell's assertions.

Shrugging those off as irrelevant, desperate ploys of his own mind to obtain some kind of magical help (he had called it Earth's mythology of a madman), Elbraith again tried praying the formulas from the Conductors' manual that he believed had moved the Watcher to action in earlier times.

Now, his limping words, remembered from a destroyed book seemed weakly to meet his cage's ceiling and to fall, trapped as helplessly as himself, to the cage's floor. The prayers died on his lips. Cleaning the toilet, washing the clothes, exercising his body, surviving his jailors' moronic sadism—these became his reality.

I am not in control. Degrading sobs shook him to his core and provided Lynch only a passing, scornful satisfaction. His guard resumed his finger weaving.

Elbraith's shield of arrogance evaporated. The Conductor became teachable.

Three more days, and the *Hoham* dropped anchor. They had reached the island which Elbraith's drug-induced interrogation had revealed to be Lady Yancey's current location. The Conductor came to his knees and wept, fervently beseeching the Watcher to spare her somehow.

Please. Help Yancey! No formula shaped his thoughts, just raw need.

Chapter 37—Leapside

On the morning of the day on which the *Hoham* would anchor near their tiny oasis, Miranda and Yancey sat sipping tea and nibbling fresh cinnamon scones on Miranda's deck. First-sunlight warmed their cozy nook. Yancey loved this spot.

From where they breakfasted, the second-floor deck thrust into whispering treetops on its right side but gave them a clear view of the green, sloping yard. Tax always managed to thrust her nose over the deck floor and huff and rub her head along the wood until someone threw her some of whatever was good to eat that day.

Miranda quipped that they should wait till Tax's slobber had watered her flowers below. Both of them grinned; they always made extra portions for this little game.

This morning, Tax alerted them to Trenell's calm entrance through the sliding doors behind them. After exchanging greetings, Yancey slipped into the kitchen and fetched an extra plate and cup. Sitting through his blessing over the food, Yancey felt like a helium balloon about to launch.

When they finished, Miranda rewarded Tax's patience handsomely. Trenell said, "It is time to go."

Yancey's heart clenched with disappointment. *I don't want to leave Mom.* Trenell looked at her with understanding and said, "Yancey, all of us will go." Her shoulders relaxed.

He said, "Each of you should dress for the journey."

Her silvery jumpsuit felt good as always to Yancey as she grasped her staff and hooked her precious barrier water bottle to her belt. Her mom favored a long skirt and a cloak with a hood.

Trenell led them downstairs and out the front door into suddenly blinding sunshine. Yancey had no sensation of wind or time, only swift movement. Her next step did not land on the cottage's front porch as it should have; instead, pebbles crunched underfoot.

She would have stumbled from a misstep if Trenell's hand had not steadied her. As it was, she lurched into Tax's front leg where the big Endi acted as escort on her left side. Her mother had no such problems. Apparently, Miranda had taken this kind of trip with Trenell before.

When Yancey righted herself and managed to look up, her eyes flew wide open and her mouth formed an *O*. Instead of tall trees framing a beach and ocean view—the view that they saw every day from her mom's front porch— Yancey now faced a winding, broad, pebbled thoroughfare leading up to a walled city. Her eyes traveled up and up the imposing skyline before her view included the tops of the highest edifices.

The road where they stood teemed with beings, carts and wagons. This part of the planet really *looked* alien. She grinned at her companions with unconcealed delight. Neither one seemed inclined to rush her wide-eyed inspection.

Passing vehicles and foot traffic jostled each other to avoid coming too near their little party with the giant Endi on guard. Her mom and Trenell completed a rough semi-circle around her.

Miranda smiled encouragingly at her, nodded toward the piled-high metropolis, and said, "Leapside." Chills coursed through Yancey's whole body.

Their giant escort moved ahead of them. With her elbow still courteously in his hand, Trenell guided Yancey into motion behind Tax. She had no fear with Trenell beside her. Her mom came companionably alongside.

Yancey's scalp lifted every hair on her head to attention as they approached the gates to her mysterious, final destination.

If Elbraith could have broken out then, he would, even if he died trying. He bowed on his knees and prayed. After two hours of this while they lay at anchor offshore, Lynch fixed his muddy brown eyes on his prisoner and observed, "Thet must be some woman."

After two more hours, Lynch snorted and risked his life: he walked to the ladder and stuck his head above-board before his shift ended. When his rolling gait restored him to Elbraith's vicinity, he spat and said, "Reckon ye can stop that now. If yer woman was on that island, she's a black cinder by now, and we ain't detected any water craft in the area for weeks, so nobody came off it since we caught you."

Elbraith's praying ceased. He fell backward to a sitting position. Not for many minutes did he scuttle backwards into the darkest corner of his cage, diagonal and thus farthest from his guard.

Arms around his knees, with his face buried, Elbraith began to rock.

Frog and Lynch changed shift. Elbraith did not notice. Now, after all else, he experienced the most effective prison: the one he had made for himself.

Along with his own, Frog ate all of the Conductor's untouched dinner instead of the half he generally confiscated as his due. Hours passed.

Frog opened the cage for Elbraith's nightly cleaning and exercise period. He threatened to cut the Conductor if he did not come out.   Frog prodded him twice from outside Elbraith's corner.

Nothing.   To prod him harder would leave a mark. Frog snorted and relocked the cage.

 Elbraith had only one thought: *Yancey is dead.*

Other thoughts came.

My life's quest has ended.

I have failed.

*Watcher, I know you are alive, but is THAT all you are? **JUST A WATCHER?** I know you see. Why don't you intervene? Evil wins on every side, and you do nothing.*

*Why bother praying? Evil, at least, is active. I've **seen** Fafnir. Destruction and violence and the shedding of innocent blood go on unchecked every day. Where are you?*

Yancey is dead.

I call to you for help. You do not listen. How can you do NOTHING? Why do you turn away your eyes?

A Scripture from the manual slammed him right between *his* eyes: "the righteous will live by faith."

Elbraith's thoughts went dead-silent.   That fragment burned through him. Like molten rock, it poured into his cranium and worked its way down through his torso.   His insides quaked with the contact.

Another followed its wake like a cool ice-flow creating hope from the fiery void the first one produced: "Now faith is being sure of what we hope for and certain of what we do not see."

He sat silent, wanting to believe.   All by itself, that second Word turned over and over in him like a computer graphic set to reveal its meaning sequentially from every angle.

What I don't see... Be sure of what I hope for but don't see.

Tears welled up and rolled from his eyes. Sweat wet his hair and clothing. His hands cradling his sunken head grew slick. He looked up.

The Watcher is personal. You are here! You do hear and see. Somehow, you have intervened. Yancey lives. Thank God. Thank God. Thank you, God!

Trenell…here he clamped down his thoughts and held the others to him instead. A disturbance penetrated his deep concentration. Frog was rocking his cage and yelling something at him. The man was hopping around as if the ground were on fire and his long feet could not stay in one place because of the heat. Streams of spittle slung away from his mouth as he croaked at his prisoner and banged the bars.

Now, if he'd only eat a fly, he'd look exactly like his namesake was Elbraith's first surfacing thought.

The second was, *What is he yelling?*

"Get out here! Come on! Now! Move!" Profanities and creative, highly descriptive names for Elbraith punctuated these frustrated commands as Frog roused his prisoner to action. The Conductor crawled out the open door.

With a few more choice names which Elbraith's mama would never have recognized, Frog yelled, "Put on this robe and get a move on! Oh! I'd like to cut ye jest a little! **Move yer wuthless carcass!**"

In this manner, Elbraith found himself ushered into the foul presence of Pithom Eldritch.

Leapside appeared to be an interesting combination of a modern and a medieval city. Oases complete with water features and with tall trees and flowering bushes invited travelers to turn aside to rest and refresh themselves along the length of the pebbled main street. The towering wall rose six stories above grassy, rocky, or brushy banks surrounding it.

Double brass gates three stories high opened out invitingly and grandly ushered the streams of beings entering and exiting. Smaller doors, one on each side of the main entrance, stood closed to traffic. Modern, sleek skyscrapers towered inside the walls. Not one motorized vehicle appeared.

Music from unseen instruments expressed a flood of sound through the massive brass gates. It united human and animal sounds of travelers on the road into the controlled chaos of flourishing life in the city beyond the entrance. The mood of the moving crowd exuded optimistic purpose.

Costumes, briefcases, burdens, tools and conveyances were as varied as the music and life forms bustling, strolling or plodding along. Like the music and other sounds, the colors were rich and felt other-dimensional.

For the first time, Yancey saw other Endi's. Some pulled massive loads. Others, it was obvious, were pets or superior transportation. She laughed to discover Tax was on the smallish side.

Some in the town knew Trenell. They would come up, and he would touch them or merely make eye contact. Some were friends; love shone from their eyes. Four visitors, Yancey saw, were healed somehow without fanfare, only a bowing of the head or a pressing of his hand for thanks.

Most of these industrious city dwellers seemed youthful in countenance. Culture, custom, business or self-focus—Yancey couldn't tell what made them miss what was going on in their midst, but so it was. *Mmmnn, I was like that back on Earth—never seeing Him,* she thought.

After navigating a series of streets decreasing steadily in size, Trenell took the lead while Tax formed their rearguard. Miranda seemed as excited as a child and told Yancey what fun they were going to have shopping. Yancey couldn't help but grin at her animation.

Leapside was vast. They walked for over twenty minutes and arrived at a generous, modern home built into the massive city wall. The silvery metal front climbed the wall's six stories to end in a pointed gable.

It proved more spacious inside than first impressions had suggested. Miranda explained that Trenell always stayed with this couple when he was in town.

Trenell introduced Sam and Pella Austen, who appeared to be in their mid-twenties. They greeted her with warm hugs that communicated "Family" at once.

Trenell, Miranda, and Tax were next. Tax had to duck her head to stand anywhere on the first floor except the foyer. The ceiling was a light panel obviously solar.

The remainder of the house climbed the six stories to the top of the wall. Here, the Austens maintained a generous kitchen garden and enjoyed a sheltered deck shaded by real but low trees. Pella their hostess showed Yancey to a room close to the unexpected oasis.

The other most significant feature of the fabulous house was a door in the outer city wall. Yancey exclaimed to her mom that she'd be worried about unwanted guests sneaking in. Miranda's tinkling laugh sounded. She replied, "Oh, but only one with a pure heart can see it, and only one with pure hands can open it."

"What? **Mom**, *I* see it."

Her mom grinned. "If you've put your trust in Trenell, you qualify on his merit." Glory beamed from Yancey's face.

Tax came and went freely through the secret, in-plain-sight entrance. Apparently, one with a pure nose could work the lock and handle with no trouble, either. With Tax, the pure heart went without saying.

After three carefree days of fellowship, shopping, and exploring, Miranda said, "Honey, it's time to talk about Leapside." Yancey felt her insides expand with a mixture of unrest and anticipation. Even though she knew his presence remained with her, she wished Trenell had not left yesterday.

Every crewman on the *Hoham* knew to walk more softly than usual around their Captain. To calm himself, Pithom Eldritch torched the whole island when he failed to find Yancey. He lost two sailors to the fire through a careless order he issued. He did not care.

When his prisoner entered with his hands bound, Pithom's hope was for some further clue to help locate the lady in question. The drugged interrogation allowed for true answers to specific questions. Two functions it could not perform, however, were to endow the interrogator with the right questions or to break erroneous replies the subject believed to be true.

Studying him closely from eyes hooded like a snake's, Eldritch commented, "You look fit but thinner, Conductor."

Elbraith remained silent.

"Have you considered that Trenell lied to you?"

Startled at the question that had plagued his weeks of captivity, Elbraith's expression betrayed the truth.

Misunderstanding which lie of Trenell's bothered his prisoner, Pithom felt pleased and proceeded to say, "It's the only way to default a drugged interrogation: the subject must believe what he says is the truth. "

"She was not where you believed she would be, and, despite the formidable storm and odd difficulties we weathered, I can tell you definitively that no ship or watercraft approached or left that island since the *Sunbird* went down. She could not have left after we captured you."

Receiving no reply, Eldritch continued, "The question is where Trenell would have taken her if not to that island? If Trenell did manage to tuck her away somewhere for his own purposes, she probably still waits for him. Since he is, um, unavailable, Lady Yancey is possibly in great danger and all alone. Otherwise, why would her Guide lie to her Conductor?"

Hating himself for listening, Elbraith nevertheless considered this new possibility. It was one he had not thought about. *Where is Yancey? If not to the island Trenell indicated, where could he have taken her? No other land lay close enough for Trenell to have returned the next morning.*

She is safe—Elbraith did not question this any longer. Yet no ship had come to remove her.

Lips quirking, Conductor Elbraith finally spoke: "Perhaps they walked off."

Pithom cut short Elbraith's amusement at his private joke by viciously punching him in the stomach. Elbraith doubled over. Smiling at his now retching prisoner, Pithom mused in his oily voice, "We have gone to great trouble to preserve your looks, Conductor. Bruises on the torso don't deter buyers."

Then to Thomas, the sailor standing guard behind Elbraith, he ordered, "Take him back to his babysitters. Wait. Tell them they have done a good job and give them both an extra ration of rum."

Elbraith's short visit settled Pithom's course of action. *Friction lives in Elbraith's mind toward the departed Guide. Somehow, Trenell got Yancey to Leapside before he died and did not tell her Conductor. The interview went well.*

Planning who might help him locate and acquire his prize, Pithom laid in the coordinates for Downy, an obscure harbor twelve miles from Leapside. He stayed up late on ship-to-shore radio assembling his team. He also contacted their leader.

Finishing around two in the morning, he relaxed back into his chair with a satisfied smile. "We will meet soon, my Yancey. No Conductor or Guide will be there to help you."

Chapter 38—Appearances Versus Reality

Eyes sparkling with admiration, Miranda held a glorious, royal blue cloak with matching long skirt up next to Yancey's face and figure. "Oh, we should add this one. The color does wonders to your eyes and complexion."

Turning to the stall keeper in the open market, Miranda added, "*Niranth lobar*? How much?"

Yancey interrupted with her hand signaling a negative, palm upwards, and said, "No! Mom! I will not wear that color! Let's go!"

Miranda captured her waving hand in mid-motion, stepped between Yancey and the saleswoman, and repeated her question. It was the first time her mother had overridden her wishes on this planet.

Yancey whirled and strode angrily back to Tax, whose huge bulk lay on guard at the entrance to the shambles. Yancey's insides trembled. Her mind crashed. *In a few minutes my mother will walk out, package in hand, and ask "Why not that color?" I do not know.*

Some six hours later and just twelve and a half miles from the shopping area where Miranda had insisted on the blue outfit which so unsettled Yancey, an unsavory character named

Lupas Warnter glided under cover of night into the opulent but externally plain building which served as Pithom Eldritch's base of operations in Downy. In an ordinary looking office in an innocuous back corner of the uninteresting first floor, Lupas placed his thumb in a depression beneath an unremarkable looking desk's rim. The visitor's chair where he sat whisked suddenly from sight.

In Leapside, his usual place of business, Lupas Warnter scraped through his crooked life as a fringe person, not received in respectable circles and required to exit the city walls when the gates closed at eleven each night. To every denizen there his wrinkled old face marked him as an untrustworthy being of dubious character.

Such aged-looking people were barely tolerated in Leapside. The town dealt in departures and promised rosy futures to those allowed to establish residence there. Youthful features were required because they indicated energy, wisdom, integrity, and growth.

The age-prejudice galled him and prevented him from entering the only society he craved: the power people. It did not, however, prevent him from doing business there, the sort of business some of the privileged did not wish to dirty their hands with.

With a heart as atrophied as his normal appearance, Lupas eagerly served as chief spy for the well-respected Head of the Universal Church. Pithom Eldritch paid well and his church was the only hope for healing for Lupas: three surgeries in his lifetime had failed, and his repulsive flesh had slickened, slumped, and finally congealed into even deeper wrinkles within months after each surgical attempt. All three sawbones, as he called them, had experienced mysterious, "accidental" deaths following these failures; after the third demise, no other doctor would treat him.

Four weeks after the third fiasco, Bishop Faldo, head Rector of the Universal Church's branch closest to Leapside, contacted Lupas. Reverend Eldritch's Church was banned from the snooty city, but many of the city's secretly faithful made their way to the prestigious cathedral sitting on a wooded hill within sight of the city walls.

Following four successful, discreet missions, Lupas submitted himself to the first "faith miracle" offered by the Church. It was, of course, actually a "Juvie" transplant from a naïve young girl who believed Bishop Faldo would enlighten her through a secret ceremony for novices. Her tissues had beaten the normal odds for Juvies her age: 60% effectiveness. The Church was, understandably, unwilling to divulge its ghoulish secret.

Unwittingly drugged by the "cup of faith" Faldo had given him, Lupas did not know how he obtained a sixty-percent gain in youthful appearance. *No miracle—no sir,* he reasoned, but it was light-years better than any medico had offered the corrupt Mr. Warnter. Although still wrinkled, he appeared forty years younger. Lupas was hooked.

His Highness, Reverend Eldritch, assured Lupas he could be the recipient of a "more thorough" miracle if he would remain faithful. The thought tickled Lupas.

More seriously, Lupas reasoned, the not-so-good Reverend stayed young enough looking—perhaps Lupas could discover why. Gradually, his steady but secret income from the Church became the backbone of his living.

And Lupas really liked the work. He liked living a secret life, and he liked having a network of powerful people both above and below him. When he was working toward a specific goal, he felt focused and valued. His more youthful look increased his access all over the city.

The disappearing chair came to rest two stories below ground in a bar and reception room where Pithom Eldritch awaited him with two glasses and a new bottle of Tattin, imported liquor which Lupas favored above all others.

Such special preparation foretold a task more delicate than the norm. Face schooled to blandness, Lupas mentally switched to "red alert."

One look confirmed the Rev', as Lupas privately called him, was not his usual serene self. Shrewdly haggling to double the price, Lupas brought news that actually advanced his Highness to a place of excitement so intense, his hands momentarily shook, and Eldritch nearly tipped his drink over.

Such clumsiness was unprecedented. Lupas' own interest rose exponentially, a fact which he carefully concealed. At this he was more successful than his boss. He sipped his drink with real pleasure.

"Yes, Reverend, two new women have arrived in town. They're lodging on the wall with Sam and Pella Austen. Both are exceedingly beautiful and appear to be in their mid-thirties, but I do not think they let the one near any reflective surface."

"I have observed them in the marketplace, and the shorter of the two communicates for both. Sometimes, Mistress Pella accompanies them. They have a favorite tea shop on Ringlet Square. A runt-of-the-litter Endi guards the two new ladies wherever they go."

Pithom sipped his drink and smiled. "Two things need your immediate, personal attention, Mr. Warnter. First, on the eighth day from now, Bustard 28th, on our calendar, Ektan will host a most exhilarating slave auction. We have among the more usual, excellent offerings, a Conductor for sale."

"I have here a list of six highborn and/or rich families which might be interested in so special a servant. Two of these, Rector Faldo will contact. The other four require your discreet and delicate attention. No link to our involvement can occur. Your four target families are widespread. No doubt your considerable network will know how best to proceed." Here Rev. Eldritch smiled, clearly on familiar ground.

"Starting bid, one million cadres—a modest beginning for so promising a prize."
"Questions?"

At Lupas' smiling headshake, his host continued, "There is a second, much more pressing matter."

Whatever this second matter is, it is the source of the good Reverend's high emotion. Lupas smelled money, mayhem, and mystery, an exhilarating trio. Lupas turned his face to reach for his drink to buy a moment's time: *what can be a matter more pressing than a Conductor for sale?*

Reverend Eldritch said, "I have crossed a desert and an ocean, spent more than two dozen crewmen from the *Hoham*, and destroyed a small island in the pursuit of one of the women you have seen."

Eldritch startled Lupas with the bald statement. Normal negotiations never revealed so plain a need. Establishing a bargaining position allowed the employer to retain the upper hand. For Eldritch to speak so bluntly, the stakes in this game had to be astronomical ...*destroyed an island?*

Eldritch flat-lined his lips in a mockery of a smile and, satisfied that Lupas gave him full attention, narrowed his hooded eyes and continued, "She is mine. Her name is Yolanda, Lady Yancey. It is she the Endi guards. One Guide impertinent enough to challenge my right to her lies dead at the bottom of the ocean."

Lupas snapped his glass onto the table, slid to the edge of his seat, and sat, literally, at attention. Killing a Guide meant an operation bigger than the slave markets or the Universal Church. Questions infested his mind like maggots under a dead log.

Eldritch's next words were music, "I will spare no expense to gain her alive. To acquire her, I have already taken great risk, but no foolish risk."

"From you and your agents, I will require the most specific Intel you have ever provided. If a man or woman can be bribed or placed in the Austen home, do so immediately. If either of the other two women you mentioned disappears with her, I will give you the extra female to sell or to keep as you see fit. Additionally, I will triple your normal fee but still pay all expenses, as usual." Lupas raised his eyebrows in appreciative surprise.

"One more thing—success in this enterprise guarantees you your miracle." Lupas gaped. He searched Eldritch's snake-like eyes and saw absolute certainty there. He nodded once to seal the pact.

"No plan for her extraction is to be executed without me. My resources far exceed yours. Eight other skilled men already are on their way here to me at Downy. We will work out times, identities, and places; but they are yours to command. We will use only out-of-town talent."

"We will have only one chance, I think, and we must not fail. The Lady's time here grows short. We must catch her before she leaps."

"I will expect daily reports from you. Bishop Faldo can reach me safely anytime."

"For either your planned time or an emergency like the perfect but unexpected opportunity, you may contact me on this." Eldritch handed Lupas a gray sphere and a modestly embossed, gold ring. Slipping it on, Lupas admired its three medium-sized gemstones, a red, a blue, and a purple.

"Press your thumbnail on red and *voila*! Instant voice link with me."

"Press the blue gem, and the two drivers and the conveyance will come immediately to you."

"The purple is a two-way communication device with your helpers…"

Pithom interrupted himself, "Be careful with that! It's not a toy! Squeeze this gray ball in your hand, and it emits a one-time dose of gas lethal enough to kill even an Endi if administered within four feet of its nose."

Lupas gulped. *That means the Endi is close enough to eat you.*

Eldritch's lips stretched nearly into a smile. "Come over to the desk and meet your crew on holo-vid. The specs for milady's transportation along with the men's locations are in this wallet which I'd like you to trade for your own. Use these wisely."

Lupas did not mention the cost of failure. Eldritch's near-smile covered the matter adequately: *that is, if the Endi does not eat me first.*

Unable to solve the puzzle of Yancey's whereabouts, Elbraith slid into despondency. He refused meals and would not exit his prison.

Being caged was maddening. He, Yancey's Conductor, had been side-lined. *I'm property.* He sat in his cage and rocked back and forth. Mindlessness made the loss of his will bearable, but mindless slaves did not sell well.

At Frog's command, the third shift after Elbraith's interview with the Captain, Lynch began beating the Conductor's cage with a knotted rope. A few of the sturdy wires actually bent from direct hits. Three welts delivered too unexpectedly for him to evade throbbed on his ribcage. Elbraith scuttled to the cage's center and could not help jerking and taking evasive action each time the rope smacked metal.

When Lynch paused for breath, Frog commanded their captive, "Eat yer food; then get out here and clean. Captain liked yer condition, and ye ain't gonter stop exercisin' now. 'Sides, yer beginnin' ta stink real bad again."

Frog, the thinker, accepted Lynch's admiration with a snort as Elbraith ate the food that had been rattled off his plate. Lynch fingered the knots with tender regard as he exited the hold.

Elbraith resumed eating and cleaning and exercising but lost track of time. *What does it matter? I am of no use to God or man—unless I count the tidy latrine and my jailors' and my clean clothes.*

After an unspecified blur of time, sounds of an anchor dropping barely penetrated his consciousness. A few hours later, Frog did.

"We're in port!" He came at the normal shift change. Slapping Lynch's back, he croaked, "Can't be long now! Captain'll wanta move him by night."

Dully, Elbraith conceded his jailors were as heartily sick of his company as he was of himself.

For the first two hours of Frog's watch, Elbraith tried laboriously to climb once again to the lofty heights of paying attention. Perhaps when they transferred him ashore, he might escape.

Frog gave him dinner. After Elbraith ate his normal half, he noticed Frog's pop-eyes focused on him speculatively. When the detestable little man made no move to eat the other half or to let Elbraith out to clean or to exercise, the Conductor chalked it up to being in port. If he had seen the cadaverously thin Saucer doctoring his food a few minutes before it came below deck, Elbraith might have expected what came next.

Instead, shock and disorientation ruled when he woke in a real jail cell. He tried to stand, but its not rocking gave him trouble after his weeks at sea. In a cell next to him, a fellow prisoner, a green-tinged Mulster from the other side of Planet *X*, emitted a high-pitched whistle through the narrow slits that served as his nose.

In Freebon, the widely spoken commercial language of the planet, the Mulster commented, "They must have drugged you enough for three beings. You've been out for two days." It came out, *"Truglar...fi-nay suna...thrusha dinang*/drugged…four suns… three beings," but Elbraith readily grasped the gist. His head felt as if something as big as Tax sat on it.

Elbraith muttered, "Tax!"

The Mulster wrapped fingers like vines around the bars and whiffled with amusement. "Tax" was the same in Freebon. Misunderstanding, he snorted, "I don't know if they charge tax, or not. The sale's in six days. Pay close attention, and when someone buys you, maybe you can find out!"

A select assortment of other beings occupied the cells around him; he seemed to be off-center in a row of six facing six others, each with a single occupant. A few of the assorted beings paced. Some moaned. A couple appeared to sleep. His light-greenish, seven-foot-tall neighbor seemed to be searching for a distraction; Elbraith figured he was it.

Elbraith asked, "Where are we, exactly?" He already knew what sale: it could only be the slave auction. Rumors of the degrading black market extravaganza circulated each year. It had seemed impossible to believe back in Conductor Training, but the manual had listed it as a possible explanation for vanished charges and unexplained disappearances, planet-wide.

The Mulster replied, "Ektan…sewer…Planet X," and punctuated its middle word with a disgusting glob of green, viscous material which it spat onto the floor. Because his neighbor specified the planet, Elbraith deduced he must look even more disoriented than he felt. He agreed, however, that the city that would hold such a barbarous auction would aptly be described as a "sewer."

Their brief, unpleasant chat was interrupted by the arrival of a rumbling dinner cart chugging to the stroke of a two-cylinder engine. When Elbraith opened the silver charger shoved through a slot in his door by a mechanical arm, the sight and smell of wonderful food, well prepared, shocked and overwhelmed his senses.

His stomach, half-starved for months and empty for two drugged days and nights, clenched. He thought he might retch. He sat down to calm himself. The aroma proved irresistible. Cautiously, Elbraith began to eat.

His options seemed clear: if this food was drugged like the last, he would pass out; if he refused to eat, he would die. What was not clear to him was why he elected to live.

His busybody neighbor the Mulster had already snaked four root-like feeding tubes from the vicinity of its wrists into the liquid suspension of nutrients it favored as high cuisine.

After it had greedily sucked down its own sustenance, the being once again turned its attention to Elbraith.

"If you don't want the tea, that is something I would relish."

Elbraith, rather short on friends at the moment, replied, "Can you reach it if I move it next to the bars?"

For answer, a brown, hairy tube snaked out from his neighbor's wrist. Sipping tea seemed to encourage conversation. He extended a second tuberous, cylindrical appendage to within an inch of Elbraith's ear. He whispered information.

"In four days' time, while we feast on the finest of food to groom us for our moment on the block, the exclusive bidders or their agents will tour our cell area to inspect subjects of interest for the auction. They already have videos and live feed available for a price. Preliminary one-on-one inspections, however, go a long way to prevent fraud."

Elbraith examined his cell. "I see no broadcasting device. How do they manage this?"

The Mulster smiled, if the widening of its vertical slit of a mouth was any indication. Through its voice tube the Mulster whispered like a wind soughing through the woods, "Your entire floor and ceiling and myriad insets in your bars are composed of micro-cellular transmitters. Some of the candid shots and noises are utterly repulsive."

Seeing no proof, Elbraith nevertheless felt the immediate dread of ceilings, walls and floors spying and recording his every movement and sound. Every hair on his body stood to attention and quivered with revulsion. He quickly whispered, "How do you know all this?"

"I perform a particular service for Oswalt, our jailor."

"Being by nature a form of plant life, I can absorb odor or smoke and purify the air in this entire building better and faster than the antiquated ventilation system. This allows our keeper to divert the system's energy and sell it to a buyer in the town."

"Oswalt makes a tidy sum; the buyer re-sells a precious, controlled commodity; and I am allowed to stretch my limbs through an opening to the outside."

"Additionally, our jailor fancies himself a fountain of knowledge, and he bears an old and ancient grudge against the chief puppeteer—Eldritch."

With teatime over, the Mulster withdrew both tubes and shaped itself into a compact green rectangle. Elbraith's next thought indicated mild hysteria: *Please, don't panic, but you appear to have slumped into a vegetative state.*

He was sure about the hysteria part when the corny joke triggered thoughts of Yancey and he erupted in loud guffaws that ended in wrenching sobs. Throwing himself on his bunk, Elbraith tried to gather himself. Knowing he was watched and possibly studied by untold numbers of secret eyes unnerved him, and he curled into a fetal ball and slipped off into a vegetative state of his own.

Chapter 39--Recognition

Pella Austen, Yancey's gracious, lavender-haired hostess softly tapped on the entrance to the roof garden Yancey enjoyed as her own. Pella carried a large tea tray. On it lay a three by two-inch, chartreuse rectangle which looked like a common vid translator.

Yancey smiled her welcome and ceased her prayers for Elbraith, who was never far from her mind. She welcomed the cup of tea Pella offered, but her hostess' manner showed she had not come for a pleasant chat.

After a few sips during which Yancey gauged Pella's agitation as high, Yancey asked, "What is it?"

Pella replied, "Today after work Sam found this device in his cloak's inner pocket. He ate at a restaurant, The Diving Cat, where he hung his outer garment on a common clothes stake near the entrance. Anyone who wanted could easily have placed it there."

"Thirty-three clips of eleven other beings are also on this viewing device, but Sam has it set to the three you need to see first. Brace yourself. The three pics are most disturbing, Yancey."

A few moments later, Yancey held the chartreuse device in her hand and looked unmistakably into the upturned face of her Conductor. New lines and a small, fresh scar were noticeable alterations in the dear face.

The second pic showed him unclothed and drastically thinner, from the side; the backdrop, also unmistakable, was the bars of a jail cell.

The third identified itself as an historical clip and showed Elbraith, clothed in his familiar off-white Conductor's garment and up to normal weight, striding confidently along a sidewalk in a brushed-out and thus unidentifiable city. Bidding started at 1,000,000c.

Fat tears rolled down Yancey's cheeks and neck. She breathed raggedly and moaned. Pella gathered her wordlessly into her arms.

Minutes passed. Yancey drew apart and mopped her face on a tea napkin.

"What can you tell me about this, Pella?"

Pella replied, "Sam has done some checking."

When her husband came to join them as if on cue, Yancey's mom came with him.

"It's a black market holo-vid. Not the norm, however, because this one should require 5000 cadres to purchase it."

"Information on the bottom indicates a special viewing day after tomorrow to potential buyers. The device itself serves as an entrance pass to Ektan and to the prison. The vid cost will be subtracted from any purchase over 10,000c on the following day when the slave auction will take place."

Yancey said, "Please, Sam, phone for reservations for dinner at this contact restaurant. Whoever placed this device in your cloak invested 5000c because more money is to be made. That might prove to be the lever we need to help Elbraith."

A flurry of disagreement ensued. Yancey ended it, "If it's a trap, we'll have to plan better than they do."

Her mother offered, "Let's pray about this before we do anything." Sheepishly, Yancey and the Austens bowed their heads.

Forty minutes later, Trenell had not appeared, but his presence was strong with them. Pella and Miranda went off to make reservations for two at the Diving Cat and hold a prayer vigil. Sam and Yancey parted to dress for dinner. Her stomach turned gymnast and practiced cartwheels as she readied herself.

Lupas Warnter felt he deserved a gold medal or two when Sam Austen and his tall, beautiful companion entered The Diving Cat to have an early dinner that night.

He studied Lady Yancey's reflection in the lounge mirror. He saw nothing to warrant Eldritch's desperate commitment.

She appeared to be in her late twenties. Her titian hair was, no doubt, glorious beneath the gold net. Her figure was commendable. At least two other women within his immediate view excelled her in beauty. Mentally, he shrugged.

When it came time for dessert, the waiter whom he bribed delivered his offer to buy coffee and whatever sweet ending they wished. Lupas turned around on the bar stool. When they looked his way where the waiter pointed, Lupas inclined his head slightly. His messenger approached and delivered their offer to join them. Lupas moved smoothly between the tables, arrived at theirs, and introduced himself.

"Good evening. I'm Lupas Warnter, a purveyor of exotic goods."

Lady Yancey said, and her voice was rich and level, "I assume you already know both of us. What can you tell us about the device you left in my friend's cloak this afternoon?"

Lupas liked her businesslike efficiency. She struck exactly the chord he had intended to establish.

Lupas described the vid translator and, following her lead, continued, "Word on the streets of Leapside led me to think you would be interested in viewing and possibly acquiring Number Eight pictured for sale as you saw him. You have set inquiries over the entire city since your arrival here."

Sam clutched Yancey's hand on top of the table and asked Lupas, "What is your position in this matter?"

Lupas passed a legitimate looking business card to Sam and answered, "I am an agent for the auction. If one of the highborn families I contact comes to the viewing, I receive a commission. If one of them makes the actual purchase, I receive another, a very lucrative one, as you might imagine, given the risks of conducting such business with the powerful."

Lupas sat very still in strict self-discipline and sipped his coffee as he absorbed the familiar contempt broadcasting from yet another youthful, patrician face. The contempt was not new; Lupas encountered it every day. He admitted to himself that Sam Austen's expression of it rated a "10."

Lady Yancey's rich contralto broke the silence. "This viewing—it is the day after tomorrow, and you arrange such a thing for a fee?"

Lupas set down his cup and replied, "I require the price of the vid translator plus fifty percent for transportation arrangements. I guarantee you or a companion of choice will arrive in style."

Tersely, Sam spat out, "And her return—how do we guarantee that?"

Lupas replied, "Please note on the card that arrivals and departures must be registered with Leapside Central Bureau. Failure to close the cycle means exile from the city, or worse, if foul play can be proved."

Lupas' insides exulted in the astronomically expensive and elegantly simple application of a custom-made by-pass loop devised by one of Eldritch's crack team to insure the departure would never be registered. His exterior expression remained matter-of-fact and sincere.
Laying a generous tip along with enough money to cover the unordered desserts and, except for his, the untasted coffees, Lupas rose to his feet.

"My contact information is on the card. I will need to hear by six o'clock tomorrow night in order to make travel arrangements. Accommodations on-site can be reserved for the auction next day if the viewing results in an interest in bidding.

Good night. No doubt you have somewhat to consider before making up your minds."

After arriving home and recounting their story, Yancey and Sam joined Pella's and Miranda's prayer efforts. The small team would fast and pray until mid-afternoon tomorrow and then come together to share their impressions.

Yancey wished Trenell would just show up and tell them what to do, but she had the impression this was vital training in walking by faith, not by sight. She shuddered, remembering the cave.

Hopelessness can spur one to dig into what he has discarded. Elbraith's traitor thoughts began to replay Trenell's words: "I will be with you if you believe." He looked around.

"What nonsense!" he muttered to himself.

Some new thoughts came to him. He believed the Mulster's word that micro-cellular cameras provided live-feed of the prisoners despite his fruitless inspection of the bars, ceiling, and floor. Elbraith did not know the Mulster. Still, he believed.

Following this train of thought, Elbraith recited to himself a list of other ideas he believed without having seen. It ranged from electrons to brain cells to the Watcher who is personal.

Some he believed with and some without personal experience. Some he believed because of who had taught him.

On board the *Sunbird*, Elbraith had learned the Watcher is personal. On the *Hoham*, Elbraith had learned he was not in control.

He rehashed the ground. *If I am not in control, and the Watcher is personal, then, judging by my recent and current situations, the Watcher must be very angry at me. Slavery and degradation are not rewards between friends. Does that mean in my former, successful years, the Watcher was NOT angry at me?*

What did I do? Break the rules? When did my life go wrong?

The G.A.L.A. was the night Yancey defied my wishes. I let myself lose track of her, and she came under Trenell's influence. I began losing her the moment HE came on the scene.

Flashbacks to his failure during his separation from Yancey replayed across the screen of his memory. *TRENELL again! Yancey and I were never the same again.*

When I lost her, I lost the purpose of my existence.

Scriptures memorized from the Bible began to pound him like hammer blows. *God demands exclusive worship:* **"Thou shalt have no other gods before me."** Elbraith thought, *I never thought of Yancey like that*, but his insides began to tremble—again—and he could not control the shaking.

I followed the rules! **"Therefore by the deeds of the law there shall no flesh be justified in his sight: for by the law is the knowledge of sin."** In his heart he admitted he'd found it impossible to follow them perfectly.

"For all have sinned, and come short of the glory of God;" The trembling increased. In that moment Elbraith met himself, the fraud.

"That if thou shalt confess with thy mouth the Lord Jesus, and shalt believe in thine heart that God hath raised him from the dead, thou shalt be saved. For with the heart man believeth unto righteousness; and with the mouth confession is made unto salvation. For the scripture saith, 'Whosoever believeth on him shall not be ashamed.'" With this portion came a shattering replay of the lightning bolt that Elbraith had convinced himself killed Trenell for blasphemy.

Again he smelled the sulphur. Again he felt blinded by the flash. In the split second before the *Hoham* crashed into and bisected the *Sunbird*, Elbraith's memory of the little yacht's deck returned. *NO BODY* was what his senses screamed at him—*Trenell vanished UP that lightning bolt!*

If a lightning bolt came into this cell and hit me as it did Trenell, there would be a body. He gasped, "Jesus! Save me! Forgive me my sins!"

Elbraith bowed with his face to the ground. Every bruised muscle and pulled ligament screamed for his attention. Some things Yancey said to him aboard the *Sunbird* came to him: "Some receive faith to heal, and some receive faith to bear the circumstances...God—a Person...buys me out of death and SLAVERY...for life and freedom." *I was a slave to sin before Pithom slated me for the auction!*

Elbraith whispered, "I'd like to be Yours from now on, Lord, no matter what."

Trenell's parting promise came with a Scriptural force that drove him flat to the floor: **"Fear thou not; for I AM with thee: be not dismayed; for I AM thy God..."**

Elbraith felt he'd been trying to read some book or print in the dark. Now, Someone kindly, simply turned on the Light. The sense of an unspeakable Presence expanded his heart with full recognition of Trenell, and the glorious Light revealed the Name, *Jesus*. He didn't know how long he worshiped there in joy before the sense of Light and Presence withdrew, but he wanted it to stay.

Peace spread within him and healed his soul. With it came the certainty: *He's in my heart now and will never leave.*

When he was able, Elbraith climbed into his bunk. He lay there confessing his sins and asking for forgiveness and worshiping his God. Exhausted, he began drifting in and out of sleep and at last, stayed.

The Mulster, curiously observing from the next cell, decided tomorrow, set for the viewing, might provide unexpected sport. Incarceration had proved too stressful. His neighbor had clearly lost his mind.

The fast at the Austen house ended the next afternoon. They reached consensus.

Trusting Lupas Warnter was out of the question.

Posing as a potential buyer at the viewing tomorrow was too dangerous: Yancey would be committing herself into the hands of the mystery being from which all had protected her since her arrival.

Danger, bondage, suffering—the Spirit had guided all four of them independently to Acts 21:11 where a prophet warned Paul that bondage and prison awaited him. All of them agreed that was what waited for her if she tried this dangerous game. Paul went anyway because God called him to go. So would Yancey.

When they came together, each one spoke all this and with anguish of heart agreed. Yancey would leave the safety of their hearts and home and place herself beyond help except by faith.

They contacted Lupas. He would send her transportation at nine in the morning, just after second sunrise. Sam demanded and received assurance he would get an itinerary and a direct code by which to contact Yancey at any time. Payment was half now and half when she returned.

Sam reported gloomily that Lupas had seemed to agree all too readily to the stipulations.

Terminating the call, the three remaining behind agreed to prolong the fast. All would pray. Meanwhile, Pella, Miranda, and Yancey had work to do.

What to wear? Yancey had to appear as one of the rich and famous. Her hair must be styled: for this, Pella made a vid-call, and a styling specialist came and agreed to spend the night. She trimmed and experimented with Yancey's hair while Pella groomed her fingernails and Miranda prepared her garments. Lady Yancey had to look more beautiful than she ever had in her life, and more carefree.

Much of the preparation was instruction from her mom and Pella concerning customs and developing a persona for someone who was obscenely rich. The sophisticated hair dresser was of invaluable aid in these matters.

Being rich was not, it appeared, as easy as it looked.

Chapter 40—Leave-taking

Lupas arrived at 8:52 the next morning in a sleek, black, stretch- hovercraft. In tasteful black and white, a liveried chauffeur sat at the wheel. A matching guard stood at respectful ease by the back.

Lupas knocked politely, made no small talk, and handed Sam the required information and a vid-phone. When Lady Yancey appeared six minutes later, Lupas' eyes widened. When out of habit to high-born ladies, he bowed from the waist, he felt secretly annoyed at his reflexive, servile display. Gauging the small audience's response, however, assured him his instinct was well received. Yancey, her Mother and hosts exchanged goodbyes.

Lupas' annoyance disappeared. Just about anyone would respond so to the Lady he now was helping into her conveyance. She wore a royal blue, long skirt and cloak with a soft hood draped down her back. An elegant white blouse peaked from the cloak as she moved. Her hair was swept up and caught with two jeweled combs.

Although he knew she played a role, it pleased him that she presented herself calmly. Her height, carriage, and youthful good looks gave Lupas second thoughts about why Eldritch was so set on acquiring her for his own.

Lupas' eyes darted nervously around looking for the Endi. He could not know that Tax had exited her private door in the wall the evening before Lupas contacted Sam.

When Lupas actually locked the door behind Yancey, he experienced the single greatest moment of his miserable life thus far. This one woman represented the threshold to the realization of all his dreams.

Aside from his remote, nothing short of a direct hit with a missile could open the hovercraft in which the Lady was now secured. With everyone in place in the vehicle, the fast, black craft glided silently off.

"Too fast" was the thought of Yancey's Mother and friends thus left behind. The mourning band, weighted as they were with the heaviness of their hearts, dragged themselves back into the house.

Sam activated the vid-phone and found it reached nowhere but a replaying, recorded message reporting the non-existence of any such party. Exchanging with the women a look welling with grief, he tossed the useless device onto a table and plodded upstairs.

He headed silently toward his prayer chair to cry to the Lord. Seeing their worst fears confirmed, the two women did likewise.

Yancey was a prisoner.

I have to admit, whoever my captor is, he provides a comfortable prison. Her elegant cell offered no door handles and no visible locks. Darkly tinted windows allowed her to see out. The tufted and buttoned seat cushions were deep and covered in faux suede in a tasteful, dark gray shade.

A small unit on the side walls covered with pearl-gray, watered silk offered cold or hot drinks and snacks. One perfect, red bloom and one warm red blanket offered the only color. A small partition between her seat and the closed-off front of the vehicle opened to a tight but adequate bathroom with a tiny sink.

I need to think. I needn't worry any longer about masquerading as a high-born lady. That's not expected of prisoners, no matter how opulent their cage.

Yancey speculated *if Elbraith actually is in Ektan as advertised, I'm probably about to become another number in the slave auction, not the rich, prospective buyer I tried to play for the viewing.*

Well, Christ came to set prisoners free. For a few minutes Yancey fought fear. God's Word rose in her and won the round.

She reviewed her other assets.

The holo-vid which was supposed to be her entrance pass must now be studied minutely. Information, no matter how insignificant looking, might make a difference. She had a small, complete Bible in her pocket alongside the holo-vid.

In her other pocket was a small journal which contained her mother's final words concerning Leapside. *I can barely wait to read that.*

This morning, for the first time on the planet, Yancey had seen her own reflection. Her mother, especially, seemed excited about this. Her excitement over such a trivial matter compared to their dire circumstances had seemed out of place until Yancey saw herself in the mirror.

Yancey gasped. She looked at herself and then at her three smiling companions in bewilderment. Her reflected image appeared as she had been some sixty years ago—maybe better!

"Is this a trick mirror? This can't be true!" Seeing their deep affection and understanding smiles convinced her it was.

"But, how...?" she continued, "Why did no one tell me? Oh, I had noticed my hair color, my hands, but this?"

"Oh, mother, you did tell me about the age reversal here....I just never considered..."
"Oh," she wailed, "how can I pass unnoticed looking like this?" Under different circumstances, the comment might have been funny.

Her mother replied briskly, "That's why you have a deep hood on your cloak." She continued, "You still haven't remembered these particular blue garments, my Sweet, but you will. Your reaction in the market when I insisted on purchasing them shows your memories are preparing to break through into your conscious mind when the time is right."

At this intriguing point, her escort arrived and conversation stopped.

With furious speed the sea passed by her left window. Yancey laid her head back to think and started with prayer. Her plush cage was soundproof and helped concentration.
She reminded herself, *Jesus is with me.* Then she reached for her mother's journal. She prayed her way through it as well as she could. Elbraith's immediate problem eclipsed her journey to her own goal just now.

Next came the holo-vid. A casual run-through showed a diverse group of beings with a common bond: hopelessness. Yancey began again to pray, this time over each being as she came to his or her pictures.

Closer inspection revealed some details: camera angles indicated a surround-feed; the place was automated; the place appeared escape-proof—there were no windows and only one door providing the sole entrance into the corridor running between the cages where the prisoners languished. The beings were not chained and were thin but healthy looking except for their listless, dejected air; one exception to this appeared to be Elbraith's green neighbor—Yancey did not understand how she knew it, but this green being did not suffer from the depression, fear, and despair visible in the others.

Her lips quirked—*it does look a bit like a green bean, er, being.*

A deep shadow penetrated even her heavily smoked windows and eclipsed the light of day belonging to this mid-morning hour. Pressing her face to the window revealed a border just crossed and falling behind them. It seemed to be the barrier between light and darkness. Although it was composed only of air, the change was as substantial as if it had been a great wall separating two kingdoms.

Yancey's skin crawled right up her back and tried to hide under her hair. This was the border yielding entrance to Ektan.

Lupas Warnter had never been involved in such high drama for such high stakes. Throughout his frustrated, smarmy life, glamour had always been reserved for others. Here, at last, was his time.

Eldritch would have his prize. Lupas would fulfill his role to gain his great reward.

First, however, Lupas simply wanted to luxuriate in one, often-dreamed of, perfect moment with himself—Lupas Warnter—as the supreme player. He wanted, for this one brief moment, to *BE* the one at the center of a great affair. He lusted to show its error to a world that had marginalized him.

Accordingly, Lupas directed his sweet hover-craft to the high-security facility where Conductor Elbraith languished while waiting to be sold. Not until his craft settled with its normal sigh of power relinquished, did Lupas thumb the red gem to inform Eldritch, once again at Downy, that he, Lupas, had delivered the package to the special jail in Ektan.

Lupas stretched internally with glory when Eldritch vehemently cursed because his captive had passed by his current position on the way to his town.

"There was some mis-communication, Pithom"—oh, how Lupas loved using the first name familiarly! "I was informed you would meet us at the Ektan facility." The lie rested on his tongue like the finest Tattin, and he savored it.

Lupas listened with deep gratification as Eldritch expressed his frustration, a temporary lack of control. Watered by his secret victory, frustrated seeds sown by all his inglorious life germinated ambition and grew. A lifetime delusion of Eldritch as all-powerful was poisoned and replaced by this new planting of possibilities. To Pithom, he made not the slightest suggestion that a foundational crack had begun in their relationship.

With perfect, dramatic timing, Lupas interrupted Eldritch's monologue: Lupas' script with himself as star required, at the very least, a dialogue that afforded himself all the best lines. "Eldritch," Lupas said firmly, "your prize is here! I have delivered her into your power. I will hold her safe at Ektan High Security Facility. A slight delay cannot alter our success. Come quickly." With this, he signed off.

Lupas knew better than to reveal his deep pleasure where Eldritch's own team could see and possibly report, but satisfaction streaked through his nervous system. He exulted in power.

Lupas walked over and with his remote, opened Yancey's door. He would keep up her pathetic charade a few more minutes to prolong his small victory. So, he handed her down and respectfully said, "My Lady, the Viewing is this way," and led her to the door to her future.

Chapter 41 –Currents

Elbraith's morning, the same morning as Yancey's departure, began, as did that of all the prisoners in his little wing, with an involuntary, stinging, automated shower. The device rumbled from one cell to the next.

The operation for all cells was the same. Elbraith disrobed to avoid being electrically shocked. Extended wands shooting, in order, jets of hot water, water with liquid soap, and more hot water cleaned both cells and prisoners in one pass.

Then a cell-size, warm blow dry. Robes disappeared by suction and new ones moved into the cells on metal paddles like commercial pizza turners. Rumble to the next cell.

Breakfast came next. *I'm ravenous.* Bowing his head, Elbraith prayed, "Thank you, Father, for the food."

He refused his green neighbor any of his tea until the Mulster whispered he had information. For the sacrifice of one of the precious two cups, the Conductor heard that five viewers were scheduled: four this afternoon, but one mystery lady this morning—a highly irregular occurrence. Oswalt was upset.

I wasted my tea on that one, Elbraith mused to himself. *What difference could any of this make to me?* Elbraith settled on his bunk and began praying for Yancey.

Perhaps an hour later, all bunks retracted into the walls. One either hurriedly stood or was scraped off onto the floor. The door to their wing opened.

Oswalt's obsequious voice preceded his noxious person. Two guards dressed in black stalked behind him and towered above his bald, knobby head.

It was the next person to enter, however, who caught the attention of each prisoner as she passed his or her cell bars. The unimpressive but well-dressed older man who followed her barely merited a glance.

Prisoners on either side of the lady and the older man heard Lupas say to her, "Just down here, *Lady Yancey*, Number Eight." He had hoped for some alarmed response to his sarcastic, masterful tone, or to his fingers hard enough to be bruising and suddenly digging into her elbow, but the oblivious woman focused on the cell and strained only to discern its captive just ahead.

When the two big guards came to parade rest on either side of his cell door, Elbraith suddenly focused on the visitors. He had been stubbornly staring at a fixed point where the bars met the ceiling. What he saw now ripped the breath and part of his heart from him.

"Noooooo!"

He recognized Yancey immediately. Her file, memorized so long ago, held numerous pictures of her from her younger years. Her whole, beautiful countenance lightened when she saw him.

No picture did her justice. Elbraith forgot for a moment where they were; in fact, for a disconcerting split second, it almost seemed they were elsewhere.

A city strange to Planet X…confusion…Yancey's arms around him…her screams and tears. She wore the same blue as she had there. Regret nearly consuming him…the almost-memory slid past.

…the reality of cell bars jerked him back to the horrifying present. As if in slow motion, Elbraith saw Oswalt place his palm on the pad at Cell Door Eight, and the door slide noiselessly to one side.

Despite the two guards, Elbraith would have sprung at the older man who guided Yancey with such obvious force to face him in his cell. Lupas, however, sensing this latest great triumph was not going according to his plan, roughly flung her stumbling straight into the cell and into the Conductor himself.

By reflex, Elbraith caught her instead of trying to demolish his enemy.

To salvage his private victory, Lupas dredged up an exit line, "This, I believe, is the being in question? Enjoy each other while you can. Eldritch arrives within the hour."

Feeling, really, bitterly deflated and much like "Puss 'n' Boots," who ran ahead of his master proclaiming how great and powerful he was, Lupas snarled at Oswalt: "Leave them until Eldritch arrives. The guards stay."

Pithom Eldritch looked at the com-link in his hand with profound surprise: Lupas Warnter, his flunky-for-hire, had just reported bungled orders and then cut the connection on him!

Even as he pressed his henchmen into leaving Downy, Pithom turned that fact over in his mind to consider what response might be needed. No one hung up on him—ever!

Hurriedly settled in his hov-craft behind his driver and personal guard, Eldritch moved on to savor Lupas' report. *Lady Yancey is mine!*

On second thought, Pithom liked it that Lupas had thrown her in with her precious Conductor. *This way, Elbraith will witness his own failure and my triumph. He'll then disappear into whatever bastion of the rich and spoiled to which the auction takes him: poor, throw-away Conductor.* Eldritch snorted in pleasure.

The hov-craft jounced. Eldritch raised his voice: "Winston, tell me how a hov-craft can bounce! What seems to be the trouble?"

His driver of several long years patiently replied, "There seems to be turbulence, Governor Eldritch (a name familiar to natives of Ektan). She's pulling to the south, always out and up toward the sea. Look at the trees on the coastal side."

Annoyed, Eldritch looked. Here and there, but not in a consistent front, the trees on that side looked like angry stallions pulling against the reins holding them earthbound. No doubt, some storm was brewing out to sea. He said no more to his long-suffering driver; both of them knew Winston was the best in the business.

Yancey's forward momentum nearly drove both of them to the cell floor.

Their first words overlapped: "Are you all right?" Their arms tightened unashamedly around each other for a few moments.

Then in anguish Elbraith spoke again, "Oh, Yancey! I had rather be dead than have you here!"

Yancey looked at him, saw unshielded love in his eyes, and replied with youthful spunk, "You really know how to welcome a girl!"

Self-consciously, they stepped out of each other's embrace.

From the Mulster's cell came a hissing sigh, "You humans sure know how to mess up a reunion. I thought I'd at least see a kiss—isn't that what you call it?"

Yancey ignored the audience and said to Elbraith, "This wasn't my Plan A, you know."

Yancey placed her forehead on his shoulder. Elbraith rested his head on hers and stood inhaling the fragrance of her titian hair.

Elbraith tilted her face up to him, stared tenderly as if memorizing her face from the living model, at last, and kissed her long and gently.

A susurration of approval whispered to them from the next cell. Outwardly, they ignored it. *Sassy vegetable!* Yancey thought.

Breaking contact reluctantly, both of them felt shaken by this new season of their relationship. Conductors and their charges never crossed this line, yet neither of them paused to consider the rightness of it, just the newness and the contradictory puzzle of its familiarity.

Moments later, Elbraith groaned, "Why are you here?"

Yancey looked at him speculatively; statements even remotely like the one she was about to make had not been well received in the past. Despite this history, she decided the full truth was the tale to tell. She began with the best part, "The Holy Spirit directed me to come and confirmed it through Mom and my host and hostess in Leapside."

Conscious of the uncertainty of their time, she spoke quickly of her time since leaving the *Sunbird* and omitted nothing of her adventures concerning Trenell. Still watching him carefully, Yancey ended, "The Watcher confirmed to each of us separately that prison and bonds waited for me and that this was his plan."

"So, here I am, Elbraith." She studied his dear face to try to gauge his response.

Elbraith exhaled heavily and swept her closer into his arms. His frame trembled, and Yancey knew he struggled to accept her words and her presence.

She questioned, "What about you?"

Elbraith's outline was brief. She read the humiliation and pain in what he carefully avoided saying.

Then he spoke the words revealing the answer to her friends' and her own day and night prayers, watchings and fasting. "I know Trenell ascended in the lightning, Yancey."

Yancey gasped with delight.

"I discovered the Watcher was angry with me. Last night I asked Jesus to forgive my sins and save my soul. He did it, Yancey! No matter what, I am His now."

Tears welled, no doubt from the river of life swelling within them, and flowed with joy down their faces. They felt the building and their cell shake as if from a mighty blast of air. They hugged, believing their God had sent his approval.

From the next cell, two green nose slits whuffed a disgusted snort of air. If this was how these beings handled joy … The Mulster drew itself into a passive rectangle determined to ignore the next scenes in this disappointing human un-drama.

The mighty blast of air Elbraith and Yancey felt came from an opened door. The wind forced itself into the stale insides of the Ektan High Security Facility and nearly wrenched the door from the hand of Lupas as he held it open for his master.

Hating Eldritch as he did it, Oswalt snapped to attention and said, "Welcome, Governor. Your prize is in Number Eight!" Eldritch flipped his hand imperiously and proceeded down the corridor in front of Oswalt.

Sullenly, Oswalt thought to himself, *Hmmph! I take the rear in my own jail!*

Eldritch did not feel grateful or even exultant as he had anticipated he would at this moment. Instead, he entertained murderous thoughts toward Lupas—Lupas whose bungled timing had exposed him to a very bumpy ride from updrafts that seemed to lie in wait for his hov-craft and from crazy winds that Winston said gusted up to eighty-five miles per hour.

Up, up the craft had been sucked without warning. The first downward plunge had crashed Eldritch—just as if he were a person of no account—face-first into the back of

Winston's seat. Stanching the bloody nose took a few minutes. His garment was stained. He bore an equally undignified, bleeding cut and scraped imprint of the gold braid from the border of that same seatback—this the result of a violent, sudden canting of the craft which nearly grounded them. Eldritch's driver had offered a hanky.

Seeing his abrasions and stained robe, Oswalt did not allow so much as a glimmer of satisfaction until he faced the disgruntled "Governor's" backside. Still, Eldritch felt his scorn.

Lupas followed meekly behind Eldritch and Oswalt. His dark eyes danced with suppressed mirth over his fearless leader's disheveled state. Keeping his head down looked respectful and shielded his dangerous humor from discovery.

Holding the lightly bloodied hanky to his face, Eldritch nearly ruined his own moment of triumph. His mood, however, altered dramatically as he stopped at Cell Number Eight. Two individuals stood in the cramped cell: Yancey, the security for his future, and Elbraith, a satisfying revenge for a part of his past.

With a gesture, Eldritch motioned for Oswalt to place his palm on the pad between the two standing guards, two of Eldritch's favorites loaned to Lupas earlier to help capture his "bird"—*at least Lupas did that part right*—and peered through the opening.

Eldritch's opening words dripped sarcasm, "Is it possible? Love birds?"

"I do not think, Conductor, that such a relationship would be sanctioned by the Rule Book. Rejuvenate charges are so very…vulnerable. Surely, it is taking advantage, leading them to love their only beacon of hope in this otherwise dark world!"

"No, no. I must break this up, for your charge's sake." At this, Eldritch stretched out his hateful hand and sharply commanded, "Come, Lady Yancey! Your destiny no longer lies with this failure!"

Yancey could not stop herself. She shrank back against Elbraith.

Eldritch said to his guard beside him, "If the Lady does not move in the next five seconds, Henry, kindly wound the Conductor in his upper thigh, not to cripple, if you please,!"

Yancey surged to right herself. A moment's thought told Elbraith a false move might cause Yancey harm if he tried to resist superior numbers and weapons. Elbraith schooled himself to immobility.

With a sardonic smile at the rigid Conductor, Pithom hauled Yancey out into the corridor and slammed the bars. He purred, "Henry, give the Lady a hand. She appears a bit unsteady."

Yancey stiffened. She snapped at Eldritch's henchman, "That won't be necessary, thank you."

She looked a last time at Elbraith. His eyes steadied her. With Lupas and Oswalt now leading the way they had come, Yancey turned and walked regally down the corridor between Eldritch and the two guards. The blue cloak billowed as the train of a queen.

With a show of exaggerated outward respect, Oswalt secured the cellblock door behind Eldritch and his burly prison gang. Passing with difficulty through the outer door, which seemed to buck in the hands of Oswalt's men who opened it, the odd party emerged into a world of shockingly black, scudding clouds. Violent gusts of wind threatened to sweep Yancey and Eldritch, the two lightweights, from their feet.

Winston did not even emerge from the hov-craft; he was too busy keeping it roughly in place. The group fought their way into the vehicle. With Lupas behind them in his heavier and so more manageable craft, the two vehicles blasted away from the prison and headed into Ektan where the buildings would afford some barriers to the powerful, horizontal winds.

Winston did not want to think about updrafts among the hovels on the edges of Ektan or about crosswinds around the buildings in the business district. From the harbor side of town pealed sounds like rolling thunder. On the water's horizon, lightning flashed in eerily long strokes if he could believe his eyes at this distance and in his struggle to fly safely.

With relief he finally piloted his sturdy craft into the sunken garage below "Eldritch's Pride," the name so apt for Pithom's lair. Lupas and his burly guards hustled to help Winston close up the garage.

In the hov-craft Eldritch had had restraining bands placed on Yancey's wrists. Now he used them to half-drag her to the elevator to his penthouse quarters above the business floors of Ektan Mining and Shipping.

The two favorite Heavies, Eldritch's pet guards, escorted their boss and his "guest" and stationed themselves one outside and the other inside his penthouse door. Bolts of pain shot up Yancey's arms from the too-tight wrist bands. Eldritch's jerking her by them loosed storms of ice-picks through her nervous system.

Once in his apartment, Eldritch motioned and Tip released her from her agony. Seeming rattled by the buffeting of the storm, Eldritch looked at Yancey's bruised wrists and, vexed with himself, muttered, "No, no, mustn't damage Saint Yancey before her time."

When his ill-favored Sumo-wrestler of a housemaid appeared and inquired about dinner, Yancey surprised herself by finding she was hungry and thirsty. She ordered, as instructed by Eldritch, who seemed suddenly affable, whatever she wanted to eat.

In Eldritch's main quarters, doors and windows to the balcony overlook as well as all other accesses to the outside world were shuttered and barred to keep the storm out and her in. Her host was in a merry mood.

The elevator dinged. At Pithom's nod, Tip, who stood by that entrance, palmed a wall panel. The door opened. In walked Lupas Warnter with an oily smile on his wrinkled, evil face.

Eldritch hoisted a glass and offered his latest guest another. He said to Lupas, "I was very disappointed with you for awhile today, but *All's Well that Ends Well*—isn't that one of your Earth plays, Lady Yancey?"

Yancey eyed him grimly. "I don't think this plot of yours will prove to be a comedy. You have not seen the conclusion of this business yet, Mr. Eldritch."

Eldritch leered at her. "I say the same to you, *Saint* Yancey! You also have yet to see the end—yes, for your sake I should, perhaps, have selected a tragedy."   Then he smiled a smile calculated to make Yancey shudder.

He made a mistake: addressing her as *Saint* was for him a sardonic reference to his evil plans for her demise. For her part, however, Yancey couldn't comprehend why he emphasized her relationship with God. It brought praise to her spirit and great encouragement each time he said it; his sinister smile completely miscarried. If Eldritch had known, he would have gnashed his teeth and cursed his professed cleverness.

Chapter 42—Escape

Elbraith stood praying through Psalm 18. Yancey belonged to God and so did he. She'd been ripped away from him—again! He had never been more thankful for the memorization required in his training manual.

No matter what, I will love YOU, O LORD MY STRENGTH. You are my Rock, my Fortress, my Deliverer, my High Tower. I call upon You, my Lord. Save Yancey and me from our enemies.

Sorrows of death and hell flood me. The ruin I face terrifies me! I call to You, O Lord! I know You hear me! Shake the earth. In Your anger at these beings, make even the hills tremble in fear. Let smoke come out Your nostrils and devouring fire from Your mouth on these wicked ones, Lord! Bow down the heavens and put thick darkness under Your feet!

Fly on the wings of the wind. Come secretly in the darkness of dark waters and thick clouds of the sky! Send hail stones and coals of fire onto Your enemies! Thunder in the heavens! Shoot bolts of lightning and put Your enemies to flight! Open channels of water to wash away their remembrance!

Save us from them, Lord! They are too strong for us! Bring us out into a large place, Lord! By You I can run through a troop and leap over a wall—here, Elbraith paused to

look around at the three sets of bars and the solid wall behind
him.

He commented aloud, "I **believe** You can do anything,
God!"

*You wrap me in Your strength, Lord. You teach my
hands to war. Deliver us from the violent man, Lord. Avenge
us and so many others on Eldritch, Lord! Thank You, Lord!
Bless You for Your mercy! In Jesus' Holy Name, Amen.*

The winds that plagued Eldritch in his latest endeavors
gusted stronger and drove large, rolling waves inland. Dark
waters stretched their fingers past Ektan's ocean-ward borders.
Eldritch, to insure readiness for the whole business with
Yancey, should it take a seaward turn, had ordered
replacements and no shore leave for the *Hoham's* crew.

Austin Poltroon, acting Captain of the *Hoham* had
thousands of leagues of sea experience and had navigated
hundreds of storms as he took "his" ship about her dark
business. Watching the sky with increasing unease, Poltroon
waited at Downy for the orders to return to the safer harbor of
Ektan, from which he had sailed his boss to Port Downy.

He watched the growing storm push increasingly
enormous waves ahead of it. It became clear that Downy, as
rough as the seas were becoming there, was on the perimeter of
the disturbance, with the center concentrating toward Ektan.
Poltroon risked Eldritch's ire by calling to see if his boss had
need of them. Upon discovering that Eldritch had departed by
land to his capitol city, Poltroon felt enormous relief.

Downy's harbor was hidden by a thin spit of vegetation
too low to weather waves over twenty feet high. Six to ten-foot
high waves were already rolling in and tossing the *Hoham* on
her anchor line like some mad helium balloon at the end of its
string; and these waves originated out on the storm's perimeter!

Poltroon signaled up-anchor. They should be able to flank the storm by steaming due north from Downy, away from Ektan. It seemed a good plan.

He set a course due north and away from the darkest concentration of angry clouds. The formidable *Hoham* had weathered seas like this countless times. Gray-black clouds rested on gray sea. Lightning flashes produced thunder like drums pounding signals for the end of the world.

Poltroon put on all speed to race his slaver safely past the activity's farthest reaches. Expecting to pass through, the *Hoham* entered the end of what looked like a bank of storm clouds similar to countless others.

What hurtled upon the *Hoham*, however, was an irresistible force. As it churned across their position, its southbound trajectory offered them no escape.

Hugging the surface of the water, racing dark clouds obscured all vision until it was too late. Not one of the *Hoham's* hardened crew, not Captain Poltroon vigilant on deck, nor Lynch and Frog off-duty and gorging in the gloom of the mess hall, saw the horizontal, rolling tube of water bloating and filling in the secrecy of the low-hanging, obscuring clouds.

The enormous low-pressure system created by warm air passing over the colder ocean surface sucked tons of sea water relentlessly upward. With cruel ease, the maelstrom greedily sucked the *Hoham* along with the sea water forty feet up into the blackness.

Like a gigantic steam roller with its cylinder rolling in reverse, the upward-surging tube of water broke the *Hoham's* ironclad timbers in pieces. The thundering back side of the rolling water dropped broken timbers and raft-sized panels indifferently ripped from sides and decks of Eldritch's once proud ship. In its wake dead bodies churned, the *Hoham's* despicable crew discarded with the other debris.

Some remainders of smashed materials and broken corpses whirled in grotesque captivity to the circling water as it picked up speed and strength. When the winds gained enough power to stand the rolling tube with its grisly freight on end, it would make landfall with its center at Ektan. A tornado six miles across, it would spawn other funnels as casually as an oak tree broadcasts acorns.

In the harbor at Ektan angry water spouts twisted their way upward to serve as auxiliary feeding tubes. The churning blackness of clouds preceded and concealed the approaching death. The spouts' pillars seemed in some demented way to support and conduct the low, funereal black canopy toward the shore—grisly pallbearers for corpses yet to be made.

A mere forty-seven minutes after destroying the *Hoham*, the storm thrust its entire horizontal tube into a vertical position. Storm clouds obscured the monstrous, killer funnel from sight on land as it had at sea.

Momentarily poised on the brink of land, the storm stalled to gather strength. Sucking tons of sea water through its feeding-tube waterspouts did the trick. A mile and a half of wet sea bottom suddenly lay exposed to the air. Whirlpools swarmed in dizzying arrays. When God commands, oceans become bare sand, Scripture says, but Ektan had never read His Word.

Whirling and teetering at first like some grotesque Slinky, miles wide and drunkenly disordered, the funnel gathered itself at last into an effective, deadly pattern. It twisted purposefully toward Ektan as if aimed at a target, which, indeed, it was.

Wind speeds gusting in excess of 200 miles per hour blasted vehicles, animals, beings, anything unfortunate or stupid or drunk enough to be caught in the open, with hail the size of baseballs. Killer waves rushed ashore seeking prey.

To announce its arrival to those farther inland, lightning strikes five to ten miles ahead of the massive center shattered the air along a six-mile front and ignited fires in the city's downtown area. Later, the killer storm would drown the flames in gouts of rain as the land and its buildings ripped tons of seawater from the funnel's swollen esophagus.

Such harbingers announced the core clouds proper, which now made landfall. Apparently impatient with its outriders gulping all the living food, the funnel itself now swallowed its first delicacies onshore in Ektan.

Softened up by thirty-foot waves, what was left of shoddy, clapboard shacks along Ektan's waterfront began to tremble and then to shake. Up and down the waterfront, roofs separated and flapped like grotesque, clumsy bird wings that flew away into the vortex that powered them.

Walls that had withstood waves smashing them like gargantuan fists were wiped from sight as if embarrassed by their suddenly uncovered state. Like the *Hoham's* crew before them, their equally hapless occupants disappeared with them. Their shocked bodies catapulted into furious air to whirl circling in the bowels of the massive system.

Almost as if it liked the flavor, the greedy funnel still hidden in its masking cloud cover whirled farther inland. Having destroyed or devoured all in its path, the monster tornado settled to feeding in the city's heart before advancing to taste what morsels the far side of Ektan might provide.

Lightning on Earth has been measured at temperatures around 54,000 degrees; iron melts at about 2700. A sustained stroke of Earth's lightning lasts 1/10 of a second yet can do tremendous damage.

On Planet X old wives' tales speak of lightning, however, whose strokes endure long enough to melt holes in the planet's surface. All who remembered those old "tales to scare children" were about to find that some old wives deserved more respect than Ektan had ever paid them.

Out in the street, "safe," closed vehicles began developing molten holes in their metal shells. Astonished drivers lost control of their machines. The racket outside and, in some cases, filthy water rushing in through newly created openings pulled those indoors from the depths of their turpitude.

Pedestrians screamed and ran for cover while dodging smoking craters. Debris-laden water surged in between the buildings and brushed running people off their feet.

Lightning strikes lasting one to two full seconds began to liquefy minerals in buildings' structures. Skyscrapers built through the commerce of slavery and company-organized vice slumped and folded; their superstructures collapsed like skeletons whose bones have suddenly melted.

Massive jags of lightning continued to split the darkening sky. Fires broke out. Cheap wood and canvas structures went up like torches and spread sparks to other structures. Dead people began to be ignored in the streets. Each being's credo became, "Save yourself!" Few succeeded.

The gigantic killer remained shielded by low clouds and sheets of rain. Whirling darkness and debris gave the only accurate revelation of the system's true nature; and once visible, it was too late to escape.

Perhaps eight miles past downtown Ektan, the squat, ugly prison that was the Ektan High Security Facility stood impregnable in its polished steel construction. Outside, hail struck the roof. As if seeking entrance, thunder pounded its storm fist on the locked doors.

Prisoners terrorized by sounds of thunder and hail, felt the walls of the cell block shaking. Inside, bluish tinged light played around the cell bars, sometimes arcing. Curses, wails and yells joined the chaos.

Only Oswalt's office section had windows. Hail hammered through a large one and pounded water through the rupture.

To escape the watery invasion, Oswalt and four regular guards came scuttling through the metal door that led to the prisoners' wing. Ignoring the prisoners' curses, they pulled up short and smacked into each other as first one and then the next saw the bluish, eerie lights dancing around the cells. Each cringed from the blue arcs between the bars.

They did not have long to investigate. Blinding light and white-hot heat shot suddenly from the midsection of cells on the right-hand side. "Anybody in that area," one guard yelled at Oswalt, "is a crispy critter fer sure."

The sustained lightning strike, if that is what it was, would most certainly have fried his star boarder, Number Eight, Eldritch's pet. This idea twisted one side of Oswalt's mouth into a briefly pleasurable grimace, and he thought, *Mebbe that's not all bad. If it hurts that snake, it does good to me.*

Pushing their way cautiously to the cell, they saw the outside wall looking as if a powerful blowtorch had peeled its way straight through. No body appeared near the still glowing seam. A small crater lay just below the glowing remnants of the former wall. No doubt the charred remains smoldered in the bottom of this pit.

The fiery condition of everything else in the cell convinced them not to explore. Besides, rain beating through the opening was producing steam as it hit the burning cell interior.

Oswalt yelled over the din of screaming beings at one of the guards and pointed at Cell Nine. He cocked his thumb at the glowing mound of charcoal that had once been his Mulster informant.

Blue flames had destroyed every micron camera, so no record would be retrievable. Oswalt wouldn't have believed his vid-cams about the real action in Cell Eight anyway.

Like the other prisoners, Elbraith felt the jail begin to shake about midway through his prayer and reveled in the raw power of his God. When he finished praying, he sat on his cell floor and felt every molecule in his body must be electrically charged.

Parts of Psalm 78: 50 and 52 passed through his mind: "He prepared a path for His anger....but He brought His people out like a flock." What occurred next, Elbraith believed he dreamed.

With a sudden, tremendous SLAM! the outer wall of his cell disappeared from view in a blinding light brighter than both suns at full strength. Dazzled, he did not see the sustained lightning bolt like a laser peel his smooth metal cell wall inward.

Intellectually, Elbraith reasoned that if any of this were real, he would be a dead man—incinerated by the lightning, if that's what it was. He squinted between his fingers. His Mulster neighbor, quite logically in his dream, had already ignited and was burning in bright orange fire.

As his fantasy unfolded, a giant seam from top to bottom gaped where solid metal had been. Its edges glowed yellow and red, smoldering as liquid metal should. Steam rose from the edges of the huge opening as pounding rain hit them from the outside. Elbraith mentally applauded the dream's detail.

It was not until rain began to wet him that the truth dawned. Elbraith leapt up. Before he could run more than three paces, an enormous, shaggy head with giant fangs that a saber-toothed tiger would envy poked through the opening.

"TAX!"

She let her giant tongue loll a second to show her own pleasure at their reunion. Then she scooped Elbraith up into her mouth. It was a game they had developed on the *Sunbird*. Elbraith remembered Yancey had screamed most satisfyingly when the two schemers had first performed their "gulping" trick for her benefit. The Lady had not been amused.

Jerking away from the hole, Tax was immediately in motion. She loped away with Elbraith peering out from behind her left fang and holding on for dear life. Her lower jaw cavity bordered by its double wall of serrated teeth provided a good brace for his feet and prevented sliding down onto the sharpened points.

Elbraith shouted with laughter as Tax surged ahead through wind and rain with tremendous leaps. Tax seemed to know where she was going. *Quite a feat in a suburb that looks like a war zone.* Elbraith gasped when he saw the black storm system blotting out the horizon along with half of Ektan.

"Yancey!" he shouted. *Downtown is where Eldritch took her!*

Elbraith did not know if the wind velocity distorted his sense of Tax's speed or not, but never had he imagined that even an Endi could cover ground so fast. Trying to focus on any one object as they passed was simply impossible. Water flooded the low places. Tax's massive weight and extended claws held them to the ground, but he felt them rock as her phenomenal muscles flexed against powerful bursts of wind threatening to overthrow them.

*If her foot lands where her claws can gain no purchase…*Elbraith suddenly rejoiced in that split second…*I do not care! We must save Yancey! It seems belonging to Jesus frees one to love others as He loved.*

Chapter 43—A Shift in Power

At *Eldritch's Pride*, Eldritch and Lupas were toasting their mutual success with their fourth glass of Tattin. Supper had been superb. Yancey had eaten heartily but had insisted on water to drink.

Outside, the wind flung itself in great bursts that sought vainly to breach the storm shutters on the floor-to-ceiling glass doors. Rain and thunking hail succeeded no better.

Eldritch, slimmer than Lupas, seemed giddy with success, the Tattin, and the power of the storm marking his day of triumph. Lupas, with a much higher tolerance for the strong liquor, led Eldritch to talk.

Yancey also wanted the answers to the leading statements Lupas fed to the self-proclaimed "Governor." Refusing the liqueur-flavored dessert, Yancey busied herself making tea.

Lupas said, "So, you're calling her 'Saint Yancey.' How come? I thought this deal was scientific business, not religious."

Eldritch smiled. Evil touched his audience. Yancey's horrified ears began to hear her future as planned by her captor. From under her lashes, she looked at Lupas; surely no sane being could approve such an agenda.

To divert her terror a moment later, she quipped to herself, *O.K., so I'm the only sane one in the group.*

Eldritch looked at her with professed sympathy. "Come, Lady Yancey, it's no different on your planet."

"W-What?" she gasped in outrage.

"Oh, come, my dear. You Earthlings clone fetuses and grow embryos for sale as 'research' subjects; and I know, as here, you have a robust trade in the embryonic stem cells of aborted babies—oh, sorry—'tissue' masses, your abortionists call them."

"Harvested eggs to be fertilized provide some women with a living. And that doesn't even include new organs from, shall we say, reluctant donors, now does it?"

Eldritch smiled with feigned innocence that sat grotesquely on his smooth face. "Dear me, now how old *did* you appear when you died back there on civilized earth? Not much older than now, was it? I must say, though, I liked that spiky blond look you maintained there better than this rippling mess."

Yancey's face burned. Every hate-filled word her enemy purred at her was partially true.

"Dad provided anti-aging treatments for me from umbilical cord or legitimate adult stem-cell sources."

Eldritch snorted in disbelief, "Come, we're all adults here and know how the worlds work! You believe the most powerful crime-boss—Daddy dearest—in the tri-metro, Cincinnati area obtained your tissue rejuvenators legally?"

Hotly, Yancey fired back, "My Dad runs the largest adoption agency for live children in the entire central United States of America!"

Lupas whistled and chimed in with "Illegal adoptions? There's good money in live children, too."

Yancey threw her water glass at him. He shocked her by plucking it out of midair as quickly and gracefully as a linebacker grabs a perfect, spiral pass. He smiled a lazy smirk in her direction and set the water glass down without taking his gaze from her.

Lupas now shocked Eldritch. His Segundo was not as much under the influence of the Tattin as himself. He jerked to his feet when the interior door to the penthouse whisked open and the guard stationed outside burst into the room. Not only Eldritch but also the whole building swayed.

"Gov'," the excited guard blurted, "something's wrong out there. Look." He activated the security screen to split images of more than a dozen views feeding from cameras around the building's perimeter.

Violent winds lashed sheets of rain. Lightning flashed impossibly long strokes. *That has to be a malfunction in the equipment,* Eldritch thought. Otherwise, darkness like night prevailed, and it was mid-afternoon.

A white-hot gash opened up as if from a laser torch in the southwest corner of the balcony wall. Struck by the lightning, Eldritch's fat housemaid with the bad attitude evanesced in a repulsive yellow sizzle that burned an ugly black blob onto the floor and ignited the carpet.

Yancey screamed. Lupas grabbed her and shouted, "The garage basement!"

Eldritch ended up behind the two guards behind Lupas and his escaping prize. Right now, it was every man for himself.

Later, he vowed, *they will pay for this outrage. How dare Lupas take Yancey as if he had a right! Even my own guards are not guarding me!*

The fleeing train of people charged down the stairwell-tower. Finding his natural coordination slightly impaired by too much Tattin, Eldritch jerked the shoulder of the nearest guard with a clawed hand and screamed, "You fool!"

The big man turned slightly on the stairwell and let Eldritch pass him. His boss was now located between the other guard and himself in their scramble to safety. Eldritch felt the ham-sized hand of his hindmost protector come under his arm just above his elbow.

The guard propelled him faster downstairs. Eldritch experienced a momentary gratitude but quickly shook off the unfamiliar sensation. They descended two more landings in this furious race.

Another searing jag of fire appeared on the outside wall at the top of floor seventeen just above them. Wind whipped the glowing metal, mixed in pounding rain, and produced steam that blasted its hot breath up the shaft above them.

Yancey thought, *If one of those hits just right, we'll all be crispy critters, or if the steam bursts over us, maybe pot-stickers.* Thoughts of her favorite dumplings did not comfort her just now.

Lupas loosed his hold on Yancey as soon as the fast-moving hulk that was Eldritch's guard—*soon-to-be-ex-guard,* Lupas thought—*maybe I can use that*—had plunged into the stairwell behind him and her with no thought for his boss.

The young woman charged after him. Yancey gathered and twisted her cloak around her left arm to reduce drag from their spiraling progress. Panting and gasping for breath, they slowed their descent about midway.

Hail slammed the reinforced steel walls of their passage and joined battering sounds with the fury of thunder and lightning. With four flights of stairs, including those to the underground garage remaining to navigate, sounds of the tornado engulfed them.

The storm shock rocked their tower. The edifice called *Eldritch's Pride* lost the battle. Winds in excess of 300 mph laid siege to his fortress; previous wounds the lightning and hail had inflicted provided crevices and weak fronts inviting attack.

The distinctive screeching produced by metal overstressing erupted in dying screams. The tracheal stairwell down which they fled shook with the sounds of the storm's victory screech cascading down the tower's stairwell.

Yancey's insides trembled. The whole tower lurched sickeningly above them.

Below them the stairs twisted and spaced themselves apart as if mad at their neighbors. The terrified quartet took the no longer horizontal descents three and four at a time and increasingly risked broken bones from wrong landings.

Lupas provided Yancey with a moving breakfront. She grasped his bobbing shoulder for balance. The first guard, still behind her, roughly propelled Yancey forward and down in giant leaps.

Behind him, Eldritch blocked the second guard from passing and so found himself equally urged and roughly assisted forward by his powerful, soon-to-be-ex-hireling. With each bruising jolt, Eldritch gritted his teeth and wasted precious breath cursing the storm, the heaving stairwell, the swaying building, his guards, Lupas, and Yancey.

Maliciously, he told himself he traveled down this hell with three dead men. Hatred helped him focus. He muttered *sotto voce* for fear his unwilling supporter might hear and throw him away like a used tissue.

The defeated building's top floors avalanched debris. The twisted channel of the tower above them delayed the tons of death cascading down.

Newly warped spots and the arms of stairs sticking out crazily deflected one large portion of the tower's crashing higher floors. Lupas with the help of the burly first guard, who now burst past Yancey, shouldered through the skewed garage door from the tower by brute force.

Behind them with no time to spare, Yancey, Eldritch, and his determined assistant leapt through the beckoning door now hanging by one hinge. The stairwell behind them disappeared under crashing rubble.

Lupas' bulk once more saved Yancey from a bad fall; she landed full-force on him and drove him to his knees. Cursing, he abraded his hands and arms and left bloody spots on pants and pavement where he crashed forward and down.

The guard propelling Eldritch and himself forward took his boss with him as they fell through the door to safety. They landed on a hov-craft. The guard broke the windscreen with his forehead, which began to bleed vigorously as head wounds tend to do.

Hitting the more flexible hood, Eldritch survived a hard knock on the head just at his hairline. The point of contact swelled into a fisted pump-knot.

Eldritch slid like some noxious slug down over the hood's raised medallion. The ornament grabbed him by his plaited braid of hair just above his goose-egg and yanked the offending impediment out by the roots. Fresh blood oozed.

He howled as his body slumped over the front and headed toward the pavement. His pump-knot thwacked on the bumper. Dazed, he sat cussing.

Yancey knew her giggle sounded hysterical, but she couldn't help herself. Temporary safety brought relief, but it was the sight of a long, substantial braid of hair dangling from the aforementioned hov-craft's hood ornament that set her off.

It had so recently graced the head of her captor. *It looks so much better on the car,* she thought, and lost it. The first bursting giggle led to the next, and she doubled over with guffaws. Tears poured down her dirty face.

Lupas and the first guard cast about for a safer place. Sounds of popping rivets, screeching metal, and crashing debris spurred them. Water cascaded in intermittent draperies through rents in the garage basement's ceiling.

The banshee locomotive sound of the killer storm in full force around them started them running. Pushing and half-dragging Yancey roughly before him, Lupas pressed forward to shelter beneath a massive inner arch built as part of the support for the entire building.

If anything could hold through such a storm, it would. He gave not so much as a backward glance at what he now considered his former boss. With equal indifference, the two guards followed Lupas and his captive.

Chapter 44—Pursuit

Tax's progress in the storm was a mission from her Maker. The winds whirled impossibly. Buildings, debris and corpses whirled with them no more than a half mile from where they raced. Fists of hail pummeled the Endi. Angry waters swirled around her knees.

Elbraith now experienced a lengthening of Tax's stride, which he would have thought impossible, given her already stellar pace through the surging waters. *A goal must be in sight.*

Suddenly everything stopped. Elbraith shuddered. *Death means we fail.*

Comparative calm surrounded them on three sides. Elbraith peered from his shelter on her bottom jaw. Rounded darkness with water gushing perhaps six feet deep around Tax's legs confused him.

A sound of impossible proportions ripped above them. The fierce wind scoured the ground in front of the city drain pipe in which he suddenly comprehended they stood. Tax's lowered head surged upward. She roared into the storm. Her song rumbled every molecule in Elbraith's body.

She had surged to safety in the nick of time. Her massive muscles trembled.

She roared still, *in praise to the Watcher*, Elbraith thought, *for deliverance from the maelstrom*. Although the whirling winds above drowned them out, Elbraith shouted with her.

Their drain pipe shelter buried under six feet of ground faced into a cement catch-ditch used for run-off. A mudslide far back in its intestinal course prevented the deepening waters from flowing fully through their haven. Back from the drainpipe's mouth, they stood in relative safety from the black whirling killer scouring Ektan from the planet.

Three majestic verses from Psalm 91 walked then through Elbraith's mind: "Only with thine eyes shalt thou behold and see the reward of the wicked./Because thou hast made the Lord, which is my refuge, even the most High, thy habitation;/There shall no evil befall thee,…"

Moving well back from the entrance, Tax lay down in the water flowing into the drainage ditch. Her tongue stirred in her massive jaws.

Elbraith leapt, did some gymnastics and pulled himself up onto her muzzle. She flicked her ear. Elbraith caught it and climbed up behind. His reward came as she drank deeply, a relief his presence in her mouth had denied her. She shuddered.

Catlike, she cleaned blood from the pads on her platter-sized feet and from her face and body where her tongue could reach them. Redness swirled in the muddy waters.

She closed her eyes to protect her face from small missiles of debris that hurled far enough into their sanctuary to reach them. When the backside of the monster funnel system rolled past them outside their artificial tunnel, Tax shook Elbraith awake in his fur-lined sanctuary. Carefully, he slid once more down onto the grit of Tax's tongue.

Again walled by giant, serrated fangs, he thanked the Watcher she did not like the taste of stale Conductor. He shook the humor from his mind and braced himself again in her maw.

Tax broke through a delta of effluvia some five feet high that had collected at the mouth of their drain tube. She leapt from the drain channel up to normal ground level. *Nothing here looks even near "normal."*

Elbraith prayed for Yancey and for their heavenly Father's help in finding her. Water surged randomly through open spaces or around obscene stacks of rubble. Partial structures and twisted metal tangled with former trees and derelict vehicles to create trash piles from ten to hundreds of feet high. Vegetation and abandoned bodies draped the ruins or merely swirled past in the mindless flood.

A mile of smashed materials would suddenly give way to another scoured area. Some of the rubble, unbalanced from its recent arrival, shed debris or toppled over. Catlike, Tax avoided these, sometimes with giant leaps that nearly flung the Conductor from his rough perch.

Nose always sampling the air, Tax cast for a scent.

Ektan had been evil, yet Elbraith wept with shock at the swiftness of God's righteous judgment. With mournful certainty he understood in his spirit that there had not been even ten righteous people in the whole canker of the city.

Tax's great tail swished; she changed direction and bounded off. Ten minutes, and Tax bowed before a twisted tower so that her jaw brushed the ground. Elbraith leapt down into perhaps a foot of water. *Eldritch's Pride* had stood on the highest ground.

The formerly gleaming, twenty-story tower pointed a stubby, accusing finger at the sky. The three remaining stories left roughly vertical sparked with fizzing electric wires like protesting nerve endings suddenly bared to the painful air. Live wires popped and writhed like Medusa's hair around the remnant. Water spouted from various places in its breached shell. It bled from water pipes broken off but still pumping from the heart of the underground system.

The entrance stood blocked. Tax charged off and disappeared from view around the left side of the massive, ruined building.

Hills of glass shed from the stories' high entrance covered the muddy ground, and marble pillars and blocks littered the place. Twenty feet away to Elbraith's right, the derelict building cast off a slide of crazed glass from a massive former window; deadly spars shot into the ground.

In his spirit Elbraith knew this was where Eldritch had taken Yancey. *If I didn't believe God saves His Own, I'd quit now.*

With a quick prayer and on full alert, the Conductor jogged toward a crack in the foundation. It was far too small for an Endi. Elbraith emerged into the travesty of the once magnificent lobby. Mindful that broken glass might as easily fall inward as outward, and leery of live wires, he trotted swiftly into the interior.

Three parts of the ceiling either lay where it had fallen or tilted at crazy angles where still attached, sometimes precariously, to the superstructure. Cavernous rents crazed the marble veneer of the floor and forced him to run a wide, zigzaging path.

Shattered glass and furniture littered ruined red and gold carpets soggy with mud. Water spurted from a former wall and cascaded through the cracked floor into the garage below.

Elbraith searched for a stairwell to lead him below-ground. The subterranean garage offered the most likely place to begin his search. He reasoned it might be completely under water and thus easy to eliminate. If it was not flooded, its massive pillars would be the best protection that running fugitives might logically seek.

Progress proved hazardous over the slick, tilted flooring. Huge chunks of ceiling debris crashed down in places and obliterated all below them.

Elbraith sprinted and dodged his way toward the right wall, which seemed better preserved than its left-hand counterpart. Midway to his goal, an enormous chunk of floor fell away from his proposed path and landed with a choking, gray cloud of dust. All over the building, materials tumbled with little warning.

Beyond the new cave-in, he saw the door which had been his goal now bent but still shut one-third of its length. *No access from that quarter.*

Disgusted, he veered left. The last twenty feet required him to crawl beneath a gigantic pile of fallen materials. Here the storm had plucked down the floor above him. The peak of the dangerous obstruction boasted broken furniture still shifting.

Dead ends blocked his progress. He moved carefully to avoid precipitating a new avalanche. Going slowly required discipline. His hands and knees trailed blood. Because of the numerous detours, he could not be sure he maintained a course that led to the door he had glimpsed before entering the maze. He would not know until he found the portal whether it would allow access to the stairs.

When he emerged from his tunnel, sweat stung his eyes. Blinking and mopping his forehead with his arm to clear his vision, Elbraith saw the door about fifteen feet from him.

He looked down a narrow, jagged corridor stubbornly holding its space against the wall in defiance of the mess of materials forming it. Even as he grasped what this passage might cost him, debris began to fall in under its own weight.

Elbraith plunged into the thin space. Jagged metal caught him across his right shoulder and blood spurted. Barely noticing, he weaved and dodged his way to the door. A cave-in rumbled behind him. *If the door leads to a closet or refuses to open, God will be rescuing Yancey without his servant Elbraith.*

He wrenched the door open as the mass above and around him began its final shift. Falling into the remains of the stairwell, into relative safety, Elbraith crashed the door shut behind him. Hearing the thunder from the room he had escaped, Elbraith thanked God.

Displaced steps in the crazy stairwell jutted at weird angles like the ribs of a lady's fan wrenched into disorder by some demented hand. Others simply were not there.

Sometimes he crawled. Often he leapt down the stairs over debris or through gaps left above thin air. Ominous darkness quivered above the entrance to the garage; rents in the tower's metal walls offered intermittent light.

His heavenly Father remained the only immovable quantity in his shifting environment. He had never heard of cautious haste, but that is how he proceeded.

Not all of the first floor has caved in. Patches of the garage below remain unburied. Oh, God, keep her alive. He continued his descent.

Governor Eldritch wasted precious breath, a loan from the Watcher to him and all beings, on curses. He cussed Lupas. He cussed the storm. He cussed Yancey, the guards, the darkness, and the pain and fear of his current woebegone state. Predictably, it did no good.

Bleeding and clawing his way to safety, he moved to outrun death *behind* his hireling, his prize, and his own two guards. *This is an outrage! When this ends, they will pay.*

Revenge was the first thought since bashing his head on the hov-craft's hood that comforted and offered clarity. Eldritch hobbled after his companions, *the deserters*!

Lupas herded Yancey, his prize heifer for slaughter, into shelter below the massive arch. Head nods situated the two guards with him into a semi-circle around her, with the solid wall at her back. *She is,* he reasoned, *why I am here. The profit from sales will cover my own reconstruction and the building of the new order—if we live.*

When Eldritch scrabbled up—he seemed to have bruised his ankle in his recent encounter with the hov-craft— Lupas was the one who linked him into the protective layer around Yancey. Lupas and Henry, the guard who had manhandled the woman down the stairwell, grabbed Pithom's arms and assimilated him into the protective half-moon.

Eldritch's splutters drowned in the storm raging outside. "Fool! Put me in the outside ring?" *You lose sight of me as your real future!* Irretrievably locked into place by their arms, Eldritch seethed.

On the far left, outside perimeter of the garage, the silver wall buckled with a shriek in the winds whirling around them. Horrified, they watched the roof avalanche as the sheer weight of the floors above their shelter crashed through.

Vehicles, roof, floor—whole sections disappeared. Furious rain pounded the rubble while mighty arms of wind muscled the upper floors into the hungry vortex that fueled it. They cowered as they looked up at undercarriages sucked aloft. The main body of the storm was passing over.

The noise became unbearable. The wind buffeted the fragile ring of men a quarter of a mile away from the breach in the building. The cave-in rushed toward their spot as if the wind were its hunting dog.

When the imploding structure reached their arch, the gaping exposure to air forked around the supporting arms of their refuge. The cave-in raced around them to each side, like stacked dominoes, for twenty more feet. Their arch held.

Untoppled by the storm, islands like theirs stood here and there the length and breadth of the place. In the spaces between, tilted rubble from the defeated building shifted dangerously. Fires from sparking, thrashing, downed wires sprang up wherever they encountered fuel.

The murderous wind exhausted itself with the last, crashing blow. The freight-train din distanced itself as the monster twister hurried to whirl through and demolish the rest of the town. Slashing rain and lightning strokes sliced mercilessly in its wake.

Yancey's guardian ring stood in silence as she did, shocked and appalled at the violence and the near miss of the caving upper regions. Still believing he led this small band, Eldritch broke their stupor with a growled command, "C'mon!

I'm getting wet!" He grabbed Yancey by the arm and jerked her roughly because no one else moved.

Suddenly blocking Eldritch's path and making no move to follow, Lupas challenged, "Go where, Pithom? How?"

Eldritch found no support, but commanded, "To Storage Bay 13 where my city patrol keeps their riot-control vehicles. Three arches converge in that section, and the walls are reinforced to withstand bombs from disgruntled citizens. C'mon."

He looked with hard insolence at Lupas standing in his way. What passed over his hireling's lips could not be termed a smile, but they stretched a fraction of a second into some inscrutable expression.

Lupas remarked, "By all means, Gov,'" and stepped back. Eldritch hid his distress as Henry and Tip—Eldritch suddenly remembered Guard Number Two's moniker—both looked at Lupas for their lead, not him.

Murderous frustration pricked him. His head hurt. Once again, he jerked Yancey. This time Tip caught her by the shoulders and prevented a fall to her knees right where Eldritch had intended to hurl her as a demo.

Lupas snapped, "Try not to damage the goods, *Pithom*! Bruised tissue requires time to regenerate." Eldritch glared at him. With his former boss towing Yancey, Lupas dropped behind.

Yancey replaced her rainproof hood—bless her Mother for insisting on the waterproof, blue cloak—and re-wrapped herself closely in its folds. Although Tip looked at her like the rescued merchandise she was to him, she whispered, "Thank you," for sparing her from a hard fall.

Eldritch snarled at Tip, "You seem to like to handle her! Keep her safe, then!" and began leading his rebellious procession easterly along the most sheltered ways he could find. It did no good. They had to thread their way among massive debris, which forced them in and out of the knifing rain.

Yancey remained the least impacted. Her trusty cloak apparently was cousins with the silvery jumpsuits of her early days on *Planet X*. Still, without Tip's alert assistance, she would have stumbled and fallen many times.

Eldritch moved from shelter to shelter. These were chosen on the basis of only one criterion: Was there room enough for Eldritch? The quartet's exposure to the deluge increased with every stop. The wind buffeted them, blowing in the backlash in gusts in excess of 100 miles per hour.

If I just spread my cloak, Lord, would I fly? Yancey thought. She couldn't have done this even if she had been serious: Tip, Henry, and Lupas formed a solid human chain with her as an unwilling link.

After torturous progress due not only to weather but also to dead ends among the shifting, falling, and sometimes floating debris, Eldritch's body language informed them he had seen something. The rain began to let up, but patches of garage, now appearing as some twisted, open-air theatre, ran in flooding water often reaching above their knees. Smashed relics of hov-crafts charged down these like guided missiles.

All of them could now plainly see the remnants of a formerly all-black number *13* painted on a giant pillar ahead. Rounding an irregular corner revealed one last, major obstacle to reaching their goal. A raging, waist-deep river with debris both large and small rushed between them and the cluster of large pillars that Eldritch had described.

Yancey thought, *if God the Watcher intended to kill me, He wouldn't have to go to all this trouble. I was already dead when He started. He knows how to save the godly.* As she gazed on the river, she was the only one not rattled by the fear of death. *I'm too tired to rattle now, anyway, Lord.*

The Watcher spoke in her heart verses she had, in love, memorized: Isaiah 43:2—"When you pass through the waters I will be with you, and through the rivers they shall not overwhelm you...3—For I AM the LORD your GOD...4—Because you are precious in My sight, and honored, and I love you, I give men in return for you and peoples in exchange for your life. 5—Fear not, for I AM with you..."

Eldritch caught the look of serenity on her face. A look of shrewdness crossed his. He refused to acknowledge the existence of any power greater than himself; however, in his vast years as Chief Shaman in his bogus church, he had sacrificed many others to idols or to fellow clients. Numerous beings who died well clung to a profession of faith in what they called God. Some he had tortured for fun to see if they would recant.

What caught his attention as he gazed at Yancey was the remembrance of a file titled, "Phenomena." He had collected reports of such incidents through centuries of his "church's" history.

Events had not always unfolded as his "church" fathers planned them: beings escaped from impossible incarcerations; resurrections had happened in rare cases; healings had occurred in response to prayer to this Deity never sanctioned by *his* outfit.

Now he roughly snatched Yancey from her place between the two guards as Lupas looked on with surprise. Tip, without thinking, moved to right her and placed his great catcher's mitten of a hand on her back to steady her. He stood at arm's length to avoid Eldritch and found success, for his High and Mightiness ignored him.

Eldritch growled, "Touch the water with your cloak!"

Yancey's mouth fell open. He bruised her arm as he propelled her forward toward the filthy, rushing waters. Yancey looked over her shoulder at him and saw a madman on the brink of losing the one thread of sanity that remained.

Too tired to think, Yancey unwrapped herself and extended the corner of her cloak into the muddy torrent. The waters to her left began piling up like a heap. Henry, Tip, and

Lupas were more terrified by this than they had been by the prospect of crossing.

Eldritch, however, let out a scream of triumph and hoisted his fist as if he had performed the miracle himself. He wrapped his arm around Yancey and half dragged her across the suddenly dry space. Even his elation could not prevent him from nervously craning his neck around and up at the waters and debris piled to a height well above their heads.

So roughly hustled, Yancey stared at this incredible phenomenon but managed to say, "Thank You, Jesus." Only much later would she remember II Kings 2:14 and Elisha and shout for joy.

Immediately, Tip and Lupas leapt in close behind them. Henry stood trembling, for a few moments paralyzed by fear.

As the others were near reaching the other side, Henry yelled, "Eldritch! My lord! Wait for me!" Henry's original allegiance had just returned and then escalated to worship. The big guard leapt into the dry zone and charged to follow his restored leader.

Eldritch soaked up the adoration even as he scuttled with Yancey in tow to less supernatural security on the other side. Yancey, with Eldritch clinging to her like a limpet, stepped out from the water's path.

No more than a step behind them, Lupas leapt out alongside Tip with no time to spare. They only had time enough to hear Henry's scream as the ceiling-high heap with its deadly freight crashed down upon him. The muddy water engulfed its latest flotsam; not one of them glimpsed his dead body as it tumbled away and out of sight.

Two parking areas away, with his direction confused by debris, Elbraith heard the scream and picked up the trail he feared he might never find. He loped off.

Outside the broken structure, a pair of enormous ears twitched and focused on the first human sound they had heard since parting from the Conductor. Tax loped off to locate the source.

Eldritch cursed Henry's stupidity. Shaken by the crossing experience in spite of himself, Eldritch jerked Yancey savagely.

When she pitched forward, he dropped her arm to let her fall. Tip, however, once again saved her from physical harm. He menacingly imposed his six-foot, seven-inch, 247-pound bulk between her and Eldritch.

Quietly, Tip offered, "Why don't you lead, Sir? I'll make sure Lady Yancey doesn't injure herself and harm our livelihood."

Eldritch snarled at Tip's hulking insolence. He ground his teeth. He darted his eyes to Lupas, who watched with a lupine hunger to see what Eldritch would do. Eldritch nodded curtly to preserve the illusion that he was still in charge.

He lusted to murder these two insubordinate nobodies. *Now's not the time. I have to get them both at once, or lose the game.*

Eldritch led toward Storage Bay 13 although any of them could have done so by now. The mountain of muscle and Saint Yancey, his little gold mine, came in the middle. Lupas trailed watchfully at a distance.

Low-voiced, Tip leaned down to Yancey and whispered, "Lady, what happened back there with the water?"

Yancey answered, "God stopped the water because I belong to Him in Jesus Christ."

Tip whispered, "I want that, too."

Glory dawned on her face.

Yancey whispered, "Ask God to forgive you for your sins and make you new. At the end, say, 'In Jesus' Name, Thank You for saving me, Lord. I'm Your man, now. Amen." Tip looked at her face and eyes for a few moments. He saw that it was that simple.

He whispered the prayer. Something like blossoming opened around the area of his heart and flooded all the way out to his toes and fingertips.

I know Jesus, and He is good. It was a clean freedom, a pure goodness—and Tip had never experienced either before. *I am new, just like she said. Why, I belong to Someone; and He has given Himself to me. Ahhh, He...why, He...loves me. How could I not know that before?*

Silent tears streamed down his stubbly jaw. Yancey, too, had tears rolling unheeded. A third One walked together with them, and both of them knew it.

Lupas' attention strayed for a moment away from Eldritch and refocused on the guard and the prize between himself and his former leader. Their backs were toward him. He scowled, sensing some undesirable undercurrent between the soldier and his charge.

Allowing him no time to investigate his observation, however, Eldritch snapped, "Lupas! Front and center! This is right up your alley!"

The slur was not lost on Lupas. It was an old-fashioned lock that needed to be picked. Burglars were the low end of the crime food chain, barely above pickpockets. Sneering at Eldritch, Lupas opened it faster than someone with a key might have managed.

Brusquely, Lupas lofted the overhead door and stepped through ahead of Eldritch. Gauging Eldritch's response correctly, Lupas pivoted like a dancer and grabbed the laser pistol that appeared in the former Guide's hand.

Eldritch fought more strongly than Lupas expected.

Nevertheless, Lupas' superior bulk turned the tide. Forcing the pistol up toward the Guide's own face, Lupas depressed Eldritch's finger on the trigger.

One-third of Eldritch's facial skin began to bubble and sizzle. A swath of braided hair disappeared; the flames blackened his scalp beneath and commenced spreading.

Screaming, Eldritch broke away beating his face and hair. Satisfied, Lupas smiled and retrieved the weapon from the floor. *I have plans for you, and they do not immediately include death.*

He pulled a half-full water bottle from his inner pocket, snagged the gyrating Eldritch's arm, and doused the man's still burning skull and what was left of his face. Both skin and brittle blackened hair sloughed off while Eldritch screamed.

From around his waist where his robes always concealed it, Eldritch clawed at an invisible pouch. In agony, he snapped open a med-kit and gave himself a shot. It was simple to see when the serum kicked in.

Eldritch looked now at Lupas with the only good eye remaining. His mouth twisted up, and he could barely form intelligible words. He raised his arm and jerked his hand palm down in a salute of surrender.

Despite the gesture, murder sat invisible on Eldritch's shoulder: *Just wait, Lupas.*

Lupas pointed to a strike vehicle the size of a small tank on Earth and equipped with a front-end loader. Amused at Eldritch's hasty salute, he experienced an indescribable bolt of pure power when the former Mr. High and Mighty backed away to take the place Lupas indicated.

The king is dead. Long live the king!

Lupas turned to find Yancey and Tip, whom he mentally was commending for prudently keeping the merchandise away from the line of fire. Except, they were not there.

With a roar, Lupas scrambled up to the control seat next to Eldritch. He pressed the starter. The vehicle roared to life. He ground the gears into submission much as he planned to do with the escaped guard. The tank surged forward with him and Eldritch once again, even if only temporarily, on the same team.

Chapter 45—One Giant Leap

Tip and Yancey stopped well back from the overhead garage door when Eldritch growled for Lupas to come pick the lock. As the latter stomped forward, they slipped backward. When the fight erupted, they ran hard to the left and turned a corner to put a great pile of rubble between them and the combatants. Their goal was an outside wall with a rent or hole in it.

The fifth turn they made scared three people and nearly set two of them to battle. Yancey prevented the latter by a joyous leap onto the new third party with a glad shout: "Elbraith!"

Tip curtailed the affectionate reunion by booming, "Lady!" Pulled back to their current reality, Yancey made hasty introductions.

An echoing thunder of repeated roaring came to their ears from a spot outside the wall to their right. Yancey and Elbraith shouted, "Tax!"

Tip had been briefed on the possibility of fighting an Endi. Lupas had said, sarcastically echoing Eldritch, who did not expect to encounter the giant beast himself, "Don't worry, Tip, it's a small one!" Fervently, Tip hoped the animal got the message he'd changed sides.

Yancey and Elbraith set off running. Only the sound behind him could give Tip's feet wings and rush him toward an Endi: the engine signature of an assault tank.

Not knowing the direction the fugitives had taken, Lupas and Eldritch veered toward a deep rent ahead in the outer wall—a half-mile south of the escapees' true target. They blasted through or raced around blockages. When they reached the hole, they reconnoitered but did not see their prey. The broken wall twisted to the pavement and blocked visibility.

Before Lupas knew what Eldritch was doing, his former boss reached past him and killed the engine. With an imperious gesture fitting his former state, Eldritch motioned Lupas to silence. Catching the idea, Lupas complied. There was a sound, all right.

The thunderous sound popped gooseflesh on their skin. Rolls and rolls of roaring that only an Endi could produce broke over them like pounding surf. Horror for the moment blocked the enmity between them.

From his ruined mouth, Eldritch grunted and frantically pantomimed. Repeatedly, he reached into his garment, then thrust his empty hand upward. Lupas scowled. Eldritch poked him hard with his forefinger and repeated the powerful gesture.

Finally, Lupas' hand dived into his own pocket and emerged holding the container with poison gas designed to kill an Endi.

Restarting the engine, Lupas slammed the sphere into Eldritch's hand and blasted toward the terrifying bellows they heard. That Eldritch grimly held onto it was a powerful mark of their changed relationship.

Tax listened. Small but clear to her marvelous ears came the cry, "Tax!" She unsheathed her nine-inch claws and worked at widening the fissure before her in the wall. Another sound prodded her: she and heavy machinery had long been enemies, and from her right she heard a powerful engine tearing toward her.

Trotting, Tip led. Elbraith traveled with laser pistol drawn to protect them rearward. He marveled at the unquestioning response of the gruff soldier to the beautiful woman between them.

When they reached the wall, they saw the great saber tooth, part of the muzzle, and an enormous golden eye through an opening in the twisted shell of the building.

Tip faltered.

Yancey surged past him yelling, "Oh, Tax! Tax!"

Elbraith snatched the big man's arm and yelled, "Come on!" Tip stumbled along with him.

Yancey leapt through the fissure Tax had widened. Elbraith shoved Tip behind her and jumped through to the outside himself.

Incredible after the murderous storm and the nightmare interior they had just exited, clear blue sky pressed down on them. Yancey's cloak blended into the cerulean atmosphere.

Tax shocked them all. She leapt mightily into the air and landed with her tense body towering sideways above them. A battle roar wrung her sides. Straight toward the defiant Endi, Lupas and an unrecognizable co-driver charged. The assault tank closed at sixty miles an hour, assault blade thrust forward and whirling.

Elbraith grabbed Yancey's hand and pulled her to shelter behind a concrete slab. Tip dove for cover with them while the armored enemy closed on the enraged she-cat.

From one hundred feet away, the charging juggernaut raked Tax's hindquarters with its laser cannon. The sickly odor of singed fur and burnt flesh immediately filled the air. She leapt avoiding three other bursts and landed atop her mechanized enemy. Its steel skin ripped by flashing incisors peeled like a sardine can's lid.

Elbraith hustled Yancey from one protection to another. He and Tip shared one goal: Lady Yancey must be spirited away to safety. Adrenaline empowered both men: obstacles were torn from their way, or Yancey was propelled up or around by strong hands. Only glimpses of the Endi versus machine battle appeared as they ran for their lives.

With the armored top-shield peeled back, Tax raked her extended claws through the exposed cab. The villains inside barely escaped. Lupas and his unrecognizable companion plunged from their seats and down among the foot controls.

Tax dived through the opening after Lupas: cat and mouse. He would be eaten alive or impaled on the spear of her incisor.

Instead, the maimed companion lobbed a grenade at the Endi. A purple flume of gas burst from the gray sphere and exploded in her mouth. Tax had no chance to withdraw her head.

One moment, she was righteous, snarling fury triumphant. The next, she crashed to the vehicle's top; her massive size and weight pulled her and she slipped to the ground, defeated. Her powerful body lay twitching, rippling with convulsions. Her great, golden eyes rolled back.

Yancey jerked free from her protectors and unbelieving, watched Tax die, her great tongue, black and pink, lolling on the churned-up ground.

Yancey screamed, "No-ooo, Ta-aax!"

"Not you! Ta-aax!" Yancey wailed. Tip and Elbraith grabbed her and forced her behind the nearest debris.

Seeing Yancey stopped her enemies' unholy jubilation over the fallen Endi. They yelled, "We've got her!"

Lupas and Pithom re-booted their machine. The two remaining threats to their plans must be destroyed. The hate-filled duo slammed the armored vehicle into gear and raged toward the shelter of their turn-coat guard and the slave-bait Conductor.

Professional that he was, Tip opened rapid, covering fire as Elbraith sprinted with Yancey across the clear space leading to the next protection. The crack guard's third shot creased Lupas, but Lupas' laser cannon burned through the big guard's heart and dropped him like a log.

Eldritch lusted to murder only two beings more than he wished to kill Lupas. One lay dead, his body still smoking. Grabbing a laser rifle from its cradle, Eldritch took careful aim with his one good eye at the Conductor whom he hated. *An easy target if you keep shielding the lady.*

Pulling the trigger with careful deliberation, Eldritch felt purest pleasure when the former Conductor dropped to the ground as if smashed by some giant fist, *my fist.* Eldritch's deformed face twisted, triumphant in hate.

He savored a moment too long. Rolling to his side to finish Lupas, he found himself looking down the barrel of his intended victim's weapon.

Lupas snarled and motioned with his laser pistol. Eldritch dropped his weapon.

With a wrenching scream, their now uncontested prize flung her body onto the ground across her downed Conductor.

Lupas' mouth quirked. He ruled the field. He would enjoy the scene. Motioning with the pistol to his reluctant, glowering servitor, Lupas prodded Eldritch. They climbed out to go claim their prize.

As Yancey swooped down on Elbraith, his beautiful eyes fluttered open. Yancey yelled, "Daniel!" *I wore the blue cloak and held him the first time he died!* Her blue cloak settled over them and shut out what was now.

Yancey held him in her arms and cried aloud into the air, "Jesus! Oh, dear God, help!" Daniel breathed out, "Jesus." He whose Name is above all names could spare their lives, or not; they belonged to Him, HERE, on this puzzling planet with this inexplicable end to all their efforts.

Yancey's next thought came from her Lord: "Living water!" She fumbled, found the bottle, and poured barrier water into her beloved's lips.

Former Governor Eldritch later grunted agreement as Lupas described the scene. Yancey's cloak blotted their view of their fallen foe and the Lady Yancey. With the premonition of defeat and helpless to prevent it, they watched the billowing garment become indistinguishable from blue air. Tax's and Tip's bodies also melted from sight.

The blink of an eye, and both the living and the dead merged with the blue, blue sky under the double suns and vanished. Lupas and Eldritch looked around stupidly, not believing the messages their eyes were sending to their brains.

Eldritch hissed hate-filled words through his broken mouth, and Lupas heard him: "She leaped! No..." Eldritch's ruined face contorted.

Lupas thought for a moment that his companion's mind had shattered like his face, for Eldritch looked around them wildly and with great terror rasped, "Trenell! Do you see him?"

Lupas irrationally feared for one second the name Eldritch spoke. The next second Lupas was grasping frantically for his own sanity.

In this already crazy scene, he discerned in the vacant, blue air a large, gently undulating face of incredible evil turned toward him and his battered ex-boss. He shook off the impression as a dog might rid itself of water. Surely, the apparition resulted from the weird angle of the two suns by whose light he had already witnessed impossibilities in these moments!

Furious about his incomprehensible loss of the lady, he savagely muttered to himself, "Whacked, that's it...whacked by all this weirdness!"

With contempt Lupas looked at Eldritch doubled in on himself and dully moaning what seemed to be, "She leaped..."

One more moment and Lupas squinted, looking again for the oil-slick vision. Seeing nothing, he shrugged it off as a trick of his mind—*things are weird enough already.* He began brutally, systematically kicking the cringing Eldritch; it helped center them both once again in the real world.

Everything around them was empty. Ektan had disappeared except for a wall here or a heap of debris there. This Lupas could see from their hilltop.

The tangled mess that had been *Eldritch's Pride* reassured them in some measure. Ruins from a giant storm were something they could understand. Lupas comforted himself, *Much remains.*

He tightened his grip on the laser pistol again pointed at his former boss. *This,* he grinned smugly to himself, *this is real.* The butt felt solid in his hand. *Oww, my old boss seems to have broken some ribs. Looks painful.* Lupas kicked Pithom one more time and felt better.

An alert observer could have seen a transparent face superimposed, this time on the assault vehicle's windshield. Eldritch was in no state to do so. Lupas only felt renewed power surge through him and ambitions far beyond the former scope of his dreams.

There is, he thought to himself, *about to be a new, more enlightened Leader of the Church Universal; and good ol' deformed Eldritch is gonna grease the way for his successor. This is gonna be fun!*

Lupas missed Fafnir's slick smile before the phantom projection became once again invisible. *Lupas has decided that I, Fafnir, am not real. I love it!* His image wavered out of sight.

Lupas dragged Eldritch and flung him limp, bloody, and whimpering on the seat beside him. He roared off toward the jail, which he suddenly knew was still standing and failed to ask himself how he knew.

Oswalt, the jailer, is good at administration. The best part is that Oswalt hates Eldritch. He should prove a valuable ally. Lupas laughed.

The again invisible Fafnir smiled. *Lupas believes he's finally in control.*

Chapter 46—Transitions are Important

Real-time with Yancey and her fallen beloved blurred from the moment they surrendered to God's will and breathed together the name *Jesus*. She felt them being transported through time and an enormous space: *The Leap*, she thought.

A moment of eternity broke through her current reality. It changed her grief over the dying Elbraith/Daniel cradled in her arms—remembrance of his identity now seemed so clear to her—and of Tip and Tax dead on the ravaged ground. *I'll see them again.*

Joy burst through. *Jesus is here!*

Fear vanished. Sorrow disappeared. Worship, the reasonable response, stirred.

She breathed Him in. Peace settled in her inmost being while the awareness of transcending space and time pressed in on her senses. His peace like a mighty, rolling river wrapped round her. Her heart within her expanded into calm.

Wide-eyed, Yancey huffed, "Lord, the last time we did this time-space thing, I died and woke up on a strange planet in a rejuvenating tank!"

The speed they traveled vied with the sensation of having all the time one could wish. She spoke intimately with her Lord. Yancey sensed He smiled at her comment as if she had successfully performed a complicated calculation.

Fully invited, Yancey posed Him a question, "Why all this, Lord?"

A song, her own personal psalm which had hummed in the Tank, arose in her spirit. Inside her now were lyrics resonating as poetry, pieces of an as yet unfinished masterpiece. *Words! Lord, I knew it had words!*

Yancey reviewed. *I died at age eighty-seven on earth but awoke on a strange planet You created with weird rules and experiences. Dangers and blessings I couldn't recognize until they were over, unknown beings that looked like friends but who really were trying to kill me, and a purpose of my own that I had to learn as I went along—all this I passed through.*

Even living my life backwards did not make for smooth sailing.

The song continued, *And You! You were with me through it all. You love me, but I had to go through all this to know it?*

At this juncture she felt Jesus laugh. In her heart, He sang back, *No. I told you in My Word! You had to go through all this before you'd believe it!*

His music surrounded and permeated her understanding like a perfect composition, matrix of all sound she had heard on Planet *X.* He continued with His counter-melody.

All of you come from Me to a planet you don't know. All the experiences and rules are weird to you. Some beings and some people do want to kill you. But they help you know what is in your heart.

All of you since Adam live life backwards: as sinners you put "me first," not Me. You set up your life's equation wrong and arrive at the wrong answer. My Father brings you to recognize and confess your need for Me and ask Me in. You lived all those decades and missed your life that could be.

I love you that much— all of you, in fact.

So much, I died in your place to raise you up at the end with Me as My Father and I planned all along.

I reached into your time where you had rejected Me and inserted a bit of eternity: it's what I do. My Father draws you, and I save. I AM the only true, alternate reality.

I made you live and freed you from the prison of your future. Your life will be alive, now, and so will your Daniel's.

Both of you are ready to go back! He sang it once more in her spirit: *I love you that much.* The sound of the chorus again felt like laughter, so great was his joy.

A split second later, a little drunk with revelation and still whirling with the Lord through time and space, Yancey erupted with giggles at the thoughts running through her head after His glorious song.

Talk about a non-sequitur! It went something like this: *A common train leaves Seattle and travels to Los Angeles at a speed of 80 miles per hour. Three hours later, a Bullet train also bound for L.A. leaves the same station on the parallel, elevated track; the Bullet train travels at a speed of 230 mph. How long before the Bullet train passes the common train?* Yancey whuffed a puff of sheer merriment.

Here I am zooming faster than both trains put together, and I come up with a math problem? I liked the song better!

"Lord, You made me an English teacher who cringes when I even imagine such a problem. It is just not funny to ask me to solve problems with trains, boats, spaceships, hovercrafts, birds, or slip-overs into eternity—especially while moving so fast with glorious songs and beautiful lights to distract me."

Then suddenly, Yancey gasped, "Ah! I get it! **X**, the unknown quantity! You're it!"

Although increasingly conscious of time passing somewhere up ahead, which it certainly did not seem to be doing wherever *HERE* was, Yancey felt no pressure. She and Elbraith/Daniel, still in her arms, began slowing.

No longer exceeding light speed, they plummeted down, dropped through a dark firmament, and continued falling and falling; glowing orange, lavender and blue painted their trajectory.

She recognized Earth below them, rotating on its axis. *Beautiful—it's so beautiful!*

As this kaleidoscopic whirl through time and space slowed more and brought them nearer their destination, Yancey's most devastating memory demanded freedom from its burial place deep in her psyche. The sense of eternity faded into time.

The precise moment of Daniel's death, which she had suppressed for sixty years, burst into her consciousness. She descended screaming. Tears cascaded down her face, and the wind stream dashed them away.

The answer to a new puzzle arose. *Sixty years before Jason Thomas ended my life with a palm laser,* Daniel *exited to Planet X in his own eternal moment to begin his studies, ironically, as my Conductor.*

I remember wearing the blood-stained blue cloak. Daniel's blood all over it—I burned it and buried the ashes along with the memory.

Will Daniel die again, now on two planets, saving my life?

She screamed one word as they drifted down to the scene that had been: "Jesus!"

Her breath broke on a sob. They settled downward in wavering, slow-motion pantomime, into the dreadful moments when Daniel had died in her arms sixty years ago.

She and Daniel had sat behind and to the right of the lectern where her Dad, the honest, then-Senator Silva, stood to announce his candidacy for President of the United States. The large, enthusiastic crowd of supporters cheered as he raised his arms like a champion.

A motion of her Dad's hand brought her to his side. His beautiful daughter and her young man would help him "milk" the crowd and interest the sentimental vote.

Only, Daniel had seen a flash of light from the barrel of a laser rifle on the seventh floor of the building across from the cheering mob and themselves. He had hurled himself sideways into Yancey, tackling her and propelling her into her Dad. Their trajectory downed her father and saved his life along with Yancey's.

The two eruptions from the sniper's rifle sliced Daniel's chest as his body drove past her. Screaming, Yancey had scrambled, too late, to shield Daniel's body. After one agonized moment, Senator Silva lunged at his living daughter and dragged her down and between their seats at the back of the stage. Three more short blasts ripped the air.

So much was what had been. Superimposed on this greatest tragedy of her life came the knowledge of what came after the funeral.

In that first reality—the one without the saving grace of Jesus—Senator Silva shortly thereafter renounced his bid for President and disappeared from the political scene. Deciding to pursue power through more direct and totally illegal channels, Duke Silva emerged.

His first act was to discover the identity of the assassin. The offered reward for Henry's head became the first grisly bounty the newly ascended Duke Silva had disbursed. These events she now remembered as clearly as her name.

Still clutching Daniel, falling straight through the images in her mind, their bodies descended into real time. Horror stricken, Yancey listened to the ending remarks her Dad and she had labored over in his acceptance speech. Perhaps two minutes remained till history would repeat itself.

In agony, she groaned loudly, "I have to DO something!"

Her Dad at the lectern paused and turned slightly toward her at the interruption. Daniel, once again whole and vital and hers, leaned toward her and whispered, "What?" Her comment bought two seconds.

Her Dad smoothly resumed his speech.

Despite the fact that she had arrived back on earth, Yancey now sat transfixed between two worlds: what had been and what was now. *Wait! Mother is onstage—wha-at? She died when I was seven the first time...it was why Grampa and Gramma moved in...*

Yancey could not move, captive to a new picture show in her mind.

She strained to move, to shout the saving words—she sat paralyzed by a force outside herself. The next two minutes would again play out, scene by scene. *And Mom...here?*

Instead of saving them all as she had dared hope, she would sit in dumb numbness and live it all over again, *somehow worse because my beautiful Mother...* She could not escape any more than a dream figure can escape from a trance.

Stop frame: Daniel squeezes her hand. He looks in her eyes. *Ah...his eyes!*

Stop frame: Dad says, "I wish to announce my candidacy for President of the United States!"

Stop frame: The crowd cheers wildly. Dad half turns and uses the microphone to say, "My lovely family! Come, join me"

Yancey tried to scream, "Down! Get down!" But no sound issued from her.

The next scene...Daniel sees the flash, throws himself to save me, but dies.

Any change to this scenario will have to be by divine intervention. She started frantically to pray. *That's it! JESUS!*

Chapter 47—Aftermath

The last thing in the world that she expected to happen occurred in the next split second.

Roars of laughter erupted from everywhere and rolled through the vast crowd. Thousands of eyes unable to see first-hand glued themselves to the massive screens surrounding the plaza.

Her Dad ceased speaking. Along with the crowd, all on the podium shifted their gaze to the giant screens set up for the rally. At the first hint of disturbance, Tip, her Dad's massive bodyguard, leapt from the edge of the stage and landed solidly in front of Senator Silva, who craned his neck for a glimpse of the screens despite his formidable impediment.

Instead of announcing his candidacy, her Dad joined with the hilarity of the audience. As his hearty laugh boomed through the sound system, it seemed the only death imminent here might be from laughter.

Broken for good from her trancelike prison by this bizarre twist, Yancey's eyes took in the images on the enormous screen immediately to her left. Her gaze traveled up the one-story-tall, brindled image she saw there. Her mouth formed an astonished *O*.

Attracted by shouts and yells from the back of the outdoor assembly, the camera crew quickly abandoned the esteemed, prospective, next President of the United States in mid-sentence. Focusing instead on what they knew would be a-once-in-a-lifetime sensation, they avidly filmed this comic interruption.

Through the crowd scrambled a truly magnificent, brindled Great Dane. From her huge mouth, magnified over and over on the giant screens, three or four streamers of red, white and blue bunting trailed.

Blown up to enormous proportions on screens all around the plaza, the buntings appeared much more spectacular waving over her back than they had on the Senator's limo.

Behind the fugitive lunged a lanky, Ichabod Crane of a man in chauffer's livery. As he yelled at the elusive animal, his lean, huffing cheeks expanded and contracted in giant detail like some indecisive blowfish. He alternated between catching his breath and calling to the prancing Great Dane.

He flailed knobby arms and disarranged his formerly dignified uniform into what looked like disjointed squares and rectangles of cloth on the giant screens. His hat sailed off behind him as he bungled in hot pursuit trying to catch bunting or dog, whichever he might grab first. The bunting slapped him inconsiderately in the face. He swore at the dog. The crowd ate it up.

The audience parted before the gaily adorned, fleeing canine as the Red Sea had for Moses but closed to thwart the angry uniform behind her as if he wore Egyptian garb. This spun out the hilarity. They called advice, encouraging the "nice doggy" and disparaging her frustrated, erstwhile keeper.

Happy slobber flew from her formidable jowls. Huge canines thus becoming visible encouraged the crowd to make way.

The bountiful bunting tangled as it streamed over her back. Helpful crowd members grabbed at it and jerked— anything to get onscreen with this show-stopping, canine sensation. Others began tripping or body-blocking her ineffective, red-faced pursuer.

All camera crews filmed the impromptu parade's enthusiastic progress through the crowd. The images on the multiple vid-screens filled all eyes.

Laughter ruled, except in the domain of the unhappy driver trying to catch her. Tip Reno, the huge guard who headed up the Candidate's personal security team and now shielded him with his own body onstage, roared, "Tax!"

A jubilant microphone wielder bobbed his ten-foot boom in front of the frustrated chauffer just in time to broadcast "Bad dog! Come back! Sit!" The crowd shouted with redoubled laughter and confusing commands of their own, some aimed at the unfortunate driver, who wisely clammed up when his voice went airborne.

Attempting to help the chauffeur catch or herd the strutting Great Dane, numerous other bodyguards charged from other directions through the convulsing crowd. One fell flat on his face, his dilemma caught onscreen by yet another member of the press, and caused the roar of laughter which had finally snapped Yancey from her horror of dread.

The screens displayed the playful tip of the huge, festooned tail as Tax eluded their collective grasps. Each evasion set off laughter from multiplied thousands of throats.

Magnified by the video screens and trotting as if on a mission launched straight at the podium, the already huge animal the color of a mountain lion continued galumphing ahead of the mortified driver and guards. Seeming almost to flirt with their touch, she stayed just out of their reach.

The bunting grew steadily shorter as the crowd grabbed what they could. The dog sailed on.

The animal wriggled with delight as she looked back at her pursuers. She stopped when she outdistanced them, play-bowed, dropped the elusive bunting, and barked thunderously as if encouraging them to hurry up! When they moved or lunged again after her, she grabbed up her colorful trophy and sprang ahead to resume the hilarious parade. Peals of laughter erupted from the delighted crowd.

In a sudden blur of speed, the gigantic dog, tail high, effortlessly launched her mountainous self onto the raised stage and straight at the red-faced bodyguard of the next President and First Lady of the United States.

One, history-altering moment later, two rapid blasts from a laser rifle sliced cleanly through the air just where the two intended victims had been peering around their guard. Tax's body sent Tip and Senator and Mrs. Silva crashing down to the ground with their huge rescuer. Daniel body-blocked Yancey down with them.

Part of a moment passed. Events crashed together in compressed time.

"Laser fire!" people shouted. The crowd panicked. Screams and escaping bodies destroyed camera angles of those onstage. The screens split, most focused now on the stampeding crowd.

With telephoto lenses, however, two cameramen with superb instincts hungrily searched opposite the stage for the skyscraper from which the blasts came. Police on the outside perimeter of the crowd charged and entered the same building.

Tip got his massive hands on the scruff of Tax's neck. Tax wriggled away. Her loose skin rose in his hands and settled back indifferently onto massive shoulders beneath. Looking as if she smiled, Tax's pink and black tongue lolled from her mouth.

Like Tip, expecting a second attempt, Daniel took hold to help move the big animal who had clowned her way to saving her family. Together they budged the massive animal's weight off Yancey's Dad and Mom and hustled them off-stage. Tongue flopping in a happy grin, Tax pranced behind them—*what's all the trouble? I just saved them, didn't I?*

In a few more minutes, with the family sheltered, Tax shook herself nonchalantly. Drool flew everywhere. It did not stop any of them from converging on the huge beast with pats, hugs and "Good Girl's." Tax's rough tongue scoured Yancey's tears from her cheeks.

Yancey's Dad fiercely hugged each member of his family, including Daniel, and helped the massive Tip and four guards he mustered to usher them around the crowd perimeter and into the waiting limo. Their long-suffering chauffeur had straightened his uniform and salvaged what dignity he could. Senator Silva said, "Never mind, Windsor. There'll be a bonus in it for you!"

Settled safely in the armor-plated limo, Yancey thought, *What was it Jesus said? "... freed from the prison of your future" into the "life that could be. I'm the only true, alternate reality."* In this new, revised reality, Yancey motioned to Tip who had boarded with them. "Were you to hand us off to Henry as we exited?"

Tip's slate-gray eyes sharpened under suddenly frowning brows. "How could you know that?"

"I didn't see him, did you? He probably had trouble making his way back through this chaos. Check the tapes, Tip. You won't find him visible. He's the one who was cozied down on the seventh floor of that building opposite us with a sniper rifle all set for Dad, and it wasn't for protection, trust me."

"Right now I bet he's resumed his guise as one of Senator Silva's special guards. In the confusion, no one will ask how he came first on the scene over there."

Tip's countenance hardened. "The Holy Spirit's still got me on 'red-alert'. This must be why. I'll need to prove this on the creep."

Tip switched frequencies on his earpiece. Speaking into a com-link, he called Henry in an excellent imitation of normalcy, totally at odds with his outrage at his hireling's suspected betrayal.

Matter-of-factly, the would-be murderer explained his absence from his post. When that "stupid dog" had charged the stage, Henry reported he had taken a detour to try to help catch her. Caught toward the back of the crowd, Henry said he then rushed the hotel after seeing the flashes.

Tip growled, "Be there in ten," and broke the link. He grabbed two of his men to come and ride home with the family. Two others followed him.

Mad clear through, Tip flashed an amazed look at Tax, "If she hadn't wriggled out of the limo and clowned her way up there …. The Lord sure works in strange ways."

When the big guard jogged purposely off, Yancey remembered Tip had died both other times—one here, one on Planet X—*not this time, please Lord,* she prayed. Peace flooded her soul and she thanked the Lord. Her God had rescued them all.

She and Daniel joined hands there in the limo in front of her family and their new escorts. They bowed their heads and thanked the One Who loved them enough to step from one reality into another to make a way for them to come home to Him and His Father.

Senator Silva watched with a questioning frown. Seeing her two loved ones giving thanks, Yancey's Mother smiled in the glory of answered prayer. *Now, Lord, for my husband,* she thought, and had to stifle her laughter.

Pictures broke through now to Daniel from another reality—sixty years of barren obedience to the Law but without the Lord Himself.

Planet *X? I never seriously considered the possibility, let alone the reality, of an invisible world all around me. It's here, though. Weird.* Daniel ran his hand over his face.

We have life and death adventures. We have a personal enemy, but lots of us don't want to believe he's even there; and he likes it that way.

God watches and breaks through all the time because He loves us. Sometimes it's with hard, painful things that get our attention. Sometimes it's with good. Whatever it is, it's always truth with grace if it's from Him.

Daniel thought all this as he relived his pride, his failure, his sin, and the one thing God required: his surrender.

With wonder, he remembered himself as Elbraith. *Trenell!* Mentally, he dropped to his knees.

Studying Yancey and her blue cloak, soiled and draped around her, Daniel suddenly remembered dying onstage back there in that first reality. Next came memories of scenes from their last battle and their leap from *X* to Earth. Violent death memories—laser blasts slamming him so hard, his hand clutched his chest.

Watching him, Yancey knew *Daniel understands! Thank You, Lord.*

Yancey looked at Daniel's beautiful eyes, perfectly remembered for over six decades. They lit in response to her gaze.

God, she thought, *changes all our realities. I got that lesson in the cave.*

I'm the Senator's daughter, soon to be, if all goes well, the married daughter of the next President of the United States. In her heart she suddenly believed the Lord would change her father as surely as He had her and Daniel.

For some reason, with this thought her eyes sought her mother's. Yancey's heart leapt as she saw the wisdom there. They exchanged a knowing smile.

Oh, I have to find out if Mom remembers our time together. She chuckled at the absurdity of her thoughts: *she's older than I am again.*

Through all this external silence, Senator and Mrs. Silva sat holding hands in a new way. Then, Duke Silva, the ultimate crime-boss who would now never appear, roughed Tax affectionately under her nearest ear.

The Great Dane draped herself in a most catlike position, a favorite habit, over Daniel's and Yancey's laps. Their legs and feet numbed as Senator Silva rubbed Tax's "sweet spot." It was a family joke that if she'd been a feline, she'd purr.

"Tax, my girl," Senator Silva crooned, "you're gonna have steak for a week whether I receive the nomination or not! And that news video's about to become a family heirloom."

Laughing with the rest of them, Daniel shoved Tax off their laps—*fine treatment for a larger-than-life-heroine*—and wrapped his arm around Yancey.

They would be speculating about their grand adventure for the rest of their lives—maybe they'd write a book! One thing, however, they knew for sure: God had chosen to intervene and change them. Suddenly, Jesus' words returned to Yancey: *You would have lived all those decades and missed your life that could be.*

Yancey's mouth quirked in humor. Her eyes widened as the two-train word-problem returned.

Aftermath, indeed. Solve for X.

Yes, even an English teacher could do that after accepting Christ as Savior and Lord. With Him, life is no longer an unknown quantity.